ON THE
Corner

OTHER BOOKS BY S.J. TAGLIARENI

Hitler's Priest
The Cross or the Swastika
Roving Leadership

sjtagliareni.com

WHAT OTHERS ARE SAYING

"It will touch your heart and ignite your mind to the endless possibilities life holds . . . even to the end. If you have ever loved deeply, grieved deeply, questioned life, or your purpose, this is a MUST READ!"

—MAK (MARY ANNE) MORAN,
Author of *God Lives in Detroit (and Vacations in Other Places)*

"This 5-star novel literally bursts with love, joy, laugh out loud humor, profound sadness and a colorful cast of characters. The 'corner friends' and Jersey City scenes evoked so many wonderful memories of bygone days and the lifelong friendships made during that time. A wonderful story!! It would make a wonderful movie."

—MARY JANE HEIART SCARCIA

"*On the Corner* is profound, heartbreaking, funny, deeply interesting and realistic in how lives progress through a lifetime."

—PETER FITIPALDI

"*On the Corner* is a masterpiece. A tale of two men and the lessons they learned as they made their way from the middle of the last century to the beginning of this one. The stories will lead you through your own memories in a profound and touching way, leaving you with fresh, sweet energy to help pursue the rest of your life."

—MARK MALONEY, Former Director of the Boston BRA

"*On the Corner* moved me as Michael and Sal struggled with the issues we all face as human beings: our search for meaning, love and loss, joy and suffering. All the ambivalent experiences that Michael and Sal dealt with, I identified with. *On the Corner* is a powerful story of two life journeys, but truly, it is also the story of us."

—JACK KAKOLEWSKI

"The reader will often find himself laughing out loud or shedding a tear while reading this cleverly written cathartic tale. The novel drawn from life teaches one the importance of never giving up the choices we always have to fulfill ourselves in life. I highly recommend this read. You will not be able to put it down."

—GAIL FORSYTH FOLGER

"I was expecting a light novel about fictional characters, Instead, I got a poignant, autobiographical, fictional work about love, loss, grief, and the difficult and often painful decisions that forge character and make life worth living. This book contains lessons we all need to learn, set in the context of two friends who grew up in the gritty reality of 1950s Jersey City, and matured into real adults, encountering success, failure, grief and God's amazing grace along the way. A voyage through the many seasons of the heart: "a time to weep, a time to laugh, a time to mourn, a time to dance.""

—WILLIAM P. ISELE

"WOW! What a story. It hit every emotion in me. I was very impressed and moved There were times when I felt transported and I could almost visualize being there The power of friendship and love."

—PATTY HEALY, Actress

"I couldn't put the manuscript down. What I loved is the concept of a lifelong hometown friendship as a support when we go through life and especially as we age. The entire book speaks of love, its nature, mystery and beauty. With love come loss also full of mystery and terrible pain."

—THERESE RAU HERO

"*On the Corner* is a marvelous novel written with tender sensibility and wonder. It takes the reader deeply into the emotional joys and sorrows in a lifelong friendship."

—DONALD HAWTHORNE

"There is tremendous heart in this novel and I found myself laughing through tears. The reader will root for Michael and Sal each step of their journey."

—GUSTAF BERGER, Author of *Death Postponed*

ON THE
Corner

A NOVEL OF LIFELONG FRIENDSHIP

S.J. TAGLIARENI

Jamaica Plain Publishing

On the Corner
A Novel of Lifelong Friendship

Copyright © 2018 S.J. Tagliareni

Published by Jamaica Plain Publishing

This is a work of fiction. Some names and identifying details have been changed to protect the privacy of individuals.

ISBN–13: 978-1-7322149-0-3

Publisher's Cataloging-In-Publication Data
(Prepared by The Donohue Group, Inc.)

Names: Tagliareni, S. J. (Salvatore J.)
Title: On the corner : a novel of lifelong friendship / S.J. Tagliareni.
Description: Jamaica Plain, Massachusetts : Jamaica Plain Publishing, [2018]
Identifiers: ISBN 9781732214903
Subjects: LCSH: Male friendship--Fiction. | Older men--Fiction. | Spiritual life--Fiction. | Loss (Psychology)--Fiction. | United States-- Social conditions--1945---Fiction.
Classification: LCC PS3620.A347 O5 2018 | DDC 813/.6--dc23

Printed in the United States of America

To the lives of Jack Murphy and Charlie Hudson
whose memories continue to inspire me.

CONTENTS

1	MARCH 1954	*The Joy and the Agony*	13
2	SEPTEMBER 1954	*The College Years*	37
3	JUNE 1957	*Tragedy in Point Pleasant*	46
4	JUNE 1958	*The Next Step, Medical School*	64
5	NEW YORK 1958	*The Golden Offer*	68
6	MAY 1960	*The Road to the Priesthood*	92
7	SEPTEMBER 1960	*Hospital Duty as an Intern*	108
8	DECEMBER 1961	*The unimaginable Tragedy*	113
9	MARCH 1962	*Dealing with the Losses of his Family*	118
10	MAY 1962	*The Aftermath*	122
11	OCTOBER 1962	*Bellevue Residency, Time of Doubts*	126
12	MAY 1963	*The Incessant Doubts*	129
13	MAY 1965	*You Are a Priest Forever*	136
14	JULY 1965	*Bellevue*	145
15	AUGUST 1965	*The Death of a Young Boy*	150
16	OCTOBER 1965	*By Your Students You Will Be Taught*	154
17	MARCH 1966	*Bless Me, Father*	159
18	MAY 1967	*Boot Camp*	163
19	JUNE 1967	*Arrival of Jack Murphy*	171
20	MARCH 1968	*Prayers Finally Answered*	177
21	JUNE 1968	*Off to Vietnam*	181
22	DECEMBER 1968	*The Consequences of Spanking*	190
23	DECEMBER 1968	*Father Ray's Views*	193
24	JANUARY 1969	*DEROS*	199
25	MARCH 1969	*Adjusting to Civilian Life*	204
26	JANUARY 1970	*The Gambler*	211
27	MARCH 1970	*Tragedies*	217
28	APRIL	*Canon 509*	220

29	MAY 1970	*Leaving Westbury for Rome*	227
30	NOVEMBER 1970	*The Search for Meaning*	236
31	1974	*Coming Out*	242
32	SEPTEMBER 1974	*In Transition*	251
33	MAY 1980	*Through the Eyes of Children*	263
34	MAY 1984	*Another Adventure*	271
35	1994	*A Bridge to Nowhere*	274
36	JUNE 2000	*A New Adventure in New Brunswick, New Jersey*	280
37	JUNE 2004	*50th High School Reunion*	286
38	SEPTEMBER 2013	*The City that Never Sleeps*	290
39	SEPTEMBER 2013	*The Golden Years*	293
40	OCTOBER 2014	*No Magic Bullet*	299
41	NOVEMBER 2014	*Thanksgiving*	303
42	DECEMBER 2014	*Damn Hard-Boiled Eggs*	305
43	2014	*The Old Sod*	313
44	DECEMBER 2014	*The Pain of Loss*	326
45	MAY 2015	*The Deer*	332
46	OCTOBER 2105	*Fox Run*	337
47	JANUARY 2016	*On the Corner*	349
48	MARCH 2016	*Unfinished Business*	358
49	APRIL 2016	*Lingering Grief and Guilt*	366
50	MAY 2016	*Memories of Fathers*	376
51	MAY 2016	*Medical Diagnosis*	383
52	MAY 2016	*Terminal Disease*	388
53	JUNE 1916	*Last Attempt at Reconciliation*	392
54	JULY 2016	*The Fox Run Gang Strikes Again*	398
55	OCTOBER 2016	*Saying Goodbye*	406

AUTHOR'S NOTE

On the Corner is a blending of real life events and fictional plots and characters. Some of the scenes are vivid remembrances while others are figments of my imagination. My hope is the work portrays the many stages of joy and pain that visit the lives of Sal and Michael. It is an attempt to be a testament to the enduring treasure of friendship.

ACKNOWLEDGMENTS

On the Corner was rattling around in my head for decades but became a reality because of the persistent inspiration of my family and friends. They consistently urged me to put on paper the memories of a lifetime. Writing a novel at times feels like you are frequently dropped in the middle of the ocean and have no sense of what to do. It is in those confusing moments when the lights of love and friendship are the life preservers that allow you to go on and swim to the island of completion. I owe a special thanks to my dear friends Jack Murphy and Charlie Hudson who in many ways are the heart and soul of the work. In addition, I am grateful to Carol Burbank who helped shape the structure of weaving two lives together. Margaret Diehl consistently raised the bar and challenged me to answer a plethora of meaningful questions that made the novel come alive.

1

The Joy and the Agony

IT WAS A DARK, STORMY MORNING with incessant rain, sleet and no visible break in the black clouds. Winter was not yet ready to abandon the city. The March wind blew sheets of rain as Michael McNally buttoned his blue rain slicker and pulled his baseball cap down to prevent it from becoming a flying missile. Michael slushed through the puddles as he walked the cobblestone streets polished to shiny marble by the rain. When he neared the corner of West Side Avenue and Conduct Street, he fancifully imitated Gene Kelly as he began to stomp on puddles. The corner usually crowded with his friends was empty due to Mother Nature's last winter mood swing. A cascade of water flew up from the tires of the #9 bus and drenched him as he crossed the street. He paused to shake the water off his jacket before he entered Lee's

Luncheonette. He spotted his friend Sal La Greca at a table in the rear of the café. Michael smiled and left his duffel bag by the door. He and Sal had known each other since the second grade, but their friendship bond was forged on a snowy February afternoon when they were fifth graders. Michael at this age, was a scrawny boy whose growth spurt had made him rather clumsy. Walking home from school he was confronted by a group of seventh-grade bullies. They called him "Scarecrow," stripped off his jacket, pushed his face into the snow, and attempted to pull down his pants. Sal, observing the incident, shouted, "Leave him alone" and rushed to his aid, fighting to defend Michael. At the end of the tussle, Sal had a bloody nose, a fat lip and a torn jacket. From that day forward, the two were inseparable.

Getting out of his soaked jacket, Michael ordered a cherry coke and a tuna fish sandwich on white toast. Sitting down at his friend's table, he was incredulous at what was happening before him. It was a Friday, and despite the rules of Catholicism forbidding eating meat, Sal was devouring two hot dogs with all the trimmings.

Munching voraciously, Sal asked, "What the hell is wrong with you, McNally? You look as though you have seen a ghost."

Michael smiled and said, "I may very well be looking at a ghost because eating meat on Friday is a sure way to get a ringside seat in hell."

Sal waved his hand and scoffed. "You buy all that Catholic hocus-pocus stuff and that is the basic difference between us. You are a follower, and I am an outside-the-box genius."

Michael responded quickly, "You better get out of the box before you someday get into the final box."

The waitress brought Michael's order. Sal laughed and said, "Wow, a yummy tuna sandwich. Bet you would much rather have a hot dog with sauerkraut, mustard and relish." He took an enormous bite of the hot dog, and his lips dripped with mustard and bits of sauerkraut and relish.

"Not at the expense of losing my immortal soul."

"Michael, that's your biggest problem—you suffer from Irish guilt. The church fills you with all this blarney, and you completely buy into it."

Michael took his first bite and asked, "Don't you follow any of the rules?"

Sal closed his eyes as if he was thinking about the question. "Well, Michael, I have to tell you that I am not worried about God sitting on a cloud sending lightning down to prevent me from eating my second hot dog. Last count, I was not responsible for sinking the Titanic, the Lindbergh kidnapping or the pathetic Dodgers losing the World Series. Outside of gluttony, I haven't committed any of the seven capital sins."

"You are hopeless, and I pray that when you go, you will at least make it to purgatory."

Sal laughed and said, "With my track record, if there is such a place, I probably already have a home in hell. If there is a heaven, maybe you and the rest of my religious nut friends will drop some water on me."

As the two exchanged humorous jabs, it was striking how their physical appearances veered from the physical stereotypes of their heritages. Sal was the progeny of Sicilian dairy farmers and Tuscan merchants. Despite this, his hair was strawberry blond, his eyes a deep blue, his skin cameo. The one feature that came directly from his gene pool was an aquiline nose, bent since the fight with the bullies' years ago. Michael, on the other hand, was the direct descendent of grandparents born in Ireland, yet he looked more Italian than Sal. He had black hair, olive skin and deep, penetrating brown eyes. Once a skinny wisp, he had become an extraordinary scholar-athlete. The *Jersey Journal* sports writer Ed Grant described him as "an agile speedster with the torso of Paul Bunyan."

They were different in appearance and temperament, but they felt for each other an abiding respect and trust. Michael loved Sal's zest for life; laughter was part of his masculinity. He knew that Sal cared deeply about others. Incidents similar to the one from the fifth grade had been witnessed time and time again. He always stood up for the underdog and never tolerated bullying in his presence. Though he teased him, Sal admired Michael's devotion to his Catholic faith and how he handled his athletic stardom. Despite being a brilliant student, Michael was the epitome of humility.

Michael, attempting to change the subject, asked, "What time do we have to be at the gym this afternoon?"

"I think Coach O'Connor wants us there by five. I am sure he's going to pump us up for the start of tonight's game. We were lucky to beat St. Peters at their place in January, and you know they will want revenge."

Michael nodded in agreement. "I know. Yesterday, I ran into Danny Middleton, and he said they are looking forward to beating us tonight."

Sal sighed. "They have a deeper roster than us, but remember, the home crowd will be deafening and hopefully will get under their skins."

"Don't count on it. They are tough, and we will have to bring our A game to beat them."

"Why did you bring your uniform and sneakers so early?"

"Guess I was too antsy at home and thought some of the guys would be on the corner or in Lee's. I just hope that tempting God the Father with your hot dogs does not deprive me of a point guard tonight."

"McNally, if it weren't for my brilliant passing ability, you'd be sitting on the bench. It ticks me off that the headline in the *Jersey Journal* is always about how many points McNally scored instead of how many fantastic passes La Greca made."

"Face it, Sal, some of us have it, and some don't."

For the next hour and a half, the two best friends traded barbs and insults before going across the street to the St. Aloysius gym. On their way, they were loudly greeted by three of their friends who were standing on the corner under the pharmacy awning. They were cheering on the two warriors headed for their battle against St. Peter's. Louie DeForge shouted, "You had better win tonight! I bet my lunch money on you." The rain had changed to a drizzle, and neighborhood was coming to life as shoppers began to frequent the stores. West Side Avenue from Holy Name Cemetery to Lincoln Park was crowded with a myriad of businesses.

Over the past thirty years, the shopping area had welcomed thousands of Irish and Italian immigrants. There was a German bakery, Judicke's, known for its strudel, Jewish rye bread and huge jelly donuts. Koph's ice cream parlor was the home of gigantic banana splits and frothy ice cream milkshakes. Lauria's pharmacy served as a well of medical advice, while Jordan's liquor store provided ample spirits for all occasions. Kelly Clothiers was the primary source for Catholic uniforms, and the A&P was the largest food store in the city.

Michael and Sal were the first to arrive at the gym, and as usual, it was freezing cold in the shabby locker room. The thought of taking a shower after the game in the adjacent room was less than appealing. Michael quipped, "It's so cold in here you could hang frozen meat." As they changed their clothes, their humorous banter suddenly turned serious. Seated on a bench tying his sneakers, Sal said, "Hard to believe that this will be our last basketball home game."

Michael, palming a basketball, responded, "Kind of sad that this is the end. I have loved these four years. We have accomplished a lot together, but this game is a legacy statement."

Sal pointed to some of the team photos on the locker room walls. "Hard to imagine that none of those great teams ever beat St. Peter's twice in the same year, especially the varsity team when we were freshmen." As they reminisced, other members of the team, as well as Coach O'Connor, entered the locker room. Bobby Brennan nodded to them as he sat at the edge of the bench and began to undress. Bobby was a master student of basketball strategy and had a kind and gracious manner off the court. However, in practice sessions, he was a possessed defensive demon, and Sal contended that most of the bruises and scratches on his body were due to playing against Bobby. In the area nearest the showers, Jackie Hartnett was putting on his uniform. He cheerfully greeted his teammates. Jackie was the center and the tallest member of the team. In stocking feet, he was six feet six and weighed two hundred and thirty pounds. He was incredibly agile for his size but lacked Brennan's killer instinct. On the basketball court, he rarely took advantage of his size, and unlike Bobby was so filled with his desire not to hurt an opponent that he never reached his athletic potential. Sal once quipped about him that if four hundred students were entering the building, Hartnett would hold the door open for all of them.

The quiet of the locker room gave way to the excited nervous talk that usually occurred before any game, but this was different. Tonight's game was the most important one of the season, and the chatter reached epic proportions. Coach O'Connor, with his glistening crew cut and stern face,) was fastidiously dressed in a navy-blue blazer, charcoal grey slacks and red striped club tie. He gathered the team together before going upstairs to the gym. Unlike many coaches, he was not a screamer, and though intensely competitive, always maintained a calm demeanor during the games. He had excelled in his college career at Duke University was in excellent physical condition, and often scrimmaged against his best athletes in practice. He assembled his players and said, "Desire and guts will determine who wins this game. We beat them once at their place but have no illusions that tonight will be easy. They will pressure the ball from the opening tap. The key is to play our game, not theirs." Coach O'Connor knelt and led the team in a prayer before leaving the locker room.

As Michael walked from the locker room to the gym, he thought about what a phenomenal year this had been for him. The first of the magical moments had been his acceptance into Notre Dame on a basketball scholarship. He was class valedictorian, editor of the yearbook and a final candidate for Hudson County basketball player of the year. Tonight could be the icing on the cake.

The atmosphere of the tiny gym, filled to overflowing with 600 fans, was electric and when the buzzer sounded for the game to begin, Michael could feel the butterflies in his stomach. The capacity crowd had raised the temperature in the gym to sauna levels, and the cheering was deafening. Last-minute instructions by Coach O'Connor were taken seriously, but Michael was only focused on his biggest challenge, guard Danny Middleton. He was two inches taller than Michael and considered the finest defensive player in Hudson County. Michael knew that he and the other St. Peter's guards would put tremendous pressure on limiting them to drive the lane. He was right to be concerned. Right from the opening tap, St. Peter's dictated the tempo. They scored the first eight points, and Coach O'Connor was forced to call an early time-out.

Though St. Aloysius was almost blown away in the first half of the game, Coach O'Connor made critical adjustments to the game plan, and the team rallied.

With a minute and a half to go in the game, St. Aloysius was losing by four points. St. Aloysius guard Bobby Brennan stole an inbound pass, dribbled the lane, made a layup and was fouled. He made the foul shot, and St. Aloysius trailed by one point. St. Peter's called time out and attempted to freeze the ball, passing it around the perimeter. Michael anticipated one of the passes, slapped at the ball, and one of the St. Peter's players kicked it out of bounds. St. Aloysius called its last time-out, and Coach Bob O'Connor set up a play with eight seconds to go.

Danny Middleton walked up to Michael as he left the time-out. He put his hand on Michael's shoulder and said, "Don't think about taking a shot, McNally, because I will be all over you." Bobby Brennan threw the ball to Sal La Greca, and center Jack Hartnett created a pick, blocking the St. Peter's guard. Danny Middleton made a valiant attempt to get around the pick but was completely blocked and crashed to the floor. Michael, now free of Middleton, took a pass from Sal and hit an eighteen-foot jump shot at the buzzer. When the ball swished through the nets, the home crowd went wild and stormed the court. Michael was hoisted in glory and carried to the locker room.

The ultimate joy for Michael was that his entire family was at the game. He was unaware that before the game started, many students ascended the bleachers to pay their respects to Mrs. McNally, who was a fixture at home games. Known for her gracious manner outside the gym, her piercing, shrill voice often was the bane of a referee's existence. At one point, her husband, a shy person, seemed uncomfortable with all the attention and asked, "Are you running for mayor?"

It was the first time that Michael's father had seen him play in any sporting event. His mother and father were both hoarse from cheering, and his two younger brothers were replaying the winning shot repeatedly. Michel had finally caught the brass ring on life's merry-go-round. His senior year was filled with so many wonderful moments, and more was to come: the prom, the state tournament, working at the Jersey Shore this summer. In the fall, he would attend his dream school, Notre Dame.

Arlene Rose Fallon was the head cheerleader and Michael's steady date for the last two years. She could have been born in Dublin or the Irish countryside because, absent a brogue, everything else about her was Irish. She had wavy chestnut hair with natural highlights, which she wore in a ponytail. Her eyes were grayish blue, becoming grayer or bluer depending on the light. She greeted the McNally's as they came down from the bleacher seats and waited with them for Michael to join them for a late-night pizza at Frank's Bar and Grill. Mrs. McNally was very attached to Arlene, and though she adored her three sons had always hoped that at some point she would have a little girl. Two miscarriages after her youngest, Donny, was born ended that desire, but over the last two years, Arlene had been fulfilling that dream. Arlene's responded eagerly to Mrs. McNally's affection. Her mother had died of cancer when she was six, and being the only girl in a family with five brothers, she yearned for a maternal presence.

Donny, ten years old, chubby with bright red hair and a plethora of freckles, was the least athletic of the three brothers. What he lacked in size, he made up for with enthusiasm and boyish charm. He was under the basket with an imaginary microphone emotionally describing the winning shot while the rest of the family chatted near the exit.

Saturday morning after the Friday night victory, Michael had plans to take his brothers to the Seton Hall-St. Peter's college game at the Jersey City Armory. He had invited Arlene, but she preferred to spend the day with his mother. The McNally's, like most families in St. Aloysius parish, lived in a railroad flat that had two bedrooms and a single bathroom. During winter, the place was a wind tunnel with constant drafts, and a shawl or blanket was essential to keep warm. In the summer months, the apartment was like a blast furnace with only floor fans to give any relief.

After the boys left, Mrs. McNally went to the hall and took a worn leather photograph album from the mahogany secretary. Placing the album on the kitchen table, she began to brew a pot of tea. When the kettle whistled, she poured the water into a tea caddy and sat down next to Arlene. Opening the album, she turned the pages and came to the photo of a young woman who bore a striking resemblance to Arlene. "This is a photo of me with my grandmother and mother when I was sixteen. I was very close to them. I still miss them every day. After we have our tea, I would like to show you something they bequeathed me." Arlene loved looking through the album. She saw hints of Michael in his grandparents' faces and especially enjoyed the photo of Mrs. McNally holding Michael in his Christening gown. She was very glad that instead of going to the game she had decided to spend the day here. "Wow, you look so beautiful," she said. I can't wait to be a mother."

"It's the best thing in the world. But take your time."

Mrs. McNally teased Arlene, who had long flowing chestnut hair and beautiful eyes by continuing, "My hair used to be dark brown, but as you can see, now it is a mousy grey, and my sparkling eyes have been somewhat dimmed through caring for my three hellions. Mark my words, beauty is fleeting! The least bit of humidity in the air makes my hair fall into uncontrollable curls, and I have the look of a wild banshee. Add the more than few pounds that I have put on since that photo, and it's hard to believe that was me."

Arlene laughed and assured Mrs. McNally that she was as beautiful as the photo in the album. "And Michael looks like a little doll."

"Don't ever let him hear you say that! And speaking of that. . . ." Mrs. McNally went into the front hall closet, removed a step-ladder and made her way to the closet at the end of the apartment. Opening the door, she motioned for Arlene to assist her while she took three boxes from the top shelf. At one point she appeared to lose her balance and became light- headed. Arlene was concerned. But Mrs. McNally deflected her. "Guess I am not as spry as I used to be. Maybe it would be better if you retrieved the boxes."

Once they had been placed on the sofa, Mrs. McNally said, "These were the prized possessions of my grandmother who left them to my mother. Many years ago, she worked as a maid for the Hague family when she was literally just off the boat from Ireland. The family was quite wealthy, and much to her surprise, when the mistress died she left these in her will to my grandmother. When she passed, they were given to my mother and then me. I hoped someday to share them with my daughter." The boxes were filled with exquisite Juneau dolls that originally came from France. The three dolls had lace dresses, bright red leather shoes, expressive eyes and beautiful bisque faces.

"I hope this will not embarrass you, Arlene, but I would like you to pick one of these as a gift."

Arlene felt teary-eyed and stammered, "But they should stay in your family."

Placing a hand on her cheek, Mrs. McNally replied, "Family is wider than blood, and I would be thrilled if you would accept this. Besides, none of my sons would have any idea of their beauty and value. If it is not a basketball or a bat, they have no interest."

Arlene smiled at those words and gratefully accepted the gift.

Michael was the conquering hero in school on Monday after the St. Peters game. Every student on their way to class stopped by his locker to offer congratulations. Finally opening his locker, he turned to see the dour face of Sal. Waving the *Jersey Journal* at Michael, Sal said, "Check the headline: 'McNally's buzzer shot buries St. Peters.' Nowhere in the article does it say that the brilliant pass by La Greca was the key play of the game. Once again, McNally, you have stolen my thunder."

Michael smiled and said, "Hit the road, goofball, or I will be late for class." Slamming his locker shut, he bolted up the stairs to the second floor and made it to his seat as the bell rang. History was one of Michael's favorite classes, and for a brief period he had considered becoming a history teacher, but medicine was his goal. He had worked at the Jersey City medical center for the last two summers and was deeply impressed by the doctors at the hospital. One doctor in particular, Dr. Moriarty, had taken a liking to Michael and one day in the cafeteria told him, "I like the way you handle yourself around here. Have you ever thought of becoming a doctor? Michael had, and this moment of encouragement was another building block toward the goal that was fermenting in his mind.

Michael was busy taking notes when the loudspeaker came on and requested that he report to the principal's office. He thought little of this, assuming it had something to do with the yearbook. Despite all his other responsibilities, he had worked tirelessly on the project and was advised that the final copy would be available for review this week.

Bouncing down the stairs two at a time, he came to the principal's office and was pleased to see his favorite priest, Father Frank McNulty, in the office with Sister Gertrude Jose.

"Good morning, Sister, good morning, Father Frank. Did you need to see me?" he asked.

Father McNulty usually would banter with Michael, but something was different this morning. The lines and shadows of his face seemed to have deepened overnight, and his eyes looked sad and distant. He placed his hand on Michael's shoulder and said, "Michael, I am afraid that I have bad news for you."

Michael was confused, thinking perhaps Notre Dame had revoked his scholarship. "What is it, Father?" he asked fearfully.

"I just received a call from your father. Your mother had a heart attack at home."

The words took the breath away from Michael. He blurted out, "Is she in the hospital? Will she be alright?"

Father McNulty's face was contorted, and he had difficulty speaking. After a light cough, he said, "I'm afraid that your mother did not survive the attack. She died."

Michael fell to his knees. "No, no, Father, she was fine this morning. She can't be dead. Are you sure? Maybe she is at the hospital, and you misunderstood the message." Words were flowing with no real logic, but it was necessary to find out that a mistake had been made. It was simply impossible his mother was dead. His mind rejected the idea like a body rejects foreign tissue. Trembling with fear, Michael tried several times to understand what the error could be. "Father, you know how words get garbled on the phone. Maybe my father was so upset that he did not understand that she is critically ill—at risk—but still alive."

Father McNulty frowned, hugged him and said, "I am afraid it is true, Michael, and nothing I can say will change it." He again lovingly placed his arm around him. "I will get your coat and drive you home. Your father wants you with him when you pick your brothers up from school. They don't know yet."

Michael could barely breathe but nodded his head. His thoughts were wildly racing through his brain; his heart was pounding, and he felt like he was going to vomit. He could not fathom how quickly his life and that of his father and brothers had been shattered. His mind was still insisting it was impossible, *not his mother,* though he didn't argue with Father McNulty anymore. Sister Gertrude gently held his hand and refrained from conversation. She knew that there were no words that would help right now.

The news about Mrs. McNally spread around the school in moments. Sal, on hearing it, almost fell out of his chair. He was completely shocked and immediately excused himself from class. He went to the principal's office and asked permission to leave school early. Michael was his best friend, and he needed to visit him and ask if there was anything that he could do. Walking briskly toward the McNally home, Sal had a flashback to an evening when he was eleven years old. His neighbor Bobby Smith came to his home at nine o'clock one evening. It was obvious that Bobby had been crying. "Sal, my father dropped dead, and my mother sent me to get a quart of milk at the store."

Sal was dumbstruck and did not know what to do or say. "I am so sorry, Bobby," was all he could think of. After he spoke, there was an uncomfortable pause, with Bobby just standing there. Finally, Bobby shrugged his shoulders turned and slowly walked down the steps. Sal was confused and didn't join him. He had regretted a thousand times not going to the store with Bobby. He told himself that this time, he was going to be there with his friend no matter what was required.

Arriving at 12 Vroom Street, Sal rang the bell. He was buzzed in and climbed the steps to the second floor. After a few minutes,

Michael opened the door. His eyes were huge; he looked lost and frail. Yet it was apparent that he was glad to see Sal. There was an awkward attempt at a handshake, but then Sal hugged Michael. "I am so sorry. How are your brothers?"

"They are overwhelmed. I am most concerned about Danny. He has said nothing and resists any attempt to talk about it. Donny is crushed and upstairs crying on his bed."

"Is there anything I can do?"

"Maybe you could be with Donny. I think it might be best if we spent some time individually with each boy. He likes you so much, and that would really help me. I want to spend time with Danny and see if I can get him to talk." Michael paused and added, "This is all new to me, Sal, and there are arrangements that have to be made. One of the things is we must provide six pallbearers; would you be one?"

"I would be honored, Michael."

After spending a few hours trying to console Donny, Sal left the McNally home, tormented by the thoughts that this could have been his mother. What would he do if his mother suddenly died? When he arrived at 202 Delaware Avenue, his mother was looking out the front window and raced to open the front door. He embraced her and held on for what seemed minutes. She kissed his cheek and said, "I am so sorry about Michael's mother. Those poor boys. I'm glad you went over there, Sal; that was the right thing to do. I hope Mr. McNally can cope."

The wake at Corrigan's Funeral Home and the funeral itself were a blur for the McNally's. During that time, Michael realized that, in many ways, his father was more lost than he. His mother had been the heart of the family, and though his father was a good provider, his wife's death left a huge hole in their home. There was no physical contact between father and sons. Michael felt an overwhelming responsibility, not to replace his mother, but to provide some of her caring for Danny and Donny. Donny was ten and as the youngest had been very attached to his mother. She always enjoyed his exuberance and constantly assured him that with age he would be as tall as his brothers. Slightly overweight and less athletic than his brothers, he was an exceptionally happy child. Michael once told his mother that Donny could get excited about a peanut-butter-and-jelly sandwich. Danny, age twelve, was quiet, athletic and already approaching six feet in height. He was relatively shy and his prime interest outside of sports was building models. As a young child, he would spend hours on his brother's erector set, and his dream was one day to be an architect.

Michael knew that in many respects he was their hero, and now he was more than that. Going to Notre Dame was no longer a possibility. He decided to enroll at Seton Hall University and live at home. Living on campus would have been more rewarding than being a day-hop student, but his family needed him. His dream of playing college basketball seemed unimportant compared to his family responsibilities.

Sal was constantly available to Michael throughout during the funeral process. He spent most of the three days at the McNally home. He ate his meals with Donny, helped him get dressed and spent hours talking to him about what he was experiencing. Michael wished to be with both of his brothers but knew that Danny was the one who needed the most individual time. Sal's primary responsibility was to be with Donny McNally while Michael attended to Danny. He chose Sal not only because Donny loved him, but because he knew that Sal would be totally dedicated to his brother now and in the future. He could count on him.

The two-day wake drained the family, with every viewing hour filled. The McNally's were a neighborhood favorite, and the waiting line was around the block with students, neighbors and employees from the American Can Company.

The morning of the funeral Mass was particularly difficult, and at one point Sal found himself holding a collapsed Donny in his arms. The small body was shaking and trembling. He could not imagine how Donny, at the tender age of ten, was going to get through this.

The main celebrant at the funeral Mass was Father McNulty. Sal was deeply moved by his eulogy. Normally, Sal tuned out sermons, as they seemed to have nothing to do with his life, but this one had an enormous effect on him. Father McNulty spoke about Mrs. McNally as a living model of the Beatitudes, the words that Christ spoke in the Sermon on the Mount.

> *Blessed are the poor in spirit, for theirs is the kingdom of heaven.*
> *Blessed are those who mourn, for they will be comforted.*
> *Blessed are the meek, for they will inherit the earth.*
> *Blessed are those who hunger and thirst after righteousness, for they will be filled.*
> *Blessed are the merciful, for they shall be shown mercy.*
> *Blessed are the pure in heart, for they will see God.*
> *Blessed are the peacemakers, for they will be called the sons of God.*
> *Blessed are those who are persecuted because of righteousness, for theirs is the kingdom of heaven.*
> *Blessed are you when people insult you, persecute you and falsely say all kinds of evil against you because of me.*
> *Rejoice and be glad, because great is your reward in heaven, for in the same way they persecuted the prophets who were before you.*

Sal understood now that those words were rooted in concrete realities that made a difference in the world. He had seen the poor being fed in his neighborhood, and everyone in the two-block area where he lived cared for widows, orphans and persons with disabilities. He had never really thought about it before, but now he understood that these powerful words of Jesus were not fairy tales from thousands of years ago. They were being lived out daily by good and caring people. This seemed especially true of his experiences with Father McNulty. He had always admired him, but his involvement in the sorrow and grief of the family deeply touched him. Sal had been a Catholic his whole life, but this sermon and the experiences of the past few days had given him a deeper sense of the value of the Church and priesthood.

At the cemetery, the wintry sky was filled with snowflakes that hung like an infinite array of crystals over the grave. The stark weather reflected the pain that the McNally's were experiencing, and the thud when the casket was lowered into the grave and hit the bottom was wrenching. Michael embraced his brother Danny as they left the gravesite. He turned and requested that Sal ride in the lead car with Donny.

Sal's mother and a few of the neighbors had arranged a buffet luncheon at the McNally home. When the guests arrived, the dining room table was adorned with a Waterford vase filled with red roses and an array of luncheon meats, salads, freshly baked breads and pastries. Sal's mother had borrowed English bone china, serving plates and silverware from her neighbors. For hours, the house was filled with mourners and the noise level was loud and consistent, but by the late afternoon, everyone had left, and the house held an eerie silence. Michael and Sal sat on the stoop, both exhausted from the past few days.

"Thanks for everything you have done this week and please thank your mother for providing all the food and for leaving the kitchen spotless."

"I will and know that I am around all weekend if you need anything." Sal paused and added, "I thought it might be a good idea if I take Donny to the playground on Saturday. We can play a little basketball and then go to Lee's for lunch."

"I think that would help, Sal." Michael was silent for a minute, and then, shaking his head, said, "I can't believe that she is gone. Over and over, I see her that morning just before I left for school. She seemed fine. Now I wish that I had spent a few more minutes talking to her. I gave her a hurried kiss and raced out the door. I would give anything to have that moment back." Sal knew that it was not the time to give advice, so he just remained quiet. Michael stood, and shaking Sal's hand, again thanked him."

"I may not be in school tomorrow, but I will see you on Saturday."

Sal left Vroom Street committed to doing everything he could to lighten the burdens of his best friend. As he walked, the realization of sudden death again hit him. He thought, what would I do if my mother died abruptly? He could barely imagine the pain of such a loss and tried to block it from his mind.

MAY 1954: ANOTHER PAINFUL REMINDER

Mother's Day, was another painful reminder for Michael and his brothers of the loss of their mother. Though grieving himself, he worried about them before he thought of himself. He had shared his grief with them in the hope that they would be able to understand that what they were feeling was normal. He couldn't answer their questions about why her, why *our mother,* but he let them ask. When he entered his brother's room, he knew that Donny had been weeping. Danny, the more stoic of the two, sat on his bed in silence, his eyes focused out the window. Michael was more concerned about him than Donny and hoped that, in time, he would share his feelings.

Michael said, "It is almost time for us to go to Mass, so meet me downstairs in five minutes." The walk from their house on Delaware Avenue to St. Aloysius Church was only three blocks, but it was brought constant reminders of what they had lost. It seemed that emerging from every house in this predominantly Catholic neighborhood were mothers and children on their way to Mass.

As they approached the church, they were greeted by Sal and his family. "My mother asked if we could sit with you in church. Also, she would love for you and the boys to join us for breakfast at Al's Diner." Michael was touched by these acts of kindness.

Although Jersey City was large in population, in many respects it was a tiny village. The St. Aloysius neighborhood was tightly knit, and everyone was aware of Mrs. McNally's sudden death. Al's diner on Communipaw Avenue was a mainstay, open 24 hours, seven days a week. It was a stopping place when the bars closed at 2 a.m. as well as the place Mass-goers would frequent on Sunday mornings. The diner opened its doors in the late 1930s and had barely changed since. It had padded blue vinyl booths, red striped curtains and dark wood paneling on the walls. It was known for solid, no-frills fare and bottomless cups of coffee and tea. The walls had bright neon lights, and each table had an individual jukebox. As they entered, the waitress who seated them turned to Michael and said,

"Sorry for your loss." Al, the owner, who was busy flipping eggs and bacon on the grill, turned, leaned over the counter and offered, "I am so sorry to hear about your mother, Michael." Michael thanked him and followed his brothers to a large table at the end of the diner.

The waitress brought glasses of water with menus and inquired, "Will the young boy need a child's menu?" she asked referring to Donny,

Mrs. La Greca put her arm around Donny. "Heavens no, we are all adults at this table." Donny proudly smiled, sat up straight and immediately began to scour the breakfast choices. He chose the he-man special: two pancakes, three eggs, bacon and toast. With the vigor of youth, he attacked the enormous plate of food. Mrs. La Greca was pleased because, in her tradition, food was the key to life even in a period of mourning.

The weeks following the funeral were particularly difficult for Michael because all the tasks of running a household fell to him. His father had never done the food shopping, could not boil water and had no sense of the daily duties that were required. Arlene was most helpful in preparing meals, doing the laundry and assisting Michael with the daily chores. Michael made his brothers' lunches every day, and at night would assist Donny with his homework. Danny was more self-sufficient and rarely required any assistance with homework. One night while Michael was helping Donny with arithmetic, Donny pushed his workbook away and asked, "Michael, do you think that Mommy sees us from heaven?"

Michael knew that this was an important question and instead of answering it directly, asked, "Donny, what do you think?"

Donny sat up straight. "I think she and all the angels see us and make sure that we are OK."

Michael was moved by Donny's innocence and deep faith. He added, "I believe that, too, Donny. She is always near us even though we can't see her." Donny was comforted by Michael's belief. He picked up his workbook, hugged Michael and made his way up the stairs to his room.

Just then the phone rang and it was Arlene. "Hi, how are you doing?"

"Okay, but I never realized how much effort went into running the house."

"Welcome to my world. No, really, I understand how difficult this time must be. My brothers do little around my house except take out the garbage. As soon as I get home from school, I have to make sure everything works. On another note, I had an idea. What would you think of taking the boys on the St. Al's boat ride in May?"

Michael immediately responded, "I think that's a great idea. They will be excited being with all of our friends."

The morning of the St. Al's boat ride, the pier by the huge Colgate Company clock was crowded with hundreds of exuberant students waiting to board the ship for the annual excursion to Rye Beach. They were jostling for position and chafing at the bit to board the boat. This outing was different than the confines of their school because boys and girls would be on the same boat and not closely monitored by the nuns. There was exuberance in the air as students checked out potential partners before boarding. Sister Mary Michael told a faculty member, "Today it's us against the hormones, and we are losing."

The weather was perfect, and Donny was ecstatic to be here with his brothers and Arlene. The ride up the scenic Hudson River took approximately two hours. There were stunning river views as the boat glided under the George Washington Bridge, but most of the passengers were more into card playing, making out and flirting than savoring the breathtaking views of Manhattan and the Palisades cliffs.

Upon arrival at Rye Beach, Michael gave both boys some spending money and arranged a meeting place where they would have lunch. Danny, who had a dry sense of humor, quipped, "Does that mean that I am stuck with Donny until then?"

Donny perked up and responded, "Bet I can beat you at throwing the balls against the dolls." With that, the two scurried off to visit the roller coaster and every other challenging ride. Arlene and Michael spent most of the day with Sal and his new date, Elizabeth Murphy. Arlene, ever the matchmaker, had paired them up for the boat ride last Wednesday. She and Elizabeth had become friends last year, and she thought the quiet beauty with the big blue eyes was perfect for Sal.

The day was a marvelous success, and Donny was so exhausted from riding the Dragon roller coaster and playing games that he literally slept the entire way back to Jersey City. It was a wonderful break for Michael as well as the boys.

Every event that spring was an experience in joy and loss, sometimes at the same moment.

Graduation was another grief milestone. The night before the ceremony, Michael had spent hours working on his valedictorian speech and was trying to decide whether he should mention his mother in the talk. His father had requested that Aunt Mary sit with the family during the graduation exercises. She had placed a picture of her sister on an empty chair so that Michael would have a symbol of his mother at the graduation. St. Aloysius Church was the site of the graduation, and fortunately, the rain of the previous day had ceased. It was a lovely spring day. The temperature was in the low seventies without a smidgen of humidity. While Michael was putting on his cap and gown, Father McNulty came over to talk to him. Adjusting Michael's graduation gown, he told Michael, "It has been my experience that every first event after a loss is most painful, and I am sure that Mother's Day was no picnic for you and the boys. One thing I know is that your mother was so proud of you, and her spirit will be present today. When you give your valedictorian speech, know that she will be at your side." Michael reached out and hugged Father Frank.

As he began to speak, he gazed out at his classmates and realized it was the end of a significant part of his life. Most of his friends were not going to college, and the days of hanging out on the corner were coming to an end. He saw Johnny Farawell and remembered the number of times they had hitchhiked down to the shore. Maddy Dolye, seated in the front row, gave the victory sign, and Michael immediately remembered the night of their grammar school graduation when his father brought home two street people to attend the party. Maddy's mother was less than happy, but his father wanted to share that proud moment with these two lost souls. Giving the valedictorian speech was a moment of achievement but also a realization that he was separating from his community of special friends.

He wondered if he'd ever again feel such a sense of belonging.

2

SEPTEMBER 1954

The College Years

SETON HALL UNIVERSITY

MICHAEL GAVE UP HIS SCHOLARSHIP TO Notre Dame because he felt a deep responsibility to help raise his brothers Danny and Donny. His mother's death was devastating for him, and he was sure it was as least as bad for his brothers—probably worse because they were younger. They needed another adult at home. His father was a devoted provider but without the love and affection of his wife was unable to care for the emotional and educational needs of his sons. Every day he would come home from his job at the American Can Company, eat his meal in silence, and then retreat to his Barcalounger. Each night was the same; he watched mindless TV and polished off a huge bottle of beer. His mother's sister Mary did everything in her power to fill the gap, but as a widow raising four children, she had responsibilities of her own. Arlene, Michael's girlfriend, was an amazing help, both in practical and emotional matters, but at the end of the day, Michael knew that it was his responsibility to help raise the boys.

Michael had arranged with a high school classmate who was to attend Seton Hall University to share the driving from Jersey City to South Orange. It was important for Michael not to feel sorry for himself. He didn't wallow in the fact that his lifelong dream to play basketball for Notre Dame would never happen. He meditated and prayed, asking God for guidance and strength. He decided that he would throw his entire being into his new college career because he didn't want college to be a secondary experience. There would be no opportunity to participate in dorm life, but despite that, he was determined to have a thorough and fulfilling experience.

When the two freshmen arrived on campus, his friend Joe went to the bookstore while Michael made his way to the college chapel. It was empty, and the only lights were the flickering votive candles in front of the side altar. Michael blessed himself with holy water and knelt in the last pew. The chapel, which had been home to Seton Hall students for almost one hundred years, was small but architecturally gorgeous. The original terrazzo floor, in the shape of a cross, led one to the stunning red coralline marble altar. The amber walls and the sunlight washing through the stained-glass windows seemed to be welcoming Michael with their beauty. Michael prayed and for the next ten minutes poured out his need for his Lord to guide him through the family challenges. Leaving the chapel, Michael felt a deep sense of peace, something he knew he would need to get through the next few years.

It was a truism in Jersey City and Bayonne that if you talked to a stranger for three minutes, you would discover a host of common friends. If you spoke for five minutes, you were related. The city connections through athletics and activities like the Catholic Youth League and summer shore basketball allowed Michael to quickly find a network of friends at Seton Hall. Almost immediately, Ted Heiart, Bert Burke, Jack Rority, and Paul Bronkowski became Michael's new band of brothers. Of course, there was also the addition of Jim Manning, affectionately known as "Maniac" due to legendary stories that were, unfortunately, all true. Michael had witnessed one of these outrageous happenings on St. Patrick's Day in New York. Maniac had somehow smuggled a woodsman's saw into a suite at the Biltmore Hotel. At one point in the afternoon, Maniac ,(completely inebriated) and an accomplice sawed a piano in half. This was only outdone several hours later when, for some reason, he held up traffic by running naked through the Lincoln Tunnel. His arrest and short stay at the Bellevue psych ward were whitewashed because his father was the chief of police in Bayonne.

On the home front, Michael had a team of experts intimately involved with caring for Donny and Danny. Father McNulty and the good Sisters of Charity at St. Aloysius daily addressed many of the boys' emotional and social needs. This was complemented by Michael's Aunt Mary and girlfriend Arlene. Michael's father was still experiencing overwhelming grief. His wife had been his only love, and he had depended on her in every way. Losing her had set him adrift. Michael's grandfather had been an alcoholic brute who was physically abusive to his wife and children. Mr. McNally's life changed when he met his wife—he adored her and had never once raised his hand to any family member—but he had let her be his rock, and she had taken on the role. She saw in him a wounded spirit but a man of infinite gentleness. He did not know how to physically or emotionally provide the necessary sustenance that the boys needed. He had never been taught how to lead and care for his family.

Despite all the responsibilities at home, Michael thrived in the academic environment of the University. As the first semester evolved, he anticipated that he would get straight A's. He particularly loved the philosophy and theology requirements and found himself regularly engaging the professors in meaningful dialogues. The Catholic environment and opportunity to attend Mass daily fortified his faith, and he laid his sorrow and concerns at the feet of his Lord.

As a biology major, one of the most challenging courses was organic chemistry. The second week of the spring semester, the professor wrote a series of answers to the main topics that would be covered in the course. Few of the students paid attention to these details, but Michael wrote them all down and memorized the answers to the problems. He was amazed later when the final exam in the course was exactly what the professor had written on the board two months prior. Before he answered the questions, he raised his hand and requested to speak with his professor. The professor made his way to Michael's desk.

Michael whispered, "The day you wrote those on the board, I memorized them, so I'm not sure that my test results would be ethically achieved."

The professor stroked his chin in amazement. "Mister McNally, you are a rare bird. Please answer the questions because if you were wise enough to memorize the answers, you deserve the grade." Michael aced the test and kept his straight-A record intact.

OCTOBER 1954:
A WHOLE NEW WORLD IN NEW YORK CITY

NYU was a whole new experience for Sal, who had spent his entire life in the predominantly Catholic environment of Jersey City. It was exhilarating for him to be surrounded by such diversity. Two of his roommates were Jewish, while another was an atheist who had little regard for organized religion. The classes at NYU, unlike his previous academic experiences in Catholic school, often proposed directly opposite views of the world. Many of the professors were not enthusiastic about religion, and some were openly hostile to Christianity. Despite his casual stance toward the rules of his church, he was deeply aware that he was culturally Catholic. The Church had been an integral part of his childhood. He thought many of the beliefs, like Limbo, were fanciful, but through the Church, he had witnessed a great deal of caring and love, especially by the priests in his parish. For the first time in his adult life, he began to more appreciate the core of his Catholic faith.

One of the required freshman courses at NYU was "Fundamental Science 101," which encompassed some chemistry as well as biology. The standard biology section of the course required that the students, in small groups, dissect a frog. The professor, Dr. Jansen, was an avowed atheist and frequently made disparaging remarks about Catholicism. He was also openly hostile to female students. On the first day of lecture hall, he requested the eight female students sit in the first row. After they were seated, he asked them to cross their legs. He then said, "Now that the gates of hell are closed, we may proceed with my lecture."

One day while the students were dissecting frogs, Professor Jansen said to the class, "When you Catholic students get to the soul, please let me see it. I have never seen a soul, and it would be a worthwhile experience for me to see one."

These remarks made Sal feel uncomfortable, but he refrained from showing any disagreement with the professor. One of the other students, John Kelly, who had a brother who was a Franciscan priest, raised his hand. Professor Jansen inquired, "Do you have a question?"

Kelly stood up and said, "Professor Jansen, may I ask you a personal question?"

"I am not sure what that would have to do with dissecting frogs, but yes, you may."

Kelly proceeded, "Are you married?"

Professor Jansen was taken aback by the question but replied, "Yes, I am."

"I know my next question is personal, but it is important for me to know. Do you love your wife?"

Professor Jansen seemed annoyed. "It is none of your business, but yes, I do. Why do you ask?"

Kelly said, "The reason I ask is that we Catholics have never seen love, so could you please bring it in and show it to us?"

Professor Jansen's face turned bright red, his lips quivered, and he was embarrassed by the laughter of some students in the classroom. He stuttered momentarily and was unable to speak.

Finally, giving up on the challenge to find a perfect response, he pounded his desk with his fist and said, with great venom, "Get out of my class this instant and do not bother to come back."

Kelly picked up his books and headed for the door. Before opening it, he turned and said quietly, "Somebody made a fool out of themselves here this morning, and it wasn't me."

Sal felt a burst of admiration for his classmate, though he was mildly surprised that the professor's disdain for his religion had sparked such personal outrage. After class, he made it his business to find Kelly and thank him for his response. "I was never comfortable with all the anti-Catholic stuff he spouts but did not want to say anything in class."

Kelly understood Sal's reluctance and said, "I don't know why, but today I could not take it anymore. I am proud of my faith, and someone needed to stand up to him."

Sal became friendly with Kelly and started to attend weekly masses at the Catholic Newman Center with him. The chaplain, Father Hallinan, was a young priest who had great rapport with the students. After Mass, Father Hallinan hosted a coffee with an open question and answer period. Sal became interested in the content of these meetings, and he grew in appreciation of the sacraments and some of the historical reasons for Catholic beliefs.

The first three years of Sal's college career at NYU were way beyond expectations. Living in a small apartment in the East Village with three other students, he fully enjoyed many of the opportunities that were available to him. The East Village was filled with artists and writers. The streets and cafes were also the landing place for outrageous characters who made Sal smile. Once in a local coffee bar, he witnessed a man dressed as the Kaiser playing a tuba and singing loudly. He pranced around the entire bar for ten minutes and then suddenly left. The owner and patrons acted as if this was nothing out of the ordinary. In addition to the zany presence of "street people," Sal could feel the vibrancy of the intellectual and cultural underpinnings of this diverse community. He did not initially know the words "Bohemian lifestyle" but began to realize that many of the writers and artists were trying to create a society that was outside the mainstream. Although the Village had been a meeting ground for artists and social thinkers since World War I, each generation made it new. He was excited when on his birthday friends took him to an evening with two of the most influential writers of the movement, Jack Kerouac and William S. Burroughs. After the lecture, they spent the rest of the night at The Composer, a local jazz club filled with people wearing berets, sunglasses, and black, roll-neck jumpers. It was a long way from life in Jersey City.

The classes at NYU were challenging and fulfilling, especially the journalism classes. One professor, Jack Franzetti, had taken Sal under his wing and was a constant source of encouragement. An experienced journalist, Professor Franzetti had a fondness for bright city kids. He attempted to avoid playing favorites and in the class treated Sal as just another student. However, in their private conferences, he recognized Sal's raw talent and challenged him consistently to raise the level of his writing. Sal loved writing and aspired to be a sportswriter for one of the Jersey newspapers after graduation. He excelled at the routine class work, but it was the writing that gave him the greatest pleasure. Often late into the night, he would write invented stories of professional athletic games that he had attended. He experienced great happiness in those hours of endless imagination. Writing was when he could unleash the creative part of his personality. Some days, the writing was fluid; at other times it was slow but it was always worthwhile. He had dreams of one day writing a series of novels. One of the things he learned from Professor Franzetti was that in order to excel as a writer, you had to accept that you begin with bad writing. Great writing comes from letting go, taking risks.

Sal often made it home on the weekends for two reasons. One was to spend quality time with his girlfriend, Elizabeth, and the other was to be supportive to Michael. He was a surrogate sibling for Michael's youngest brother and included him in many family activities. Donny loved being with Sal and often would attend family dinners at the La Greca home. Over the past year, Sal had seen so much of himself in Donny, who had become more than a responsibility; he had, in essence, become a younger brother. For Sal, living in New York was a marvelous opportunity to be separate from the family home and at the same time visit at least twice a month, eat great food and have his laundry done.

3

Tragedy in Point Pleasant

THE SUNLIGHT BURST THROUGH THE CURTAINS in Michael's room on a beautiful June morning. He had been awake for hours and was trying to focus his feelings. This was his wedding day, and he felt a mixture of joy and sadness. He knew that Arlene was a remarkable woman, and he loved her beyond measure, but he was sad that his mother would not be present on this most special day. He could imagine how thrilled she would be. She had always loved Arlene and in her last year of life had many occasions for private time with her. Sometimes when he had seen them together, he felt a kind of jealousy—that female closeness that he couldn't be a part of. But this was a small thing; mostly he was tremendously glad they cared for each other and now, especially, glad that Arlene had known her.

He remembered that the characteristics that Mrs. McNally always mentioned about Arlene were her kindness to all of her sons and her marvelous sense of humor.

He glanced at his watch and knew it was time to gather the boys. He dressed and walked down the hall to his brothers' bedroom. Danny was awake, but Donny was still asleep with the blanket completely covering his head. Michael sat on Donny's bed, placed his hand under the blanket and gently stroked his hair. Donny sprang up and said, "Am I late?"

Michael chuckled and said, "No, but it's time to get dressed." His brothers were to be his best men, and Donny had been selected to be the ring bearer. At 10:15, Aunt Mary arrived and supervised the dressing of the younger boys. She smiled as Donny struggled to make a Windsor knot for his tie. He made a flurry of attempts. Aunt Mary refrained from helping him because it was important that he accomplish this challenge on his own. Finally, he was satisfied with the tie, and Aunt Mary put on his jacket and placed a carnation in his lapel.

At precisely 11:15, the family left for the five-minute walk to St. Aloysius church. As they approached the side entrance, they were greeted by Sal, who was to be a groomsman. Sal whistled his approval at Donny's outfit and was quite impressed when Donny showed him the wedding rings. They entered the church, which was relatively empty. St. Aloysius was a mammoth granite edifice that was an exquisite combination of Renaissance and French Classic design. It had been patterned after The Santa Maria della Pace in Rome. Its massive granite bell tower was a copy of St. Mark's Campanile in Venice. The setting next to the lovely grounds of spacious Lincoln Park made it as beautiful as any church in New Jersey.

St. Aloysius was more than a church for the McNally and Fallon families. It was the place that had welcomed their ancestors, the new Irish immigrants. It had become the center of their educational and social lives as well as a buttress against the many forms of prejudice that greeted them in this new land. The church had additional meaning for Arlene and Michael because every significant family event for decades had transpired there. They had each gone to their first wedding there. They had seen, cousins and siblings celebrate first communions and baptisms. This sanctuary had also embraced them in moments of death and sadness. Both the mother of the bride and the mother of the groom had been buried from this church. Arlene and Michael were devout Catholics, and the church was their reservoir for guidance and a beacon on how to lead their lives. This parish had been the center of their social, intellectual and spiritual lives. Their faith was never viewed as a burden but rather a loving path that would lead them to the fulfillment of their hopes and dreams. As Michael waited for his bride, he felt the presence of his mother, not in a ghostly way but as a strong memory of love and acceptance.

Father McNulty entered the sacristy, and as he began to dress, he playfully bantered with the group. Donny proudly told him that he was holding the wedding rings and was one of the best men. Father McNulty was quite impressed and asked to see the rings. Donny reached into his pocket and was so excited that he dropped one of the rings and it rolled under a vestment cabinet. For the next five minutes, the wedding group tried to reach it. After several futile attempts, Father McNulty suggested they get a yardstick from the cloakroom. This proved to be successful, and Danny monitored further ring showing. The organist had started playing Pachelbel's "Canon," and Michael peeked into the church, which was rapidly filling up. The altar was radiant with magnificent red roses thanks to the generosity of Aunt Mary. Sal was busy ushering friends and members to their seats. Father

McNulty, fully dressed in white vestments, put his arm around Michael. "Time for us to get in position."

They walked out to the altar. Michael was initially somewhat subdued, but when he came to the communion rail, he felt a burst of emotion. The beauty of the fully lit church overwhelmed him. As he gazed at the stained-glass windows of St. Patrick and St. Bridget, the wonder of this day elevated his soul. The church was now fully packed, and there was an air of anticipation as the organ became silent. The stillness gave way to a burst of chords that bellowed through the rafters. As they rose, at the back of the church the bridesmaids in their pale green dresses, the color of the first buds of spring, began the procession toward the altar. After the last bridesmaid made it to her place on the altar, Arlene and her father appeared. They began to slowly walk down the aisle, and Michael was breathless. He was enveloped by the wondrous beauty of his bride. He had seen the wedding dress on a hanger in her home, but he could not have imagined how alive and glorious it would be on Arlene. It appeared to him that Arlene was not walking but rather gliding toward the altar bathed in a luxurious silk and satin dress, her veil, dotted with seed pearls, floating from the crown of her head over her shining face. As Arlene and her father arrived, he shook Mr. Reilly's hand and placed his hand in Arlene's. Father McNulty had officiated at many weddings, and his opening line always broke the tension. "Arlene and Michael, please smile or relatives on both sides will think you picked a lemon." Michael was emotionally under control until he faced Arlene and mouthed his vows. The tears came as he said, "I do." She lovingly smiled and caressed his forearm.

When Father McNulty said, "You may now kiss the bride," the entire church broke into spontaneous applause.

After greeting friends and family on the receiving line, the wedding party moved to Lincoln Park to take photos. Most of the pictures were taken in front of the mammoth fountain in the center of the park. It was the largest concrete monument in the world and was adorned with 365 frog spouts and 150 lights. Donny playfully imitated the sounds of a frog during the photo session. Once this was accomplished, they arrived at the exclusive Casino in the Park restaurant for the wedding reception. Normally, the wedding reception would have been held at the Veterans of Foreign Wars Hall, but due to the generosity of Arlene's older brother, the reception was at the Casino in the Park.

Arlene and Michael entered the building and were duly impressed by the marble fountain of Aphrodite with its charming sound of cascading water. Michael kissed Arlene on the cheek and whispered, "We are really acting like swells today." She smiled and caressed his arm as they walked to the dining area. The main ballroom was stunningly lit by seven sparkling crystal chandeliers, and the French doors at the back of the ballroom led to the patio and a lovely view of the man-made lake. The sixty guests applauded as the couple entered the room and were seated at the head table.

After the initial dance, the married couple sat at the head table. Donny and Danny approached the microphone and read their toasts perfectly. Donny had a huge grin on his face as he raised his Shirley Temple to toast the bride and groom. Sal spoke next. He said, "If ever there were two people made for each other, it is Arlene and Michael. I have known them for most of my life, and their love has been an inspiration for each of us. I raise my glass to toast them and hope they will be blessed with many years of love and joy."

After the reception, the newly married couple drove to Belmar for their honeymoon. Aunt Mary had vacated her home for a week, and they began their married life at the shore. It was a lovely cottage only one block from Lake Geneva, the small body of water that separated Belmar and Spring Lake. It was a week filled with nights of wondrous intimacy and loving, tender moments. Michael had long anticipated complete union with his wife, but had not come close to imagining what fulfillment he would feel. It seemed to him no other man had known such happiness, and he marveled that the world went about its business as if love were not the supreme mystery. How could a married man ever be in a bad mood when he had this sweetness, this miracle, awaiting him? Was it possible one came to take it for granted?

They greeted the rising sun over the water and picnicked on benches as the sun crested into the deep blue ocean. Every day they held hands and experienced the joy of being fully together in their long walks on the beach.

The following week Aunt Mary and Donny and Danny joined the lovebirds for an extended vacation. Michael had a job at the Monmouth resort in Spring Lake as a tennis assistant, and Arlene returned to her job as a legal secretary in Jersey City. Every weekend she would make the trip back to the shore. Friday nights were usually spent with friends Sal and Elizabeth at one of the local pizza parlors. Over the 4th of July weekend, both couples met at Francesco's house of pizza in Belmar. After showing proof of age, the waitress brought a pitcher of beer and the two women immediately launched into talk about weddings. Elizabeth and Sal had been a steady couple for over three years. Their romance began after Arlene played matchmaker in their senior year on the annual boat ride to Rye Beach. Like Arlene, Elizabeth had been a cheerleader and was voted the best female dresser in their graduating class. She was taller than Arlene and wore her blond hair in whatever was the most fashionable style of the moment. She was a genuine devotee of stylish clothing. Her job as a salesperson at the fashionable Rene's clothing store on Journal Square allowed her, through employee discounts, to consistently be beautifully dressed.

Arlene pointedly asked, "Well, are you guys getting engaged soon and have you starting making arrangements for the big day?"

Michael stood up and said, "Sal, let's go see if the pool table in the back is free before these two plan the rest of your life."

Arlene scoffed at her husband and said, "McNally, you have never had it so good."

As they took the pool cues from the rack, Michael whispered, "She was right about marriage, Sal, and I can't recommend it more strongly, but I will never admit it." While they played a few games of 8 ball, Elizabeth showed photos of her mother's wedding gown, a slender ivory column in the style of the late 30s, and asked if Arlene would be one of her bridesmaids when the blessed day arrived.

"Try to keep me away," said Arlene. "I set you two up, you know."

"She'll never stop reminding you of that," Michael said.

One Saturday at the beginning of August, Michael had the day off, and he and Arlene took the boys to the bay in Point Pleasant. The ocean in Belmar had been quite rough with dangerous riptides due to a recent storm and was precarious for swimmers. Arriving at the bay, they picked a spot at the northwest corner of the pier, which had a series of picnic tables. They were all in bathing suits, having changed at the home of Arlene's cousin. Eating was the last thing that Donny wanted to do, and he wolfed his sandwich in record time. He could not wait to go swimming, but Michael enforced the one-hour rule before going into the water. Every five minutes, Donny asked if the hour had passed. Michael and Arlene were amused by his persistence. Finally, Michael gave the sign that the time had arrived. The swimming area was crowded, but Donny led the parade and performed a perfect cannonball off the pier into the water. Shrieks of joy and playful dunking were happening all over the area. Michael dunked Danny and was in turn submarined by Donny.

After an hour or so, Donny swallowed some water and decided to swim to the ladder and take a short break. He was unaware that an electrician was working on a neon sign that had blown down during the recent storm; two of the connecting lines were touching the ladder. The electrician had forgotten to cut the power when he went to his truck for a Phillips screwdriver. Donny, who had one leg on the ladder and the other in the water, accidentally touched one of the wires. The electrical current jolted through his body. The electrician, on his way back from the truck, witnessed Donny convulsing on the ladder. In horror, he raced to shut off the current.

Once the power was off, Donny appeared to let go of the wire and fell from the ladder into the water face down. The electrician and two other men leaped into the water and raised him up the ladder and onto the pier. One of the men said "Hurry, call a doctor; he is still breathing." The electrician was in a state of panic and kept rubbing Donny's hand while the other rescuers were trying to remove the water from his lungs. One of the observers raced into the ice cream parlor and called the local hospital. Arlene and Danny were still in the water but suddenly became aware of crowd activity on the pier. Michael looked around but could not find Donny. He swam to the area of the commotion. Climbing the ladder, Michael noticed that there was a large group of people at the edge of the pier. Michael was calling Donny's name as he made his way through the crowd, hoping that his brother was somewhere in the area. He was overcome with fear when he saw Donny cradled in the arms of two men. Michael raced to Donny and held him in his arms, shouting, "He's my brother. What happened to him?"

The electrician was hysterical, saying, "I am so sorry, I had no idea the wires were close to the end of the pier. I would never want to hurt a child; you have to believe me; you have to believe me."

Michael's fear turned to anger, and he pushed the electrician away, saying, "Get the hell away from me." At that moment, an ambulance arrived on the pier, and two emergency technicians rushed to Donny's aid. Michael was requested to let them attend to him. After frantic attempts to revive Donny, one of the attendants asked Michael if he was related to the young boy. Michael, beside himself, sobbed, "Yes, he is my brother, are you taking him to the hospital?"

The technician sadly responded, "I am sorry, he is gone. There is nothing we can do but take him to the hospital morgue." Michael collapsed to his knees, and Arlene and Danny embraced him. Losing his mother was wrenching, but this death was a mountain that Michael would have to climb for years.

Sal was working in Belmar as a waiter at the Crab Shack restaurant. Upon hearing what had happened to Donny, he began to weep uncontrollably. He was so upset that he was not sure if he could even drive a car to the city. He asked one of the other waiters to cover his shift and walked from the bay to the ocean. Sitting on a bench, he gazed at the waves. He felt as though he had lost a part of himself. After two hours, he had drained his body of tears and had enough stamina to return to the restaurant. He asked for three days off and made his way to Jersey City. He had to pull over to the shoulder on three occasions because he was blinded by his tears and feared he would cause a major accident. When he finally arrived at Corrigan's Funeral Home, the place was packed to overflowing. After waiting on line for a good twenty minutes, he reached Michael. Their eyes met, and Michael rose to meet him. They hugged, and both men began to weep. "I am so sorry, Michael."

"I am devastated, Sal."

They sat silently for a few minutes, and Sal realized that others were waiting to speak with Michael. He rose and went to the kneeler in front of Donny's casket. He reached out and touched the body. It was so stiff and cold. The image of Donny laughing and having so much fun with Sal the past year was more than he could bear, and the tears flowed again. He felt a cold shiver down his spine and despite the heat in the parlor began to shake uncontrollably. He tried to compose himself, rose and hurriedly walked to the foyer. Sal was the youngest member of his family and Donny had become a little brother to him.

The smell of the flower arrangements near Donny's casket was overpowering. Mr. Corrigan had removed some of the larger ones due to the huge crowds that had visited the first afternoon of the viewing. There was not an inch of free space in the main parlor, and the room temperature was suffocating. The blistering summer sun had baked the funeral home, and the two floor fans merely circulated the humid air. Michael had spent moments staring at the casket in sheer disbelief that his brother was dead. "My God, my God, why have you forsaken me"—the words that Jesus spoke on the cross—kept going through Michael's mind like a broken record as he sat in stunned shock staring at the coffin of his thirteen-year-old brother. His head was splitting, and he could not hold down any solid food. The heat in the room was so oppressive that he probably was dehydrated. On more than one occasion, he was wobbly when he rose to greet a friend or relative. There was very little in Michael's life that meant more to him than his Catholic faith, but he had never felt so tested. How could he reconcile the tragic death of his innocent brother with the image of a loving God? It was absurd to have a rational perspective, remembering Donny splashing joyfully in the water, with his young body now lying still in a coffin. The steady stream of visitors at the funeral home did little to assuage his confusion. Statements like: "Be strong and offer up your suffering for the souls in purgatory," seemed so ridiculous that he wanted to shout at his fellow mourners. He understood at some level that they were well-intentioned, but they did not for a second help him. There was a moment when he almost exploded.

One of his neighbors, Mr. Doyle, said, "Thank God you still have Danny." When he heard those words, he felt a rage that terrified him. The blood in his veins seemed to be a tidal wave that would launch him to violence. He feared that he would physically strike his neighbor who had uttered that ridiculous statement. He excused himself and hurriedly made his way out of the room. Walking at a rapid pace, he found the staircase leading to the basement and, shaking with anger, opened a storage door. In a moment of rage, he picked up a bottle of cleaning fluid and threw it against the wall. It shattered, and his shoes and pant cuffs were stained with bleach. He began to scream and shout. He started beating his fists against the door and thought *How could anyone believe that something good could come from this tragedy?* He was soaking wet from perspiration and felt as though his head was about to explode. After five minutes of calming self-talk, he realized that Mr. Doyle was well-meaning but didn't know what to say. He slowly went up the stairs and resumed his position at the head of the line next to his weeping brother and father.

Michael could control his anger on the outside. The more difficult challenge was dealing with the rage that was eating him up on the inside. Michael had never experienced anger on so many levels. He was angry at the electrician for carelessly leaving electrical power in an area where people were swimming. He was angry that it took so long for the ambulance to arrive at the scene of the accident. He was even angry at God for taking his mother and adding a second burden. How could allowing Donny to die help his faith? He had accepted the first loss, but this was beyond the pale. These were all targets for his anger, but most of all he was angry at himself. Why had he decided to go to the bay instead of the beach? Why had swimming become a priority instead of throwing a football around? Why had he lost sight of Donny in the water? It was his responsibility to take care his brother, and he felt he had failed miserably. Every waking moment he was inundated with details of that fateful day.

The next few days were a violent storm of emotions: dealing with the funeral home, the burial Mass, and the torturous image of seeing his brother's coffin placed in a grave. He had barely slept since that horrible day at the bay, but despite his fragile state of mind, somehow, he was able to spend hours talking with Danny about what had happened. After his mother's death, Danny had been relatively close-mouthed about his feelings. Michael had made sustained attempts to get him to talk about what he was experiencing. The first night of the wake, Danny came downstairs and sat next to Michael. He had no facile answers for Danny but knew that he must find ways to tap into the pain and confusion that he knew his brother was experiencing.

After many attempts, Danny finally shared his feelings. "It's not fair, Michael. I don't understand why God took Mom. I miss her every day but why Donny too? He never did anything to hurt anyone. He was so happy at the bay and . . ." Danny began to weep. He took out his handkerchief. Michael remained silent, waiting for him to continue. "The night before we went to Point Pleasant, he kept me up half the night yakking about all he was going to do the next day. I wanted to sleep and at one point told him to go to sleep and shut up."

There were no pat words, so Michael merely said, "I understand that, Danny. There were times I felt guilty that I did not spend enough time with him and Mom."

Danny was quiet for a bit. "I find it hard to pray, Michael, and I am mad at God for taking them, but maybe God did not take them and they just died."

Michael said, "I feel the same way, Danny, and it is hard to understand, but I also believe that they are with God and that helps me a lot. I need you, Danny, and I never want you to feel alone, so please promise me that whenever you have feelings you will share them with me."

Danny quietly said, "Okay, I will. Thanks, Michael."

Sleep for Michael since Donny's death had been almost non-existent. Each night was an endless twisting and turning filled with the nightmares of his brother's death. He imagined Donny pleading with him for help. He often woke up shouting out Donny's name and shivered in grief and guilt as Arlene tried to soothe him back to sleep. His grief found no respite.

Closure was a word that he had often heard, but he knew all too well that there was no clear path to understanding the deaths of his mother and Donny. Grief after the death of a loved one is not a process that has a terminus. It is not something that finishes and can be relegated to the past. It lingers and hits forcefully at moments that aren't predictable. Grief over the death of someone you love is so powerful that the fear is that it will never dissipate. There is no haven that offers solace, and as others receded into their lives, Michael's pain became more and more searing. The rituals of a funeral service and burial are not the end but rather the beginning. Each morning brings the clarion announcement that it was not merely a nightmare. He woke to the real, tangible declaration that his mother and Donny were dead, that these two-irreplaceable people, whose hearts were so entwined with his own, were somehow, incomprehensibly, no longer on earth. The sheer force of that knowledge had shaken Michael beyond imagination, and the hurdles in his path were mountains of pain, guilt, and self-doubt. He began to examine whether he should continue to study medicine. With only a remnant of his family left, he pondered the thought that instead of medical school he should spend most of his days with Danny and Arlene.

Arlene was his love and the harbor of his heart. With her, all facades could be dropped. She was there to wipe the sweat from his forehead when he woke shouting Donny's name. She listened for hours in loving silence to the anger and guilt that seemed to penetrate his soul. She understood that grief persisted after the calls and cards had dwindled to a few, and the casseroles and meals were no longer left on their doorstep. She allowed herself to be the catch basin of Michael's anger, pain, confusion, and loss of emotional equilibrium. At no point did she dismiss the choices that she believed were not ones that would lead to solace. She indulged and encouraged the myriad attempts that Michael made to clarify his situation and feelings. Despite his confusion, she held an unflinching belief that at some point he would choose to turn his pain into service for others. She understood the temptation for him to give up his dream of being a doctor. It was based on his desire to protect Danny and dedicate the rest of his life to being by his side. Arlene recognized the roots of this belief, but she also knew it was a choice that would not only limit what Michael could bring to others; it would also limit Danny's growth.

SEPTEMBER 1957, DECISION TIME

The time for decision was almost at hand. One evening, Arlene inquired what Michael was going to do regarding Seton Hall. She was increasingly aware that the man she loved was becoming a shell of himself. She had always loved his strength and courage and marveled at how he had given up his dream school to stay home and raise his brothers. This conversation was not merely about him. It was also about her and her needs and desires for the future. She understood his pain and confusion, but she could not stand by and let him bury all their hopes and dreams with Donny. There was a fine line between being supportive and seeing her dreams evaporate. She firmly asked him, "What are you going to do about school?"

Michael stared at his hands for what seemed an eternity before softly replying, "I don't know. Somehow medical school seems unimportant and distant at this moment. I am not sure I have the energy that rigorous academic pursuits demand." Arlene made no attempt to sell a solution but kept asking him what he saw in their future. She adored him, but her life and future were also in peril. For hours, they talked about their vision for him, Danny, her, and their children if they were blessed to have them. Her non-judgmental loving presence and honesty eventually led Michael to spend days probing all the options. He concluded that medicine could be a place to turn his grief into loving service to others.

By the time that classes were about to begin in September, Michael had regained enough emotional stability to begin senior year. He had signed up for the three-day senior retreat, which was to be delivered by Father Charles Hudson, a hospital chaplain. Father Hudson was born and raised in Jersey City and had a well-earned reputation as an outstanding speaker. He could make everyone in his retreats feel as though he was speaking directly to them. His talks were filled with powerful stories and penetrating human insights. He was known for his self-deprecation and marvelous sense of humor. Michael responded immediately to Father Hudson's inspiring words.

The last session of the second day was entitled Working through Grief and Guilt. Michael was so touched by this two-hour session that when it ended, he approached Father Hudson and asked if he could speak with him. Taking off his cassock, Father Hudson responded, "I was just going into town for a sandwich and a beer. Why don't you join me? I would love the company." Michael was thrilled to have this opportunity, and they briskly walked to the Miss Florence Diner, which was ten minutes from the campus. The diner was a mainstay in the college community and had not changed its appearance or menu in the last twenty years. Many of the leather stools at the counter were torn, and the grill had a couple of inches of grease from all the fast food items. Their waitress, attired in a vintage black and white uniform, had apparently worked at the diner since it opened. She gave them menus and said, "It looks like there are unlimited choices on the menu, but trust me, stick with the specials."

Father Hudson asked, "How is the meatloaf?"

The waitress smiled and said, "A heck of a lot better than most of the other specials."

Father Hudson laughed at her honesty and said, "I'll have the meatloaf special and a beer. How about you, son?"

"I'll have the same."

The waitress raised her eyebrows and sarcastically asked, "Would you like root or birch beer?" She had been around the college town for years and knew that Michael was underage.

Michael considered bluffing, but he knew that she would ask for proof. He softly replied, "root beer."

Father Hudson teased him. "Are you the only college kid that doesn't have a fake ID?" Michael ducked his head and grinned.

Once the food arrived, Father Hudson asked, "What's on your mind, Michael?"

That question opened the emotional floodgates. Michael poured out his anguish and pain. "My kid brother Donny was electrocuted at the beach this summer, and I can't get it out of my mind. I relive that day, and no matter what I do, I can't change it. I can't sleep, eat or go anywhere without thinking about what happened to Donny. He was my responsibility, and I let him down. I should have watched him. I am possessed by what happened. Last week I went to the movies, and there was a scene where a convict was about to get the electric chair, and all I could see was Donny being electrocuted. I began to sob and bolted from the movie. His death was on top of the fact that my mother died of heart attack a few years ago. I feel totally lost."

Father Hudson listened, not saying a word until Michael finished. He took a deep drag on his cigarette before quashing it into an ashtray. "Michael, you have been dealt a tough hand by life, and no words can make it all go away. Grief is so damn personal, and no one can fully understand where you are. Every day as a chaplain I deal with death, so I have some degree of understanding. It is always sad and difficult, but sudden death rips your heart to pieces. My sister Tina was killed by a drunk driver when she was twenty-two. Despite my faith, I was a basket case. I was angry at the guy who killed her, angry at God for allowing her death and even angry at Tina for dying. Coupled with that, I felt overwhelming guilt. She called me the night she was killed and invited me to the movies. I declined because I had appointments at the hospital. I beat myself up with a ton of magical thinking that if I had gone to the movies, she would still be alive.

"I finally concluded that Tina did not want me to live with grief and guilt forever. I believe that is true for your loved ones also. Don't run from the grief, Michael, but you are guilty of nothing. You have a life ahead, and there will always be scar tissue, but you will heal. I know from experience that your mother and Donny do not want you to be emotionally buried. The pain will always be close by but living your life as fully as possible keeps them alive."

Michael was speechless, and as he wept, Father Hudson reached across the table and grasped both his hands. The last morning of the retreat, he realized that he had choices—to feel betrayed by God or fully accept on faith that God's love was ever present and had nothing to do with his tragedies. He chose to accept God's love and took a conscious leap of faith.

4

The Next Step, Medical School

MICHAEL HAD BEEN ACCEPTED TO HIS first choice, Jefferson Medical College in Philadelphia, but there were immediate financial concerns. He and Arlene had an unbelievably low monthly rental apartment, and he knew that the cost of housing in Philadelphia would be double what they were paying in Jersey City. Fortunately, Arlene's brother was in the wholesale produce business, and one of his clients had a grocery store in South Philadelphia. The owner had a son who was starting medical school at Jefferson. In addition to this coincidence, Stefano Pittelli owned an apartment building three blocks from the school. Arlene's brother had discussed the McNally's' situation with Stefano, and he graciously rented them an apartment at family rates.

The youngest child in the Pittelli family was Joseph, and he was an Italian clone of Michael McNally. They were both incredibly bright, athletic, and had been valedictorians in high school and college. This dynamic duo soon latched on to a third medical student who would be part of the Philadelphia Three. Catherine Salvato fit right in with Joe and Michael. With her brilliant mind, can-do work ethic, and fabulous sense of humor, she could hold her own with her male counterparts. Jefferson, like most medical schools, was a good old boys club, and some professors were less than enthralled that women had been accepted. Catherine met this bias with grace, but it was difficult for her.

The three new students became as close as family.

The academic schedule of medical school was far more rigorous than undergraduate work, but Michael, Catherine and Joseph continued to excel in the classroom and labs. Michael almost immediately adjusted to Philadelphia. He compared his new city to the one of his birth but added, "It is a hell of a lot larger." Most days he was engulfed in his studies, but there were days when the losses of his mother and brother weighed heavily on his heart. It was in these moments that his faith and love of God brought him solace. This was especially true when he had the opportunity to fit Mass into his schedule. The moments after receiving communion enabled him to believe without reservation that his mother and brother were living blessed lives in heaven.

Financially strapped, Michael and Arlene would occasionally drive to the airport and watch planes take off and land. On one of those occasions, Arlene mentioned that a dream of hers was to board a plane with a child and go to some magical place for vacation. Michael thought that would be wonderful and hoped that someday they would be blessed with a child. Arlene leaned over, placed her hand in his and said, "Do you have any idea where I went on Thursday?"

Michael said, "What does that have to do with vacations and children?"

Arlene tousled his hair and, moving closer to him in the front seat of their car, responded, "It has everything to do with it, silly."

Michael, for all his brilliance, still did not have a clue what she was talking about. "What does Thursday have to do with it?"

"I had a doctor's appointment."

For a fleeting second, Michael experienced panic. "Arlene, are you alright? Why did you go to the doctor's?"

Arlene could no longer hold back her news. "I went because I had a suspicion, and it was confirmed." Michael could barely breathe, suspecting a new tragedy. "Michael, we are going to have a baby."

Michael sobbed with joy when he heard the news and could not speak for minutes. He had known the ravages that death leaves in its wake, and now he would experience the wonder of the birth of a child. This gift was a blessing and a sign that his faith in the goodness and love of God had been rewarded.

There was a new vitality in Michael's step after Arlene's news. When the day arrived, he drove Arlene to the hospital and stayed with her. He had secured permission to be with Arlene during the entire birth process. When the baby arrived and began to cry, Michael wept in unison with his son. He had hoped but not believed that the joy of new life was even greater than the grief of loss. At this moment he thought of his mother (how happy she would be) and Donny (how proud to be an uncle). Somehow, for this moment, all was in balance.

Michael Jr. was all wet and wrinkled, but Michael thought he was beautiful. He held him gently as he wrapped his tiny body in a blanket, trying to keep him warm. Michael felt such joy and elation at the sight of his newborn son. For the next few days, he would leave class and race to the hospital to spend time with

Arlene and Michael Jr. He told Catherine and Joe that they better plan to become parents because holding his son in his arms was beyond description.

5

The Golden Offer

THE SUBWAY CENTER AT GROVE STREET was like a boiling cauldron. Hundreds of people sweltering in the heat were waiting on the platform for the next train from Jersey City to New York. At the height of rush hour, the crush was unavoidable. Sal, waiting in the crowd, felt an uncomfortable similarity to a mussel pressed against stone. The claustrophobic Sal had no desire to get on the subway. The train screeched to a halt in the station, and Sal, dressed in a damp seersucker suit, jostled past his fellow travelers and took a place near the door. Lurching around the curves, the train sped toward Wall Street as the temperature in the packed car rose. Finally, the train arrived at the Wall Street station. Sal straightened his tie and carried his jacket as he climbed the stairs. The walk to his office at Wertheim Brokerage was short, and to his joy, the elevator to the fourteenth floor was almost empty. Making his way to his desk, he exchanged morning greetings with his fellow employees, and, despite the heat, poured himself a cup of coffee. As he looked around, he felt grateful for the position at the firm, though it lay far from his dreams of journalism. His plan, however, was to pursue journalism after his upcoming stint in the army. Ever the optimist, Sal dismissed any concern about the future and began to attend to his responsibilities.

Mid-morning, Sal received a notice from the secretary of the managing director that he was to report to the director's office at 11:30. For all his confidence, his heart beat a little faster. He buried himself in his work, but found that every few minutes he gazed at the clock on the wall at the end of the corridor. At 11:25, he put on his jacket and reported to the director's office. Robert Emanuel was respected for his calm, caring leadership. He was brilliant, yet down to earth, and made it his business to regularly interact with all the employees. He was gifted with the ability to remember the character and interests of all those who worked for him. Sal had met him briefly on the first day of his employment and was impressed with how much the director knew about him.

Nervously fidgeting with his tie while waiting to be summoned, he was more than slightly apprehensive about this meeting. When the secretary told him to enter, Sal knocked and heard a voice call, "Come in!"

"Please have a seat and feel free to hang up your suit jacket." Mr. Emmanuel came from behind his desk carrying a manila folder and requested that Sal sit in one of two leather chairs positioned next to each other. Before opening the folder, Mr. Emmanuel asked, "I know that you have been with us for almost two months. What has it been like working here?"

Sal cautiously selected his words, "I am grateful to be here and have been pleased with the work and assignments that I have been given."

"Good," replied Mr. Emmanuel. "I see in your dossier that you were a journalism major. Am I speaking to someone who will write the great American novel?" The question was accompanied by a smile, and Sal felt relaxed by the director's friendly manner.

"Most likely I will have to spend two years in the army. When I am discharged, I will pursue a career in journalism. I had hoped to land a junior position at a newspaper, but my draft status prevented that."

After a short silence, the director responded: "You have made an excellent impression on everyone who has worked with you in your brief stint here, and I am sure you are wondering what the purpose of this meeting is. I have called you here because of an idea that came to me this weekend."

Sal was amazed by the fact that the director would think about him over the weekend. The director continued, "You may not know it but the firm has many wealthy clients, and through the years they have requested that we do more than manage their stocks and investments. They often request our assistance in managing their wills, charitable involvements, family trusts and issues which are not always directly related to stocks and bonds. My idea is that it may be time to have someone in charge of these matters because dedicated service to our clients benefits us as well as them. This is where you come in, Sal. I am considering having you take a new position that will eventually make you responsible for dealing directly with a select number of clients on these issues."

"But Mr. Emmanuel," Sal cried, "I have no experience. How will this work?"

"I will not throw you into the lion's den," the director replied, smiling. "Not, that is, without prolonged training. My initial thought is that if you accept this, I will personally guide you through a development program, probably over a two-year period. I would envision a position where you would become a member of my staff. In addition, there would be an education component. I don't expect you to make an immediate decision. Should you choose to accept, the details will be worked out later."

"Thank you, Mr. Emmanuel, but honestly I had no idea why you wanted to see me. I am overwhelmed at what you have just proposed," Sal said, catching his breath. "I am most grateful that you have such confidence in me but never imagined that this would happen. Also, I must remind you that I could be drafted."

The director paused and, standing up, walked over to his desk and took a cigarette from his pack. He offered one to Sal, and both lit up. Taking a deep drag, the director said: "There are a couple of things that I need to say. First, when we are together here or at a meeting, there is no need to call me Director or Mr. Emmanuel. I would prefer that you call me Bob. Is that agreeable to you?"

Sheepishly, Sal nodded his head.

"The second thing is that I would like you to take a week or so to make your decision. Is that agreeable?"

"Absolutely, and please know how grateful I am for your taking the time to consider me for this position."

"You are perfectly welcome." The director rose from his chair and shook Sal's hand. It was obvious that the meeting was over.

The rest of the day found Sal constantly rehashing the morning meeting. The whole day had a dream-like quality. Sal couldn't understand his feelings. He was excited and flattered by the offer, yet he was still uneasy. It was more than his dreams of journalism holding him back from the opportunity. There was some reason that he wasn't sure about this job, but he couldn't put his finger on it. The day flew past, and he barely noticed the work that passed before his eyes. Glancing at his watch, he realized it was time to return home. Sal walked to the subway and boarded, so preoccupied with his thoughts that he didn't even notice the heat or the crowd. He was so oblivious that he missed the Grove Street stop and went on to the Journal Square station. Instead of taking the number 9 bus home, he decided to walk. When he arrived at his corner, he kept walking, all the way to Lincoln Park. Arriving at the park, he made his way to his favorite spot, a bench next to the beautiful bronze statue of a fireman. He sat down and tried to collect his thoughts. His lack of excitement made no sense. This job was security, not only for him but any family he might have. It meant a house, benefits, everything a rational man could want. It didn't fulfill that dream of journalism, but when it comes down to it, he thought, how many can really follow their dreams? And who knows if that dream would even make him happy? All of this seemed so reasonable and should have dispelled the discomfort, but somehow none of these hit the core of what was troubling him. Deep within his soul was the need to make a real difference in the world. The idea of handling the entire portfolio of a select wealthy few was appealing because it was the road to significant personal financial security for him, but it seemed meaningless. There was no passion. He was almost angry that the new job proposal did not meet the standards of his soul. He sat on the bench for nearly an hour before he heard the familiar sound of the church bell. It was from the bell tower of St. Aloysius church, making him aware that he was late for supper.

Rising slowly, he began to make his way home, but when he came to the corner where he should go left, he kept walking straight to the St. Aloysius rectory. He rang the bell, and a woman answered the door.

"May I help you?" she inquired.

"I would like to speak to Father McNulty."

"I am sorry," she said, "but he is having his dinner."

Undaunted by this response, he offered: "Please tell him Sal La Greca needs to speak to him."

The request did not seem to please her, but she said, "Come in and wait in the vestibule." After a few moments, Father McNulty appeared with his napkin in hand and smiling.

"What a pleasant surprise." He led Sal to a nearby office and said kiddingly, "Well, what is so important that you pulled me away from my dessert?"

Sal sat there in almost catatonic silence and then blurted out, "I think I want to become a priest."

Sal was almost as shocked at his confession as Father McNulty. For the next hour, the two men sat and discussed the desire that was weighing on Sal's heart. At the end of the conversation, Father McNulty advised that Sal should think and pray over this. He counseled Sal not to share his thoughts on the matter with anyone else until they had the opportunity to chat again.

The next few weeks were exceptionally difficult for Sal. He cross-examined himself constantly, repeating over and over the reasons not to become a priest. He had a phenomenal job opportunity, a wonderful young woman whom he believed he was in love with, and the possibility of children someday. How could he abandon all of this for an idea that had hit him like a lightning bolt? He scoffed at the idea that, like St. Paul, he had been knocked off his proverbial horse and was destined to follow Christ. He thought perhaps it started when Michael's mother had died. Father McNulty's involvement in the family was so profound that it moved him emotionally. All those times with Kelly in New York going to Mass and spending time with his brother Father Kelly had made a difference too. Some of the trappings of his religion—seen through the judgmental eye of youth—had blurred the core of things that meant a great deal to him, espe-cially at times of severe emotional pain. The symbols of caring and community in moments of joy and sorrow were intimately tied to his Church and the priests that served the community. He was more deeply connected to being Catholic than his glib surface attitude evidenced, but this growing awareness also fright-ened him. Realizing the value of his faith and appreciating the service of the priests he knew was one thing, but how could he give up the life he lived now and the one he'd been envisioning? He knew real love, and he'd seen the happiness of its fulfillment in his friend Michael. How could he walk away from that? From Elizabeth? There would be no family, and he would have to live a celibate, childless life. It seemed a terrible sacrifice, as it always had—the barrier he knew many young men felt when they gave any thought to the priesthood.

Somehow all this reasoning did little to dissuade the thought that was constantly plaguing him that perhaps he should study for the priesthood. In the past, one of the biggest obstacles would have been his apparent lack of religious feeling. He didn't care about most of the dogma and the rules he had been taught in childhood. He used to tease his friends, saying: "Being Italian, I believe that all rules are suggestions." However, lately he was deeply moved by so many of the sacraments. He loved taking communion, and attendance at Mass had always been special for him. He had found continued comfort in the presence of his parish priests and often thought they made a difference in the world. No matter how he tried to dismiss the thoughts, nothing could remove them from his mind. This priest thing had to be fully explored, and to his amazement, he found for the first time in his life he resorted to prayer. He asked for peace of mind if this step was truly the right decision. The presence of Christ in his life was becoming more real as he pondered the question of the priesthood. He began to envision what the role of living as a priest would be. The idea of following in the footsteps of Christ took on a meaning he could barely explain to himself and which he thought few of his friends would understand. It had to do with being a teacher—with helping others find the joy of living in the presence of God. It had to do with the purity of those stories, the gospels, which once seemed simple but now glowed with a message that touched him to the core: this is how to live. This is what love of God looks like in the world.

After spending most of his waking moments thinking about the direction of his life, the time for a decision had arrived. He made an appointment to see Father McNulty, hoping that further counsel would make the issue even clearer. He confided to Father McNulty that he had struggled mightily with the decision over the past few weeks, and he had concluded that he should try to enter the seminary as soon as possible. Father McNulty explained that there would be no way that he could go directly into the major seminary, but, because he had a college degree, it would be feasible for him to spend one year at Seton Hall University taking courses in Latin and Greek. Then, if all went well, he would go to the seminary. Father McNulty added that after spending the first year in the seminary, Sal would skip the second year because he had a bachelor's degree. After their discussion, Father McNulty inquired as to how Sal wished to make this decision public. Falling back on his usual comical self, Sal said, "I think the biggest challenge, Father, is that most of the people who know me will think that I've completely lost my mind. They will probably demand I see a psychiatrist."

Father McNulty burst out laughing, and finally composing himself, said, "I'm sure that you will find a way to make everyone understand your decision. Please keep me posted."

Sal shook his hand and said, "Thanks, Father, I certainly will."

The easy part of making it public was to tell his mother and father. His mother was elated because she had a deep commitment to the church and regularly attended daily Mass. Her parents were devout Catholics, and the priesthood in their family was considered to be a special gift from God. She was born in America and had attended the New York School of Design. For two years, she was an apprentice clothes designer in New York. This ended when her oldest child, Tina, was born. It was not acceptable in the Italian culture for a mother to work outside the home. Instead, she became the gratis dress and wedding designer in her neighborhood and made splendid wedding gowns for many. Her faith was a gift that she enthusiastically shared with her children.

This belief was not shared by Sal's father. He was not anti-clerical but was far from being a devoted Catholic. He had come from a small town at the top of the Cammaratta Mountains in Sicily. As the youngest of eleven children, he had been taught by his brothers that in Sicily the clergy only cared about the wealthy. His brothers joked that a Sicilian man goes inside a church three times: when he is hatched, matched and dispatched.

When he arrived in America, he was eleven years old and could not speak a word of English. He worked six days a week in the awful unsanitary conditions of a burlap factory. Each day he was covered with soot and working in a closed environment with little ventilation, which caused a lifelong lung condition. Fortunately for him, when he was eighteen, his brothers purchased a laundry in Jersey City, and he eventually became the manager. He had been able to support his family and purchase a two-story brick home in a lovely neighborhood . . . his children, he knew, would live better than he had.

He deeply loved his son, but this choice made little sense to him. His boy had gone to college, gotten a job on Wall Street; he could do anything. This was America! But what he said to Sal was, "I will be behind you no matter what." Then he paused. "I do have one question for you though: have you told Elizabeth about this decision?"

Sal shook his head and said, "That may be the most difficult part of this. I plan to do that this weekend." Elizabeth was the part of the equation that was the most harrowing. They had dated exclusively for four years and recently had long conversations about the timing of their engagement. They had even started to scout out places for their wedding reception. The major decision was whether to be married before or after Sal finished his two-year stint in the Army. He feared this loss the most. He was powerfully attracted to Elizabeth, and though they had never been fully intimate, he had long dreamed of his wedding night, of the marriage bed. What would it be like to know a woman that way, not just once but for years?

He also was troubled at losing the opportunity to father children. He worried that being "Father" to many would not be the same as having his own children. Elizabeth filled so many needs; because of her, he had never known loneliness. Elizabeth was not only his dear friend; she was the love of his life. There was nothing that he could not share with her—at least until now. She trusted him, and he was going to break her heart. Until recently, he had no clue that this priest thing was even a possibility, so he was certain that she would be totally shocked.

The thought of hurting her at this level was so painful that he tried to find all the reasons why he should not follow this crazy priesthood whim. What if it was just a passing fancy; was it worth shattering someone he loved so dearly? What if he started down this path and later changed his mind? Would she marry someone else? Of course, she should; she was a loving woman who deserved a husband and family. But where would that leave him? Days went by without any perfect plan, and he realized that

procrastinating would solve nothing. During this period he began
to imagine what it would be like to be a priest. He could picture
the moments when he would be saying Mass or hearing confessions, but he was moved more by the images of being involved in
the everyday life of parishioners. He thought there would be endless occasions to bring hope and comfort to those in pain. There
would d also be opportunities to teach children and be enmeshed
in the foundations of their education. Each day he was becoming
more and more concretely aware of what his life would be like as
a priest. The concept of the priesthood was becoming more real
and visual and was so attractive to him—an open door beckoning
him to walk through.

How would he handle the role? Would he be good at it? It was
almost an ache in his muscles to try, to *just do it.*

Sal called Elizabeth and arranged a date for Friday night. Her
initial response was to tease him about the fact that he had not
called her in a week. She playfully said, "I thought you had been
kidnapped." Sal told her that he had been exceptionally busy and
hoped she was free for dinner on Friday. "Great! Where shall we
go?"

"How about Ilvento's?"

"Wonderful. I love their fish specials."

"Okay, I will make a reservation for eight and will be at your
house at 7:30."

Ilvento's was mobbed, and the noise level was ear-piercing,
but fortunately, they were escorted to a table in a corridor off the
main dining area. It was relatively private, but Sal decided that he
would not discuss his issue with Elizabeth in a public place.

The waiter brought menus and inquired whether they would
like anything to drink. Elizabeth ordered a glass of chardonnay
and Sal a glass of chianti. Once the wine arrived, they clinked
their glasses and the waiter related the specials of the day. Since

it was Friday, Elizabeth ordered the flounder and a garden salad. Despite it being forbidden by the church, Sal desired the filet mignon but thought that would be inappropriate based on his status; he also ordered the flounder.

Once dinner arrived, the chatter seemed light, and Sal was sure that Elizabeth had no inkling of what was to come. At one point, the conversation drifted into an area that caused great discomfort for Sal. Elizabeth said, "My mother asked me this morning if we were going to get engaged at Christmas. I told her that was a possibility, but we had not decided yet." Elizabeth smiled and added, "You know, Mother is always trying to look ahead and sometimes can be a pest."

Sal was trying to figure how to duck the issue without being forced into the bigger questions. He motioned for the waiter. "Could we please have more bread?" Fortunately, the noise level even in their area had risen, and Sal took advantage of it. "I can barely hear you, Elizabeth. Let's chat about it after dinner." He did it in such an easy manner that he was certain that she did not see his request as avoiding the issue.

"Fine. How is your dinner?"

"Great, the fish is delicious."

The rest of the meal flowed smoothly, and there was playful banter over the desert menu. They chose different treats, and when the desserts came they shared mouthfuls, and Sal flirted openly with Elizabeth. She kissed his cheek and gently wiped the chocolate mousse off his lips. Her smile and laughter were captivating. He felt love and fear at the same moment. He could not deny his love for Elizabeth and was sharing a meal with her in a way that enhanced those feelings; yet in a short while, he was going to break her heart.

Leaving the restaurant, Sal suggested that they walk instead of taking the bus.

While they were walking, Elizabeth sensed that something was amiss. Sal was quiet and seemed preoccupied. She turned toward him and asked if anything was wrong. Sal could feel dryness in his mouth. He knew that the moment had arrived, but he wished there was some way he could avoid telling her his truth.

"Elizabeth," he began, "I have struggled with a lot of things lately."

"Like what?" she asked.

"It is complex, and I have had difficulty sorting it out. Last week, out of the blue, the managing director of the brokerage offered me a new job. I don't really understand it, but after a two-year training period, I'd be responsible for helping wealthy clients develop and maintain their money. . . . The director told me that this was a phenomenal opportunity."

"Sal, how wonderful. You must be thrilled."

Sal shook his head and slowly continued, "I should be, but I wasn't. Instead, I felt somewhat confused. Instead of going home after work that day, I made my way to Lincoln Park to our favorite spot. I sat there for over an hour talking to myself. While I was there, I heard the church bells ring, and for some strange reason, I went to see Father McNulty." Elizabeth could not follow the connection between the new job offer and going to see Father McNulty. She decided to wait and see where this was going. Sal continued, "I interrupted his dinner, and after a short conversation, I blurted out what I'm about to tell you now."

The look on Elizabeth's face changed from interest to concern. "Sal, what is it that you are trying to tell me?" she asked fearfully.

Sal swallowed and said, "Elizabeth, I'm going to study for the priesthood."

Elizabeth laughed and thought this was typical of Sal. The whole prelude about the job was leading to this punchline. She thought that he was teasing her. Suddenly, she realized it was not a joke. "You can't be serious!" she exclaimed. "I don't know of anyone who is less religious than you."

"I thought that was true, but I am seeing and understanding things about the Church that had escaped me before this."

Elizabeth looked at him in perplexity. "Are you thinking about studying for the priesthood just because you don't want to take this job?"

"No, Elizabeth, I don't believe that's it. The job offer was a catalyst for ideas I didn't even know I had. I realize how it sounds."

On the verge of tears, Elizabeth spoke in a voice that was rushed and uneven with emotion. "Do you? Sal, I am stunned by this. What about us? You and I had a future together! We had so many plans for marriage and a home and children. You, out of the blue, with no conversation, are telling me that those plans are dead. I can't believe they are all gone." Elizabeth took out her handkerchief and struggled to keep the tears from flowing.

"Elizabeth, it did not make a hell of a lot of sense to me either, but I can't shake it. I have spent hours and even days on end trying to understand the attraction to becoming a priest."

Elizabeth had so many things running through her head. Just last week she had her mother's wedding dress altered. She had honestly believed that Sal was going to propose to her on Christmas Eve. She stuttered, hoping that maybe he was just confused because his dream of being a journalist had not happened. "Sal, does this have anything to do with not having any opportunities in journalism? If that is the issue, I will support your dream of being a writer. "

"I wish that were it, but it is a need to make a difference. I watched Father McNulty last week working with a group of little kids in the Duncan projects. They loved him, and his presence made a huge difference in their lives. I saw the powerful effect that a priest can have on the lives of others."

Elizabeth bitterly responded, "So loving me and raising a family means nothing?"

"It's not that, Elizabeth, and giving you up scares the hell out of me. But no matter how hard I try, the idea of becoming a priest keeps coming back."

"I think it is terribly unfair that you never mentioned any of this to me. You take me out to dinner and make me feel so loved, and then you tell me we are through?"

"You are right. I guess I hoped that it would go away. I see now that keeping you in the dark was wrong. Elizabeth, I am sorry. I wish I didn't feel this way, but I do. Please don't think this is casual on my part. I've struggled and struggled, and I can't get it out of my mind."

Her deep hurt had now turned again to anger. "Then why didn't you tell me that this was a possibility before now? I feel like I have nothing to say about a decision that changes both of our lives."

"I understand how shocking this must be for you. The last thing in the world that I want to do is hurt you, but I feel compelled to try this. Maybe I will realize that this is not my call, but for me to stay with you and ignore my heart would be wrong for both of us."

The rest of the walk was silent. When Sal took Elizabeth home, he held her hand and said, "I'm sorry that I have hurt you. I would have done anything to avoid that short of denying this truth. You're probably going to need time, but please let us not stop talking to each other." He stared at her face, fixing it in his mind: the lovely mouth, grave eyes—the way her hair sprang up from her forehead—the way the porch light shone on her left side, while the other half lay in shadow. The sadness he saw, the hint of tears she was holding back—oh God, that hurt. She would have been his *wife*.

Elizabeth, who was heartbroken, gently replied, "I don't know what to think at this moment, but I certainly don't want this to be something that tears us apart. "

Sal turned to walk away. Elizabeth had trouble unlocking her front door. As she entered, she almost collapsed. She barely made it up the stairs to her room. She threw herself face down on her bed and wept uncontrollably, her body wracked with sobs. She kept repeating the words that Sal had spoken, "I am going to study for the priesthood." Those words had shattered everything she had believed was going to happen in her life.

Almost immediately after confiding in Elizabeth, Sal began the process of informing his friends of his decision. He couldn't let himself think of her pain too long; he was afraid he'd do something stupid and tell her he'd changed his mind. Surely, she would despise that cowardliness, as he would himself.

The fateful moment took place at Frank's Bar and Grill where he and his cohorts spent most of their free time. A good percentage of Sal's friends did not attend college, and so Frank's Bar and Grill became their stopping-off place after work. Sal and a couple of his other buddies who were in college attended at least once or twice a week. The average weekend for Sal and his friends was spent shooting pool, drinking beer, eating Italian food and lovingly trading insults. Frank's was the place where the gang had a good old time. Loudly greeted as he entered the bar, Sal was thrilled to see his buddy Michael McNally was in town. Michael would understand, or at least not be disappointed. He had no other friend to whom the Church meant so much. *Ah, genius,* he thought. *Maybe that was a clue.* They warmly shook hands and briefly caught up on what had happened since their last meeting. Sal selected a barstool and playfully traded remarks with some of his closest friends. After about an hour and a half of shooting pool, drinking beer and eating pizza, Sal decided it was the moment of truth and that he should make an announcement. He asked the bartender for a spoon and loudly tapped his glass.

"Gentleman," he began, "I use that term very loosely because as I look around this room, it is very difficult to believe that any of you are gentlemen. However, I think that some of you may want to sit down because I'm going to tell you something now that may take your breath away. I have been offered a very wonderful position at Wertheim, one that means that at some point in time I could even buy a little cottage in Avon by the sea. However, I don't think that job is my future because after a great deal of thought, and by the way, very little alcohol, I have concluded that Wall Street is not where I want to spend the rest of my life."

Impatiently, Louie De Forge loudly chimed in, "You're going to join the Foreign Legion because seven women have come forth and claimed you are the father of their children."

This was followed by Maddy Doyle's remark, "You are going to become a famous author and write a book finally admitting that the Italians have no war heroes." Johnny Farawell almost fell off his bar stool with that remark.

Sal let this typical banter go on for a while before getting serious. "Okay, guys, let me get to where the rubber meets the road. I am completely shifting gears here. I have made a decision that I'm going to study for the priesthood."

There was immediate silence followed by shouts of disbelief and a loud roar of laughter on the part of all of his friends. Even the bartenders and the waitresses howled. Michael said, "I am a devout Catholic, but if that happens, I have to tell you that I'm going to start shopping for something else besides Catholicism. You can't be serious; are you kidding me?"

Sal could see in his eyes that, joking aside, Michael was happy for him.

And he was. It felt right to him. Despite all the past exchanges they had about God and the Church, Michael thought that Sal was one of the most honest, caring men he knew. He thought Sal would be a tremendous priest."

One of the waitresses said, "Oh my God, Sal! You mean that the crush that I've had all these years now has to be put into the desk drawer?" One by one, a waterfall of humorous remarks challenged the statement that Sal had shared.

Sal sat with a big smile on his face, weathered the storm and finally said, "Okay, I get it, but I'm telling you this is not a joke. I've spoken with Father McNulty, and the deal is that I will enter Seton Hall University for one year. If all goes well, I will enter the major seminary at Darlington next May." No one in the bar could believe that this was happening; however, at some point, the humor turned to acceptance. It was apparent that Sal was really going to study for the priesthood.

Over the next couple of weeks, one of Sal's friends decided to create a betting pool on how long Sal would last in this crazy decision. To enter the pool cost ten dollars. There were sixty-seven people who participated. The longest that anyone thought that he would last was twelve weeks. Despite this fact, they decided they should probably wait and see what happened. If, by some miracle, he made it, then in May they would have a priestly version of a bachelor party for him.

As time passed, it became apparent that Sal was not going to leave Seton Hall before the year ended. The pool was over, and the announced winner, Emily, one of the waitresses at Frank's Bar and Grill, had won with her estimate of three months. With the reality of May approaching, his closest friends decided that they would have a gala bash at Frank's to give Sal a sendoff to the major seminary.

Once the news of Sal's decision to enter the seminary became public, Elizabeth became a bit of a recluse. She consistently avoided anyone who knew her and Sal as a couple. Rarely did she go out on the weekends, and Sunday Mass presented a real conflict. Her faith had been a cornerstone of her life, but she felt an abiding resentment toward God. She prayed that the bitterness she was experiencing would lessen over time.

One morning she lay in her bed and watched the lace curtains dancing as the breeze came through her bedroom window. She was almost motionless as she cycled through her emotions of grief and abandonment. Finally, she rose, put on her robe and went to the kitchen to make coffee. She sat at the table while the coffee percolated and heard the sound of her mother on the stairs. Her impulse was to avoid any morning conversation, but it was too late, as her mother had arrived in the kitchen.

Elizabeth's family had been most concerned about her, but it became increasingly difficult to discuss the topic with her. This morning, her mother could no longer remain silent. "Elizabeth, I have tried not to interfere, but I am concerned about you. You have not been the same for months."

Elizabeth poured herself a cup of coffee and bluntly stated, "Mom, I don't want to talk about it."

"I have understood that, but I cannot stand by and see you so miserable without saying something."

"Mom, there is nothing to say. I have spoken to myself for months, but nothing seems to help. Sal is going to the seminary, and there is not a damn thing that I can do about it."

"Elizabeth, maybe it would help if you would talk to me about your feelings."

Elizabeth hesitated before responding, "What's the use? The ending will still be the same. I had so much to look forward to, and now I feel that I am constantly in a fog."

"I can't pretend to know what you are feeling, but is there anything I can do to help?"

Sarcastically Elizabeth said, "Yes, call Sal and tell him to change his mind."

"I don't think that would have any effect because I haven't always been his favorite person."

Elizabeth smiled, "Mom, he has always said nice things about you. That's not always true about your weepy daughter."

"Have you spoken to Sal recently?"

"A couple of times on the phone and we are going to have lunch on Thursday. Not looking forward to it because he leaves for the seminary on Saturday. I am so stuck because if it were that he had cold feet or it was another woman, I would fight for him. How the hell do I fight God, whom he thinks is calling him? I find myself putting silly deadlines on my life. Maybe he will only stay a year and then come back to me. I even pray that he is not really called to be a priest, and then I feel guilty."

"It's called Irish guilt, sweetheart. You come by it naturally from both parents." Despite the hurt, her mother's words made Elizabeth laugh.

"I have no magic wand, Elizabeth, but I honestly believe that if this is real for him, at some point, you will let him go. In the meantime, please know that being a mother has no time limits. I am always here for you." Elizabeth stood up and hugged her mother.

The evening before Elizabeth was to meet Sal, she decided that it was too difficult to share her feelings in person so she would write him a letter.

Dear Sal,

I am writing you this letter because, despite the time that has passed, I am still heartbroken. We had a wonderful life plan, and it has been shattered by your decision to study for the priesthood. There was no way for me to know that you would suddenly leave me, and I am left with so many questions. Could I have been more loving in our relationship? Did my not making you feel loved enough contribute to your decision? I feel lost without the ability to understand why this has happened, and my biggest fear is that time does not seem to help.

There is not a day that goes by that I do not think of us. I even dream about us most nights. The thought that there is no longer an "us" is to me the most painful part. The memories of our years together still warm my heart, but they are not enough. I still want all the plans that we had shared to become reality.

I have tried to listen to the words of those closest to me about getting over us, but nothing seems to help. It is my fondest hope that they are right, but now those bits of advice do not help. The reality is that I still love you and there is nothing I can do that will bring you back to me.

Love,

Elizabeth

As Sal sat in Lee's, he nervously fidgeted with his napkin. Every six seconds he would look at his watch. While waiting for Elizabeth, his mind was flooded with troubling thoughts that seemed to have no answers. Why had he decided on the priesthood? The question had been burning in his mind and soul because of what he was giving up. Elizabeth was the love of his life, and he had thought that they would spend the rest of their lives together. In his mind, he saw children, a home, and summers at the shore, and now it had all evaporated. Not only that but he had wounded the heart of one who had done nothing but love him. Why was he trading this life that meant so much to him for a life of loneliness? Celibacy seemed like a huge price to pay for this path that he had chosen. Was this really a calling or a temporary search for relevance? When it first came into his mind, he could not grasp this intense attraction to something that did not seem to fit into who he was. Could he give over his free spirit to a life of obedience and rules? He knew he was to some degree a rebel, not one who made fun of the rules but one who lived just outside the rules he didn't take seriously. During this emotional turmoil, he was steadied by the cornerstone of the Christian message, Christ's words in the Sermon on the Mount. They were so powerful and different from some statue with his eyes raised to heaven, which was the compelling attraction for others. He knew that being a priest was complex, and there would be rules and regulations that would have to be followed, but in the Beatitudes, Sal sought a path that he could grasp and follow. He didn't know if he could fully commit to this quest, but he believed if he did not try he would spend the rest of his life looking over his shoulder. In addition, the year at Seton Hall had deepened his faith, and daily Mass had enhanced his love for the liturgy and the sacraments. He had started to understand the role of the priesthood and shed some of his prior shallow beliefs about Catholicism.

Selfishly, he would like to hedge his bet and imply to Elizabeth that there was some degree of uncertainty in his decision. However, he knew that was wrong. He had to let her go, and today, before leaving for the seminary, was the time to do it.

The door to Lee's opened and in walked Elizabeth, looking more beautiful than ever. She was wearing a pale blue dress, which highlighted her golden blond hair and penetrating blue eyes. She radiated a kindness that made her irresistible. Through their courtship, men envied Sal, and many women had sought her friendship. How could he give up this wonderful woman who had loved him so intensely for years? He stood, undecided what to do. Should he shake her hand or hug her? He just stood there and beckoned for her to sit. "What would you like?"

"Just a cherry coke. I am really not hungry," she replied.

"I appreciate your coming and honestly don't know what to say, but I needed to say goodbye."

The word goodbye created a twinge in Elizabeth's heart, but she had resolved that this meeting would not be overly emotional. "I wanted to come, and I am glad that in the past few months we have had opportunities to meet and talk." Elizabeth paused and said, "It has been a roller coaster year and a half for me, and I have had more than my share of ups and downs." Sal grimaced at this statement. "I know that your decision to become a priest was not meant to hurt me, but it has been so difficult. I have had every emotion possible."

"I can imagine."

Elizabeth continued, "There were times when I was so angry at you, but that has faded."

"I can understand that, Elizabeth, because there were so many moments when I asked myself *What the hell are you doing?* There are tons of doubts in my head, but I could not hold onto you. That would not be fair."

"I now understand that and realize that you must follow your heart. I will not lie and say that I have fully come to grips with it, but I do believe that we will both be okay."

Mr. Lee brought Elizabeth's coke, and she took a long sip. She momentarily reached for her purse, which contained the letter, but chose not to give it to Sal.

Sal haltingly said, "It may seem silly, but in my heart, I wish you the best and hope that we will always be cherished friends."

The word "friends" was the end of their relationship.

Elizabeth stood and said, "Goodbye, Sal. May God bless you for the rest of your life." With that, she turned and left. He momentarily felt more alone than he ever had before, but he experienced some comfort in the thought that many of his needs would be filled by bringing parishioners to a deeper understanding of God's love. The last year had been filled with many spiritual moments when he believed that he was truly called to be a priest.

6

MAY 1960

The Road to the Priesthood

THE NIGHT BEFORE SAL WAS TO go to major seminary at Darlington, reality started to set in that this was not some kind of a lark. A going-away dinner attended by his parents as well as his sister and brother was heartwarming. The house was filled with the aroma of eggplant parmigiana, lasagna, peppers and sausage. His mother wanted the send-off meal to be all of Sal's loves, and she topped it off with espresso and cannolis.

He was thrilled that his sister and brother would be at the going- away dinner. His brother Russ had always been his role model. Currently an FBI agent, Russ had, throughout the years, taken him under his wing, and Sal aspired to be like him. Russ was voted most likely to succeed in his high school class and was a loving husband and father. Russ had inherited the zany La Greca sense of humor from his father and shared the gene with Sal. Tina was the oldest child in the family and had in some respects been like a second mother to Sal. The ten-year difference in their ages did little to impede their friendship. Tina was always supportive of Sal in any decision that he made. She was every child's idea of the perfect aunt, and her Christmas presents were wrapped as though they were works of art. She was an avid reader and a wonderful conversationalist as well as being the communication directress for the extended La Greca family. She was in constant contact with all of her cousins and kept everyone aware of key events and happenings. The evening had been filled with stories, laughter, wonderful food and even a few tears.

The past year at Seton Hall University had been relatively easy because he came home every day, but this was a whole different kettle of fish. The desire for service was still strong, but he had no idea what it would be like to be resident in the seminary for five years. He began to pack and realized that he was smoking one cigarette after another. His level of apprehension was intense. He got little if any sleep during the night; he kept tossing and turning with fears that he had made a mammoth mistake. Was it too late for him to turn back? Would anyone think poorly of him if he decided that he didn't want to go through with this? His mother seemed happy with the choice, but his father had serious reservations and could not fathom that he opted to study for the priesthood over the Wall Street job. The night seemed endless. Every time he looked at the clock on the wall, he realized that only ten or fifteen minutes had gone by.

At one point, he must've drifted off into a deep sleep because he heard his mother say, "Sal, I think it is time for you to get up."

Sluggishly, he opened his eyes and said, "Okay, Mom, I'll shower and get dressed and come down for breakfast." The water cascaded over his body in the shower, and he realized that never in his life had he been this nervous. Most occasions Sal handled with a great deal of calmness, and almost always he felt self-assured. This was different because it was so unknown and so removed from what he had experienced. What would it be like to be confined, every day, within a very stringent set of rules and requirements? He wasn't particularly holy and knew very little about the Catholic faith tradition, even though he spent twelve years in Catholic school, and if you count college, sixteen years. But during all those years, he took with a grain of salt much of what he had heard about the Church and its rules and regulations. He wasn't sure that he subscribed to heaven and hell and thought that limbo was one of the silliest ideas. But this past year had also produced some changes regarding his faith. The beauty and wonder of the sacraments had a real impact on him, and the growing experience of other men willing to pledge their lives to a solitary life absent of their own family edified him. He was handing over his life and freedom to the unknown, and for the moment, he was unsure about that decision.

After showering and going down for breakfast, he tried to fake that he was hungry, but he was pushing his food from one side of the plate to the other. When his mother wasn't looking, he took what was left over and threw it in the garbage. Climbing the stairs, he told her that he was going to finish packing. He lit a cigarette as he sat on the side of his bed, wondering whether this was the appropriate time to tell them that he had changed his mind. After an hour and a half of vacillating, he concluded that there was no way he could turn around now. If need be, he could leave later on.

His father asked him if he wanted to drive from Jersey City to Bergen County where the Darlington Seminary was located, but he refused, saying that he would enjoy watching the scenery. The reality was that he was so nervous he thought it would probably be a bad idea to get behind the wheel. The ride, which under ordinary circumstances would be probably forty-five minutes to an hour, seemed interminable because there was a great deal of traffic. The first part of the trip looked familiar because the highway went through towns that to some degree resembled Jersey City. However, as they progressed, he realized they were entering what he would refer to as the countryside. He became keenly aware that the seminary, at this point, was probably no more than ten minutes away. He could feel his chest tighten. There was very little saliva in his mouth, and he was tapping his fingers on the side of the door. Fortunately, neither his mother nor father had any realization of how nervous he was when they entered the gates of the road that led directly to the seminary. It was his most difficult moment of the entire year.

The seminary was exquisite, the former residence of a Mr. James Darling. It was built by James Crocker, and the construction took six years, concluding in 1907. It was a magnificent residence that rivaled the palaces of Europe. The mansion was a replica of Bramshill, the residence of the Prince of Wales, built in the sixteenth century. Crocker imported Bavarian sculptors to help craft the beautiful building. The walls, ceilings, and staircases were all hand carved, and the great ballroom had glittering Tiffany chandeliers. When Sal's family pulled up to this mansion, they were greeted by a group of seminarians, who gave them instructions on where to park and unload the luggage. The older seminarians were very friendly, and eventually, after they had parked the car, led them into the building where most of the newcomers and the families had gathered. There were informal introductions on the part of seminarians dressed in cassocks despite the summer heat. Once Sal's name was checked on the list, one of the seminarians told him that he would take him to his room. The seminarian seemed down to earth and shook

Sal's hand. He was rather tall and had the appearance of being an athlete.

"Sal, my name is Jim Maselko. I have been here for almost five years and the first time I entered this building I was totally scared. Believe me, it will get better. I now love being here." Sal momentarily took some comfort from this statement. Upon entering the small chamber, he was gently instructed to put on a cassock and come downstairs sometime within the next thirty minutes. This was a new experience for him, and as he put on his cassock and Roman collar and looked in the mirror, he was shocked at what he perceived as a major transformation. He felt like it was Halloween, and he was about to attend a party. However, this was not some lark; this was real, and he felt like an imposter. What the hell had he gotten himself into? He went downstairs and made his way to the cafeteria where many of his new classmates and families had gathered for refreshments. After a brief period, a priest came into the cafeteria and strode to the microphone. He was a rather heavy-set man with horned rim glasses and a cassock that was much more ornate than everyone else's simple black cassocks. His had red piping and a bold purple sash.

"Good afternoon. My name is Monsignor Charles Brady. I am the rector of the seminary, and I welcome all of you to what I know will be a wonderful experience. In the next hour or so, we welcome you to tour the grounds as well as the chapel. When the church bells ring, it will be an indication that the formal seminary life of your sons has begun. It will be at that moment that we would ask you bid farewell, as there will be a church assembly for the new seminarians."

The next hour sped by. Once the church bell rang, Sal's mother and father embraced, kissed him and said, "We love you, and we know that this will be a wonderful time for you." Sal returned their kisses and embraced them. He hoped that they were right.

His longing for flight at that moment was overwhelming. All he could think of was that he wanted to get in the car with them, but he knew that was not something that he could do. After watching them drive off, he followed the rest of the seminarians to the chapel where he was to begin his new life.

Sal's first night in the seminary was anything but peaceful. He tossed and turned most of the night, and at one point got up, sat in a chair and stared out the window. Unlike the city, there were no buses, police sirens or the bellows of patrons leaving the bars at 2 a.m. He was unused to falling asleep in total silence. After a few more fitful starts, he dozed off. The next sound he heard was "Benedicamus Domino," a voice in the hallway beckoning him to greet the new day. He had learned the night before that he was to respond with, "Deo Gratias." Quickly rising, he splashed cold water on his face, which reinforced the fact that this was no longer a dream; he was in the seminary. As he shaved, he stared into the mirror and thought, "Well, here goes nothing." Opening the door, he joined the procession of equally dazed seminarians making their way to the chapel.

The schedule identified this time before Mass as a period of meditation. Sal had never meditated in his life. He gazed around the chapel and noticed that most of the seminarians, especially those who were tabbed as deacons, had their eyes closed. He closed his eyes, but he didn't know exactly what he was supposed to be doing. Hundreds of thoughts were running through his anxious mind. Finally, the bell indicated that the Mass was about to begin. The rector came from the sacristy, and the celebration of his first liturgy at Darlington began. After Mass, the seminarians proceeded to the cafeteria. One of the deacons offered a blessing in gratitude for the food. After the blessing, it was permissible to speak. There were introductions as each seminarian became acquainted with the other people at the table. Sal was encouraged because it seemed that everyone at the table was as anxious as he was. Most had very little knowledge as to what would transpire for the rest of the summer. After breakfast, the new seminarians were instructed to go to their rooms and collect their notebooks. At precisely 8:45 they were to go to the mansion where they would have class from nine to twelve. The summer classes for the new seminarians consisted of two courses. One was entitled The Gentlemanly Priest, and the other was Introduction to the Holy Rule.

Entering the classroom, Sal observed that there was a table at the front of the room, which had place settings. His initial reaction was that there would be a snack during a break between classes. What he didn't realize was that the faculty seemed to be under the impression that every priestly candidate had been raised in a barn. The course, which could have been a parody at a comedy club, introduced the new seminarians to the fundamental eating rituals that most civilized human beings experience in the first eighteen years of their lives. The instructor was a young faculty member who had the unenviable task of teaching seminarians where to put the napkin, where the knife and fork went, and how to have civil discourse at a meal. This marvelous revolutionary information was followed by other breakthrough concepts like shining your shoes, combing your hair, brushing your teeth and how to shake hands when at a social event. Whenever there was a break in the course, and the students would move out onto the veranda to have a cigarette, the comments were priceless.

The second course focused on spirituality. The seminary was built on a set of religious beliefs. Silence was a major part of this tradition. There were significant periods during the day when seminarians were expected to be silent; whenever the bell rang, their silence was to be immediate without exception. The spiritual advisor who taught the course conveyed the belief that these periods of silence were based on the need for seminarians to reflect on their relationship with God. He indicated in every lecture that, over time, following this religious rule would shape and form them spiritually. Sal, ever a chatterbox, found these periods of silence difficult. Initially, he followed the law to the letter, but he could not see the great value in this requirement. Sal had promised himself that he would not question every single rule or belief because if he were going to be here, he would try to be as passionate and committed to the process as possible. This course was certainly more thought-provoking than The Gentlemanly Priest. The faculty member who taught it was the seminary spiritual director, who had been a naval officer before he entered the priesthood. He was a feisty, no-nonsense man who spoke straight from the shoulder. He more than occasionally warned the new seminarians not to take themselves too seriously. One of his favorite lines was "Put a Roman collar on a broomstick, and someone will fall in love with it." During the summer, on one particularly hot day, the spiritual advisor had just on slacks and a sports shirt, and on his left arm was a large tattoo that he had acquired sometime in his naval career.

Sal was pleased to realize that whenever you gather a group of individuals together in a confined milieu, humorous behavior follows. The seminary was a prime example of this despite the religious setting. During the summer, every room had a transom window, which was kept open for air circulation because there was no air-conditioning in the building. Sal was immediately aware that not only were the windows opportunities for the free flow of air, they also provided perfect access for water balloons. That summer the idea of floating a water balloon through the transom was transferred from the deacons to the new seminarians. This bit of juvenile behavior was also accompanied by short-sheeting people's beds, and especially during the grand silence, you could hear the person trying to get into bed. Occasionally the Lord's name would be used, often in vain. The highlight that summer was that at noon, before lunch, the seminarians would gather at the chapel for a spiritual reading. At a point in the reflections, one of the brethren let loose a huge, loud fart. The entire chapel exploded with laughter. Finally, the laughter dwindled, and the reader continued with the next line, which was "Lord save us from the plague that lays waste at noonday." The entire chapel exploded again, and the faculty member gave in to the reality that it was hopeless to return to order and allowed everyone to leave the chapel.

Sal survived the summer but was incredibly grateful that there would be a vacation at the end before they would begin the new school year. When the vacation was over, Sal's level of apprehension was not nearly as high as the first time he had visited in June. Meditation, prayer and his fellow seminarians had altered positively some of his prior views. However, he was still somewhat doubtful as to whether this was the right path for him to follow. Some of his anxiety was lessened by frequent contact over the summer with Bill Meade and Mike Keating. He had known Bill from high school. He was not only a close friend but also so down to earth that Sal confided some of his apprehensions. Bill shared that along the way he was also unsure. That was part of a normal route to the priesthood, he said. Mike Keating was different in style and temperament than Bill but also someone that Sal admired. A history major at Boston College, he was more of a challenger than Bill. He wanted reasons and logical rationales for many of the seminary rules and regulations.

NOVEMBER 1960

Whenever a group of persons are placed into a common environment, there is almost always a bonding experience that occurs.

This was certainly true in the seminary, and Sal's life was enhanced by many of his fellow seminarians. Very quickly, total strangers became a band of brothers who stood side by side in common cause. One of his closest friends was the ever-zany Rocco Constantino, a former politician from Bellville, New Jersey. Rocco was the consummate professional who never missed a funeral, party or opportunity to kiss a baby. Rocco, whose rather corpulent body was reminiscent of the Little King cartoon character, had a personality that could charm the devil himself, and his outrageous behavior brought laughter and acceptance from everyone. Once, while on vacation at the Jersey Shore, he and seven seminarians entered a pizzeria. Without hesitation, Rocco marched into the kitchen and said to the chef, "Hey, shorty, start making pizzas and don't stop till I tell you." The chef roared with laughter. If Sal had said that, he would probably be running down the boardwalk avoiding a knife-wielding chef. On another occasion, early in the morning, Rocco leaned out his window at the seminary and shouted to the local bakery deliveryman that he and others were being held hostage and to call the state police. However, there was a more serious side to Rocco, which on different occasions he shared with Sal. Once, during a recreation period, Rocco confided to Sal the reason why he had chosen to enter the seminary. "As a politician in Bellville, I was involved with many families but never connected at a level that was deep and spiritual. I couldn't; I didn't know how, and it was not my place. That's not what people expect from the local pol, you know? I was doing good work, but I knew God's love was what would make a difference in their lives. Having that in my life, I wanted it to share it with others."

Joseph Michael Ryan was perhaps the brightest and most well-read person Sal had met in his life. Joseph had a library of over a thousand books. He was not only a friend to Sal; he was a primary mentor. He had a range of interests that went beyond what seminarians were supposed to be reading and had the uncanny ability to teach without ever being patronizing or pedantic. Sal's understanding of topics that were outside the scope of the seminary curriculum was widened and developed through Joe's loving guidance. They often had conversations about psychological growth and how that connected to spirituality. In these conversations, Sal became more aware of the connections between the two worlds—spirit and psyche—and was able to create a view of priesthood that was compelling. Joseph introduced him to Teilhard de Chardin, the Jesuit author of *The Phenomenon of Man* and Sal practically inhaled the book. Chardin's views of the world of matter and spirit being one, a synthesis he called "spirit-matter" deeply resonated with Sal. That's how he saw the role of a parish priest. Joseph said that he envisioned the priesthood as being a life enmeshed in every aspect of the parishioners' lives. "The ordinary situations that they face," he said, "must be connected to the religious experience that we offer them. That is the job we have to do—to show them, again and again, where the spiritual and the material worlds touch, how God's love is woven into every fiber of their being, every mundane circumstance."

It was thrilling to Sal. The world seemed so much bigger after one of these conversations—glorious, sad, beautiful and brimming with possibility.

Not that everything was on such a high level. Jim Herbert was another luminary who opened Sal's mind, plus he was one of the funniest guys in the seminary. He once said that his brother had married a wealthy woman who was into thoroughbred horses. He told Sal, "My brother is a great guy but out of his league with that crowd. Until he met her, he thought every horse had a cop on it." Sal was fortunate to have his first parish assignment with Jim. It was in a poor section of Newark; their job was basically to run a camp for ten-year-olds. Jim fractured Sal by making shoeboxes into altars during arts and crafts. In a moment of great frustration, he said, "If I make one more Popsicle cross, I may become a serial killer."

If you were an organized, detailed person who enjoyed the sameness of a rigid schedule, then the seminary would've been nirvana. However, for a personality like Sal's, the rigid schedule could at times be pulverizing. Sal found that one of the ways to survive the sameness of the seminary was to have short-term goals about making it to the next vacation. He loved the camaraderie of his friends and never quite took his eyes off the prize at the end of the process. All the requirements that at times seemed tedious would lead to a path of service to others. With very few exceptions, many of the courses in philosophy and theology were not the primary subjects of Sal's interest. He intellectually grew through the guidance of some of the older seminarians like Joseph Ryan. He had become more aware of the need to widen the scope of his intellectual pursuits. Joseph's ideas about God were wider then what was being taught in the seminary. He believed that God could be found in literature, science and everyday lives. On many occasions, Sal sought out Joseph, and a great deal of the learning that he gained was not in the classroom. With Joseph's help, Sal was creating a middle path for himself. He could not completely adhere to the single model that was being preached in the seminary. Nor could he consistently be a rebel, going against the grain of tradition. He had to meld the two choices into a personal approach to the priesthood. He had grown in his understanding of the importance of spiritual symbols and value of the sacraments. The liturgy was the bringing together of the community, and the bread of life in the Eucharist bound him to Christ. The pulpit and spiritual messages assisted people in their search for ways to lead moral, meaningful lives. He realized that prayer and meditation were positively impacting his personal relationship with God.

The faculty at Immaculate Conception Seminary would have been a fertile field for someone like director Woody Allen. The Rector was an austere and brilliant scholar who would never be mistaken for a "touchy-feely" type. He was glacially distant, and when in his presence one felt like the Spanish Inquisition had been renewed. However, those who knew him well viewed his distance as shyness, and had loyalty to him despite his aloof aspect. Unfortunately, he suffered a massive heart attack during Sal's first summer at the seminary and died instantly. For a two-day period, his body lay in repose in the main ballroom of the mansion, which was referred to as the "Magna Aula." Sal was assigned to be one of the seminarians serving as escorts in the room, and it was actually quite creepy to be in a room filled with only candlelight and the corpse of the Rector.

The Dean of Students was a former jock, tall and handsome, who could hit a softball a mile. He was the scourge of anyone whom he believed was in any shape or form effeminate. There was an outspoken policy at the seminary regarding "particular friendships"; everyone understood that it was a code for men the Dean perceived to have homosexual tendencies. He knew that Sal was an athlete, but Sal never shared with him that he loved opera and classical music. Those two devotions would have moved Sal off the favorite list to the suspect file. The Dean was not an unkind individual but seemed locked into a focus on how a manly priest should look and behave. He was constantly on the prowl to make the lives of anyone whom he sensed was less traditionally masculine difficult.

One of the senior faculty, Monsignor O'Brien, was a hypochondriac. When he spoke to you, he covered his mouth because he had the intense fear that a germ might escape your body and infect him with a death-dealing virus. Sal always believed that he probably had the first constant Lysol automatic spray mist in his quarters. He was an affable man, but his virus fetish was one of the standing jokes among seminarians.

The primary head of the philosophy department was a true intellectual who was, in the finest sense of the words, a "space cadet." There was a story that he was musing about Descartes while mowing his sister's lawn and allowed the power mower to ascend up the base of an elm tree.

Another member of the philosophy department was a gracious soul who had a kind word for everyone. Despite his gentle demeanor, he had a sharp mind and a great sense of humor. Once taunted by a brash young member of the theology department who asked him to say something stupid, he responded immediately, "Okay, you say something and I will repeat it."

The primary homiletics professor was nicknamed "Jolly Jack." He pranced around like a peacock in full Monsignor's regalia every chance possible. He was very affected, and although he had a doctorate from Columbia University, one sensed that his education had stopped the day he received his terminal degree. He was politically astute and made no bones about his desire to become a member of the hierarchy. The rumor was that he had a bishop's outfit on call in case it ever happened. The book on him was that he was truly a genius because he spread five minutes of prepared material over four courses.

One of the favorite faculty members was Monsignor Henry Beck, a world-famous church history professor. He was a magnificent teacher who could engage the students in meaningful dialogue. He taught a course on the Reformation in the context of art, politics, music and every facet of medieval life. His classes were so vibrant that when the bell for the next class rang there was always a tinge of disappointment.

The faculty had some degree of intellectual autonomy, but it was ever apparent that Rome had specific ideas on priest formation that were non-negotiable. The current Vatican Council may have been somewhat radical, but those in charge of seminaries were still holding fast to ancient rituals in order to send the message that they were still in charge. Rome issued a document entitled *Veterum Sapientia*. The meaning focused on the ancient wisdom of Latin and why it should govern curriculum. The news that all courses would now be taught in Latin caused a great deal of anxiety, especially for American seminarians. The day after notification of this impending doom, the first class of the day was Church History. As he was fluent in Latin and Greek, the seminarians knew Monsignor Beck would immediately implement the frightening new document that came from the bureaucratic side of Rome. Monsignor Beck came to the next class after the dictum had been received and said: "Gentlemen, the Holy See has spoken. We will begin immediately. *Non habemus bananae hodie. Non habemus bananae hodie.* For those of you not familiar with the mother tongue, I have said twice in Latin we have no bananas today. That will suffice for the semester. If Rome does not like it, they can lump it." The students howled with glee and had another reason to love Monsignor Henry Beck.

The faculty members were different to a man, but Sal always had the sense that as a group they cared about the seminarians and had tried to create an environment of warmth and caring. In the hands of these scholarly and religious men, seminarians were to be shaped and molded into pious and dedicated servants of the Church. As one who had always been a private contrarian, Sal bought some of the guidance and dismissed some of it out of hand. He was never overtly confrontational or disagreeable but always intellectually challenged their "My way or the highway" path to the Christian message. Before Sal entered the seminary, a lot of what he called the "hocus pocus" dogma seemed nice but not particularly relevant to the service he imagined. This began to change as the faculty clearly connected much of dogma and theology to their essence in the priesthood. This growing understanding enhanced his anchor in the Beatitudes, the words that Christ spoke in the Sermon on the Mount. No one ever lives them fully, but he thought if he could pattern his life on them, then all else would fall in line.

7

Hospital Duty as an Intern

THERE COMES A TIME IN EVERY profession when the study part recedes into the background, and the experiential part begins. It was rewarding to have family and friends heap praise and admiration on Michael, Catherine, and Joseph, but now was the time when they would practice patient care. This was the reality in their third year of medical school. Michael was assigned to Lankenau Hospital in Philadelphia, Catherine stayed at Jefferson, and Joseph began his medical internship at Hunterdon Medical center. The night before internships began, they had a few beers at the bar in the Billings Hotel. Their laughter and teasing were thin facades that covered the anxiety of the unknown. Academically, they had mastered their coursework, but this was different. From tomorrow on, they would not be merely responding to a professor but involved in the direct care of patients. At the end of the evening, they agreed to meet the following Sunday to discuss their medical adventures.

Michael always, as was his custom, arrived at the hotel bar fifteen minutes before Catherine and Joseph showed up. He was ashen from lack of sleep and had absorbed too much caffeine every day for a week. Catherine and Joseph were no less exhausted and the evening began slowly, with none of the three willing to begin recounting the week's experiences.

Finally, Michael broke the ice: "I was nervous before making rounds but checking myself in the mirror and putting on what I thought to be my 'professional doctor face,' I arrived at the door of my first patient. Sidney Bernstein was a fifty-five-year-old man who had been hospitalized with a heart condition. I entered his room and said: 'Good morning Mr. Bernstein,' and before I could say another word, the guy makes a grunting sound and slumps over in the bed. In sheer panic, I raced to the nursing station and called the resident. Mr. Bernstein had died. Not a great way to begin patient care, I said to myself."

Next, it was Catherine's chance to describe her initial voyage into patient care. "Professor Larkin has little affection for female medical students, so he assigned me to change the dressing of one of his patients. The patient had been caught by his wife in bed with another woman. Her response was to shoot his penis off. My first moment as an intern was cleaning what was left of his private area. I thought to myself while cleansing the area that this is not what my mother had in mind for her daughter, the doctor."

Michael and Joseph roared with laughter, and then Joseph took his turn at true confessions. "My first patient was a forty-year-old man who needed a cast. He had fallen down a flight of stairs and had broken his right leg. I started out well but had a hell of a time getting the damn thing even on both sides. By the time I finished the cast was so heavy that the guy could barely stand. He asked me if the cast was larger than normal. I immediately told him that the reason it was so large was because his injury was the most unique one I had ever treated."

The first week of the "Three Musketeers" medical careers had passed—to be followed by months of lack of sleep, monumental challenges, and the growing knowledge and confidence that this is where they would make a difference in the world.

Michael Jr. was an absolute delight, and what little time Michael had as an intern was spent with Arlene and the baby. Michael loved the fact that he lived so close to the hospital for his second rotation. Michael Jr. was so energetic, and he would light up when Michael walked through the door. This delightful explorer of everything in the apartment would be joined in two months by their second child. This news came at a time when Michael was trying to decide whether he should continue his studies and explore residency programs. He had been counseled by professors and peers that he would make an outstanding pediatrician or gastroenterologist. The good news about these options was that they were short in duration. He concurred that these opportunities would be fulfilling, but the one rotation that captivated him was surgery. The hesitation on his part was that a surgical residency would be four more years of a crazy lifestyle, and he questioned how fair that would be for his family.

Arlene could always sense when Michael was thinking over the issues involved in a major decision. In many ways, she knew him better than he knew himself. One night after they had put the energetic dynamo to bed, Arlene said, "Mrs. Pittelli knew you would be home tonight and offered to babysit while we went out for your favorite meal, a Philly cheesesteak." Michael jumped at the offer not only for the culinary delight of Geno's on South Street but because it provided an opportunity for some adult time together.

Michael ordered the house special cheesesteak, flank steak, peppers, American cheese and grilled onions and said, "I have been thinking about devouring one of these for days." He offered a bite to Arlene, but she chose only to order a coke.

Arlene started to probe their future as Michael wiped the last trace of cheese from his lips. She said, "I know that soon you must decide whether you are going to seek a residency and wondered where you were leaning." At this request, Michael smiled and realized that Arlene had emotional radar that was always on target regarding anything that he was pondering.

Michael said, "I have been meaning to talk to you about possible next steps, but there has been no opportunity. I am having difficulty with the implications for you and the children. I am barely home now and fear that a residency program may be worse. There is also the question of Danny because I know he has had great difficulty dealing with Donny's death."

Arlene reached across the table, cupping both his hands, and asked, "Which was your favorite rotation?"

To his surprise, he immediately responded, "Surgery."

Arlene followed her initial question with a series of gentle but probing inquiries. Michael apparently had thought at least at the subliminal level a great deal about surgery because he gave chapter and verse about its appeal. His insightful wife asked, "What is standing in the way of your following your dream?"

"The realization of the sacrifices you and the children will have to make over the next four years."

Arlene said, "I understand your concerns, but after all you have lost, I believe that you taking a surgical residency will be worthwhile for all of us."

Michael touched her cheek and said, "If I were just a general practitioner, we would have a more normal life."

"Michael, you well know there is no such thing as a normal life. I vote for a surgical residency."

Walking back hand in hand to their apartment, Michael stopped and kissed Arlene. "What would I do without you?"

"Don't worry, Doctor; you will never have to lose me. However, I have one request from here on out. You must share whatever your concerns are about any important decision." Michael agreed and felt Arlene's support had made his future clearer.

8

DECEMBER 1961

The unimaginable Tragedy

MICHAEL HAD FEW DAYS OFF FROM the grindstone of the intern life. He was looking forward to a four-day break around Christmas because his brother Danny was due to visit. Since the deaths of their mother and brother, Danny and Michael had been very close. Danny, like Michael, had an exceptional athletic and academic high school career, and was currently a junior at St. Anselm's College in New Hampshire. He was the second-leading scorer on the varsity men's basketball team but was hampered due to a wrist injury that had not healed properly. Michael suggested that during his visit to Philadelphia he see a hand surgeon at Jefferson Hospital to get a second opinion. College had matured Danny in many ways, and he had become more outgoing and comfortable in social settings. His desire to become an architect had been fortified by the internship he had at a New Hampshire architectural firm last summer.

By the time Danny visited, the wrist had become a non-issue. He was fully healed and cleared to resume full basketball activities. Fortunately, the men's team had a ten-day break in the schedule, so Danny decided to spend an entire week with Michael and Arlene. It was a wonderful time to see the historic city of Philadelphia, and thanks to the kindness of Mrs. Pittelli, who offered to babysit, Arlene could be his tour guide.

The evening of the second day in Philadelphia, the Pittelli's hosted a sumptuous dinner, and their son Joe was also fortunate to have a few days off. During the dinner, sports banter took over, and the question of who was the best basketball player at the table became a point of contention. All three of the jocks had impressive high school careers, and the burning issue was which city had superior basketball, Philadelphia or Jersey City. The noise level rose as each of the participants gave chapter and verse to support their position. Finally, Joe said, "Enough with the talk. Let's actually see who the best player at this table is. I can get us a pickup game at Roman Catholic High tomorrow morning. Are you up for it, or is the Jersey baloney just talk?"

Danny smiled before answering, but Michael immediately said, "Pittelli, you are about to get your clock cleaned."

Arriving at the school around 8:30, they dressed, and entering the gym, were pleased to see members of the alumni warming up. There was to be an alumni varsity charity game played tomorrow night, so the old-timers were hoping to work some of the kinks out in preparation. Joe chatted with a few of his friends, and after a few minutes, they picked the team members for a scrimmage. Joe was on one team, and Danny and Michael on the opposing squad. Initially, the game moved slowly, but after a few minutes, the competitive juices kicked in, and the game became quite physical. Danny was clearly in the best condition, and Joe could not contain him. At one point, Danny switched hands on his dribble and blew past Joe for an easy layup. On the inbound pass, he stole the pass and again made an easy layup.

Joe, breathing hard, said, "McNally, if it weren't for your kid brother, we would wipe the floor with your team." Michael laughed and responded in kind. Danny who had been the star up to this point called a time out and started to walk off the court.

As he neared the bench, he suddenly stumbled, tried to gain his composure and then collapsed. Michael, who was getting a drink of water, rushed to Danny, as did Joe. Michael was in a panic because it was obvious that Danny was having trouble breathing. One of the other players ran into the hall to call 911. Meanwhile, Michael was frantically performing mouth-to-mouth while Joe was doing compressions on Danny's chest. Michael could not believe that this was happening again. Michael was frantic and was having trouble breathing himself. In a few minutes, an ambulance pulled up to Roman High and three ET staff raced to the gym. They administered oxygen and hurriedly placed Danny in the ambulance and took him to the emergency room at Jefferson Hospital.

Joe and Michael drove to the hospital, but by the time they had arrived, Danny, despite valiant attempts by the staff, had been pronounced dead. Michael upon hearing the news collapsed in Joe's arms. He felt as though all of his limbs were made of lead and had trouble standing. His vision was blurred as though he was immersed in fog. His body was flooded with perspiration, and he was so unsteady that if it had not been for Joe holding him, he would have fallen to the floor. All he could think was that he had become the modern-day Job. He had lost his mother and two brothers without warning. Had they died after extended illnesses, it would have been difficult, but the suddenness of each death was a trauma in its own right. The next few days were a blur, and Arlene and his faith were the only things keeping him from the abyss of despair. If he gave up the idea that somehow, somewhere, there was a loving God, he was lost. He rejected the possibility that the God he believed in sent this awful test. His faith would sustain him; no matter what the cost, he would never abandon his deep belief in God.

Sal's mother called the seminary and received permission to speak to her son. The news was unbelievable. He immediately remembered the pain and anguish he felt when Donny died. He had carried that confusion for months. Sal felt that, somehow, he had to be by Michael's side. It was seminary policy that you could only attend the funeral of an immediate family member, but Sal went to the office of Father Gibson, the Dean of Men, to plead his case. Sal explained his friendship with Michael, the sequence of tragedies, his deep need to provide emotional support. At the end, Father Gibson reminded him of the rule.

Sal thought for a moment and said, "Father, the McNally family has suffered more than anyone I know. In my heart I believe that Jesus wants me to be with them at this time." Father Gibson was moved by Sal's words and granted him permission to attend the Funeral Mass.

As Danny's body was being carried from the hearse, Michael, his father and Arlene were in the vestibule. Coming to greet the body were Father McNulty, the acolytes and a familiar face. Michael was surprised and moved that Sal had made it to Philadelphia. He shook Father McNulty's hand and then embraced Sal. "You will never know what it means to me that you are here."

"I had to be with you. Michael, I am heartbroken."

Michael looked at him with the faraway eyes of shock. "Yes. We all are."

After the Mass, Sal accompanied the family to Holy Name Cemetery for the burial. The vision of the empty grave and the huge mound of dirt made Sal shudder. The only thing he could add to his friends was his silent physical presence. He led the final prayers before the casket was lowered and arm in arm walked with Michael and Arlene back to the cars. He shook the hand of Mr. McNally and hugged Aunt Mary before entering his car. The ride back to the seminary found him filled with sadness. He silently prayed for the McNally's and asked his Lord to be ever present in the impossible months ahead.

That evening, Michael sat with his father in the living room and offered his father a glass of beer. In the past few years, Mr. McNally had become a different person. He had spent more time with the grandchildren, and Michael began to understand that he just did not know how to show affection when his children were younger. The grandchildren adored him, and he also had helped financially in so many ways. "Michael, there are no words that can describe the pain I feel. When you called me I immediately hoped it was a dream. How the hell could I lose three-fourths of my family like this? I don't know how to go forward . . ." Tears rolled down his cheeks until he could no longer speak. Michael got down on his knees and placed himself before his father who now had buried his face in his hands. "Dad, I don't know where we go from here, but please believe that Arlene and I have never needed you more than we need you now."

"I know, son. I know. I'm not leaving you."

9

MARCH 1962

Dealing with the Losses of his Family

THE SCHEDULE AT THE HOSPITAL WAS unrelenting and in a way allowed Michael the opportunity to avoid consciously dealing with his grief. He buried himself in his work and tried valiantly to avoid thinking about his losses. With the knowledge that he had Arlene's complete support, he prepared himself for what was referred to as "Match Day" because the medical student filled out his preferred residencies and rated them in order of preference, and the hospitals did the same thing. Michael had five hospitals on his list, but his number one was Bellevue Hospital in New York City. Two months after he had submitted his paperwork, he was requested to come to Bellevue for an interview.

Michael had a college friend, Bert Burke, who had an apartment overlooking Central Park. When Michael called and requested they meet in the city for dinner, Bert informed him that he would be out of town but invited his college buddy to stay in his apartment. Michael was thrilled to be in the city that night, but he was very anxious about the interview and had trouble sleeping. He rose early and started to review the questions that he anticipated would be asked during his interview. Leaving the apartment, Michael made his way to breakfast. Two blocks from the hospital, he stopped at a local diner. After ordering his breakfast, he took out his notebook and began to practice the answers he presumed would be part of the interview process. After finishing two eggs over easy, bacon, hash browns, and two cups of coffee, he felt less anxious.

Michael paid the bill, left the diner, and as he walked began to collect his reasons for why he had chosen to pursue a surgical residency. Within ten minutes, he had arrived at the behemoth hospital complex. His first impression of the exterior of the buildings was that the hospital had seen better days. The faded facade of each building needed sandblasting because harshness of the East Coast climate had clearly stripped the original color of the buildings. Some rain gutters were broken, and there were more than a few cracked or broken windows. As he walked through the heavily stained-glass front doors and made his way toward the information desk, he was keenly aware of the gritty appearance of the reception area. Ceilings had large water stains, as well as floors littered with candy and cigarette wrappers. The walls were peeling and in dire need of a new paint job. The semi-darkness indicated that some of the ceiling lights had burnt-out bulbs. There was a musty odor in the waiting area, which was filled, and the foul language of those present resembled longshoremen at their best.

Weaving his way through the clientele to what was billed as the information desk, he inquired as to how he could find Dr. Forneris. The person behind the desk reading a newspaper responded as if he had insulted her family, answering with a scowl, "On the third floor." Her annoyance grew to complete disdain when Michael asked for the elevators. She responded, "At the end of the hall." As Michael left this cheerful introduction to the hospital, he was aware that the hallway next to the elevators was filled with gurneys with patients on them, but no one attending to their needs. Exiting the elevator, he was unsure of whether to go left or right. He scoured the names on the doors—at least those that had names. Finally, he found a door that had most of the word surgery on it. Apparently, the 'ER' had faded, and all that was left was 'SURG--Y.' He knocked, but there was no answer, so he opened the door and walked in. At that precise moment, out of the next door came a physician holding a large group of files. Michael introduced himself and said: "I have a 9:00 a.m. appointment with Dr. Forneris."

Dropping some of his folders, the physician bent to pick them up and said, "I am Dr. Forneris. Come into my office and have a seat."

Dr. Forneris initially seemed almost annoyed that he had to interview Michael. His clothes were completely wrinkled, and his white jacket appeared to have coffee and food stains. He glanced at his watch while opening a large metal filing cabinet in his office, and, after a few minutes of shuffling through the files, pulled out what Michael suspected was his dossier. Seated behind his desk, Dr. Forneris read the file and began by asking Michael some basic questions about his life and experience at Jefferson. After this, he closed Michael's file and looked directly at the young man.

"Let me begin by telling you that at your graduation, everyone will be praising you and calling you doctor. However, in my

opinion, you will not really be a doctor. After your surgical residency, you will be a doctor. Here, you will see and experience
things that you will find nowhere else. We are the catch basin for
every person that walks the streets of the city. There are those who
use this facility as a hotel, and there are many who have no other
place to go. For the alcoholics, some mental patients and street
people, the hospital is reduced to 'three hots and a cot.' You will
be attacked, cursed, spit on, have puke on your shoes, and wonder
a million times why the hell you chose this place. Your television
images of performing complicated surgeries and saving lives are
merely fantasies. You will work for thirty-six hours straight and
then have twelve hours off. You will be the bottom of the medical
totem pole and perform often-routine scut work."

Michael, during this expose, momentarily wished he would be
accepted by his second choice of hospital. However, after sharing
all that was wrong about the place, Dr. Forneris explained why he
chose to stay at Bellevue. "In spite of all that I have just laid out,
the experience of being a doctor and surgeon here is phenomenal.
Though often completely exhausted and working with minimal
resources, you will make a real difference here. I am privileged to
work with an outstanding team of nurses and doctors. This is a
community that serves with unbelievable dedication any and all
who come through our doors." As Dr. Forneris went on, Michael
could see the commitment that this man had made to others.
His initial fear that he would be accepted at Bellevue now was
transformed into the hope that this would be the place where he
would spend his surgical development.

10

The Aftermath

AFTER DANNY'S FUNERAL, DR. FRIEDMAN, the head of the medical school at Jefferson Hospital, arranged for Michael to take a few days off. During this period, Michael was sending thank you notes to all who had written or had left Mass cards. In the pile of mail was a large manila envelope. Michael opened it and inside was a book and a short note that said, "Hope this helps. Love, Sal." The book was *Man's Search for Meaning* by Viktor Frankl, a Jewish physician. Michael intended to only skim the book, but once he started reading, he could not put it down. He was yanked out his own grief by learning that the author had lost most of his family and so many other vital parts of his life during the Nazi years. One passage seared his soul: "When a man finds that it is his destiny to suffer, he will have to accept his

122

suffering as his task; his single and unique task. He will have to acknowledge the fact that even in suffering he is unique and alone in the universe. No one can relieve him of his suffering or suffer in his place. His unique opportunity lies in the way he bears his burden." This and the rest of the book did not put an end to his mourning but made him search for what meaning these losses could provide in his life. He found some avenues in his treatment of patients and their families.

It took great effort to remember that his care and skill were precious, no matter how empty he felt. He marveled that Frankl could suffer so many losses and stay vital, still be active in his concern and treatment of others. Despair was the enemy, a powerful one. He prayed that even when time had passed and life seemed good again, his losses would remind him to never see medicine and patient care as routine. He made the conscious decision that no matter how great his losses were, he would choose to make that pain a way of helping others.

The next few months were a time of great darkness, lightened only by the love of his family and the awareness of God, but every day, every week, every month, his faith grew stronger. On the one hand, he felt blessed that this was so. On the other, he felt a great ferocity when he heard anyone disrespecting religion. He had no issue with other faiths or even those of no faith though he pitied them; but when faith itself was mocked, he was flooded with righteous anger.

In March, Michael found out he had been accepted to the surgical residency program at Bellevue Hospital. Within a few short weeks, he would be immersed in his new environment. One of the key challenges for Michael and Arlene was to secure an apartment as close to the hospital as possible. Residency paid a paltry salary of $100 a month, and they realized that this would not adequately cover Arlene and the family's living expenses. They had a small savings account, but since Danny's death, Michael and his father had become extremely close, and his father had pledged a degree of financial help while Michael was studying to be a surgeon.

One of Michael's professors at Jefferson, Dr. Rodger Friedman, was most supportive of Michael's decision to pursue surgery. He was keenly aware of the trials that Michael had experienced and had apparently shared the tragic story with his wife. Two weeks before the McNally's were to move to New York, Mrs. Friedman called Arlene and invited her to lunch.

It was a beautiful clear day, and Arlene was grateful to have the opportunity to enjoy a social event that did not require planning or money. When she arrived at the Capital Grill, Mrs. Friedman rose to greet her. "Good afternoon, Arlene, it is so nice to see you.

Arlene responded: "Thank you, Mrs. Friedman. It was so kind of you to invite me to lunch."

Mrs. Friedman sat and said: "Please call me Phyllis. Mrs. Friedman is too formal, and I feel that I somewhat know you."

For the next ten minutes, the two women exchanged pleasantries, but it became apparent to Arlene that there was a purpose to this invitation. Phyllis said, "I have been the wife of a surgeon for over thirty years, and I can still remember Rodger's residency years. Many of his colleagues and friends of ours were in the residency with him, and almost all were married. It is somewhat sad that many of those marriages did not survive the surgical residency."

Arlene could not fathom why Phyllis was sharing this history. Phyllis continued, "I tell you this, Arlene, because I care about what you and Michael are about to experience. In no way do I want to be a busybody or a know-it-all. However, I would like to share some of the things I learned along the way. Would it be alright if I did that?"

Arlene had a sense that Phyllis was genuine and caring, and this introduction had completely engaged her interest. Arlene said, "Please continue because this is a whole new challenge for us."

"It is critical that you find time together. In the immortal words of the poet, Rodger and I did not have a 'pot to pee in' but we found time to have dates and even a yearly vacation. We made tough choices financially to do this, but it created the moments for us to be truly together without all the other distractions. Also, don't look at the whole surgical residency. I suggest that you approach it with short-term goals. You will find that it is easier to not only get through the grueling times; it will give you a sense of accomplishment.

"Flexibility has to be something that becomes central in your lives. So often, an emergency at the hospital will take precedence over your plans. You may feel resentful, and Michael will feel guilty. Reflect on and share your needs and feelings with each other. I would also urge you to be inventive. I can't tell you how many times I took the boys to see their father at the hospital. We would take him a sandwich or bring some of the kid's drawings. They loved it, and so did we. It truly connected us and allowed the entire family to share in the residency. We also refused to be boxed into the holidays of the rest of the family. It was too much pressure, so there were times when we had a Seder three week after the regular Passover date. It allowed us to live in the present while at the same time looking forward to the days when this phase would be over."

Arlene felt as though she had sat at the feet of a mistress of learning and could not wait to share Phyllis's counsel with Michael. At the end of the meal, she embraced Phyllis and agreed to take Phyllis up on her offer of regular phone calls and communication.

OCTOBER 1962

Bellevue Residency, Time of Doubts

WHEN THE ALARM WENT OFF AT 4:00 a.m., Michael slowly rolled out of bed. He had been at Bellevue for six months and was completely exhausted. The last twenty-four hours he had received six phone calls and had seen patients with various surgical complications. The most serious was a seventy-year-old woman whose incision was draining blood, which indicated internal bleeding. Almost immediately he called the attending surgeon, and she was rushed into surgery. Later in the evening, the surgeon stopped by his room and said, "Good call tonight, kid. She is stabilized. You probably saved her life."

Washing his face, he quickly shaved and began to make the rounds of the patients on his clipboard. The first was Donald

Walsh, a fifty-eight-year-old man who used Bellevue as his primary hotel. Still wet from his last alcoholic binge, he was always hostile and treated every staff member with complete disdain. He was not remotely interested in a twelve-step approach to sobriety, but ever the optimist, Michael attempted to believe that even Donald was capable of positive change.

"Good morning, Donald, are you feeling better?"

"Go to hell," Donald said in a disdainful voice. Michael smiled, having accustomed himself to the various loving ways in which a good portion of his patients responded to ordinary greetings. Unmoved by the poetic use of foul language that followed, Michael examined Donald and momentarily thought about addressing the consequences of continued drinking but decided to move on to the next patient.

Walking down the hall, Michael recalled the words of Dr. Forneris in his initial interview. "You will be cursed at, struck, have vomit on your shoes, and treat many who may utterly disrespect you. However, you will make a difference and truly will become a doctor who fills the gaps for those who have nowhere else to go."

The last part of that counsel was made vivid in the next part of his rounds. Mildred was a twenty-year-old woman who was dying from aggressive breast cancer. Michael had seen her two days before and spent twenty minutes chatting with her. That amount of time was a luxury, but she, like everyone he treated, could not be reduced to notes on his clipboard. He had been counseled both in med school and here not to become emotionally involved with his patients, but though he respected that wisdom, he rejected it. Mildred was dying, and at her bedside were her parents and younger brother. They rose to greet him. He smiled and sat on Mildred's bed. Gently holding her hand, he spoke to her by whispering in her ear. Hearing is the last thing that goes in the death process, and he wished to let her know that she was surrounded by loved ones. He then spent a few minutes speaking with her family before going to the cafeteria for a quick cup of coffee and a bagel.

Glancing at his watch, he was unaware that one of his favorite persons in the hospital had sat down next to him. Nurse Janice Brewington was an outstanding O.R. nurse who made it her mission to make sure the new residents fit into the culture and rules of Bellevue. "Good morning, Dr. Michael," she said cheerfully. "How are you?" She was aware that he had been on call for approximately thirty hours.

Michael took a long gulp of coffee, hoping the caffeine would sustain him for the rest of his shift. "I am on the downside of my shift, so I guess I am okay."

"I noticed that you had the wonderful experience of being Dr. Skeffington's whipping boy at conference two days ago."

Michael grimaced at the memory of being humiliated in front of his peers. "I think that he doesn't believe that I belong here."

Nurse Janice smiled and said, "Get that out of your head. Every year he picks out the most intelligent and caring new resident and tries to completely embarrass him. You are this year's winning contestant. But let me tell you something: I believe he is jealous of someone like you. He has zero bedside manner and is a compete egotist. His idea of the perfect home would be ten thousand feet of mirror. Don't let him get to you." Michael burst into laughter at the last comment. He thanked Janice and went back to the next few names on his clipboard.

12

The Incessant Doubts

S AL HAD NOT ONLY SURVIVED THE first four years of seminary life; he was now approaching ordination. This goal had
seemed so far away for years, but now he encountered a constant
issue, and that was the intensity of the doubt. It was one thing
to be a seminarian where there was always the chance that at any
given moment you could walk out the door; quite another to
face the stark reality that ordination would change everything. He
had heard over and over from faculty members that doubt always
shadowed the route to the priesthood. When he assessed himself
in relation to his classmates, he almost always concluded that he
might be the least religious person in his class. He had friends and
acquaintances who were such marvelous human beings that even
though he had a very healthy self-image, he thought they were
much more profoundly prepared to be priests than he was.

His time here had changed many of his beliefs, and he no longer saw dogma and theology as separate from the desire to offer constructive service in a parish. The loneliness of the future was never distant from his concerns, and the celibacy requirement was something he hoped would change. The church was going through a renaissance, and there was a remote possibility that in the future priests would be able to marry. He believed this would benefit the whole parish.

There was so much a priest's wife could do to help the community, especially the women who wanted to talk to someone about intimate matters; sex, childbearing, the management of difficult husbands. Even the whole question of how a marriage works—Sal knew something about it, having grown up in a family, being a keen observer, but he knew his parishioners wouldn't always trust his knowledge, and he couldn't blame them. He remembered things he'd heard growing up: respect for priests, always, but also a sense that there were things they didn't know.

The ever-present thought of worthiness became more than a casual conflict when Bill Meade left the seminary just before he was to take the major step of ordination. Bill was brilliant and possessed a consistent level of kindness towards others. Also, he was not only a great athlete but a poet and an excellent public speaker. If you were to develop the poster boy for the Archdiocese of Newark, Sal's first choice would have been Bill. When Bill left the seminary, Sal's immediate reaction was *If someone as worthy as he leaves, what am I doing in this place?*

For days Sal struggled. His anxiety was compounded when a week later one of his closest friends, Mike Keating, also decided to leave. Mike was one of the funniest people Sal knew as well as a real intellectual. Michael had a lot of the Joseph Ryan characteristics in that he was not entirely focused on philosophy and theology but realized that there was a greater world out there.

Mike had a fascinating opinion on almost everything. Two tremendous human beings who had been a profound influence on Sal's life, and suddenly they were gone. This was more than a casual doubt: it created a real crisis in his life. Coupled with this was a wedding invitation from Elizabeth that had arrived this week. He was torn between happiness for her and a lingering pang at losing her as an intimate part of his life. Celibacy at this stage was not a choice that he had to make; there was still the option of leaving the seminary at any time. Yet despite these doubts, Sal had been changed in many ways during his seminary tenure. His depth of knowledge about the church had been expanded, and prayer and meditation had been vital avenues to his spiritual growth. However, these realities did not fully remove questions about making a final commitment to the priesthood.

One night during study hall, Sal concluded that it might be time to quit the seminary. He was not at all influenced by the fact that many people had moved from great initial skepticism to the belief that he would soon be ordained a priest. He could no longer keep this to himself and decided that he probably ought to give it one more shot and discuss his impending decision with his spiritual adviser. Study hall was a period where one was not allowed to leave the room, but there were exceptions to this rule and one of them was that any time you could go in to spend time with your spiritual adviser. Sal left his room, walked to his spiritual adviser's room and knocked on the door. For the next two hours, he shared his doubts and concluded that he thought it was best that he leaves the seminary and returns to his home in Jersey City. The spiritual adviser was a warm and friendly priest who had spent a good portion of his priesthood in a parish. He had been at the seminary for six years and had a positive reputation with all the seminarians.

After Sal's complete catharsis, the spiritual adviser offered him a cigarette. "Sal, I am sure that you think that along the way I never had any moments when I thought about leaving the seminary."

Sal lit his cigarette and said, "I am sure that you did not have persistent doubts."

"Sal, if I had a dollar for every time I almost packed my bags I would have more money than Rockefeller." Sal was shocked at this admission; he had thought that his experience was unique. His advisor continued, "I have never met a seminarian who has not experienced significant doubts along the way. It was true for people far saintlier than I."

One of the examples he gave was that Camillus DeLellis had serious doubts and yet became a wonderful priest. Sal had never heard of Camillus, and his initial reaction was that he was probably a recently ordained priest. He also thought he was certainly not from Jersey City because, with that name, he would have had eighty-five beatings before the sixth grade. For some reason, he did not ask if he could speak to Camillus. That was a good thing because as the priest kept speaking, he found out that Camillus was a saint who had lived in the Middle Ages. Somehow, that brought a smile to Sal. At the end of this intense conversation, he reassessed and thought that he would stay at least a little while longer. The months that followed found Sal more and more at peace with the decision to stay and to willingly accept the vocation, which he now believed was his destiny.

APRIL 1965

Two months before ordination, Sal was called to the Dean of Men's office and informed that his mother was seriously ill. His father had called to say that she had suffered a heart attack, and the prognosis was not positive. Sal received permission to go home to be with her. Sal smiled when his father told him on the phone that she insisted walking to the ambulance so none of the neighbors would be upset. Typical of her unending concern: even in this dire moment, others came first. Sal's mother was the kindest person on the planet. He had learned many things at his mother's knee, but probably the most important was that everyone deserves to be loved and respected. In his entire life, he had never met anyone else who was absent of racial or ethnic bias. As a young child, he had uttered an ethnic slur at the dinner table, and she immediately sent him to his room without supper. When an Italian mother sends you to your room without food, you don't have to be a rocket scientist to know that you are in serious trouble. After a few moments, she came to his room and lovingly explained why what he had said was offensive. This attitude was unusual in that culture, especially in someone whose own brother regularly employed racial slurs. Sal once overheard her say to him, "Rudy, every night before I go to bed, I pray that you will wake up tomorrow and be black."

The ride to Jersey City seemed to take forever. Once home, Sal borrowed a car and drove to the Jersey City Medical Center. When he was entering the parking lot, a cop was shouting at a woman that she could not park in a reserved spot. She was annoyed and questioning his decision. Spotting the Roman collar, the cop waved Sal into the spot she had vacated. The woman began to give the officer heat for letting the priest park in the vacated spot. Hoping to alleviate the tension, Sal rolled down the window and said, "Thank you, officer; I have an emergency."

The cop bolted in front of him and shouted, "Get out of the way; Father has an emergency.

When they reached the elevator, which was filled with doctors and nurses, the cop ordered everyone off so "Father" could quickly reach his emergency. Sal was terrified because although he had on a Roman collar, he was not yet a priest. When they reached the intensive care floor, Sal used his street smarts and said, "Thank you, Officer, but I can take it from here. If she sees you, she will be frightened." The cop saluted him and left. Sal uttered a sigh of relief, but now the real concern would begin. Seeing all those tubes in his mother was quite a jolt, and watching his father gently speaking to her was tough. She was semi-conscious and did not recognize Sal. His mother had always been robustly healthy. Certainly a few pounds beyond slender but with enormous physical stamina. Now her red hair had turned a shocking white, and her perfect facial skin was an ashen gray. Her breathing seemed labored, and there were hitches in it that alarmed him. He could not even remember her having a cold. She was a woman who was constantly helping ill or infirm neighbors with chores; it was part of her regular regimen. The woman in the bed before him was barely recognizable.

The attending physician came in to examine her, and Sal and his father waited outside. Sal asked his father to go back and hold his mother's hand because he wanted to speak with the doctor alone. Sal asked him not to pull any punches. The doctor told him that the next night and day were critical. If she made it through that period, she had a chance. He casually told Sal that there was the possibility of her arresting during the night. He said if that happened and there was no one around, he should bang heavily on her chest. He indicated how this should be done. Sal was shocked and terrified that he might have to perform this intervention.

Sal sent his father and sister home and sat in the darkness for hours. He kept glancing at the heart monitor, hoping that it wouldn't flat line. Around two-thirty, he was thrilled to see someone enter the room. He noticed that the figure had a stethoscope around his neck, and he was relieved that he would get a medical update; suddenly, he heard a familiar voice. "Hi, Sal, how are you doing?" Incredible as it might seem, this was his buddy Michael.

Sal was almost speechless. "How . . . ?"

Michael said, "Mike Henry called and told me about your mother. I was not on duty tonight, so I came from Bellevue. If it's okay, I will spend the night with you." Sal was so grateful and told Michael what the doctor had said about pounding on his mother's chest. Michael laughed and indicated he could handle that while Sal would probably be better at the prayer responsibilities. Michael reminded Sal that he had been there for him when his mother and brothers had died, and he was thrilled to have the opportunity to respond in kind. All through the night, the two shared life experiences since they had last seen each other. Michael enjoyed Sal's stories of the seminary, and Sal was awed by Michael's experience saving lives.

When Michael left the next morning, Sal's mother had stabilized, and her prognosis had improved. By the time Sal returned to the seminary, she was cooking up a storm for the family and had made a miraculous recovery. Her indomitable will had carried her through the crisis.

One humorous note was that during that period when Sal was home, he went on a series of errands for his father. Losing track of the time, he came back to his car, and there was a cop writing a ticket. He saw him and said, "Is this your car, Father?" When he replied in the affirmative, the cop said, "Thanks a lot, now I have to look for another '57 Chevy." It could only happen in Jersey City.

13

MAY 1965

You Are a Priest Forever

THE SEMINARY YEARS WERE ENDING. He had survived the rigid schedules and the lack of intellectual freedom. There had been a tightrope approach to his years in the seminary, but he had been changed by the experience and now had a new reverence for much of what he had dismissed as a younger man. There had never been any disrespect in his heart, but he now realized that while service to others was vital, a spiritual foundation was equally important. Classes ended in the middle of May, and then all the deacons would go on a weeklong retreat. This would be followed by a trip to Sacred Heart Cathedral, where they would be ordained priests by Thomas A. Boland, the Archbishop of Newark.

The week before ordination, the deacons were separated from the rest of the seminarians. The ritual at the seminary reminded Sal of an athletic contest because all of the seminarians were lined up before the chapel and cheered and slapped the back of each deacon on his way inside. The raucous shouts and cheers gave way to absolute silence as the deacons entered the chapel. This was to be a week of prayer, meditation and silence. The reality of the moment was overwhelming, and each day Sal tried to keep focused on what was to occur on the following Saturday. He would move from the confines of the seminary to the challenges of parish life. He spent the entire week reminding himself that this was not a time for pride or a belief that he was somehow above those that he was called to serve. His guidepost and anchor became Christ's words in the Sermon on the Mount, and he tried to infuse those guidelines into his soul.

Ordination was not the end for Sal, but the beginning of his service to the daily lives of others. He yearned to embrace the role of the priesthood but not to preach from a pedestal. The role was not about his own worthiness. Some of his classmates had more easily adapted to the seminary; the process fit them like a glove. The seminary was more difficult for him despite the value of being in the presence of so many wonderful people. Sal's life had been enriched by classmates and teachers, but he was glad to be able to experience more freedom of thought and practice.

On a brilliant May morning when the sky was deep blue, and the sunlight beamed crystals of light through the trees, Sal made his way from his family home to St. Aloysius church. He was to celebrate Mass in his parish church for the first time.

His first Mass was the high point after ordination. He remembered that when he struggled with the decision to enter the seminary, this church had been the sanctuary that solidified that choice. One day, when the church was literally without a soul other than him, he knelt at a side altar and with the votive lights flickering in his face pleaded with God to let the confusion pass and lead him to the choice in peace and certitude.

The church was more beautiful than he had remembered. As he walked from the rear of St. Aloysius to the main altar, each pew was filled with persons who had been vital in his life. Elizabeth was there with her husband. She reached out to touch his hand as he made his way toward the main altar. In the second row was Michael McNally with a Cheshire Cat grin as Sal nodded to him. He and Arlene had been such loving friends, and he truly treasured them. In the first two rows, the people who meant the most to him were beaming with pride. His mother, father, sister, and brother embraced him before he ascended the two steps to the main altar. He was thrilled that so many of his relatives and friends were in attendance. As he reached the altar and looked out at the pews, he was overwhelmed by the view of everyone in his life who had all contributed to this moment. St. Aloysius was a church filled with memories of countless acts of love and kindness. He was deeply touched with gratitude when he gazed at the pews that contained vital pieces of his life. It was an out-of-body experience to see all the relationships as a mosaic. Who he was and what he had become was largely because of those present at this glorious celebration. He paused before beginning the liturgy to savor all the love and caring. At the point in the liturgy that called for the "kiss of peace," Sal turned it into a spontaneous love fest. Instead of merely greeting the first few rows with an embrace, he went down the entire church, hugging those on the aisle seat of each pew. The most touching moment of the Mass was when he gave his mother Communion. Months prior, he had thought she would be dead from a serious heart attack.

After placing the host on her tongue, he caressed her face and wiped the tears from her cheeks. At the end of the Mass, when he gave the final blessing, the entire congregation applauded and rushed to embrace him as he left the altar.

One of the neighborhood wits, Jimmy Colgan, said: "The National Guard had to be called out to protect an entire area of Jersey City homes from looting because everyone was at Sal's first Mass." It truly was a marvelous experience, and Sal felt humbled by the reverence and love that were showered upon him.

The next two weeks were a whirlwind. Sal couldn't wait to hear the location of his new parish. Finally, the day came, and he was informed that he was to be assigned to Holy Trinity Parish in Westbury. Hearing those words hit Sal like a sledgehammer, despite his usual upbeat approach to life. Holy Trinity was known in clerical circles as one of "The Stations of the Cross." The pastor, a ninety-year-old priest, went through priest's year after year who would be transferred to yet another "Station of the Cross" parish.

After the initial disappointment, Sal had a long chat with himself. The seminary had been no picnic, and yet he had survived. Service to others had been the prize, and though there were days when he was ready to walk out the door, he stayed. He had survived because there was a goal that resided deep in his soul. He had been transformed into a person with rock-solid spiritual convictions. It had begun with the desire to serve and make a difference, but now it was more than that; he now believed in so many of the Gospel's teachings. This was the time when all that emotional juggling would have a payoff. There would be people in this parish whom he could serve, and though he could not control the circumstances of Holy Trinity, he could still make a difference. If this were the place that he was assigned, then he would make it the best assignment in the class.

JUNE 1965: THE PARISH ASSIGNMENT

In the words of the old cliché, this was the first day of the rest of Sal's life, and his anxiety and anticipation were beyond measure. His mother had made a marvelous breakfast, but he merely feigned enjoyment. After breakfast, he packed his suitcase and put on his Roman collar. It was a rather warm day in June, but not yet humid. Kissing his parents, he left 202 Delaware Avenue, and as he drove to the end of the street, he saw a few of the neighbors who had assembled at the corner to wave goodbye. He returned the waves and headed toward the New Jersey Turnpike. Many times, on a Saturday, he had taken this road as the first part of his ride to the shore, but this was different. The destination here was not a rowdy weekend with his friends; this was his first parish assignment. The seminary was preliminary; this was the main performance. Unlike the past five years, there was no script.

The traffic was growing, and Sal knew that it would get much heavier once he got on the Garden State Parkway, which was the main thoroughfare leading to the shore. No sooner had he exited the Turnpike and entered the Parkway when the traffic came to a screeching halt. For the observable horizon, all Sal could see was a chorus line of brake lights. Gazing into his rear-view mirror, he saw a police car speeding on the shoulder. As the car whizzed by him, it suddenly came to a halt, and at breakneck speed, the patrol car reversed. When it was parallel with Sal's car, the officer rolled down his window and said, "Follow me, Father; there is an accident a mile from here."

Sal turned his car to the shoulder and tried to keep up with the patrol car, but he wasn't used to going ninety. When they arrived at the accident scene, both cars had substantial damage, but there were no serious injuries. Sal, with holy oils in his hands, removed his stole from his neck and returned to his car. The officer came by and said, "Thanks, Father, glad it was a false alarm. As soon as the tow truck clears the road, you can be on your way." Fifteen minutes later Sal was again moving rather quickly, despite the traffic. He was only three exits from Westbury. Again, the traffic came to a dead halt. As he glanced into the rear-view mirror, he saw a patrol car speeding on the shoulder. This time there would be no need to back up because, apparently, the officer was searching for the priest again.

Smiling, the officer waved at Sal with a motion that indicated he should follow. Steeling his nerve, Sal pulled on to the shoulder and with pedal to the metal stayed on the officer's tail. Arriving at a three-car fender bender, Sal realized there would be no last rites given but was now shaken by the realization that he might be late for his first day in the parish. Exiting his car, he walked over to the officer and said, "Officer, it's not that I don't enjoy playing bumper tag with you, but I am on my way to my first parish assignment, and if this keeps up, I will be late."

The officer introduced himself, saying, "I am officer Darcy McGill, and I am afraid you have a problem, Father." He took out his pad of tickets, continuing, "Let's see, Father, I have you for speeding, riding on the shoulder and tailgating a state police patrol car. I think there are enough points for you to lose your driver's license. Only kidding, Father, get back in your car, and I will hold the traffic for a few minutes to give you a head start. By the way, what's your name? We are always looking for chaplains who can really drive fast."

Sal sped away and was relieved once he saw the sign for Westbury. Getting off the exit, he drove three miles up South Street and made a left onto First Street. Arriving at First Street, he presumed that the gray building next to the church was the rectory. It was a faded 1920s structure that was in dire need of a paint job and new gutters. The sidewalks in front were cracked, and some were raised due to the roots of a large oak tree. Taking two long breaths, he opened the trunk of his car and, suitcase in hand, climbed the four steps and rang the bell. A middle-aged woman with what he perceived to be a German accent answered the door. He greeted her, saying, "Good afternoon, I am Father La Greca."

"Yes, Father, we were expecting you; please come in." It was bright and sunny outside, but Sal felt like he was entering the catacombs because there was almost no light in the hallway. "You can put your suitcase down here, Father," she said, leading him to the end of the hallway. They entered what appeared to be an office as she said, "Monsignor, Father La Greca is here." At the end of the room in a leather chair, smoking a cigar, sat the pastor, Monsignor Henry Masterson. He barely grunted at the news that his new curate was present, and Sal thought he looked like Ebenezer Scrooge. His face had a thousand lines, and Sal barely could see his eyes, so bushy were the thick grey eyebrows that topped them. His cigar smoke permeated the room; there were yellow stains on the windows from the constant presence of cigars. Also, in the room were two other clerics.

The older one, Father John Flannery, extended his hand and said, "Welcome to Holy Trinity."

He was a middle-aged man with a perfectly tailored suit, an out-of-shape body, and a slight tremor in his right hand. His rosy cheeks gave the hint that perhaps he was a drinker.

The other priest, Father Gene McCoy, the youngest member of the staff, warmly shook Sal's hand, and offered, "When you are ready, I will show you to your room." He was on the short side and looked younger than his thirty years. Sal remembered that he was an excellent public speaker from their time in the seminary. Father McCoy had been ordained two years ago and had so far survived without being transferred. The pastor continued to smoke his cigar and watch *Wheel of Fortune* while Sal stood twiddling his thumbs. After a pause, Father Gene indicated that there would be no breakthrough conversations on the horizon and said, "Let's go upstairs to your room." 'Upstairs' was a fancy word for the attic where Sal would be housed. The room had a low ceiling and was furnished as if the Goodwill had dropped off the latest donations. The temperature in the room absorbed the rising heat from the lower floors and had only one small window for ventilation. Gene said, "You really could use a window air conditioner, but you will have to provide it yourself. The pastor squeezes the nickel till the buffalo farts."

Sal laughed, and Gene then started to give chapter and verse about what he had learned at Holy Trinity in two years. Gene was most helpful in conveying some of the parish ground rules and advised Sal that they would leave to hear confessions in an hour. Sal unpacked, undaunted by his initial entry into parish life.

At five to three, Gene McCoy called up from the hallway and said, "Time to go, Sal." Together they walked to the church, which was only a hundred feet away from the rectory. The church was dimly lit, and Gene said, "Get used to it. The Lord may have said 'Let there be light,' but our pastor never heard him. Leaving a light on is more sinful than murder in Holy Trinity. Your confessional is the one at the front on the left." As Sal entered, there were six or seven persons waiting to have their confessions heard. Seated in the confessional, he slid the panel open and almost immediately heard an older male voice say, "Bless me, Father, for I have sinned."

When the penitent had finished, Sal gushed forth a tidal wave of thoughts that he had waited years to share. He spoke about how forgiveness was vital to spiritual growth and how deeply Christ loved to forgive us our sins. He expounded on the belief that when you accept God's forgiveness, it allows you to grow in many ways. He added psychological gems regarding the positive connections between faith and mental health that he hoped could transform this man's life.

When he finished the voice on the other side of the screen said: "Could you repeat that, Father? I am very hard of hearing."

14

Bellevue

O N DUTY ONE NIGHT, MICHAEL WAS summoned to the OR. A serious accident had occurred in front of Radio City Music Hall. A family of four was crossing the street when a drunken driver ran a red light and plowed into them. The parents and one of the children had been killed instantly. The youngest child, a boy of five, had been critically hurt and was being transported to the hospital.

As Michael scrubbed, he looked at the x-rays, and his immediate impression was that, at best, the child had a fifty-fifty chance to live. There were multiple fractures, probably internal bleeding, and it was too soon to ascertain the extent of brain damage. During the intensely delicate surgery, Michael had a fleeting memory of his brothers and was aware that he felt a wave of sadness. It did not interfere with the technical issues that he was addressing, but he was surprised that it had occurred. He had become used to keeping his emotions distant while performing surgery. After six hours of surgery, the child had been stabilized but was in a deep coma. Michael was most concerned about what the child would experience if his brain function were restored, and he was informed about what happened to his parents and sister. Had he been saved to be all alone in the world? How can one get through trauma without love?

Daily, Michael checked on the child and found out that his name was Robert. At the end of each surgical shift, he sat by his bedside, often whispering in his ear. He could not define why this child had become so special except that he reminded him of his past. He often thought of his brothers Donny and Danny. He remembered those days after their deaths when he had longed to comfort them, when even the idea that they were in Heaven didn't seem enough. The need to love, to show love, to protect, had been so strong. When he asked her about it, the hospital social worker, Anne Torregrossa, informed him that there were no immediate close relatives and that the boy would be placed in foster care if he survived. Michael wondered what would have happened to his brothers if it had been he and his father who had died instead.

Michael had not shared his interest in Robert with Arlene, but she had a sixth sense about his concerns and challenges. One night after dinner, she approached him while he was making dinner on the grill. Arlene was busy negotiating the countless squabbles between the children and, having finally prevented World War III, walked down the steps to the grill area. She delivered the family choices. Michael was monitoring the charcoal fire, waiting for the right temperature. He was busy coating each hamburger with the marvelous McNally recipe. It was made up of sea salt, onions, parsley and a sprinkle of Pabst Blue Ribbon beer. Arlene paused before returning to the kitchen and said, "Well, Mr. Mystery Man, do you want to chat now or after dinner?"

Michael smiled and sheepishly said, "You should open up a fortune-teller shop, my dear. Let's wait until all the kids are asleep."

Arlene teased him by stating, "With our four wild kids, that may be never."

After the apartment became silent, Arlene took two cups of coffee to the patio where Michael seemed deep in thought. "Let's have it. What is going around in that wonderful Irish brain?"

Michael was not sure where to begin, so he started by telling her about the accident in front of Radio City Music Hall. "I saw that on the news, terribly sad," she said. "Did the whole family die?"

"No, the parents and the older sister died instantly, but the youngest child, Robert, is still alive. He is in a deep coma and had many fractures as well as internal bleeding. The biggest concern is whether there is brain damage because there is significant swelling."

Arlene sighed. "Oh, that poor child. It must be difficult for you to treat him."

"It is, but there is more to it than that. He is for all practical purposes an orphan, and I am deeply concerned that if his brain function is restored, he will be overwhelmed."

"Michael, I know you well enough to believe that this conversation is going somewhere."

"Arlene, somehow I have connected Robert to Donny and Danny. It may seem out of the blue, but he has no immediate family. He has no one to help him make sense of grief. The best option for him if he recovers is foster care." Michael stopped, took a long swig of his coffee and said, "If he survives, I would like us to consider adopting him."

Arlene stood and put her hands-on Michael's shoulders. "Very few have been as blessed as we have, and if you feel this strongly, I will enthusiastically support adoption."

Michael stammered, "Don't you want time to think about it? We already are barely making it financially. This will put an extra burden on you."

"What is there to think about? The man I adore wants this, and that is good enough for me. We have always found a way to make ends meet. Soon you will finish the extra year of residency, and we will be in better financial shape."

Four weeks later, Robert came out of the coma and began a period of extended physical rehabilitation. He would need many future surgeries and years of speech therapy. His upper thighs had braces that would stabilize him, and he required a cane to maintain his balance. The McNally's became his family, and the children loved and treated him as one of their own. Michael Jr. established an immediate bond with Robert and daily they would spend time together reading and drawing. Michael Jr. was the first to be aware that despite some physical and mental limitations, Robert had exceptional art ability.

Despite his ailments, Robert continued to develop his artistic abilities and related well to the McNally children, who were all kind to him. "I'm so proud of our kids," Arlene said. "We've done something right." There were moments when Robert's mood would go dark, when he'd cry about his parents and sister's deaths.

At those times, he liked looking at their pictures, running his fingers over the colored paper, and recounting the memories that held the most meaning. Michael listened, though this was difficult for him—his empathy was sometimes painful. His own memories rose. But he spent quality time with him and tried to address the questions that were lingering in Robert's mind. Robert had, over a period of time, been able to call Arlene and Michael Mom and Dad, but he still had questions about his biological family. Once while they were building a sand castle at the beach, Robert asked, "Dad, are my parents and sister in heaven?"

Michael was touched by the question and responded, "I believe they are."

"What do you think it's like there?"

Michael paused and asked Robert what his idea of heaven was.

Robert put down his shovel and asked Michael to help him sit in the beach chair. "Maybe it is a place where you are always happy."

Michael thought that was a good description. "I think that is it, Robert. They are very happy and close to God." This seemed to satisfy Robert, and he asked that Michael help him back to the beach house.

15

The Death of a Young Boy

I T WAS A HOT, SUNNY DAY, typical of the East Coast: the heat was difficult, but the sweltering humidity made the heat index dangerous. The local junior varsity football practice began with the normal stretching and jumping jacks. After an hour, the practice moved to contact without pads, and the coaches kept verbalizing the need for toughness. Requesting water or breaking the routine was defined as the acts of sissies. These challenges impacted the young men; none of them wanted to be identified as weak. As the sun bore down, fatigue set in, and yet there was no pause in the practice schedule. Angelo, a vibrant fourteen-year-old, began to experience blurred vision, but he didn't share this with the coaches. He was extremely thirsty but did not wish to be labeled a sissy, so he continued despite his thirst. After finishing the exercise of tackling the dummy, he had trouble catching his breath and stumbled as he returned to the end of the line. Feeling disoriented, he attempted to speak, then collapsed. The coaching staff responded immediately, but they were unable to revive him. After frantic attempts with mouth-to-mouth resuscitation, the emergency technicians transported him to Summit Hospital where he was pronounced dead on arrival.

The Westbury police had a policy that if anyone who died in an accident had a religious affiliation, the church or synagogue would be notified. Sal was on duty when a policeman came to the door and told him what had happened. Their records showed that the family was Catholic, and the officer requested Sal to come and break the news. Sal had never told anyone that there was a death in their family, and the circumstances in this case were overwhelming. On the way to the family residence, he was filled with anxiety. What could he say to this family that would make the reality that their young son had died any easier to bear? He vividly recalled Donny's death and remembered that he was so broken up that he was unable to drive a car. He had loved the little boy, but Donny wasn't his own brother or child. Yet those hours of being devastated, looking at the ocean when Donny died, had cast a spell of sadness over him that now rose, almost as strong as it was the first time.

He prayed for guidance but could not relax enough to feel any answer.

Accompanied by a policeman, Sal shuddered as he rang the doorbell. The woman who answered could not initially fathom why a priest and a policeman were at her door. There is no easy way to tell someone that her fourteen-year-old son has died, so when the words came out, she screamed and collapsed. Sal and the officer carried her limp body inside, and they stayed with her until family members arrived. The news spread quickly in her neighborhood, and her brother, who lived a short distance away, came and tried to comfort his sister. Before Sal left, the brother contacted the funeral director and made the necessary arrangements for the funeral.

Angelo's uncle called the rectory later that day and informed Sal that the mother wished to bury her son in Fairview Cemetery, the nonsectarian cemetery, because it was close to her home. She wished to visit the site daily. In his naiveté, Sal did not think that there would be an issue. He was amazed when he was informed that, as a Catholic priest, he could not bury the child in unconsecrated ground; Catholic burial would be refused if they chose that site. Sal knew there had to be rules, but this was antithetical to caring for someone in such pain. A young boy had died, and the Church's response was to deny burial? He thought there must be a way around this decision. If he created a rational solution to the dilemma, then all parties would be satisfied. Sal offered to go to Fairview and bless the ground, but this alternative was denied. In a last-ditch attempt, he went to the chancery office to plead the case. Fortunately, the priest who was on duty was a priest Sal knew from the seminary. Sal believed that the rule would be waived considering the circumstances. His position was that if this mother were to kill herself because she was so immersed in grief, the Church would not deny her Catholic burial. The presumption would be that she was so disturbed that she could not make a rational decision. If that were the case, he argued, what was the difference here? Her grief at losing her son was so vast; it was the foundation behind the decision to bury the child at Fairview. His rationale was based on the premise that such profound grief had prevented her from making a better decision. He believed that his argument had merit, but again, the request was denied.

When informed by his priest friend Vinnie Boylan that he could not bury the young man at Fairview, Sal could not contain his shock and anger. "Vinnie," he said, "this is an absurd position, and I am sure you feel the same way. How the hell can we contribute to this family's pain by refusing Catholic burial?"

Father Boylan put his hand on Sal's shoulder. "I hope that if I ever get into a position of authority, I would make a different decision."

Sal did not reply. *He thought to himself,' by that time you will be so co-opted you would respond in kind'.*

Sal turned and left the chancery office but could not accept the verdict. He had taken an oath of obedience, but who and what was he to be obedient to? Was he to be like a sheep, following the dictates of ecclesiastical bureaucrats who had lost touch with the ordinary people in the parishes? Or was it to Christ who had dedicated his life—loving and caring for the poor, the sick and the suffering?

The morning of Angelo's funeral, Sal went to the Episcopal Church where Angelo's service was to be held. Entering the sacristy, he introduced himself to the priest who was preparing for the funeral: "Good morning, Father, I am Sal La Greca, a curate at Holy Trinity."

The celebrant of the liturgy, Father Clark Hunt, was a tall, regal-looking man with jet-black hair who immediately grasped Sal's hands and warmly welcomed him. He asked, "Would you like to participate in the service?" Sal gratefully declined and explained the circumstances. Father Hunt shook his head and with sadness in his voice sighed, "When will we clerics stop getting in the way of Christ's love and compassion?" They chatted for a few minutes, and Sal left the sacristy and sat with the family. His decision was an act of disobedience at face value, but in his opinion, it was an act of witness.

16

By Your Students You Will Be Taught

IN MOST PARISHES, YOUTH ACTIVITIES ARE an essential part of the ministry, but there was no parish youth organization at Holy Trinity. Also, the pastor held the belief that the only children that should receive attention from the priests were those that attended the parish schools. Gene McCoy had tirelessly ignored this belief and, though he had no resources financially, did everything possible to make every child in the parish welcome. Coupled with Gene's dedication to the children of the parish was the passion of a long-standing group of parents who over the years had pleaded with Monsignor Masterson to start a Catholic Youth Organization. Finally, they wore him down. He consented but told them there would be no money spent on the organization. Rightfully, Gene McCoy should have been given this assignment, but probably perceiving that the new curate would be less troublesome, the pastor gave the assignment to Sal. After soliciting Gene's input, Sal asked two students to be joint presidents for the new organization. One was a football hero at the public school, and the other, one of the most popular female students at Holy Trinity High. In Sal's opinion, it was the perfect opportunity to model gender equality as well as stating that all of the children of the parish were important. Sal and Gene also hired Joe Hayes, a former Broadway actor, to create a parish show that would support the organization. Hundreds of kids from both schools became involved, and the shows were a howling social and financial success. The high point for Sal during opening night was when one of the soloists came down with the flu, and the conductor decided to cancel that number. A junior, Dianne, who was relatively shy, asked if she could substitute for the sick child. Sal was proud of her for taking a chance. She belted out the song "Downtown" and wound up with a standing ovation. It was a cherished moment for Sal as well as the rest of the audience.

One of the parochial assignments for each curate at Holy Trinity was to teach daily in the parish high school. Sal welcomed this opportunity to be involved in the lives of the teenagers, and it became one of the highlights of his ministry.

There are two lines from Broadway shows that stuck with Sal as he began his teaching career in the parish. One was from *The King and I*. It went, "When you are a teacher, by your students you will be taught." The other was from *A Man for All Seasons*, the play about the life of Saint Thomas More. A teacher was begging Thomas More for a position in the King's Court. Thomas replied to the request, "But William, you are a wonderful teacher."

William scoffed at the remark and said, "Who will know if I am a good teacher?"

Thomas said: "God will know, you will know, and your students will know, and that is a wonderful audience."

Sal's assignment at Holy Trinity High was to teach Religion to high school juniors. There were three groups, and for some bureaucratic reason, they were labeled as the A, B, and C groups. This system could not have been driven by any true evaluation of their intelligence or capabilities because there was not one iota of the difference among the three groups. It was based on a purely numerical evaluation of an IQ test they had taken before freshmen classes began. For Sal, teaching was the highlight of his day, and he put a great deal of time and effort over the summer into developing a curriculum so that the classes were rigorous and at a high level. Sal never bought into the old teaching adage that you should not smile until Christmas, and he found the students to be not only bright but engaging. High school juniors are a separate breed because a great deal is at stake regarding their futures. They have matured past the sophomore year but have not retired on the job like many of the seniors.

One of the major benefits of teaching was that the personal bond between teacher and student often led to trust relationships where students would confide all sorts of issues. Sal was privy to personal as well as family issues and what was going on in the community. One Wednesday, at the end of the day, he was leaving the building when he saw one of his students hanging around for no apparent reason. Sal realized that there was something serious on his mind. After ten minutes of conversation, the boy shared that there was going to be a robbery at Dewey's Pizzeria over the coming weekend. He would not give Sal the names of the robbers but assured him that they were not students at Holy Trinity. That information did not matter as much as how he could warn the proprietor of the pizza place without causing a panic.

That evening Sal and Gene endured another ghastly meal in the rectory. Aggie, the cook, had been an institution at Holy Trinity for the last forty years. She was now in her middle seventies and suffered from a bevy of ailments. Hard of hearing and blind in one eye, she had a limited repertoire of culinary choices and had never heard of Julia Child. She also had a chronic cough from years of smoking. For dinner this night, she had served a mystery meat they believed to be pork covered with a huge amount of heavy dark gravy. This delight was accompanied by overcooked broccoli the drab green of an army uniform and tasting much the same as Sal imagined that would and a burned baked potato. Sal pushed most of it to the outside of the plate to give the appearance that it had been eaten. After dinner, Gene retreated to his room to eat a sandwich that he had bought that afternoon.

Sal needed to convey information about the impending robbery so he visited the pizza parlor on South Street and engaged in small talk with the Italian owner while eating a Margherita pizza. They covered a host of questions like Dewey's interest in Sal's father's Italian village. Finally, Sal asked, "Do you have a security system in the restaurant?" The tone immediately changed. Sal shared that he had some information that Dewey needed to take seriously.

Dewey pressed Sal for the source of this threat. Sal assured him that he would convey to the source that he had been warned and that he could not say more.

Sal was back at the rectory no more than twenty minutes when a local detective rang the doorbell and asked to see him. The detective pressed hard for Sal's source, but Sal told him, "If I give you a name, I will have no credibility with these kids in the future."

The detective kept up the pressure but at the end graciously said: "I understand, Father. Thanks for tipping the owner off." The good news is that apparently the word made the rounds and there was no robbery then or ever in the pizzeria.

17

MARCH 1966
Bless Me, Father

ON A CRISP WINTER SCHOOL MORNING, two weeks before Christmas, Sister Eucharia had arranged for her second-grade class to have their confessions heard. They had all received their first communion in May, but the experience was still daunting for some of the children. At precisely ten o'clock, Father Sal arrived at his confessional. All of the students stood and said: "Good Morning, Father." Sal returned their cheerful greetings and entered the confessional. None of the children had killed anyone or lusted after their neighbor's husband or wife, so the litany of so-called sins was not earth-shattering. One child confessed that he was always making noises with his back. After a few seconds, Sal realized he was referring to farting.

The greatest challenge of the morning was that one of the boys was so nervous about the experience that he had wet himself. Embarrassed, he did not want to leave the confessional. Sal told him to stay there and went out and told Sister Eucharia what had happened. He inquired if there was any way she could get some dry clothes and take the children back to school so that the boy could be dry and unashamed. Sister Eucharia was a delightful, understanding person, and she immediately gently knocked on the other side of the confessional and asked the little girl to return to her pew. She then told Sal that she would invent a story about the boy not feeling well. She winked at Sal and said, "This won't even be a venial sin on my soul."

Soon, she returned with new underwear and pants. Father Sal instructed the boy to change his wet clothes, but after he was dressed, he still refused to leave the confessional because the entire floor of the confessional had a puddle of urine. He feared that the next child would know that he had peed and would tell everyone what had happened. He had no way of knowing that the good sister had told a white lie to protect him. When he returned to school with different pants, the presumption would be that he had thrown up. Sal asked him, "What is your name, son?"

The boy spoke barely above a whisper, "Tommy."

"Okay, Tommy, when I count to three, you and I will both go out, and they won't know who did it." Tommy returned to school, and no one was the wiser.

Another confessional episode occurred because it became common knowledge that Holy Trinity had a priest who could hear confessions in Italian. Almost every week Sal had more than the occasional Italian-speaking penitent. He could speak the Tuscan dialect, which had over the years been selected as the official language of Italy. Many of the dialects spoken in the major areas of Italy and Sicily were very different and at best difficult to understand. Sal's father, who had been raised in a small village at the top of the Cammarata Mountains in Sicily, spoke a version that was a combination of Italian, Greek, and Arabic.

On one Saturday evening, an elderly Italian woman confessed her sins in what Sal thought was a dialect from the Bari area. He understood about half of what she said. He blessed her and in Italian told her that God loved her, and she should say three 'Ave Marias.' There was silence, and she did not leave the confessional. Again, she began to speak, and Sal could not understand why she was going through the same list of peccadilloes. When she finished, he repeated: "Please say three 'Ave Marias,'" thinking that this time she would say thank you and go her merry way. There was still no movement to leave the confessional, only silence, and then once more time she went through what Sal thought was her list of sins. He honestly thought her sins could not be so terrible. He doubted that she was confessing to being a serial killer. So again, with great patience, Sal said, "Good night, Signora, God loves you and please just say three 'Ave Marias.'"

Sal thought little of this, but it was the custom in the parish to stand in front of the church on Sunday mornings to greet the parishioners before and after the Masses. One of his favorite people, Antoinette Mone, was laughing hysterically as she greeted him. "Good morning, Father," she said. "Last night my mother came to you in confession because she knew that you spoke and understood Italian. I gather you had trouble with her Calabrese dialect."

"Why do you say that?" Sal inquired.

Laughing even harder, she said: "My mother told you she has bouts of gas and feels the urge to relieve herself when she goes to Mass. She asked you what she should do, and you advised her to say three 'Aves.' That did not make sense, so she repeated herself twice." Sal let out a roar of laughter and once again was reminded never to take himself seriously. Sal was sure that story made the rounds of many Italian dining rooms that Christmas.

18

Boot Camp

I T WAS RARE IN A RESIDENCY PROGRAM that there was any fanfare to the appointment of chief resident. The person in that position was largely responsible for creating the weekly surgery schedule, which was more of a nuisance than an honor. However, this was not the case for Michael in his fifth year of the program. Dr. Patricia Stewart, a much loved and respected vascular surgeon, had campaigned to have a formal nominating process for the position and use the person selected as a role model for the new residents. Michael was unanimously selected by his peers and the surgical staff. He had developed outstanding technical skills, but what made him extraordinary was his ability to create bonds with the entire staff as well as the patients. Along the way, the story of his tragic family history had surfaced, and even Dr.

Skeffington, his first-year nemesis, had written favorable reports on his stay at Bellevue.

To formalize the new responsibilities, Dr. Stewart had arranged an early morning coffee where she spoke glowingly about Michael. At this event, there was also the opportunity for other residents, and a few seasoned staff members, to chime in. It was an hour of praise and to some degree a roast. At the end, Michael was requested to say a few words. Dr. Stewart asked him to develop the basis for his approach to the care of patients not only in the O.R. but post-surgery. Michael was somewhat embarrassed by the praise of the morning and wanted to keep things light before everyone went back to the chaotic schedule of the hospital.

"I want to thank Dr. Stewart and all of you for taking time out of your day to honor me with your praise and pathetic attempts at humor. I find it hard to believe that this will be my last year at Bellevue. Thanks to the staff and the patients, I now believe more deeply in the words spoken to me in my interview for the residency program. Dr. Ron Forneris told me that even though I had the title 'Doctor' coming out of med school, I was not truly a doctor. That title would have genuine meaning only when I became immersed in the surgical world of Bellevue. Ron's words were precisely on target. I am sure that you will find through the peaks and valleys of being residents that, in the end, it is more than worth it."

Before closing, Michael focused on the world of pain and suffering that happens every day in the hospital. He said he had been touched by so many experiences, and that suffering can be something that leads to personal growth for the patient and the surgeon. All those in attendance were aware of the tragic history of Michael's family and were anticipating that he would recount what he had been through. Michael began, "I must admit that I know suffering at a level that is beyond imagination. I have been a New

York Jets fan for years, and no one suffers more than a Jets fan."
The gathering, braced for the tearful history of Michael's family,
roared with boisterous shouts and laughter at the statement.

Leaving the conference room after the gathering, Michael
stopped by his mailbox, which was filled to the brim. In his office,
he began to drink his third cup of coffee of the day and sat at
his desk sorting through the mail. Most of it was immediately
filed into the wastepaper basket, but one was strikingly different.
It appeared to be from the United States Government. Michael
opened the letter and could not believe his eyes. He had been
drafted and ordered to report to Camp Pendleton in San Diego,
California. Being married and the father of children, there was
the possibility that he could receive a deferment, but he had an
intense sense of patriotism and believed it was his duty to serve.
As he did whenever he was confronted with any serious issue, he
made his way to the hospital chapel and prayed for guidance. He
decided that despite his concerns for Arlene and the children, it
was his patriotic duty to serve.

Michael spent two weeks on vacation with his family before
reporting for military duty. It was wrenching for Arlene and his
father, to whom he had grown closer in the last five years, to
have Michael placed in harm's way. He left with the assurance
that his father and Aunt Mary would keep a close eye on his
family.

Before leaving, he contacted Sal and drove to Westbury. Sal
met Michael at the Jolly Roger Restaurant, and after ordering,
they began to catch up. "How is parish life treating you?"

"Before I answer that, how are Arlene and the children?"

"Great. It has been hard on her because I had so little free time
during my residency, but she is able to juggle everything. The kids
are all growing rapidly."

"Terrific. I will give her a call and hopefully on my next day off will spend the day with Arlene and the kids in New York."

Michael was pleased and said, "She will love that but better wear plated armor because my kids may do you bodily harm."

Sal smiled and offered, "I have plenty of practice dealing with that every day at recess with the grammar school kids."

Michael took a long gulp of coffee and inquired about Sal's experience in the parish.

"At times it is overwhelming because we have four thousand families, and there are only three priests. We teach, cover the hospitals and participate in the ordinary and extraordinary events of the parishioners' lives. I am often exhausted at the end of the day, but I love it. How about you?"

"Well, I can certainly relate to the exhausted bit because I am on call for thirty-six hours in a row, but it has been fulfilling. I deal with every conceivable medical and surgical issue. Like you, we are grossly understaffed. But the experience is phenomenal."

Sal agreed. "You and I are lucky to be so involved in people's lives at the times when they most need help." He felt a deep bond with Michael at that moment—a bond that had always been there, but not always something he was conscious of. *This is why we are friends,* he thought. *We are alike in the ways that matter.*

Their meals were served and Sal raised his glass of wine and said, "Michael, you chose to go to Vietnam, didn't you? I wasn't under the impression they drafted fathers of twelve."

Michael grinned. "It does seem like twelve sometimes, believe me. " He went on to say that he could have received a deferment, but after reading about the conflict, he was convinced that it was his duty to serve. "These young men are risking their lives, being wounded every day, and they need doctors. I swore an oath, and I see this as part of that oath. And the war itself—well, it may be a distant country, but Vietnam is key to what will happen in Asia.

The Communists can't beat us directly, so they are using stealth. We are so fortunate to have grown up in a free country, where we can worship as we choose. I think we owe it to those less fortunate to help out."

Sal did not concur with Michael's view of the war and had privately been involved in the anti-war movement. He was less sure about the reasons for US involvement than Michael was, but he did not share his belief that the war was wrong. He knew many who agreed with Michael and understood that changing minds was a slow and difficult process. All that would come of voicing his ideas now was argument, and he wanted the lunch to be a rewarding experience for both of them. Sal again raised his glass and said. "May God protect you and bring you safely home to Arlene and your kids."

Michael thanked him and said, "I won't pretend I'm not afraid—especially of leaving Arlene a widow and my kids fatherless. But this is what I have to do."

"I understand that." *And you better come home, Michael,* he added to himself. *I'm not sure I could go to another McNally funeral.*

Arriving at San Diego airport at 2:00 p.m., Michael made his way to the information booth in the center of the main terminal. He was informed by one of the military police standing near the booth that there would be a bus leaving for Camp Pendleton within the next fifteen minutes. Michael followed the Marine's directions, went outside and saw a group of about thirty men waiting for the same bus. Once the bus arrived and everyone had boarded, there were introductions and constant chatter. Not every physician on the bus was a surgeon. There were many different medical specialties present, and it appeared that the physicians had been drafted from all over the country. After a forty-minute drive, they arrived at Camp Pendleton. As they left the bus, a Marine sergeant with a clipboard checked off their names and assigned them to a Quonset hut across from the bus stop.

In the supply barrack, they were issued uniforms and military gear and given the number of a hut where they would be billeted for the duration of boot camp. Upon entering Quonset hut number six, Michael was thrilled to see his old colleague Joe Pittelli. The immediate response from the Philly wise ass was, "McNally, if I knew you were coming, I would have fled to Canada. Your presence tells me that the war is lost." Michael laughed and warmly shook the hand of his dear friend. After the initial teasing, the two settled into a serious conversation and tried to ascertain what this experience would entail. It did not take long for that question to be answered.

The doors of the Quonset hut opened with a loud bang, and a short, stocky, tough-looking Marine sergeant entered and barked, "Attention on deck; everyone is to report immediately to the communications center." Michael, Joe and the rest of the new inductees followed the sergeant to the largest Quonset hut on the base. They were instructed to be seated, wait for further information and remain completely silent.

The Marine sergeant stationed at the door shouted, "Attention, officer on deck." With those words, a tall, well-built, handsome officer entered the room and walked to the podium. This impressive officer walked with a noticeable limp and had a patch over his right eye. The sergeant who had led them to the stage shouted, "Salute and then be seated." Without as much as a "good day" or welcome to the base, the officer launched into a verbal barrage that stunned and scared the new officers.

"I am Colonel Dennis McCormick, your commanding officer. My task today is to make you aware of what you are about to experience for the next year of your lives. You may think of yourself as the high priests in the world from which you have come, but I want to take that illusion away from you immediately. This is not a place where you will be fawned over by staff, patients, family, or anyone in your social circle. There will be no special reverence for your title, no privileged parking spaces, no perks, and no one spending their lives praising you. Ordinarily, when a man enters the Marine Corps, he goes through a grueling eight weeks, which in many respects shapes him into a combat Marine. Parris Island is a real boot camp. I refer to these five weeks that you will experience as 'Pussies Camp.' Because you are officers, you will not be humiliated and screamed at by drill instructors. However, in my opinion, you have not earned the rank. You receive it solely because you are physicians. It is critical for you to understand that where you are going is a world that is foreign to you. I would strongly suggest for practical purposes that you take most of what you know regarding philosophy, morality, and even maybe parts of the Hippocratic oath and throw them out the window. You will eventually go to base camps in Vietnam where you will meet and treat the finest human beings that you have ever met.

"The Marine Corps is at war with the most savage bastards on the planet. Besides caring for other Marines, you can bet your sweet asses that you better learn how to kill. The war zone does not provide cushy jobs for anyone; that is one of the reasons that you are issued a firearm. At any given moment in Vietnam, you may find yourself face to face with a gook hell-bent on taking your life. In a few short weeks, you will live in a country where men, women, and even children will be dedicated to killing all the Marines on your base. There is no safe place for you, even within the confines of the camp. There will be Vietnamese men and women who give every appearance of being loyal to you, but these same people may plant explosions in your Quonset hut or aid the enemy with military information. We call them 'sappers.'

I am telling you now that every time you trust one of these monkeys, you not only put your life at risk but the lives of others around you. In some respects, I envy you because, having been in Vietnam for over two years, I know that you will see extraordinary heroism and will be overwhelmed at times by the dedication that Marines have for each other. They are dedicated to God, country and the Corps. You have come from a world where a lot of chicken-shit protesters have no sense of the bravery and dedication of those fighting this war. Those cowards believe that we should quit and run."

Colonel McCormick walked out of the room as Michael gazed at all his fellow physicians. He could see that this is not what they had anticipated. When they got back to the Quonset hut, there was an explosion of chatter, and Joe Pittelli, in his usual fashion, said, "Well, Michael, I look forward to all of the other endearing Colonels that we will meet along the way. Seriously, Michael, you must admit that living in Canada is more appealing than it was yesterday."

19

Arrival of Jack Murphy

THE FIRST TWO YEARS OF SAL'S assignment to Holy Trinity parish were ending. There had been so many inspiring moments during that period. Sal was deeply moved and grateful to be a priest, but his relationship with the pastor had gone completely south. Sal did everything he could to avoid confrontations, but the rigid rules imposed on the curates were almost always in contradiction to the critical needs of the parishioners. Sal understood he was probably going to be transferred. Yet despite going to another 'Station of the Cross' parish, he would be eternally grateful for the time he had spent in Westbury.

It was a sad evening the night before the clerical assignments were to be announced. Sal offered to take Gene out for dinner. In the middle of the meal, Sal thanked Gene for all he had done for him, and Gene responded in like manner. The two had forged a mutual respect and shared a common vision of service to others. It was the end of their joint venture, but there were many moments of laughter through the meal. Neither man could wish ill to befall the pastor despite all that they had experienced. However, they both admitted that every night before they retired, they asked the Lord if he had forgotten to call anyone to eternal life that day.

When the meal was over, both priests drove back to the rectory. Sal made a theatrical gesture of goodbye to Gene and ascended the stairs to his attic domain. In anticipation of his coming departure, Sal had packed his bags that evening, certain that there would be a special delivery message for him in the morning. He stayed up half of the night going over so many meaningful moments that had occurred in the last two years. The joys he felt at marrying persons so deeply in love as well as the painful moments during family tragedies. He smiled at the marvelous educational growth of those in the high school and the wonder of watching adolescents mature. When the alarm went off, he was groggy and had a difficult time getting ready for the inevitable. He said the first Mass of the day and implored God to help him accept with the fullness of faith his next assignment. When he returned to the rectory, he was met at the door by Gene, who said, "I have been transferred, Sal, and am to report this afternoon to Sacred Heart Parish in Newark." Sal was speechless and again thanked Gene. He wondered who his replacement would be.

Sal did not have to wait very long. Father Flannery informed him at breakfast that the pastor had shared the name of Father John Murphy, one of the newly ordained. Sal searched his memory but could barely envision the new member of the team. He remembered that there was a "Jack Murphy" two years behind him in the seminary but knew little about him.

Precisely at one o'clock in the afternoon, the doorbell rang. Sal thought it might be the new curate, so he answered the door. Standing in front of him was a thin, immaculately attired priest with a suitcase in hand. Clark Kent glasses and a winning though nervous smile adorned this lanky visitor. Before Sal could speak, the stranger said, "Hi, Sal, it is great to see you again." He offered his hand, and Sal, charmed by the fact that Jack even remembered him, shook his hand and led him into the rectory. "Place your bag down," Sal said, "and I will take you to meet the pastor." Entering the office at the end of the hallway, Sal gently knocked on the door and said: "Monsignor, Father Murphy is here." As had happened two years ago, the pastor, smoking a cigar and watching *Wheel of Fortune* in his overstuffed leather chair, did not attempt to greet his new curate. Sal motioned for Jack to come with him. Instead of confining Gene's replacement to the Siberia of the attic, Sal led him to Gene's old room. They chatted for the next hour. Sal did not realize that his life would be dramatically changed by the presence of Jack Murphy.

It did not take very long before Sal and Jack had developed the steel bond of a common vision. Aware that there would be significant challenges from the pastor, they strategized and developed a series of clandestine ways to move the parish forward. Sal was immediately impressed with Jack's intellectual capabilities but more taken with his compassion. He had an inviting way of immediately making parishioners feel comfortable in his presence and a talent for reaching out to many who were often overlooked.

Sal's first awareness that Jack Murphy could be zany occurred in November of his first year at Holy Trinity. He knew Sal loved the opera, so he decided to treat him to dinner in New York for his birthday. The restaurant he chose was famous for having good food, and the waitresses and waiters were all opera singers. It was a bitterly cold night, and, dressed in normal suits and ties, the two clerics were at the end of a very long line to get into the restaurant.

Jack was impatient, and out of the blue he walked past everyone and entered the restaurant. After about five minutes he reappeared and motioned for Sal to join him. Whispering, he said: "Take off your overcoat and drape it on your shoulders the way Italians do in Rome."

Knowing that something was off the tracks, Sal asked, "Okay, lunatic, what have you done?"

He smiled and said, "I merely told the owner that it was embarrassing that the famous Italian heart surgeon Dr. La Greca from Rome had to wait in line." With those startling words, he ushered Sal into the restaurant where the owner was rushing to greet him.

Now, Sal spoke Italian well, but Signor Asti would immediately know that he was not native-born Italian. He greeted Sal with a flurry of Italian, and thinking quickly on his feet, Sal answered in English with a very heavy Italian accent, "Signore Asti, when I am in America, I only speak English." He embraced Sal and led him to the finest table in the front of the room. When the restaurant was packed, Mr. Asti announced what a privilege it was to have Dr. La Greca from Rome in attendance. He motioned for Sal to rise and be greeted by the adoring crowd. Sal was forced to endure a standing ovation.

Sal was hopeful that there would be no further notice of him, but almost immediately a soprano and a tenor dedicated the next aria to Doctor La Greca. By this time, Sal was in full-blown terror mode, fearful that he would be discovered as a fraud. Meanwhile, Jack was sipping his drink and savoring the hoax. Sal leaned over and asked Jack, "What happens if someone in this place has a heart attack?"

He never missed a beat. "Just jump on his or her chest and start pounding away."

JANUARY 1968

Meals at Holy Trinity rectory were almost inedible. The cook, Aggie, was truly a lovely person who took great pride in her work, but all of her meals were overcooked and bland. Sal and Jack would joke about all the seasonings she had never heard of—garlic, of course, and herbs, pepper, wine, even salt—but they also went to extraordinary lengths to avoid hurting her feelings. On more than one occasion, they brought large mailing envelopes to dinner and placed their food inside. Then they would joke about to whom they should mail these offerings.

The worst meal of the week was on Saturday when Aggie melded all of the leftovers into some sort of a stew, or perhaps casserole. "Goulash," said Jack.

"Goulash can actually be very good," said Sal. "I used to order it in a little Hungarian restaurant in the East Village."

"Yeah, but if you'd never had it, just heard the word, this is what you'd think it tasted like."

Once the dinner was over and Aggie was out of sight, they opened the back door and discarded them in the garbage cans. On Thanksgiving, when Aggie brought the turkey to the table, Jack whispered to Sal, "It looks like it was hit by a Greyhound bus." One saving element was that Father Flannery was a gourmet cook who would at least once a week create a superb meal for Jack and Sal.

By this time, Jack had mastered his sea legs and was making a significant impact on the parish. He had the uncanny ability to attract persons who often were marginalized by society. An example of this came, when a visiting priest from Washington was using Jack's confessional. The penitent, who had a serious speech difficulty, believed that Jack was in the box. The penitent made a series of guttural sounds, and the visiting priest found it impossible to understand the words. Flustered, he finally blurted out, "Whatever the hell you did, don't do it again."

One night while Sal was on duty, the phone rang at three o'clock in the morning. Sal bolted out of bed and while picking up the phone began to get dressed. Calls at that hour of the morning were almost always an accident or tragedy. "Hello, this is Father La Greca," Sal said.

A female voice responded, "I would like to speak with Father Murphy."

Sal inquired, "Is this an emergency? If it is, I will try to help you."

She responded after a long pause. "Father, it has been a very difficult day, and I am trying to figure things out."

There was another long pause before she continued. Sal patiently waited. "I usually talk these issues through with my husband, my boyfriend, my therapist or Father Murphy. The problems are doozies. Tonight, I was not sure who to talk to, so I put all their names into a baseball cap. I shook the names up and wound up picking Father Murphy's name. I really want to speak to him."

Sal said, "If you will wait on the line, I will go and get Father Murphy." Sal walked down the stairs to Jack's bedroom entered and shook Jack. "Wake up, Jack, you just won a lottery."

20

MARCH 1968

Prayers Finally Answered

IT HAD BEEN THREE YEARS SINCE Sal had been assigned to Holy
Trinity. His time with the parishioners had been so fulfilling.
He had on many occasions witnessed persons with great burdens
who were sustained by their faith in God. This was especially true
of the Mount family. Jeanne and Chet Mount had five children,
and life seemed normal for the first eight years of their marriage.
Jeanne, an accomplished pianist, was lovingly raising the children, and Chet had a thriving tire and auto repair service business
in the neighboring community. This idyllic life ended suddenly
one morning when their oldest child, Eldeen, aged eight, woke
up and had completely lost her sight. This horrible event was
only the beginning of Eldeen's nightmare. She began to experience gran mal seizures and this beautiful child had bodily and

facial changes that were debilitating. Jeanne and Chet searched every medical avenue for answers, but initially, no one could understand the origin of her illness. Chip, the second child in the family, was fine, but shockingly, Eldeen's illness also afflicted the next two children. Neil lost his sight at age seven, and Tommy at aged eight. Neil rapidly progressed to have all of the same symptoms as Eldeen. Peggy, the youngest, was still fine, but no one knew if she would stay that way. Eventually, it was determined that the children suffered from a rare genetic illness—the result of a recessive gene in both parents—that medicine had no cure for.

Jeanne and Chet were devastated but responded with a degree of love and dedication that defied the imagination. It would have been expected that people would avoid being around such tragedy, but in the case of the Mounts it was the opposite. Their home became a magnet not only for caregivers but children and teenagers. Sal loved them, and every Saturday night after confessions, he would go to their home and play cards with Chip and kids from Westbury high and Trinity. Eldeen was bedridden, and Neil was rapidly deteriorating, but Tommy was still the life of the party. He was a marvelous guitar player and had a great sense of humor. He loved to tease Fr. Sal. On every visit, Jeanne and Chet said Sal's presence gave them comfort, but in fact, he gained more from them and marveled how their faith and love sustained them during these tragedies. When Eldeen died, Sal said the Mass and drove in the limo with Jeanne and Chet to her burial place in New York. The pain of this day was that soon her two brothers would accompany her to an early death.

Tragedies were part of a parish priest's life, but there were other areas that were difficult for him. One was the Church's position on birth control. Over and over in the confessional, he heard the difficulties and strains that the Church's positions had put on couples. In some cases there were medical concerns; in others, there were issues that prevented intimacy. He had over and over examined the Church's position but found it weak and rooted in a few isolated biblical texts. In addition to this moral dilemma, there was also the constant restrictions and admonitions from the pastor, which were draining. Monsignor Masterson had been a dynamic leader at one point in his priesthood, but now, in his advanced years, he was hell-bent on resisting change. He had no thought of tendering his resignation, so the only choice for Jack and Sal was to bear it and keep trying to work around the prohibitions. Jack kiddingly said, "Our only hope is that the flu bug will hit Westbury and sent our beloved pastor to Heaven." He gave his famous penetrating laugh after this statement, but he and Sal thought that might not be a bad daily request to the Lord.

Suddenly, their prayers were answered. The archbishop had decided to retire Monsignor Masterson. The initial joy at hearing the news was somewhat tempered by Jack reminding Sal, "The devil you know may be better than the one you don't know." Fortunately, the new pastor was Monsignor Charles Murray, an affable, kind man who would be a sharp contrast to the current pastor. He wasn't a hands-on leader, and though they learned that he was terribly disorganized, he had few rules. He was very conservative theologically but had a strong pastoral bent. He genuinely cared for the flock and had a very gentle way of dealing with the parishioners. Sal appreciated his kindness and felt that all the plans that Jack and he had developed could now be implemented.

The going-away dinner for Monsignor Masterson was quite lavish, and it was only fitting that the new pastor lovingly praised him for his countless years of service. Sal and Jack bore no ill will against Monsignor Masterson, but they realized this was their golden opportunity to launch the plans they had conceived in secret over the past year.

The first strategic move was the creation of a dynamic adult education program. Jack devoted himself to building the equivalent of a university in the next six months. The talent in the parish was beyond belief, and the wisdom and experience on a range of current topics flowed seamlessly. The curriculum was a combination of theology, psychology, and sociology. The response was overwhelmingly enthusiastic. Both Jack and Sal taught in the program, and the process had the support and blessing of the new pastor.

The only downside for Jack regarding the new pastor was that Jack knew nothing about sports, which the pastor loved. In addition, the pastor bubbled with enthusiastic, cheerful conversation from the moment he entered the dining room. Jack, despite his endearing, warm personality, did not really respond socially until he had two cups of coffee at breakfast. The pastor would go on endlessly about some sports events, and Jack would not know how to react . He decided that before breakfast he would knock on Sal's door and get a one-liner that would start the conversation and then he could just occasionally murmur a yes to the ongoing story that the pastor was recounting. Sal would give him lines like, "Did you see the Knicks game last night? Boy, Willis Reed was a beast on the boards." Jack would not know Willis Reed from Jack in the beanstalk, but the ploy worked, and everyone at breakfast was happy.

21

JUNE 1968

Off to Vietnam

D UE TO GALE FORCE WINDS AND torrential rain, Michael's commercial flight to Hawaii was canceled. It appeared that he would be spending the night in an airport chair, stranded with three Air Force officers. One of the officers suggested that instead of waiting until the next morning, they take a cab to Travis Air Force base and try to hitch a ride with one of the regular flights to Hawaii and then Vietnam.

Michael, who was having reactions to the preventive injections that he had received at the naval base the day before, was willing to take that chance. A cargo flight was headed for Hawaii, and then on to Vietnam, and the pilots were more than happy to provide rides to the stranded group. The flights were anything but smooth, and on two separate occasions Michael made his way to the rear of the planes and regurgitated. Eventually, after hours of turbulence and motion sickness, Michael arrived at the Da Nang airport. After exiting the plane, he was immersed in a sea of civilians and military personnel. It took him twenty minutes to find his way to an information area. He was informed that one of the chopper pilots would give him a lift to the Marine base and was escorted, after a review of his orders, to a spot behind the main runway. Michael waited for almost two hours before a chopper landed in his area. It was at the close of the day, and dusk was settling on the area. Suddenly a chopper appeared and landed almost thirty yards from Michael's area. After the blade stopped spinning a tall, lanky pilot opened the cockpit door and dropped down to the ground: "Where are you headed, sir?"

Michael eagerly responded, "To the Marine base at Phu Bai."

"Hop on. I am Frank Jorgensen, but everybody calls me Jorgie. I see by your papers that you are a physician. Is this your first time in country?"

Michael nodded, "Yes, it is."

"I don't envy you, Doc. I have carted more dead and mangled Marines than anyone should see in a lifetime."

Before Michael could respond, Jorgie had started the engine, and the whirling sound of the propeller made conversation impossible. Once airborne, the light faded almost completely, and the flight was engulfed in darkness.

"I had hoped to get you to the base before complete darkness, Doc," he said, "but it is too late, so I am going to have to drop you."

"Drop me?" Michael asked, horrified. "Where the hell are you going to drop me?"

"About five minutes from the base. We have patrols out, but they are involved in a firefight, and we would be sitting ducks for a VC missile. Normally, I would land five minutes from the base, and five Marines would escort you to the base. I will land in an open area and pick you up at daybreak once our patrols are out." Michael was terrified at the thought of being alone on the ground in this strange war zone.

Jorgie asked, "Do you have a weapon, Doc?"

Michael, in a feeble voice, replied. "No, I don't."

"Look behind the back seat. There should be an M16. Take it. During the night, some of our patrols are out, but if anything comes out of the tall cane grass, it is probably going to be VC. Open fire before they have a chance to shoot at you." Michael thought that Bellevue was a picnic compared to this insanity. Jorgie dropped Michael off in a clearing between two areas of large weeds, saying, "See you in the morning, Doc."

As the chopper flew away, Michael sat on the ground, and over the next three hours glanced at his watch every twenty seconds. He had been through so many harrowing experiences as a surgeon in New York, but never had he been so frightened. How insane was this moment, lying on the ground in a totally foreign environment with not the slightest idea of what to do if there was a crisis? The heat and humidity were far worse than a New York July. His entire uniform was soaked with perspiration, and his heart beat so rapidly that he was close to passing out. It was a still, clear night, and suddenly he was aware that the cane grass about thirty yards from him was moving. He could barely breathe, and there was no saliva in his mouth. He thought of Arlene and his children. How would they be able to get through his death? Closer and closer whatever was in the cane grass moved, and with trembling hands he pointed his weapon, ready to fire. He tried to remember the rules of rapid fire that he had learned at the range in Camp Pendleton. What would it be like to kill a man? What if there was more than one?

Before he could even think about those questions, the cane grass suddenly unfolded, and 500 pounds of Indochinese tiger sauntered out. For what seemed like an eternity, Michael and the tiger were face to face. The tiger halted, a mere twenty feet from him, seemingly startled. They were both frozen. Suddenly, there was a low guttural sound that seemed to come from deep inside the beast, followed by a deafening roar. Michael knew nothing about how to prevent the tiger from attacking but realized if he ran, he would not have a chance. Somehow, he was aware that he could not turn his back on the tiger. Thousands of thoughts were racing through his brain. Would they ever find his body? The reality of Arlene and the children living without him was unbearable. At that moment, he remembered what his uncle had told him when he was hunting deer. If you come upon a bear, don't run. Make yourself tall and yell at the top of your lungs.

Michael said a quick prayer, hoped to hell tigers responded like bears, and stood on his toes, trying to make himself taller as he shouted and cursed. Michael's hands were violently shaking as he imagined the horror of the tiger landing on him, tearing his body to shreds with claws and teeth. He realized that the tiger could be upon him before he got off a shot, and even if he pulled the trigger this instant, chances are he would only wound and enrage the beast.

The tiger, so immense in the moonlight, beautiful and deadly, continued to snarl but remained motionless. Michael worried his shouting would devolve into squeaks. Finally, the animal slowly turned and strolled back into the cane grass. Michael collapsed to the ground and immediately threw up. His bones felt like jelly; he didn't think he could walk to save his life. He shivered despite the intense heat and did not sleep a wink for the rest of the night, acutely aware of every little noise, every shadow. In his imagination, the tiger came back with his mate; crept up behind him; kept its golden eyes on him, waiting for him to drop his guard.

True to his word, Jorgie appeared at daybreak, and setting down the chopper, immediately helped Michael on board. "Have a good night, Doc?"

"You have no idea. I have never been so happy to see anyone in my life."

Jorgie laughed. "That's what they all say, Doc, when I escort them back to the base." Michael wondered if this were some kind of hazing. It made no sense, but this was Vietnam. From what he'd heard, a lot of things didn't make sense here.

After landing, Michael had his papers and I.D. scrutinized by the MPs. He was escorted to a large wooden building where he would be issued all the necessary items for his stay at the base. Once he had gathered his equipment, a Marine corporal led him to the living quarters, which he would share with five other physicians. After placing his gear in his storage locker, he was taken to the office of the chief medical officer, Colonel Barry Bultz.

Michael was greeted by an officer who looked as though he had just gotten out of a swimming pool. His disheveled uniform dripped with sweat. Michael guessed that Colonel Bultz was in his early forties, when in fact he was fifty-six. He had a voice that sounded like a foghorn, and his feet were the size of snowshoes.

"Good morning, Michael," he said. "Pardon my appearance but I just came from surgery, and it was so damn hot you could fry eggs on the floor. I am sure you feel that you are a long way from Bellevue." It was apparent that Colonel Bultz had read Michael's dossier. "Welcome to your new home. Your stay here will be vastly different than any other part of your medical career. It might help if I give you my background as a frame of reference. I was a vascular surgeon at Case Western and held an academic position on the medical faculty. I thought before Vietnam that I had experienced every conceivable form of surgical trauma, but I was dead-ass wrong. I have encountered medical challenges here that are beyond the scope of any surgical experience in any trauma unit in the States. Most of what is natural to you as a surgeon is almost useless here. There will be challenges beyond your skills and training. Every day, you will make immediate life and death calls. There will be no pre-surgery conferences, and at times you will be one of three surgeons performing surgery on a Marine, all at the same time. You will work under conditions such as enemy shelling, insects, intolerable heat and at times the least sterile environment possible. You will see injuries that are not in any textbook, and at times you will pass a wounded Marine who is still alive but soon will be dead to attend to another that has a chance to live. Triage is the name of the game out here." Michael thought the image being portrayed was rather dark, but he listened intently.

"Our job here is to keep these kids repaired and ready for combat. There is no time for opinions about the war. Realize that you are here as part of a Marine unit at war. My last bit of advice is not to let your emotions or feelings get in the way. These are mostly kids who, a year ago, were playing varsity basketball and going to their high school prom. It will sear your soul if you allow their stories to penetrate your heart, so try to keep the diagnosis and surgery your focus."

The heat and humidity in Vietnam surpassed even the record-setting days that Michael had experienced at Bellevue during July and August. Because of the humidity in the barracks, he had slept fitfully and was drenched with perspiration when he woke up at five o'clock. Dressed in fatigues and a t-shirt, he made his way to breakfast and felt that he was living in a sauna. After making morning rounds in the infirmary, he thought perhaps taking a shower would at least temporarily lower his body temperature. The coolness of the water flowing over his head was so refreshing. Suddenly he heard a sound that was to be part of every day in Vietnam. The whirling blades of the choppers spawned immediate activity within his barracks. All the stuff members raced to the triage area. Quickly drying off, he rapidly dressed and joined his colleagues.

As the wounded Marines were transported from the choppers, nurses and physicians immediately decided who could be treated and who was so severely wounded that they were beyond help. One Marine had most of his brain exposed. A nurse held his hand and did her best to comfort him in his last few minutes of life. The nurses and physicians appeared to have a sixth sense about who needed to be treated immediately, and how. Michael was stunned by the injuries and their severity. He took his lead from the rest of the staff members and began to involve himself in the treatment and decision-making.

The next helicopter unloaded a headless Marine, two with severe vascular injuries and two others missing limbs. Michael realized that the traditional medical approach to trauma was woefully inadequate, and as Colonel Bultz had said, "Even in a major city like New York you would never see this number and degree of injuries." Performing a tracheotomy on one the wounded, he was amazed at the response of the young nurses in the triage area. Many of them were in their early twenties and barely out of nursing school. They were the backbone of the triage process, and often the last person to speak with a Marine in the final minutes of his life. Michael had learned long ago that excellent medical care depends on a collegial approach and that nurses were vital to excellent health outcomes. That belief was never truer than in this war zone.

That first triage experience was to be repeated day in and day out, and Michael was counseled by his fellow physicians to guard against personalizing each patient. This advice was offered with all good intentions. He was advised to see them, not as kids from Iowa, Indiana, New York, or any other state, but as cases of multiple surgeries to be treated. One physician told him, "If you personalize their lives, you will be overwhelmed by the horror of this war." Michael did not easily dismiss this counsel, but it went against the very fiber of his personality and spiritual beliefs. He tried to implement a detached approach but quickly reverted to who he was at his core.

Michael had been in Vietnam for several months. Though it would be impossible to completely adjust to the circumstances, he found himself more settled with his duties as a combat surgeon. He marveled at the number of severely wounded Marines that his unit was able to save daily. In his opinion, this was attributable to certain factors. The first was the heroism of the helicopter pilots, who faced constant enemy fire to transport wounded Marines immediately to the triage area. Time was of the essence. In many cases, within two hours, severely wounded Marines would experience multiple surgical procedures that prevented them from bleeding out. Second and third were the ability to almost immediately hydrate the wounded, and the use of synthetic sprays that automatically froze a great deal of bleeding. As in all wars, the triage team did not depend on approved medical devices and practice but used what worked to save lives. In addition, there was also the process of triage, the ability for nurses and physicians to make immediate decisions, which ultimately saved many lives. However, some of the injuries were so grave that it created painful medical decisions. Often it was possible to save a shattered body, but not without enormous consequences regarding the future of the Marine.

Once, Michael decided that despite the extensive wounds of an individual Marine, he would operate and try to stabilize his condition. Despite losing both legs, part of his right arm and having his cheekbone exposed, the young Marine was still conscious. As Michael leaned over him, he said, "Son, we will be able to deal with all of your injuries."

The Marine, aware of the loss of his extremities and the degree of his injuries, pleaded with Michael: "Let me die, Doc. There's no way I want to spend the rest of my life as half a man. Take care of some of my buddies. Please, let me die. I don't want to go home in this condition."

This was the kind of decision that made being a physician in Vietnam intensely painful. Here was a young Marine pleading for something that he felt he had a right to, and Michael was caught between painful choices. His job was to try to save him, knowing how difficult his life would be.

Three days after the surgery, Michael visited the Marine in the infirmary. Heavily medicated, the young man, seeing Michael, said: "What are you doing here, you bastard? I hope you feel good about keeping me alive, but I hate you." With that, the Marine turned his mutilated torso and buried his face in a pillow. Michael understood the anger and left the infirmary burdened with sorrow and the awareness that his decisions had consequences for years to come, consequences he could only barely imagine.

22

The Consequences of Spanking

SINCE THE ARRIVAL OF MONSIGNOR MURRAY, work in the parish had tripled. This welcome change plus additional responsibilities found Sal overloaded. Besides all the day-to-day work, he was on the diocesan personnel board and was finishing a master's degree in counseling. He honestly believed that there were not enough hours in the day. For weeks, he survived on three hours of sleep a night. One of the rare opportunities to catch up on sleep came through the grace of a terrible ice storm. The streets and roads were so bad that neither humans nor other creatures ventured outside. Jack and he ate an early dinner, chatted for a bit, and then Sal climbed the stairs for what he hoped would be eight hours of sleep.

His head had hardly hit the pillow when he fell into a deep slumber. The sleep was so deep that, initially, he did not hear the calling of his name. Slowly waking, he heard a knock on the bedroom door but thought it was a dream. The housekeeper opened the door and said there were two policemen downstairs who had requested to see him. He hurriedly dressed and went downstairs, hoping that he would not again have to tell a family that someone had died in a tragic accident. The officers were quite apologetic but said that there had been a serious domestic dispute, and the shouting had alarmed the neighbors, who called the police. When the police arrived the couple requested to speak with Father La.

The ride from the rectory to the other side of town was harrowing, and Sal was glad that he was not the one driving. After a series of skids and one actual complete spin, they reached their destination. There was no need to ring the bell because the husband and wife were waiting for them in the foyer. They were both subdued, dressed in pajamas and bathrobes. The wife seemed sheepish and finally asked what Sal thought of spanking. He inwardly bemoaned a good night's sleep ruined for a talk about child rearing. Somewhere between annoyance and downright anger, he mustered his best advice, starting with, "It depends on the circumstances and the degree of spanking." Sal added that he was personally opposed to hitting children because it teaches them that violence is acceptable.

The couple looked confused, and the husband said, "Father, we are talking about sexual spanking."

Sal had egg on his face and tried quickly to regain balance in the discussion. The wife added, "He wants me to spank him during sex, and I don't want to do it." Trying to say something that could be remotely helpful, and realizing that the two cops were howling in the living room, Sal had no idea how to respond.

He stumbled through some ridiculous advice and then made his way out to the front door.

In the car, Sal teasingly said to the cops, "I am sure that this tale will be told this morning at the station, but remember you are both Catholics. If you ever come to me for confession, the penances will be severe. Not only that but if you proceed me in death, I have the power to refuse you Christian burial." They both laughed and added that this had made their day.

23

Father Ray's Views

MICHAEL HAD NEVER SEEN MASS AS an obligation but rather a source of strength and spiritual fulfillment. The opportunity, despite his chaotic surgical schedule, to attend Mass daily on the base was his anchor in this sea of madness. Michael's Catholic faith had enabled him to deal with great personal losses, and he believed that it would sustain him in the combat zone. Father Ray, a Jesuit chaplain, celebrated Mass when it was possible each morning and would make the rounds in the infirmary distributing communion and blessing all the individuals under his care. Father Ray was affectionately called "Father Nails" because he was an extraordinary man who was deeply admired by everyone on the base. While on patrols with other Marines, he never ran when the firefights began. He tended to the wounded and dying with

194 | S.J. TAGLIARENI

a calmness that defied logic. He also possessed a fabulous sense of humor. One beastly hot day, his sermon was brief but to the point. He told those attending Mass, "Remember, Jarheads, there are hotter places."

One late morning after making surgical rounds and receiving communion, Michael was invited by Father Ray to have a beer and a smoke outside the infirmary. The two sat on the steps of the hooch and, clinking two bottles of beer, sipped the ice-cold brew.

Father Ray took a pack of cigarettes from his pocket and offered Michael a cigarette. Michael had never had a cigarette in his life and waved his finger at Father Ray in a dismissive fashion. He told Father Ray smoking was a habit that would have dire health consequences. Father Ray smiled and said, "Living in this hellhole, you believe that smoking is even near the top of the things that can do personal harm to me? Every day I deal with deadly snakes, rashes, dysentery, sniper fire, monsoon rainfall, and you think I should be alarmed because of my smoking?"

Michael laughed and said, "I guess on the list of the things that would impact your health, smoking is probably very low."

Father Ray took a cigarette out of his pack, lit it, took a deep drag, and said, "How are you holding up, Michael?"

"I guess as well as could be expected, Father. It's overwhelming to deal with so many lives that have been changed forever."

Father Ray took a deep drag and said, "There are things that you and I see that will be embedded in our minds forever."

Michael nodded in assent and said, "However, I have to tell you in some way I feel privileged to be here. I am humbled by the approach of these young kids toward their buddies. Frequently, while attending a wounded Marine, the first thing he will say is, "I'm okay, Doc, take care of my buddy; he's a hell of a lot more wounded than I am." These kids are so brave that I feel privileged to operate on them. Also, I have developed a strong love for the Marine Corps and the sacrifices these kids are willing to make."

Father Ray was silent for a few seconds but finally responded. "Michael, this may come as a shock to you, but the reason I asked for this assignment has little to do with the Marine Corps or with the US involvement in the war."

"I'm not sure what you mean by that, Father."

Reaching for another cigarette, Father Ray responded, "I don't believe in war, Michael, and I am here only to minister and help. I take no pleasure in the killing, and though I keep it to myself, there is no joy for me in viewing the bodies in the rice paddies that are referred to as 'gooks.' Those are just like our kids; they are persons."

Michael was not used to anyone on the base feeling this way and had difficulty digesting Father Ray's words. "Don't you believe in the just war theory?" he asked.

"Michael, I think the just war theory is bullshit. Every day you and I deal with the horrors of the so-called just war. There has to be a better way for people to behave in this world."

Michael immediately responded, "But there is evil in the world that must be addressed."

"Michael, people in high places start these damn wars, and young people pay the price. Those kids on the other side believe as deeply as our kids that they are fighting for some noble cause. Or they are fighting to protect the life of the kid next to them. Once war starts, morality flies out the window."

Michael was shocked by Father Ray's beliefs. "I gather that you are of the school of Father Berrigan and all the protesters in the States."

"I know Dan Berrigan and do not always agree with his tactics, but I completely agree with his position on war."

196 | S.J. TAGLIARENI

Michael did not wish to turn this into a confrontation but wanted to understand Father Ray more deeply. He asked: "Would you disagree that the United States should have fought against the evils of Germany and Japan during the World War?"

"No, I would not; my point is that war is always the result of human failure, political failure, social injustice, poverty, greed and a host of other moral failures."

"I respect your views, Father, but I guess I'm still very patriotic and believe in the righteousness of what we're trying to do."

"I'm also patriotic, Michael, but not blind to the false premises of all politics. Every time I cradle a mangled kid and anoint him, I am filled with anger for all who cannot see the insanity of the situation."

Two factors had an impact on Michael in the ensuing months. The first was the ongoing conversations with Father Ray about the purpose and value of the conflict. His belief in the righteousness of the war had not waned. He accepted that the Communists were godless and that their plans included the slaughter of all religious believers in Asia. Ho Chi Minh, in his mind, was the equivalent of Hitler. He could not readily dismiss the impact of Father Ray's beliefs, and his respect and admiration for Father Ray were so profound that he was forced to examine his own reasons for defending the US involvement. At the end of the day, his political and religious reasons for continued US involvement had not changed. The daily treatment of the wounded and dying continued to be the foundation for the commitment to his belief in the value of fighting for freedom against the forces of the godless enemy.

The second circumstance that concerned Michael was the visible impact that the daily triage had on members of the staff. Frank Paulson, a cardiologist from New Jersey, appeared to be wearing down emotionally, and there were a series of incidents that gave Michael a feeling that Frank was on the verge of coming unglued. In the past, he and Frank had a series of conversations about family and religious beliefs, which had been sources of bonding. Frank was a practicing member of the Lutheran Community and served on the board of directors at the Somerville Lutheran hospital. He was a man of deep and abiding Christian faith and neither smoked nor drank alcohol. He was a gracious gentleman, known to have a sharp wit. He had a degree of fame due to his one-liners that often alleviated the tension in the triage process.

Lately, Frank seemed more aloof, and there had been a series of shouts from him during the night, obviously caused by nightmares. Michael noticed in surgery that Frank's hands trembled, and though the O.R. was very humid, Frank was often drenched in perspiration even before surgical procedures. Michael had tried to probe his concerns, but Frank waved them off with the statement that he was just tired.

One morning at breakfast, Michael received the news that Frank had been reassigned overnight to a hospital in Japan. This seemed strange and abrupt, so he visited Colonel Bultz's office and inquired about Frank. Colonel Bultz never ducked a direct question from a staff member. He shared with Michael that Frank had experienced a difficult period and in his opinion, was a classic case of "battle fatigue."

"He was on the verge of a mental breakdown," the colonel explained. "I would appreciate your keeping that information under your hat."

Michael assured Colonel Bultz that he would honor this stipulation but added, "I knew that he was having difficulty, but not to the degree that he would have to leave."

Colonel Bultz poured himself a cup of coffee and said, "Michael, if any of us stays here too long, we may wind up in the same boat. I am at the stage where I hope that in the next few months I will be reassigned to the States." Colonel Bultz hesitated and then asked, "Are you able to handle the job without any of Frank's symptoms?"

Michael paused. "The downsides are obvious, but what we do has such value that, at least for now, I think that I can handle it.

"Alright, Michael, but if it ever gets out of hand, don't hesitate to let me know." Michael rose, and for some reason, both men extended both their hands in a double handshake.

24

DEROS

MICHAEL HAD PICKED UP A WORD that seemed to be on the lips of all of the combat Marines. He often heard them in the mess hall refer to DEROS. This acronym stood for "Date Eligible for Return from Overseas." Even the most hardnosed vets in the group, who lived daily with the possibility of being maimed or killed, had this as their daily mantra. Michael, at least at the subliminal level, had subscribed to watching the calendar. He was only months away from returning to the States.

Father Ray's tour of duty was ending at approximately the same time as Michael's, and one evening he invited Michael to the mess hall for an early dinner. The two men, who were on opposite sides regarding the purpose of the Vietnam conflict, had created a bond of friendship that went beyond their views. Father

Ray began the conversation. "It's hard to believe that I have been here for over eighteen months and soon will be finished with my Vietnam tour of duty."

Michael drained the rest of his coffee and said, "If they run out of fuel for the choppers, they can add this coffee. I like it strong, but this is beyond jet fuel."

Father Ray smiled. "Soon you will have others bringing you coffee and donuts in the surgeon's quarters."

Michael said: "From your lips to God's ears. What's next for you, Father?"

"I will be teaching theology at Fordham University."

This news was a positive for Michael. "I am glad to hear that because I will be somewhere in New York City."

"What are your options?"

Michael, despite his prior comments about the coffee, refilled his cup. "My first choice would be the Hospital for Special Surgery and hopefully an academic appointment as well. I have always enjoyed teaching."

Father Ray lit a cigarette and searched for an ashtray. "It's odd, Michael, but in many ways, I will miss being here."

Michael concurred. "If you were not part of this base, people would think you had lost your mind with that statement. I feel pretty much the same. This morning while making rounds in the infirmary, I thought, *My life will soon change for the better while many of my patients will face a lifetime of complications and hospitalizations.* I hope they can retain the belief that their sacrifices were worth it."

Father Ray hesitated before responding. "I am not sure that any of this is worth it, and when I get back to New York, I will get involved in trying to bring this war to an end."

"Don't you think that will be viewed by some who know you on this base as a betrayal?"

"I am willing to take that risk. If no one does anything, this war will go on and on, and thousands of kids will die."

"Please don't get arrested because, currently, I have no money for bail."

"I will be respectful, Michael, and protest within what the law allows." With that, both men started to eat.

Packing the last few items into his duffel bag, Michael closed his locker and readied himself to catch a helicopter to Da Nang where he would board a flight to Hawaii. He was too excited to eat but had already imbibed three cups of coffee and was on a caffeine high. This base had consumed his every waking moment for months, and leaving was exciting but also difficult because serving these kids was a privilege. He felt a twinge of guilt that soon he would be leading a safe life while these Marines would daily be confronted by the horrors of Vietnam. So many would not survive their war. He yearned to see his family but felt remorse departing a place where he had been so enmeshed in the lives of wounded Marines. He had been personally involved with those he had treated; never was any patient defined by his wounds. He cared about them individually and always found time to listen to their hopes, fears and dreams. As he walked to the chopper landing area, he turned and gazed wistfully at the medical unit. He wondered about so many who had gone back to the States. It was difficult not to consider what their lives were like, especially those with multiple injuries. There are so many kinds of courage in the world, he thought. He had been tested by brutal emotional trauma; how different was it to endure terrible physical pain, ongoing disability, loneliness, and reduced opportunity? He would never be completely reconciled with what God had ordained for his life, but he knew he would not have wanted to decide: this and not that. Hurt me here, not there. Take my eyes, my hands. My wife, not my brother. *Who hath known the mind of the Lord?* Who could bear to?

For once, the whirling sound of the chopper blade did not mean triage. In this case, it was the first step back to his life after Vietnam. He ducked the blade, slung his duffel bag on board, and hopped on. He was amazed to see that the pilot that had left him in the open field on his first night in Vietnam was still flying.

"Good morning, Jorgie," he said. "Do you remember me?"

"Sure, Doc, how are you? I never forget a face, especially a terrified one."

Michael laughed, saying, "I am surprised that you are still here!"

"I am a lifer, Doc. As long as there are kids to be transported to the base, I will stay."

Arriving in San Francisco after two long flights, Michael almost immediately realized that being in a military uniform was an issue. In Vietnam, everyone was in military dress, and as an officer he was respected and often admired. In the airport, he felt as though he was an object of scorn. No one said anything negative to him, but he was aware by their facial expressions that they disapproved of him. He had heard stories about people believing every soldier or Marine was a baby killer but that seemed too ludicrous for him to believe. However, he was suddenly aware that the country had changed since he left for Vietnam. While in the war zone, there was little time to read about the war, but he had heard a few stories about atrocities that had occurred in Vietnam. He sensed that his uniform represented something other than the pride and honor of those who wore it. It made him angry. They seemed to have no awareness of the evil that the Vietcong presented to Asia and the world. They had not witnessed the heroism and care for their comrades that Marines evinced under horrible conditions. Had some soldiers committed atrocities? Perhaps. war brings out the worst in some men. But the vast majority— all those Michael had known—were good men struggling under horrific conditions. Not many of these protesters, he thought, could bear up under such soul-wrenching losses.

25

MARCH 1969

Adjusting to Civilian Life

I T TOOK MICHAEL WEEKS TO GET adjusted to normal life. There were no firefights, no shelling, and helicopter blades and the moans of the wounded had vanished. It was a completely different world. Even the silence and stillness of the nights initially made it difficult for him to sleep. It was marvelous being with Arlene and the children. He spent hours reconnecting with each child and every morning at breakfast would prepare their lunches and engage them, asking about what they were learning in school. He loved watching each child become interested in some new aspect of the world, their questions revealing minds greedily absorbing and growing. So often, he and Arlene would marvel at their offspring, each personality so distinct.

He loved his sons, but he treasured his daughters. Their trust in him—it staggered him sometimes. They didn't think of him as just a man doing his best; he was Father in a way his own father had never been. He guessed he was doing a better job, though it didn't feel like that so much as a great and mysterious gift. Arlene joked that they were dazzled by that aura of invincibility all surgeons learn to project.

A shadow fell over him at her words.

"What, Michael?"

"Arlene, there were so many I couldn't save." She laid her hand on his cheek. He leaned into it.

In truth, he missed the daily schedule of surgery and making medical rounds attending to the wounded. Going from a war zone to the slow pace of having no medical responsibilities was disconcerting. To his pleasant surprise, he had three job offers the fourth week he was home. The jewel of the three was a position at the Hospital for Special Surgery. He was unaware that one of his former colleagues at Bellevue, Janice Brewington, had become the head of nursing at the hospital. She was notified by the head of surgery that Michael had applied for a position, and she gave him a rave review. She told the search committee that Michael was the most outstanding surgeon she had the privilege of working with in her career.

The position at the hospital was accompanied by an academic appointment to Cornell University's medical faculty. Michael would begin as a lecturer with the possibility of becoming a tenured professor. It appeared that the stars were in alignment, and over the next six months, Michael made the successful adjustment to civilian life. There was an occasional flashback, and at times loud noises brought back the memories of shell-fire, but these were rare, and he had settled into his new life.

The health system at the hospital was vastly different than Vietnam. There were surgical conferences, perfectly equipped operating rooms, and four surgeons were not required to performed surgery on a patient at the same time. Michael never took any operation lightly, but in fact, most of his operations were simple and paled in comparison to the work he had performed in a combat zone. Occasionally there would be an incident where the patient had multiple injuries, but these were rare and done under almost perfect conditions. Michael's surgical skills had improved under pressure—he was faster and surer—which was immediately noticed by staff members. His collegial approach to every member of the team was exceptional. The surgical skills were complemented by his bedside manner and ability to relate to the patients and their significant others on a personal level. Even those—the majority—who had no idea of Michael's history felt like here was a man who knew what loss was, what pain was. The news spread rapidly that the hospital had landed a star, and Nurse Brewington was praised by the administration for her recommendation.

Michael never forgot his experiences in Vietnam, and though he was not forthcoming in bringing up what he had experienced, when asked, he occasionally shared stories about the war. Like most veterans, he preferred doing this with others who had served. But he felt it was important to answer questions, especially from the young, later from his children, about what Vietnam, and war, was really like.

He often didn't feel like he was successful in explaining sacrifice or the bonds of men in combat. He was upset when these were looked at only through the lens of politics. But he did his best.

BY 1970 Michael had been at the Hospital for Special Surgery for over a year, and his practice was thriving. He had gone from being broke to being able to afford a townhouse in one of New York's most desirable neighborhoods. The townhouse was a beautiful nineteenth-century edifice close to Central Park. It was over 3500 square feet with three full bathrooms, and a half bathroom on the first floor. The building had double parlors, a wood burning marble fireplace in every room, and a cherry wood ceiling in the formal dining room. Arlene and he loved that despite contemporary upgrades, the Queen Anne architectural splendor had been maintained. Both were very conscious of their good fortune and in no way did they act as though they were above anyone.

Michael remembered the words of his grandmother in her inimitable Irish brogue when one of their neighbors was putting on airs, "You know, Michael, you can't shine shite." Their roots were in Jersey City and they never once felt the urge to be pretentious.

Michael's time was limited at home, but he spent as much time as possible with the children. Arlene often arranged brief picnics at the hospital—as Phyllis Friedman had advised her years ago—so that they would have steady time with their father. He loved showing them where he worked, introducing them to his colleagues and sometimes patients. There was a deep satisfaction in bringing these two pieces of his heart together.

The only difficulty that Michael could not resolve was his relationship with his oldest son Michael Jr. Michael challenged him regularly, seeming to bridle at the very idea of a father's authority. Initially, Michael thought it was just the normal process of pre-adolescence, but he soon realized that it went deeper. Junior was disdainful of everything that Michael valued, including the Catholic Church. He resisted going to Mass every Sunday morning, which was a constant irritant for his father. "While at church, he paid no attention to the liturgy and never received Communion. He had refused to attend confirmation classes, and whenever Michael tried to engage him in conversation, it usually ended up by Michael losing his cool. "You're too young to know what you think!" he'd roar knowing these were not the right words, and Junior would roll his eyes.

"Well, Dad, if that's the case, how come I know what I think?"

There appeared to be no avenue to reach his son. Although Jr. was a gifted athlete, he did not try out for the grammar school basketball or baseball teams. Michael knew from their summers at Long Beach Island that his son was an excellent swimmer, and it was on those days at the beach that he seemed happiest. Michael encouraged Michael Jr. to try out for the city's swimming team, but the boy failed to show up for the trials. . Junior was an exceptional student with an extraordinary IQ. Due to his intellectual gifts, his son had skipped two grades. The current bone of contention between them focused on where Junior would attend high school. Michael insisted that he take the exam for Regis High, and though dismissive of this choice, Michael Jr. agreed to take the test.

Michael received a letter from Regis stating that his son had failed the entrance exam and would not be admitted to the freshman class. He was angry at this result, believing that Junior had failed the test on purpose. Rarely did Michael resort to influencing decisions like this, but he had an ace in the hole. His friend Father Ray was teaching at Fordham. Perhaps he could intercede and get his son accepted at Regis. The request worked, and he was notified that after new consideration, Junior would be welcomed as a member of the freshman class. Overjoyed at this news, Michael did not realize that this victory was doomed to be temporary.

Michael Jr. failed every subject in the first month, and at the teacher conference, his parents were informed that if his performance did not improve, he would be asked to leave. This news fostered a major confrontation, and Arlene tried to mediate a resolution. After the shouting, she counseled Michael to back off and give Junior some space. She believed that sooner or later he would find his stride and recommended that they include Junior in the decision as to where he went to school. Initially, this went over poorly, but eventually, Michael agreed. However, in a very real sense, Michael began to further distance himself from his son.

He didn't want to be constantly angry or disappointed. He felt like he must have failed as a father, although he didn't know how. Arlene didn't know, and Junior was on the wrong track—so who knew? Who could tell him how to correct course? These thoughts were so painful and confusing, it was easier to put them out of his mind.

Michael Jr. felt isolated because he didn't realize that what he was experiencing was normal. Most if not every boy of his age goes through similar changes. His physical appearance was striking. His facial features were similar to his father's with his smooth skin and leather-brown eyes that appeared to catch every occurrence around him. He was taller than everyone in his class despite the fact that he was two years younger than most. His hair was dark, coarse, and despite requests from his father, flowed to the middle of his back.

Because of a host of physical changes, he was unsure about so many issues. He felt more comfortable around his mother because she seemed able to give him more breathing room. His father, on the other hand, seemed perfect, and though he did not say it expected his oldest child to be like him. Michael Jr. did not know whether he believed in God. Parts of the Catholic services moved him, but the dogma seemed archaic and not related to how most people lived today. The world was changing. He felt strongly that he could not—and shouldn't have to—blindly accept all of his father's beliefs. He kept hoping his father would say something to the effect of, "Well, you think very differently from me, son, but that's fine; we're different people," but that seemed like it would never happen. He knew at some level that his father loved him, but at this age, he felt very uncomfortable in his presence. His father's confidence was like a wall he was constantly battering himself against. His mother tried to tell him his father had doubts and vulnerabilities too, but to Michael Jr., this was hard to take in. If his father did have a softer side, he didn't want to show it.

He withdrew into himself. He was absorbed by mathematics and could work for hours on difficult equations. He had friends because, though he didn't realize it, he had much of his father's charm and moral compass, which drew people to him, but he rarely confided much of what he was thinking with anyone. The two people who he felt most comfortable with other than his mother were his siblings Mary and Robert.

26

The Gambler

I T WAS THE BEST OF TIMES, it was the worst of times." These
words of Charles Dickens could certainly have described the
1970s. The nation was embroiled in a war that split families
apart, the cities were exploding with racial riots, and the Roman
Church was struggling with social and moral issues. The flip side
was that persons of every diverse background were challenging
the status quo. Women were starting to express their desires for
more freedom in the workplace as well as the church. Civil rights
were openly discussed, and the president had signed a bill that
gave black people the rights and privileges that had long been
denied. Interracial dating was more and more accepted at least
among the forward-thinking young, a general shakeup of social
norms created not only turmoil but energy and optimism. Also,

science had made many leaps forward and the country had placed a man on the moon. The parish was involved in all these issues in microcosm, and Sal believed as priests they walked a fine line. He never liked labels, so there was no comfort in defining himself in a particular camp, but in essence, on most issues that mattered, he was progressive. The danger in that was one could get caught up with serving only those of like mind. All of the people in the parish were his responsibility, not only those who saw the world as he did.

The changes in the world had mammoth effects on the laity as well as the priests. To accommodate the need for more involvement, the diocese established parish councils and a priest's senate. The parish council was to assist the pastor in the day-to-day operations of the parish. At Holy Trinity, despite the fact that Monsignor Murray was a congenial man who loved the people, the council was a paper tiger. The parish had so many talented business people who would provide valuable council, especially regarding finance, but Monsignor did not wish to relinquish his power. Two of the most talented members of the council resigned after a few attempts to change the system.

The priests in Holy Trinity were blessed to have many persons committed to social justice. Not everyone was rich in Westbury, but by and large, it was an upscale community. However, some of the local citizens lived in abject poverty. One glaring example of this was Cacciola Place. The housing conditions on that street were scandalous, and people whose families had spent decades in the community were being fleeced by unscrupulous landlords.

Sal brought this to the attention of his informal kitchen cabinet, and they immediately responded. One was the general counsel for a major corporation, another the managing editor of the *Herald Tribune*, one a chief financial VP for a multinational.

There was a host of other professional women and men. Together they decided to change the culture of poverty on one street by providing decent and affordable housing. The Federal government had an outstanding program: home ownership with a forty-year mortgage at one percent. The requirements were community involvement by those who were to benefit from the program and private personal or foundation money as a down payment.

The group generously ponied up the seed money, and the project was fortunate to solicit the aid of Mary Withers, a resident of Cacciola Place. She was dynamic, fearless, and a natural born leader; with her assistance, the project seemed headed for success. The first challenge was to plan the homes one at a time so that none of the current residents would be forced out of the community. The second was the necessity of securing the town administrator's permission and buy-in. Public hearings were arranged. At one of the meetings, a gentleman stood up and said he thought it was a foolish program and should be denied permission. In the middle of his plea for rejection, he said, "Let's face it; the properties will not be cared for and soon will become dirty eyesores."

Mary Withers stood, faced the gentleman, and with no venom in her voice said, "We have been doing a pretty good job of keeping your houses clean for decades. I am sure we can keep ours clean too." The administration voted unanimously for the program thanks to Mary's words.

On the priest's side of the equation, Sal was elected by his peers to the Senate, which was an organization that, in theory, was to assist the Bishop in policy and practice. The Bishop, as always, was kind and considerate but, without open conflict, ignored the Senate. Naively, Sal brought three outstanding human resources executives to the group to assist the diocese in structure and practice. The meetings were phenomenal, but the recommendations were ignored by the Bishop.

One area of the Senate that worked well was that any priest without permission could seek the counsel of any member of the Senate. One evening about 8:30, Sal received a call from a priest, Father Bill, who was one of the finest members of the club. He had been a priest for over twenty years and was deeply loved and respected. He asked if Sal could meet him without wearing a collar at a diner on Route 22. Sal agreed and, because he was not on duty, changed clothes and drove to the diner. It was relatively empty, and almost as soon as he sat and ordered coffee, his brother priest came and poured forth his dilemma. For years, he had been a compulsive gambler, and though his parents had left him and his sister a small fortune, he had lost it all. In addition, his bookie had no idea that he was a priest, and when he found out he was a member of the clergy allowed him one last chance to get even. This, like all other bets, failed, and now the bookie was being pressed by those above him to collect or get heavy.

Sal listened to him and finally asked, "How much do you owe?"

He was astounded when his brother priest said, "Thirty-six thousand dollars." Regaining composure, Sal assured him that as a member of the Senate and the personnel board, he would not divulge his secret but would arrange for him to get professional help. He also requested that he contact his bookie and set up a meeting to resolve the situation. Every nickel Sal had in this world came to a little over ten thousand dollars. There was no other way of raising the money without making the priest's reputation vulnerable.

Two days passed. Sal's priest friend gave him a number to call. He presumed it was the number of his bookie. Sal called and explained who he was, but there was little response. Finally, a gruff voice gave him an address in Hoboken where he was to be on the following Thursday at 11 a.m. Sal was told in no uncertain terms that he was to come alone and not tell anyone about this meeting. He ignored the second part and sought the counsel of his brother who was an FBI agent, as well as a Federal prosecutor who lived in the parish. Both insisted that he not attend this meeting. Sal was conflicted but decided that if he did not, his friend might come to harm.

Sal drove to Hoboken and with great effort found the address; it was a decrepit old warehouse. He parked the car and walked to the front entrance. There were two huge men at the door. They let him in and then, apparently searching for a weapon, performed a complete body frisk. After this, they led Sal into the open part of the warehouse where a man was sitting on a vegetable crate. The entire warehouse was musty and had an odor that smelled like rotten fish. All Sal could think about was the old Sicilian adage about "sleeping with the fishes." The only objects in this massive building were two crates, which served as seats. He motioned for Sal to sit down on the crate next to him. In an angry voice, he asked: "Do you have the money?"

Sal hesitated and finally said, "All I could raise was ten thousand dollars. There is no possibility of anything more."

The man, with a face like sandpaper, stared at Sal. With great anger in his voice said, "I don't give a damn that a priest owes this money. I am going to take your ten grand, but if he ever gambles again in New Jersey, he is a dead man. If you report this meeting to the cops, you will join him." He said those words in a chilling fashion. Finally, after giving Sal a death stare, he took the envelope from his hands without looking inside. He stood and with no emotion said, "Now get the hell out of here."

He did not need to tell Sal a second time. Sal bolted and drove back to Westbury, grateful that he had survived this harrowing morning. Months after this, he received a call from Father Bill. He confided that he had regularly been seeing a psychologist and attending meetings of Gamblers Anonymous. He had realized some of the reasons for his addiction and was grateful that Sal had helped change the destructive path he was on.

27

Tragedies

THERE ARE MOMENTS OF GREAT JOY that happen in parish life, but there are also moments of pain and sorrow that touch the very heart and soul. Jack and Sal had told six families during a year that someone in their family under the age of thirty had died suddenly or in an accident. One such tragedy occurred on the New York State Thruway when a twenty-year-old woman was killed instantly. She was on her way to meet her parents in Westbury; they were to vacation for a week in Martha's Vineyard. Sal had the unenviable task of telling her parents that she had been killed. The memory of her father collapsing when he heard the news was a moment that seared Sal's soul. Another was the tragic death of two brothers returning home from a third brother's wedding. Jack had viewed the mangled bodies of those young brothers and, in an act of great compassion, stood in front of the father and blocked him from viewing their bodies at the morgue. He pleaded with the distraught father, urging him not to look because he did not wish for him to have that as his last memory of his boys.

There was also the burial of an Army lieutenant killed in Vietnam and the murder of a young schoolteacher two weeks before her sister's wedding. These moments called for presence—and often silence—because there are no words in the shadow of such grief.

There were even occasions when the tragedy unfolded literally before the eyes of Sal and Jack. One rainy cold November evening, they were in a barn folding clothes that had been donated for the poor. Sal was called back to the rectory because he had a counseling appointment, but Jack continued to organize the clothing. Patty, a young woman of nineteen, entered the building. Jack did not initially see her. She called to him, and as he turned, she lit a match, touching it against her body. She burst into flame, having already covered herself in gasoline. Jack responded immediately: he tackled her, rolled her over, and extinguished the flames with a blanket. His hands were burnt, but he put out the flames and raced outside yelling for one of the neighbors to call 911.

Patty was one of five children with wonderful parents who had tried everything to assist her in her mental struggles, but nothing had worked. Critically burned, she was immediately rushed to Overlook Hospital. Sal and Jack visited every night after office hours, but despite the loving care of the staff, she finally succumbed. Her family was devastated by the loss. The mother spoke to Sal at the funeral parlor and said, "The pain is unbearable, but it is the first time I won't be in agony worrying about her while she is gone. She was such a loving person but tormented for years with voices and nightmares. I know that she is finally at peace."

The incident was very difficult for Jack, and Sal encouraged him to talk about it. Jack confided that he had more than a few dreams of seeing her ablaze. "I know that I acted immediately, but I sometimes wonder if I could have done more to help her before the incident."

Sal nodded. "I get that, Jack, but do you now believe that in any shape or form you missed helping her?"

"In my head, I don't, but honestly, I don't always feel that way."

"Murph, I think that is part of the price we pay for having the privilege of being involved in so many lives in pain."

The tragedies that occur almost daily in a parish bring forth the goodness of many of the parishioners. Jack and Sal's work would have been impossible without the myriad volunteers who stepped forward in their every hour of need.

28

Canon 509

WHEN SAL WAS IN THE FIFTH grade, he was put into the cloakroom for an entire afternoon by Sister Mary Michael. She accused him of heresy because in her lecture she had told the class that we could offer God nothing. It was, in her opinion, a "one-way street."

Sal foolishly raised his hand and asked, "Then why should we love God?" He could still see her red face as she grabbed him by the scruff of the neck and sent him sprawling into the isolation of the cloakroom. There had always been that part of his personality that never bought into some of the absolutes. An example of this was that he never believed that the Catholic religion was the one and only true Church. He loved the Church, but never saw it as the only route to a loving God. This belief caused him some grief along the way.

An area that caused some cognitive dissonance in his psyche was the absolute requirement that in a mixed marriage, the non-Catholic partner had to agree to sign a form stating that all children of the union would be raised Catholic. Westbury had been largely a Protestant community before the Second World War, so many of the marriages were of mixed faiths. The bulk of the Protestant community had little exposure to a Catholic priest, so Sal did all he could to make them comfortable in the pre-marriage discussions with him. This did not always go the way that he desired.

On one occasion, the young woman in his office was obviously very nervous being in the presence of a priest. Her fiancée was a graduate of the Naval Academy and, though at sea, would soon be home. Sal tried to break the ice by inquiring about him. "How long is your fiancée's furlough?"

She seemed stunned but replied, "About seven inches." She must have thought that the Catholic word for penis was furlough. Sal was dumbfounded and carefully tried to work his way around that misstep.

The requirement to sign away the rights of future children was a real obstacle for Sal, and he believed that it violated the personal beliefs of the non-Catholic party. It was imperative that he find a path around the requirement because, technically, without it, the marriage would not be valid in the eyes of the Church. There was a way around this boulder in the road called Canon 509. Canon Law was the roadmap for all of the requirements within the Church. This particular canon assumed that a mistake had been made, and to avoid any obstacles to a marriage rectified whatever issue had not been properly fulfilled. In order to make sure that the union would be recognized by the Church as valid, when the bride was coming down the aisle, Sal used this as a way of getting around his moral dilemma. He mentally pronounced that the marriage was covered by Canon 509. The problem was that he was performing so many marriages that the records were filled with tons of Canon 509s. One Saturday after performing a wedding, he came back to the rectory and was greeted by the sullen face of his pastor. He said, "Sal, there is someone to see you in the living room."

His visitor was Monsignor Clark Reiger, a member of the official Diocesan hierarchy. "As the Bishop's representative, I am here to inform you that you are immediately forbidden to perform any future marriages until you have fulfilled all of the necessary documentation for the Canon 509 marriages that you have performed. You well know that your utilization of this canon was against the spirit and intention of the law." Sal was suspended until all the required paperwork was produced. Jack took the weddings for a couple of weeks, and they decided the only hope they had to get Sal back on board was to produce all the paperwork quickly. Jack loved this challenge; his innocent Irish face hid the heart of one that loved to stick it to the system. He stroked his chin and began to plan the great ecclesiastical counterfeit plan. He informed Sal that the first step was to go to the Jewish synagogue and all the churches in town and gather their official forms. The plan was to rework these documents so that they would provide the necessary documentation that could get Sal reinstated.

Sal was mortified that he had lost the opportunity to perform weddings. They were such joyous occasions and often balanced out the painful experiences that occurred weekly in the parish. For two solid weeks, they spent hours together forging the required documentation. Jack said, "The only payment I will accept for my involvement in this caper is a bottle of Chivas Regal that will be imbibed as we work." Jack was an excellent typist and a willing collaborator in the episode. At the end of the "great forgery," Sal was reinstated and never used Canon 509 again.

The friendship that had begun in their first few months at Holy Trinity had grown deeper. They trusted each other without reservation and seamlessly handled so many of their parish responsibilities. There was no sense of territory closed to either one of them. They recognized that their styles and personalities attracted different parishioners and found that to be one of the pillars of their relationship. They also had grown from sharing skills and making them their own. Jack had learned to adapt his sermon speaking style to Sal's, and Sal had finally employed Jack's perfect attention to detail in filling out paperwork.

Sal was on duty one morning in the office filling out a series of forms that were due for the next personnel board meeting. The phone rang, and he answered it. "Good Morning, Holy Trinity rectory." The voice on the other end did not respond. Again, Sal said good morning.

"I want to speak to Father La Greca."

"This is he."

Again, there was a pause. "I need your help, Father."

"How can I help you?"

"Father, this is Bill Evanston and I . . . . . ." There was another pause. "I have decided to kill myself, and I don't want to go to hell. I need you to give me absolution before I do it."

Sal realized this was a very delicate situation and weighed his words carefully before he responded. "Billy, there is no way that I can do that over the phone, but if you give me your address, I will come right over and give you absolution."

There was a momentary silence. "Will you come alone?"

"Yes, I will."

"Okay, as long as you will come alone, I live at 2207 Windemere Road."

Sal drove to the address in one of the most fashionable neighborhoods in Westbury. Getting out of his car, he gathered himself and prayed that he could prevent this young man from taking his life. He ascended the steps and rang the doorbell. When Billy opened the door, Sal immediately recognized him as one who had been involved in the youth program. He was alarmed that in his right-hand Billy held a forty-five pistol. Billy led him into the living room and asked, "How do we begin to give me absolution?"

Sal knew that he had to buy time, so he began with a host of information about the requirements of absolution. "One of the first steps, Billy, is that I need to know a little bit about you and why you decided to do this." Billy was hesitant initially but soon began to tell Sal that he had failed at so many things. Particularly painful was the reality that he could never meet his father's expectations. Though his parents were divorced, his father had made it clear that he was not pleased with his son's athletic achievements. Billy was an exceptional amateur golfer on a college scholarship but had not made the travel team this year. This was not uncommon, but the father interpreted it as a failure.

Sal, who was a golfer himself, turned the conversation to golf and asked if Billy enjoyed the game. "When I am playing, I love it, but I am tired of worrying about each putt and whether my score is low enough." At one-point Billy seemed antsy and asked, "How much longer before you forgive me?"

Sal responded, "Billy, this is taking some time, but I know that you want me to do this right so that it will be perfect. Billy, will anyone be sad that you are gone?"

Billy placed the gun on the coffee table and pondered the question. For a moment, Sal thought about trying to grab the gun but realized that this caliber of gun could kill Billy if the gun went off in the attempt. "I guess my mother and maybe a couple of my friends."

"What will they feel like when they hear the news?"

Billy seemed touched by this question. "I . . . don't know, but I guess they will be sad."

"Will they miss you?"

"I am not sure."

Sal thought if he could gently pursue this line, it might change Billy's decision. "I would imagine, Billy, that you would be missed. I know that any time a friend has died, I really miss them. I still miss some who died many years ago. Could you tell me a little bit about your mother?"

"She is a nurse. She works at Overlook."

"Do you have any brothers or sisters?"

"No. I am an only child."

"What is your best memory of you and your mother?"

Billy seemed irritated. "What does that have to do with absolution? I want to get on with this." He reached for the gun and placed it in his hands.

"I need to have a full picture of you and your life before I anoint and absolve you," Sal said gently, though his heart was beating fast. He took the stole out of his pocket and put it around his neck so Billy would see that the ceremony would soon be finalized.

Billy thought for a moment and then said, "Last summer at the beach. We played golf in the morning, had lunch, and then went for a swim."

"Where was that?"

"In Avon."

"How did your mother play that day?"

For the first time, Billy smiled. "Terribly. She is a hopeless golfer. We spent a lot of time looking for her ball."

Over the next hour, Sal continued to probe. Whenever Billy's words gave him the chance, he'd point out indirectly that there were other choices. Billy seemed to relax as he spoke. Sal thought his confidence in himself was slowly growing as he experienced being listened to.

Finally, Billy said, "You are right. I am not going to kill myself." Sal felt relieved and even a little proud, but this statement was only the beginning. Billy pointed the gun at Sal and said, "Instead, I think I will kill you. "

If it were not so dire a situation, Sal might have humorously felt that Billy's initial decision was a better one. Slowly, with great care, Sal talked about who he was and why he cared about Billy. He never pleaded or asked Billy not to kill him, but he made himself more of a person—a son, brother, friend. A young man like Billy, just a bit older. After twenty-five minutes, Billy began to sob, and Sal asked him to place the gun on the coffee table. Billy responded immediately, and Sal slowly stood up and picked up the gun and placed it on the sideboard. He embraced Billy and led him to the kitchen where he called his friend Dr. Raftery and had Billy taken to Overlook Hospital. After Billy arrived, Sal searched for Billy's mother and informed her what had happened. She was, of course, upset and horrified, and had a lot to say, many questions about what to do next and was her boy safe. Sal spent as long as he could with her, then arrived back at the rectory and asked the housekeeper to refer all calls to Father Murphy. He went to bed and was so traumatized that he slept for sixteen hours.

29

MAY 1970

Leaving Westbury for Rome

SAL'S FIVE YEARS IN WESTBURY FELT like no more than one year. He knew that this part of his life was ending. He had recommended as a member of the personnel board that priests should be reassigned every five years. This practice was a way to refresh the priest in his ministry. This was, in theory, an excellent idea, but on a personal level, it was difficult to leave Westbury. Sal had lived through so many marvelous experiences in the parish, and the bond between him and the parishioners was ironclad. This combined with the tremendous partnership he had forged with Jack Murphy made the decision even more difficult.

The one bright spot on the horizon was that Sal, through Bishop Donnelly, a friend stationed in the Vatican, had become aware of an intriguing graduate program at the Gregorian

228 | S.J. TAGLIARENI

University in Rome. Two Jesuit psychiatrists had created a doctoral program that centered on melding philosophy, theology and psychiatry. It was an opportunity to spend four years in Rome and each summer at a psychiatric center in Chicago. Sal applied and was accepted.

Jack and Sal were referred to by the parishioners as the "dynamic duo." They had different styles and personalities, but both were driven by the need to serve. The twosome was about to be separated, but they had avoided discussing the fact that soon Sal would be transferred from Westbury. What Sal had not yet told Jack was that he was going to Rome. Sal realized that before the news became public, he needed to share it personally with Jack. One Sunday in late May, both were off duty and planned to meet at their favorite restaurant, Mayfair Farms. After selecting some appetizers and ordering a bottle of Gattinara, their favorite Italian red, the two engaged in casual conversation. "Jack, I am sure you are aware of the new personnel policies that the Senate has implemented."

"Are you referring to the five-year change policy?"

"Yes." Sal paused. "You know that I have been in Westbury for five years."

Jack dropped his eyes. "I know that but have completely blocked it from my mind." Sal was equally hesitant but said, "I actually will not be going to another parish because I have been invited to spend the next four years at the Gregorian in Rome studying for a doctorate in psychiatric pastoral practice. Each summer I will come back and work in a Chicago psychiatric clinic."

Jack mustered enough enthusiasm to say, "That sounds like a perfect assignment for you," but his heart was not into talking about where Sal was going. The conversation became quite difficult. Finally, Jack said, "Sal, your leaving is tough for me to accept. I cannot imagine someone taking your place." Sal was touched by this but did not immediately respond. Partially because he was choked up, but more importantly, he was aware that Jack was not finished. "My time in Westbury has been way beyond what I could have imagined. I was terrified coming here because of Masterson's reputation, but you made it so easy for me. Hell, from the first minute I arrived, you were there for me." Jack paused and took a sip of wine. "I have learned so much from you, and we clicked from day one. I never felt one down in the relationship and always knew that you had my back. Even in the days when things were really tough, I always knew I could go to your room, and we would laugh about the craziness of the place. It is difficult to know that I will not have that after September."

Sal, filled with emotion, slowly responded to Jack's heartfelt words. "Jack, I am touched by what you just said, but you must know that for the last three years you have been my anchor. I hardly knew you in the seminary. When you first arrived, I was actually quite fearful. Gene McCoy and I had been a team, and I did not know how you and I would connect. Almost immediately, I understood that your idea of service to the parishioners was the same as mine."

Jack added, "That was a relief to me because, like you, I was struck by the wonderful people and how many ways we could serve them."

Sal went on, "And after that incident on my birthday, I knew you were as nutty as me. Almost everything that we have achieved over the last three years is because we have seen the same needs and agreed on the solutions. Before long I recognized that there were people who would prefer one of us to the other. I never once felt that this was my territory or yours, and you are largely responsible for that. Jack, you have been the most remarkable partner. You are my rock, and being with you has changed me for the better. I will never forget the time we have spent together."

Jack was touched and reaching back for his dry sense of humor said, "It is really not fair that you will be wined and dined in Rome as I continue to nightly dine at Chez Aggie."

ROME 1970

Since arriving in Rome in September, Sal had been mesmerized by the splendor of the city. He was living in the graduate house for priests, which was located a stone's throw from the Trevi Fountain. Each day, he and his newfound friends took advantage of the opportunity to walk through the eternal city. His favorite experience was visiting the area that overlooked the Roman Forum. He would often sit at the edge of the Campidoglio for hours, gazing at the site as the sun set over the Roman Forum.

Sal and the other American priests had many visitors at the college in Rome, and it was not rare for a member of the hierarchy, either from the States or Italy, to say Mass and then have dinner with the student priests. On one occasion, they had an Italian bishop who was diminutive in size but exceptionally warm and friendly. He spoke some English, but there were certain words that he did not pronounce properly. After dinner, he stood up at the head table and wished to give his blessing of peace, not only to the priests but to their families and the world at large. He began in a loud voice, saying: "Piss on you, piss on your mother, piss on your father, and piss on your family. Piss on everybody." Needless to say, all in attendance were biting their lips, as they did not wish to offend this kind soul. However, they shared his singular blessing among themselves as they encountered each other for days to come.

Another momentous occasion occurred the following week when Sal and a group of his friends attended a public audience by the Pope in Saint Peter's Basilica. In the middle of the Pope's words, there was a commotion in the back of the basilica, and the police rushed in and with a great show of force carried a man outside. The story was that in the middle of the crowd, the man had exposed himself and was apparently trying to press against a young woman. The woman screamed, and other pilgrims intervened and held him until the police arrived. Sal later learned through the grapevine that the culprit's defense in the magistrate's court was that he was so taken by the Holy Father's words that he could not breathe. To stop from fainting, he loosened his pants, and his private part just slipped out. After the entire court howled at this ingenious defense, the magistrate levied a very severe sentence.

The one major obstacle for Sal to overcome was that his program had been canceled. The Jesuits were rather vague about why this decision had been made. Sal did not want to pursue a doctorate in theology, but that appeared to be his only choice. He enrolled at the Dominican School of Theology and would begin classes in late October.

Sal had easily adjusted to Rome and was excited that Jack Murphy was to visit in November. They had spent a week together in Rome a year ago, and Jack loved the city as much as he did. He had plotted out the time they would spend together. He arranged for them to visit all the exquisite historic sites of the city. In addition, through the courtesy of Bishop Donnelly, they would be able to attend a small private audience with the Pope.

It was a beautiful morning in Rome on October 23, and Sal had just had coffee at the Piazza Navona. He spent hours reading the paper in the shadow of one of the most beautiful fountains in Europe. As he perused the *Herald Tribune*, which kept him in touch with the States, the beauty of the Fountain of the Four

Great Rivers enthralled him. The magical sound of the water flowing over chiseled marble gave the fountain a lifelike feeling. Sal thought how lucky he was to be here in this magnificent city as a student and to have the opportunity to roam through the annals of history at will. The city was so full of treasures that Sal had to resist his instinct to become a tourist. It was and is a city of living moments that leap from doorways, fountains, and cobblestone streets. The voices of the Forum can still be imagined as the sun glances off the Palatine Hill. Rome did things to his heart and soul, and Sal almost thought that he had lived there before. With all this poetic nonsense rushing through his veins, he finished the last drop of coffee.

There was no immediate need for him to race back to the Graduate House of Theological Studies, located on Via dell' Umiltà, so he went for a promenade toward St. Peter's Square. Along the way, he met a group of American tourists and offered his services as a tour guide to escort them through St. Peters. It was fun hearing the familiar accents of New York and New Jersey, which immediately brought him back to the land of his birth.

After an hour of pointing out what he knew, Sal bid them farewell and made his way back to the college. He had been in his room for about ten minutes when the switchboard rang and told him that he had a call from the States. Sal was pleasantly surprised but couldn't imagine who it was. Once connected by the operator, the voice at the other end said, "Is that you, Sal?"

"Yes," he replied. "Who is this?"

"It's Tom Daly." (Tom Daly is the priest that replaced Sal at Holy Trinity.)

"Tom, it's great to hear from you." At that moment Sal could tell from Tom's tone of voice that something was wrong. He immediately thought that it was one of his parents, but if that was the case, he wondered, why weren't his brother or sister delivering the news?

"Sal," Tom said, "I have terrible news. Jack Murphy was killed in an accident last night." Sal blanked out on the rest of the conversation, muttering that he would take the next plane home.

Sal couldn't believe that Jack was dead. Somehow, he was dead while Sal was in Rome, but Sal continued to believe that he would wake in America and find out that it was all a bad dream. The thought came over and over, and none of the tragedies he'd lived through made any difference: this death was still not possible, not acceptable. Sal had given up smoking, but due to his anxiety asked a fellow passenger if he could borrow a cigarette. Before he knew it, the old habit had fully reared its head, and he smoked one cigarette after the other. The flight seemed endless as Sal attempted to process the unbearable reality. How could this happen? Was it a dream? Part of him wanted to believe that, but having experienced so many deaths as a parish priest—where not once did it turn out to be a dream, a mistake, reversible—Sal knew in his heart that Jack was dead. The torrent of feelings was not only about losing his best friend, bad as that was; this death was also a poignant reminder of his own mortality. He had blithely assumed death was decades away but losing someone as vital as Jack obliterated that belief.

When Sal arrived at Kennedy Airport, the reality of Jack's death began to infiltrate every aspect of his being. He was nervously smoking cigarette after cigarette, and his hands trembled from too much coffee on the plane. As he approached the luggage area, he saw friends from Holy Trinity who had come to give him a ride to Westbury. As they approached with their drawn faces and funereal gait, they looked like messengers of doom. The sight of these friends renewed the realization that he had not come home on a visit but was there to attend the funeral of his best friend. He momentarily had the urge to turn and walk away from them. They were another step toward the awful truth that Jack was dead. Finally, he gathered enough stability to walk toward them. The warm hugs and embraces of friends momentarily abated the profound loss that Sal was experiencing. It was exceptionally painful to listen to them as they shared the details of Jack's death. A tidal wave of memories poured forth as each one of them hugged him. These were some of the persons who had their lives enhanced by the dedication and compassion of Jack's presence, and like Sal, they hurt intensely. The ride from the airport to Westbury seemed exceptionally long, and conversation was difficult because everyone observed that Sal was emotionally fragile.

Upon arriving at Holy Trinity Parish, Sal felt like he could not get out of the car. It was as though grief had paralyzed him, and he could not move his legs. One of the parishioners opened the door and assisted him. He slowly left the car, grabbed onto the handrail and stumbled up the steps into the lobby of the rectory. Monsignor Murray opened the door and warmly greeted him.

"Welcome home, Sal," he said sadly. "I am sorry it is under such circumstances. I know how much Jack meant to you."

Sal shook his hand and said: "Thanks, Charlie. I still can't believe it." With these few words, Monsignor Murray stepped aside, and Sal slowly walked down the narrow corridor that he had walked down thousands of times before. The back parlor was filled with guests and family. Jack's parents, brothers, and sister rose to greet him and, as if he had turned on a switch, the tears cascaded as they embraced each other. Words seemed useless, and he could not honestly remember what he said to them, but he remembered staring at the casket that contained his best friend. Sal knelt by the casket and could not contain the water that flowed from his eyes. Little did he know that as painful as this moment was, it would be easiest part of the grieving process.

For the next three days, Sal preached eulogies about his friend, and when Jack was laid to rest, Sal naïvely believed that he was prepared to deal with his loss. Staying with his parents for a few days before returning to Rome, he took great comfort in their presence and the number of friends and family who reached out to him. All too soon, however, it was time to go back to Rome.

Upon arrival at the graduate house of theology, Sal went to the mailbox and there to his amazement was a letter from Jack Murphy. The note was in typical Jack Murphy fashion. It was filled with humor, friendship and excitement that once again that they would be together in a place that they both loved. Sal's hands trembled as he opened the letter. He read it repeatedly as if reading it would somehow bring Jack back. In a way, the letter made it even more difficult because it had the ability to capture the wondrous boyishness that Sal had come to so respect and enjoy.

30

NOVEMBER 1970

The Search for Meaning

THE LOSS OF JACK IN THE blink of an eye shook the roots of Sal's belief in immortality, which is the province of the young. Notwithstanding all the accidental deaths he had experienced or the teenagers he had buried, he had felt that because of their tender age, he and Jack were on a road with no exit to death or illness until beyond middle age. Unspoken, illogical, but so real, that myth was visceral, and when it shattered, the pain and confusion positioned Sal on the precipice of depression. It was a great deal to comprehend that Jack, a person so alive, with all the energy and dynamism of youth, had ceased to be. The pain was searing and floated to the surface without notice through a familiar song, a favorite place, or merely the mention of his friend's name. There were no insulated places where the residue did not seep to wound again.

He was immersed in thoughts that were overwhelmingly sad and morose. How could such a vital life be obliterated in a blinding crash? He reminded himself over and over that he was no stranger to death. He had seen it in its gasping last breaths and ashes as he anointed one burned to death in an automobile accident. He had knocked on doors with horrible news. He remembered the deaths of Michael's brothers, gone so abruptly. All of these losses had pulled at his heartstrings, and he always exhibited care and compassion to the families, but this was different. This pain so wounded him that he had no exit, no harbor and no guarantee that it would at some point end. Depressed and feeling so alone, one morning he began rereading *Man's Search for Meaning*. The words of the book were so powerful that he felt as though the author had him in mind when he wrote it. He almost dropped the book when he read, "It is through the crucible of pain and suffering that we humans achieve our greatest *humanity.*" Frankl was not talking about avoidable suffering but that tidal wave of pain that drowned one suddenly and without warning. Somehow, Sal knew that this book would be the beginning of his healing. He had no idea that Doctor Frankl would radically change his life and that in a few short weeks he would meet him in Vienna. He knew that Doctor Frankl was teaching at the University of Vienna and decided that he would like the opportunity to study with him.

His pain was not alleviated, but it had turned to action. He called the University and requested to speak with Doctor Frankl. To his amazement, Doctor. Frankl answered the phone. After a few moments of conversation, he invited Sal to visit him at the University. It was easy to fly from Rome to Vienna on the following Tuesday. The plane ride was smooth, but Sal's stomach was in knots at the thought of being in the presence of someone whose work and life he had so admired. He practiced over and over what he would say, but by the time he arrived at the University, he was a nervous wreck.

Waiting in a room near Doctor Frankl's office, he was told that Doctor Frankl would soon be with him. Finally, the moment arrived when he was ushered to Doctor Frankl's private office. His initial impression was that this intellectual giant was physically short. He had a mane of shocking white hair, thin glasses that were perched at the end of his nose, bushy, wiggling gray eyebrows and electric blue eyes. He was taken immediately with the ability of the good doctor to listen without interruption. When Sal finished explaining why he wanted to study with him, Doctor Frankl said: "You are the perfect student for me, and it will be a pleasure to have you in my classes."

Winter in Vienna with the overcast skies, frequent snow and bitter cold reflected Sal's emotional state. His saving grace was the daily opportunity to listen to Doctor Frankl. Although the classes were in German, he had enough language ability to follow. Frequently, in the middle of his class, Doctor Frankl would personally direct remarks toward him in English. He had marvelous emotional intuition and could tell that Sal was struggling.

Vienna was probably gorgeous in the summer because it was filled with lovely parks, but in winter it was dreary and dark. Sal found no solace after leaving sunny Rome and was engulfed in days of sadness.

One evening, Sal went to Doctor Frankl's office and for two solid hours unloaded his grief and confusion. He had temporarily forgotten all that Frankl had endured during the Second World War. Frankl had lost his parents, wife, relatives, profession and country, and was incarcerated in four concentration camps. He had been beaten, starved, suffered frostbite and typhus. Despite this tragic personal history, he listened to every word intently and never interrupted Sal's emotional catharsis. When Sal had finally finished, he said: "You are in great pain because your dear friend is dead and you loved him. There is no recipe to make that pain evaporate, but I also know that at some point, you will have to make a choice. You will decide to emotionally get in the grave with your friend, or despite the grief go on with your life. If you bury yourself with him, I don't think you really knew who he was."

Those words changed Sal's life. He knew at that moment that there was no way that Jack wanted him to be a prisoner of grief forever. Viktor challenged him to incorporate Jack's caring for others into a leadership role. "You have had a great gift in such a friendship. Share with everyone you encounter the treasure of this man." He also began to introduce Sal to Holocaust survivors, telling him, "Now that you know, you must be a witness."

The graphic stories that the survivors shared made the Holocaust personal. He could imagine standing naked on a line, holding the hands of children, observing people before him being shot and falling into a lime pit. One story, in particular, overwhelmed him. He interviewed a Polish immigrant who had been from a tiny village near Warsaw. One day while he was restoring his roof, the Nazis occupied his village. In horror, he saw the young men taken to the woods and machine-gunned. This horror was replicated when they took the children and all the other residents to the woods. The young women were forced to disrobe and were marched into the synagogue. After an hour or so, the soldiers in various forms of undress left the synagogue and placed horse carts in front of the building. They poured gasoline around the perimeter and ignited it. He heard the shrieks of those being burned alive and knew that his wife and sisters were in that inferno.

Sal had always thought the Holocaust was tragic, but stories like this bored deeply into his soul. He wondered how anyone could possibly get over such tragedy in his life. He could not fathom how Frankl handled his losses. His capacity to forgive was beyond Sal's comprehension. He once asked him, "How do you not hate the Nazis?"

Frankl took off his glasses and reflected for a moment. "Salvatore, they took everything that I loved and prized. If I hated them, what would I have left? Love is more powerful than hate, and that is why though I cannot forget, I can forgive."

After weeks of studying in Vienna, Sal's new mentor and friend Viktor invited him to join him on a visit he was making to San Diego. He had been invited to spend the spring semester at the International University in California and had suggested that Sal pursue his doctorate in human behavior and leadership. He explained that if he accepted this offer, he would spend three years in San Diego and function as his teaching assistant for the semesters that Frankl would be in San Diego. Sal was thrilled to join him. Each day in his presence was like being in a laboratory filled with wisdom and learning. In addition to his incredible mind, Sal was privy to the innumerable letters from all over the world telling Frankl how his book and work had dramatically changed their lives. The concept of finding meaning in life resonated not only in the academic world but also amongst people experiencing all kinds of personal tragedies and challenges.

It wasn't only his brilliant mind that captivated Sal. Frankl taught lessons both in his classes and in the kind of life he lived. Besides his genius and gifted teaching style, he possessed an uncanny ability to see the humor in so many situations.

Sal learned many things including:
- No matter what the circumstances there are always some choices within your control.

- The past does not determine the future.
- Every human person desires and seeks meaning.
- Love will always overcome hatred.
- Everyone has value and is worthy of love and respect.
- You become great by not seeking greatness but rather by service to others.

He was at the center of the University, not only a magnet to students, but also to other heavyweights in the field of psychology and psychiatry. He took Sal everywhere with him while he was in San Diego. One-night Sal was at a restaurant with Viktor, Carl Rogers, Harold Greenwald, Everett Shostrom, and William Shutz. He thought, *what is a kid from 202 Delaware Avenue, Jersey City, doing at this table?*

31

1974

Coming Out

MICHAEL, IN MANY ASPECTS OF HIS life, was quite progressive. He consistently researched the new technologies that were evolving in the surgical world and enthusiastically embraced those that supported better outcomes. His surgical teams were the envy of the hospital because he included every occupation in the hospital as valued colleagues. He modeled a collegiality that supported the health and welfare of the patients. However, he had no enthusiasm for what he perceived as a breakdown in the social, moral and cultural fabric of society. A devoted Catholic, he enthusiastically followed the teachings of the Church and feared that the Church itself was becoming involved with these changes. In his mind, the new threat was the preaching of situational ethics. Faith was a gift that was never meant to be easy; removing the absolutes would lead to moral chaos. The Church and Christ had been his foundation and had enabled him to weather tragic events in his life. When he had lost his mother and brothers, he had experienced a moment when he decided that God's love would sustain him then and in the future. He firmly believed in the official positions of the Church on birth control and abortion. As a physician, he realized that many colleagues held other beliefs. Bellevue exposed him to every conceivable lifestyle and belief both from patients and colleagues. He was never judgmental about their convictions but chose to follow the letter of the Church's laws.

The one constant irritant for Michael in his personal life was his unresolved situation with his oldest son, whom he experienced as being reflexively opposed to Michael's bedrock beliefs. There were many differences of substance, but these had become emotional triggers; they didn't discuss anything anymore. Both were civil to each other around Arlene, but that was the limit of their interactions. When Junior left for Cornell at the end of the summer, Arlene experienced the wrench of the firstborn leaving the nest. Michael, on the other hand, was relieved and glad that there would not be any more awkward moments around the house. He loved his son deeply, but he had exhausted ways to bridge their gaps and instinctively knew the issues were more than adolescent rebellion or withdrawal.

Cornell was somewhat a plus and a minus for Michael Jr. He loved the immediate freedom that campus life provided. However, he was experiencing more than a casual identity crisis. He had been aware for years that he was more attracted to males than females, but the implications of that reality were daunting. He knew that there was no way that his father could accept the possibility that he was gay, and though Michael Sr. would not have believed it, his son desperately wanted peace in the family and a return to the closeness he'd felt in childhood. Junior handled the dilemma by believing that the attraction was a phase, and at some point, he would be able to find a woman who could fulfill his physical and emotional needs.

His avoidance did not withstand the second week of the fall semester. He had become friends with Steve Jefferson, and the two of them worked out together at the gym on a regular basis. Casual conversations led to questions of sexual preference, and much to Michael's surprise, Stephen admitted to being gay. This made Michael, who'd been feeling isolated by his preference, both excited and uneasy, and he did not know how to handle the information. The one thing he did know to do was assure Stephen that it made no difference to him.

One Friday night, the two of them and a group of classmates attended a frat party. Michael was not much of a drinker, and after two hours at the party, he was rather tipsy. The group decided that because it was such a warm night, they should walk down the hill and go skinny-dipping in Lake Cayuga. As the group stripped, Michael thought being naked wasn't weird at all. The water was nice and cool and had a sobering effect on most of the young men. Stephen playfully splashed Michael a few times and then encouraged him to swim to the bank. When they jumped out of the water and sat down, they were still naked, and the little bit of breeze cooled them off. Suddenly Stephen put his arms around Michael and kissed him on the cheek. Michael pushed him away and turned to see if any of the other friends had seen what just happened. Most were still in the water and at the other end of the lake.

Stephen said, "Not trying to make you nervous, but I would like to get to know you better. You're gay too, aren't you?" Michael did not know how to react but did not move away when Stephen put his arms around his neck. As they stared into each other's eyes, Stephen gently kissed him. The initial kiss was followed by a series of more prolonged kisses. Michael was overwhelmed with sensation and a feeling of rightness. He did not resist. Stephen said, "Let's get dressed and go back to my room. My roommate is out of town, and we will have total privacy."

When they arrived at Stephen's room, they chatted for a bit, and then Stephen pulled out a six-pack and said, "Let's get hammered." Before long, they were both naked in bed, and Michael experienced his first sex with a man. More than just pleasure, it was vindication and belonging.

Over the next few months, any doubts about his orientation evaporated. He was ecstatic to be having a sex life but feared the consequences of this new reality. Stephen had come out of the closet with his own family. It was difficult, he said, but worth it. His parents were overcoming their prejudices and grief about the loss of the expected future daughter-in-law and grandchildren. He counseled Michael to do the same. It seemed impossible, though. "My dad is a great guy, but he is deeply religious and could never accept this."

"What about your mom?"

"I could be wrong, but I think she could handle it."

"Up to you, but living your life in secret will eat at you. This society is hard enough on us as it is. If they love you, they will learn to live with it."

Michael thought about his conversation with Stephen. He realized how much his secret *had* eaten at him—how it had cast a shadow over his adolescence, which he had blamed on himself. He finally concluded that at Christmas break he would divulge his newfound identity.

The train ride from Ithaca to Penn Station seemed all too short, and when he arrived, he saw his mother waiting on the platform. She ran to greet him and hugged him for quite a while. "I am so happy to have you home. We have missed you." He smiled but thought the 'we' should be changed to 'I.' He did not believe that his father missed him at all.

Arlene said, "Before we go home, why don't we have lunch in midtown? It will give us a chance to chat before you see your father and the rest of the family." Michael agreed and tried to reinforce his courage because this might be one of the few times he would have his mother to himself. They arrived at the Plaza Hotel, and Arlene said, "Have whatever you want. I am sure that it is a lot better than cafeteria food." Michael scanned the menu and ordered fries, a hamburger and a coke. Arlene smiled and realized that adolescent tastes had not changed for generations. She selected a salad and a cup of coffee. "Tell me how the first semester has gone."

For the next hour, they chatted about Cornell, the family and a host of other safe topics. Michael Jr. was particularly interested in hearing about his brother Robert. Arlene reported that Robert was well and had been accepted into an accelerated art course at the New School. Robert had both hips replaced and was facing a series of surgeries and skin grafts on both legs. His vision had dramatically improved, and despite his many physical hardships, he was becoming an accomplished artist.

The restaurant by now was almost empty, so Michael thought this would be the most appropriate time to confide in her. Arlene sensed that something had changed in the last few minutes but did not wish to interrogate her son. If there were an issue, he would discuss it when he was ready. Michael lowered his eyes took a deep breath and said, "Mom, I have something to tell you." The nervousness in his voice led her to prepare for a bombshell; silently, she prayed that he was not ill. The McNally's had more than their share of such tragedies.

"Alright, Michael, please tell me what is on your mind."

Michael was not sure that Arlene would know the word "gay" so he thought he would explain what had happened before using the word. "Mom, as you know I never really had a steady girl-friend in high school though I dated quite a few."

Arlene thought, *oh my God he has gotten someone pregnant* but said nothing.

Michael continued, "I now know the reason for my not having a steady. I have many female friends, Mom, but I am not attracted to them in other ways." Michael gulped. "Mom, I am attracted to men. I have finally admitted to myself that I am gay."

Arlene had tears in her eyes and reached over to hug him. "Thank God. I thought you were going to tell me you were seriously ill."

"Mom, I am not sure you understand what I just told you."

"Michael, in so many ways I think I always knew, and it makes no difference to the way I feel about you."

Those words penetrated Michael's soul, and he began to sob.

When both had composed themselves, the hard question had to be answered. "I need to tell Dad, but I am terrified at how he will react."

His fears were real, and as a mother, Arlene probed to find a way to prepare her son for what might happen. "I understand your fear. Your father adores you even though the two of you have been at odds for years. You see your father as perfect and believe he is always in control. That was not always true, Michael. He suffered unimaginable losses when his mother and two brothers died suddenly. He was fragile and drowning emotionally, and the life preserver that saved him was his Catholic faith. He has a deep love for his church, and we both know he will not take this well. You may find it hard to believe that your father loves you deeply.

He will not reject you or stop loving you but please give him time to understand you. This will be a great challenge for him as it has been for you. I need you to promise me that no matter what happens that you will not cut yourself off from a family that so loves you.

"I will arrange for everyone else to be out of the house tomorrow might, and you can tell him after dinner."

"Will you be there when I tell him?"

"Of course. Now let's find a cab and go home."

Arlene had successfully emptied the house, and it had been a pleasant dinner. Michael had put his best foot forward and seemed genuinely interested in Jr.'s first semester. When Arlene brought coffee and dessert out, she winked at Jr., indicating it was time to speak up. Jr. slurred his words and the prelude to the big announcement was clumsy. Michael initially was silent but at one point interjected, "Son, is there some message at the end of this? Because I am lost."

Junior understood that the moment had arrived. He was extremely pale and nervous, but there was no other way but to be direct. "Dad, I am trying to tell you that I have finally come to grips with who I am. Your son is a homosexual."

Those words were like a branding iron to the stomach. Michael stood and said, "Like hell you are." He searched for words and finally said, "You go off to college, and this ridiculous idea comes into your head. You are not a homosexual."

Arlene tried to mute Michael's response. "Michael, let's calmly discuss this."

"Calmly? Are you crazy? Did you know about this beforehand?"

"Yes, I did."

Junior had a choice to retreat or affirm. He chose to restate who he was. "Dad, I have known for a long time."

Michael was angrier than confused. "And how are your mother and I expected to take this news?"

Arlene, who had been silent, said, "Michael, this is not a complete shock to me. I think I have known it for a long time as well."

"Then why the hell didn't you say something? We could have gotten him some help."

Those words shocked Junior. "I don't need help."

Michael angrily responded, "Then what do you want, applause?"

Arlene said, "Michael, don't be cruel. This isn't easy on him either."

Michael sat down to collect his thoughts. "You are my son, and I love you, but I cannot support a decision that I believe is unnatural and wrong."

That word "unnatural" made Junior want to curl up in a ball—and then it made him furious. "I guess there is nothing left to say." Junior stood and started to leave the room.

Arlene tried to intercede, "Come back, son," but Junior opened the front door and left. He had expected this. He knew it would be painful but it hurt more than he had imagined. He felt like his father was trying to annihilate him.

Michael and Arlene sat in total silence for the next ten minutes. Michael was seething and said, "Why the hell didn't you tell me? I feel like you set me up and now I am the villain."

"I knew it was more important that he tell you himself. I respect your religious convictions but think that you need to more clearly see them in light of your love for your son."

Michael fumed at this. "I don't know how you can accept this. We have to be on the same page, or he will not give this up."

Arlene shrugged her shoulders. "Many men are gay, Michael. You know them; I know them. I have rarely heard of anyone 'giving it up.' I hope that someday you will see the pain that your words cause him, me and the rest of your children."

Michael left the table and went to his bedroom. It was the first time in their married life that they slept without discussing an unresolved issue.

There was no real communication between father and son for the rest of the week. Michael returned to Cornell feeling totally alienated from his father.

32

In Transition

SAL'S FRIEND NAVY CHAPLAIN JIM FARROW had asked Sal for help. Jim said that it was almost impossible for him to meet all the needs of the Navy as well as lending a hand to the San Diego Archdiocese. He requested that Sal say Mass at the Mission church in San Diego on Saturday afternoon and at the naval submarine base on Sunday morning. Of course, Sal agreed. He had a friend who was a puppeteer, and after lengthy discussions with Jim Farrow, they decided that they would focus the liturgy at the naval base on the children.

The first time they did the puppet show, the main story concerned the lost sheep. All of the children came up to the altar, and Sal led the search for the lost sheep throughout the church. The children immediately responded to the puppet Masses, but in fact, Sal believed that the parents enjoyed them more than the children. All they heard in the next few weeks were compliments, and the parents were thrilled they could engage their children in the story of the week.

When Sal celebrated Mass at the Mission church, it was packed to overflowing. San Diego is a marvelous city with hundreds of possible activities, and a five o'clock Mass on Saturday met the needs of all sorts of parishioners. The golfers could still fill their religious obligations while making early tee times on Sunday. This was also true of boating enthusiasts and also those who wanted to sleep in or have a long breakfast session reading the papers.

When Sal ascended the pulpit, he gave his usual short sermon. He usually began with a story and then developed the theme for today's Christians. He had learned from his former parish that one of the best compliments that one could receive was when people said, "I wish you had gone a little longer." When he finished his sermon, he was stunned at the reaction of the entire church. The parishioners all stood and applauded. After he gained his composure, Sal thought, "Boy, they must hear some terrible sermons."

Life in the following months continued to be quite hectic in San Diego, and Sal found himself drifting more and more away from the life that he had known as a parish priest. He began to think that the priesthood was not, in fact, his destiny. The concepts of being authentic and finding meaning and the realization that decisions change with new information and experiences had a genuine effect on him. He did not love the Church any less than the day of his ordination, but life and his role in it had been altered. His studies had allowed him to realize that the role of ministering to others was not confined to the institutional Church. The theories of Harold Greenwald who taught at the University on the ability to change your life through making different decisions at life's crossroads influenced him powerfully. He knew that the search for meaning had always been within him, regardless of whether he was wearing a collar or not. His decision to become a priest had channeled his desire to serve and his particular gifts in one direction, but that was not the only possibility. *He* had made that choice. And now, older, he could make a different one.

He harbored no resentment or regret about becoming a priest; in fact, he couldn't imagine his life without that tremendously powerful experience, but he believed that the rules and narrow passage should not be where he spent the rest of his days. He had difficulty accepting the Church's positions on birth control, the prohibition against a female priesthood and the burden of mandatory celibacy. These seemed to him like the political decisions of men, not the word of God.

The openness that the Vatican Council once offered seemed to be ending. The Church was becoming more distant from the needs of the people. In his studies, he found a level of comfort that had been eroded in the past few years. It was not an easy choice to leave the active ministry, and there were troublesome feelings because he knew this decision would be harmful to some who believed in him. The temptation to find a way to stay, to not court conflict, was quite strong, but it would be the wrong decision. He would be acting out of cowardice and would inevitably become only a shell of what he hoped to be. In a way, this was not so different from his original struggle to choose the priesthood, hurting Elizabeth, confusing his friends.

Many of those he had served would be disappointed, and this weighed heavily on his mind. One person whom he thought would have major difficulty with his leaving was Michael McNally. Although they had not been in frequent contact recently, Sal thought of Michael as his best friend. He decided that he would write Michael a letter about his decision so that he would not receive the news from anyone else.

Dear Michael,

I cannot believe how long it has been, and I realize that we have not connected for years. Although there has been this absence of personal time together, I often think of you and Arlene. I hope all is well with you and that the family is thriving.

I have recently returned from Europe where I was studying and am now pursuing a Ph.D. in human behavior and leadership in San Diego. My five years in Holy Trinity Parish were marvelous, and I will always be grateful for that experience. I am sure you as a physician can truly appreciate the rewarding relationships that are forged with the people who come to us.

In the past year, I have had growing concerns about my life, and especially regarding the question of priesthood. I have loved the Church, as I am sure you do also, but find it increasingly difficult to follow some of the Church's positions. This is not a casual process. For years, I questioned many of the dogmas and moral guidelines. All of this has led me to the decision that I will request that the Archbishop start the process of my laicization. I wish to be restored to the position of a layperson and will probably in the future marry and raise a family.

The decision is not easy because I realize that many will be disappointed in my choice. Some may see it as betrayal. You have always been like a brother to me, and I did not want you to hear the news from someone else. Your friendship has always been an anchor, and as soon as the dust settles, I hope that we will be able to get together in New York.

    Love to Arlene and your family,

    Sal

Having decided to leave the active ministry, Sal returned to New Jersey and made an appointment to see the Archbishop. The irony of this meeting was that even though the Most Reverend Thomas A. Boland was most conservative theologically and Sal most progressive with regard to current moral issues, there was a bond of friendship between them. He was always especially kind to Sal, perhaps because the pastor in Sal's original church was his immediate aide.

Sal, wearing his black suit and collar, sat in the ornate waiting room of the Archbishop's residence. The door opened, and the Archbishop walked briskly toward Sal and warmly shook his hand. He seemed to be less formal than usual and made no gesture for Sal to kiss his ring. He listened to Sal's desire to leave the active ministry and began a series of questions. "Are you leaving because you believe you are in love?"

"No. I am not involved emotionally with anyone but imagine at some point I may marry. "

"I know that your years at Holy Trinity were difficult but also fulfilling. Would it help if I assigned you to an academic position?"

"No, that is not the reason I am asking to be released. I have tremendous love for the Church but can no longer ignore the issues of conscience that have led me to ask to be released."

The Bishop said, "I wish that you would take more time, but I am pleased that you came to talk with me in person." He rose from his chair and gave Sal his blessing.

After returning to San Diego, Sal felt quite relieved and knew that it was time to start making plans. His years in Westbury were treasures of the heart, and he would not trade them for fame or fortune. He would ever be grateful for all that transpired in those five years. Despite the shedding of the collar, the need to serve and find meaning was still vibrant and compelling. Frankl's words and more important his modeling was a blend of the Sermon on the Mount and existentialism. The University was where Sal's views on spiritually had matured and he realized that in many ways his life had officially changed, but his search for personal involvement with others had not radically been altered. He immersed himself in developing a framework for leadership. All of the academic theories were coming together to provide a way forward. There was a peace in his soul that he had not known for months.

OCTOBER 1974

Sal received word from Rome that his application for leaving the active ministry had been rejected. He had a suspicion that the Archbishop had not supported his decision, and he completely understood. He believed that the Archbishop was hopeful that Sal would change his mind. However, it was now time for him to move forward and to follow the urgings of his heart.

One of the parishioners from Westbury had moved to the West Coast and was currently an executive vice president with the Dymo Corporation in San Francisco. Luigi Contini was a brilliant executive and a phenomenal developer of junior staff members. He had a wonderful family, who had been very gracious to Sal when they lived in his parish. Mary, his wife, was truly one of a kind, and everyone privileged to know her was changed for the better. They had seven children, and when invited to their home

Sal felt like he might be an imposition with an extra person at the dinner table.

Mary smiled and said, "One more makes no difference because every night at our home is a dinner party."

One night during dinner, Luigi, with his steel-trap mind, explored what Sal was studying in graduate school. "I understand that you have focused on leadership. Do you think that your studies would be helpful to a corporate executive team?"

Sal explained his belief that leadership was not static and that every environment could flourish by adapting what he was learning in his graduate program. He focused on the concept of Roving Leadership.

"Luigi, it is my conviction that leadership is not the sole responsibility of those at the top of the pyramid. Leadership permeates an organization, moving from person to person dependent on the challenge, the required skills and desired outcomes. I have learned that the belief in a singular leader is limiting to the potential outcomes of an organization."

Sal described the benefits that Roving Leadership would have to an organization, and at the end of the meal, Luigi offered Sal a consulting opportunity. Dymo was undergoing a cultural transformation because their business had grown exponentially in the past two years. Luigi wished that the senior management team could be on the same page and thought Sal could accomplish this through a leadership program tailored to the business goals of the company.

Excited by this opportunity, Sal agreed to accept Luigi's proposal and engaged one of his professors to assist in the project. The weekly trip from San Diego to Oakland gave Sal the opportunity of reconnecting with a friend from Westbury. Mary Ellen was a surgical nurse who lived with another nurse, Emily, and a physician, Helen, who was doing a residency at San Francisco General

Hospital. He stayed in their apartment during these visits. In lieu of a paying a hotel bill, Dymo allowed him to take them out to dinner on a weekly basis. Luigi approved this but teased him by saying, "No hundred-dollar bottles of wine, Sal."

Most nights there were the four of them, but one evening Mary Ellen and Emily were on duty, and only he and Helen were free. Sal admired Helen, and over the past few months he had extended conversations with her, mostly about her background and why she had chosen emergency medicine. He knew that she came from a community in upstate New York and her family was rather successful. Her rationale for why she chose a residency that served mostly people who lived on the margins in San Francisco was impressive.

During these conversations, he couldn't help noticing how beautiful she was. No matter whether she wore jeans or a dress, her appearance was elegant. Her hair was light brown with streaks of blond highlights, complementing her glowing skin that was almost a translucent cream. Her voice had a warm lilt that reflected her kindness and emotional warmth. The absence of the other two roommates gave Sal the opportunity to spend an entire evening with Helen. She was interested in having dinner together, and they decided that they would go to a Greek restaurant that had entertainment and a reputation for outstanding food at moderate prices. Helen, as usual, was elegantly turned out, wearing her grandmother's pearls. Her friends at Georgetown often teased her that even in the midst of the protests against the Vietnam War, she was always perfectly dressed with every strand of hair in place. Sal was intrigued by the quality of her attention: she listened as if nothing else was happening around her, her eyes fixed on his face. And she didn't only listen; she was forthright and passionate about her ideas. She was comfortable with a range of subjects that Sal was studying and was familiar with the work of Doctor Frankl, which was an immediate connection.

Besides her obvious intelligence, she had a marvelous exuberance. When the waiters encouraged all the customers to join the crowd on the dance floor, dancing to the Greek music, Helen immediately engaged, getting into the spirit without hesitation. She howled as Sal took the napkin from their table and launched into his version of Zorba the Greek. With his long, fiery hair and beard, he figured he must look more like a madman. Who cared; she laughed. The evening, which started out as two strangers sharing a meal, became more and more intimate, and by the end of the night when they arrived home, Sal was smitten.

Following the dinner at the Greek restaurant, Sal could not stop thinking about Helen. His years as a celibate had not diminished his attraction to women, but he had refrained from becoming involved in any intimate relationship. Now all the desire and love that he had held at bay for years came gushing forth. Not since his time with Elizabeth had he felt so passionately about anyone.

Helen was remarkable. Her work as a doctor was only one way she expressed her compassion and dedication to the lives of others. During her medical school years at Georgetown, she spent all of her summers working at a camp for physically disabled children in Virginia. It didn't matter that she had grown up in the affluent community of the Troy country club crowd; she had no sense of superiority. Her privilege gave her a foundation from which to explore the world, and she didn't hesitate. She didn't want an easy life but a meaningful one, an interesting one—and dating a recently laicized priest was not a leap for her; she liked the twists and turns of Sal's story, the passion of his choices, his enthusiasm.

The evening at the Greek restaurant was the beginning. They couldn't stop talking, and Sal couldn't stop thinking about this bright, beautiful, enchanting woman. Despite their crazy schedules they began to spend most weekends together. Either Helen would fly to San Diego, or Sal would hop on a plane to San Francisco. What had begun as a casual friendship had blossomed into the love affair of their lives. Endless conversations over dinner or drinks, expeditions to movies, lectures and art events, time at the beach, in coffeehouses and the houses of friends, time alone building their private world—all of it ultimately led to Sal's proposing.

He hoped she would say yes; he was afraid she would say no. She was so much younger—still in her twenties, just starting her career.

But she didn't say no.

They were married by Jim Farrow in the Contini's exquisite garden and spent the next three days on their honeymoon in Carmel by the Sea. They had only enough money to stay at the Normandy Inn for three days. When they arrived in Carmel and went to their room, they spent hours talking about the magic of the wedding day. The friends, the flowers, the food, the music, the gorgeous weather. "I know this is heresy," said Sal. "But I'm not sure there could be a day this beautiful in Jersey City."

"I've never been to Jersey City."

"They have a crookedest street in the world there too, but they call it Main Street."

"I want to see where you grew up."

"You will, sweetheart. But not this week."

Sal thought of all the weddings he'd performed and reflected that even feeling the august and joyous weight of the sacrament, he had not imagined the happiness that resides in being at the heart of the ceremony, stating in public the private knowledge of the heart.

"Do you know what a miracle it is to have a wife? For so many years, I thought I'd be alone. I still find it hard to believe," he said.

"I was afraid you would forget your place and start officiating," she said. "Then I would have had to marry that young man, what's his name, the nephew?"

"You wouldn't dare. No one could love you as I do."

"Or you as I do."

The gentleness of their touches led to the wonder of completely sharing their bodies and souls for the next three nights. During the day, they roamed the magnificent Carmel beach for hours and at night danced on their patio as the moon rose over the ocean. Emotionally rich but financially strapped, their daily splurge was breakfast at the Tuck Box, the lovely British tea shop one block from the ocean.

He loved watching her do simple things—put jam on her toast, milk in her tea. She had a natural grace that made his heart stutter. He loved her laugh—the sound of it and how easily it came; how she enjoyed things. She loved that he could make her laugh and also make her think, that he never grew tired of talking about ideas or people. They both agreed that there was no way to separate ideas from people; the lives we live are the reality of our ideas, the visible argument.

He loved that she read the books that mattered to him. She loved that he told her what frightened him and that he didn't mind when she worked late—if she apologized, he'd hush her, saying the world deserved her too.

The first few years of their marriage were filled with the realization that together they became more complete as persons. Sal had been in love before, but no one had been able to so quickly gain his complete trust. He marveled that Helen could accept his high energy and impulsive decisions with such calm acceptance. She would listen for hours to his stories and dreams, and he loved the way she made him feel about himself. One day he opened a dresser drawer, and a box of gold medals fell clanging to the floor. Sal asked what these were for.

Helen answered, "When I was younger I did a bit of swimming." In fact, she was the New York State breaststroke champion in her age group. Her humility was characteristic and endearing.

Helen was equally enthralled by their relationship. She had dated before, of course—he preferred not to hear too much about it—and claimed that many men did not know how to listen. "I suppose it's all those hours in the confessional," she said. "You had practice."

"No, I'm just used to sitting at the feet of my superiors."

"You mean your sister?"

"Well, she is ten years older."

However, as in all new stages of marriage, there were certain things that needed to be negotiated. Saturday, for Sal, was a time for long leisurely breakfast with many cups of coffee and reading the newspaper from cover to cover. Helen had a different view, and Sal noticed, while seated at the kitchen table, that Helen would scurry by and give him a scornful look. Finally, Sal asked, "Okay, why the puss?"

Helen said, "I could use some help around here." When Sal realized what the issue was, they negotiated the desired household chores and peace was restored.

33

MAY 1980

Through the Eyes of Children

ELEN AND SAL MOVED TO CUPERTINO and purchased an eleven-hundred-foot square foot house. The benefit to the house was that it was situated on a triple lot on the corner. It was four months before they realized that their house was the same as every other house on the street. The California climate enabled tract houses to appear different because trees and plants matured in record time. They were not skilled at carpentry, and one of their initial projects turned into a disaster. They bought a new front door and instead of planing the door, they planed the frame. After many hours, they were able to close the door but could not reopen it. As usual, the Contini's came to their rescue.

Sal continued to work at Dymo and had become an executive on the management board. Helen took a position at El Camino

Hospital in the emergency medicine department. They carved out a lovely life for themselves in this quaint California community. Because of the extensive lot size, Helen became an avid gardener and a gourmet cook. After the door tragedy Sal developed some carpentry skills, built a cedar fence in the backyard and created a wall in the family room from antique wine boxes. Their schedules did not always mesh, but they often found time to attend auctions and antique sales.

One day Helen came home and invited Sal out for dinner at the quaint El Torro Mexican restaurant in downtown Los Gatos. It was a beautiful evening weather-wise, and they chose to eat on the patio, which overlooked the fountain and the formal gardens of the town hall. The area had a multi-colored glow from the sun, which was positioned over the Saratoga hills. Before ordering, Helen began the conversation in a manner that Sal thought was unusual. Helen folded her napkin and placing it on her lap asked, "It occurred to me recently that I never really asked you about your feelings regarding leaving the priesthood. Do you ever miss being called Father?"

Sal thought this was rather out of the blue but answered, "Truthfully, I loved that honor but have no regrets that I left the active ministry." The waitress appeared at their table and Sal asked, "Are you ready to order because I skipped lunch and am rather hungry."

Helen said, "You go ahead."

Sal ordered a margarita and the cheese enchilada special. Helen selected a fish taco and an iced tea.

Sal said, "That is the first time in history that you have passed up on a margarita. Are you feeling okay?"

"Never felt better."

The waitress brought their drinks, and again Sal asked, "Help me understand why I am drinking alone."

Helen raised her glass and touched it against Sal's. "Sal, I wonder whether you again would like to be called Father?" She raised her ice tea. "I would like to make a toast to the La Greca's, Sal, Helen and the new arrival." Sal was momentarily confused. "Sal, I found out today that we are going to have a baby."

Sal rose and moved to hug her. He was ecstatic and cherished the thought that he would be a father. The loss of that possibility had been one of the most difficult things about becoming a priest, and though he and Helen had always intended children, he knew that often things don't turn out as we wish. He would have been happy enough just with Helen, but this! He felt a wordless thrill at the recognition that he was creating further bonds, not only to his wife and child-to-be, but to his parents, siblings, nieces and nephews, and Helen's family. He thought about the community he'd grown up in, how close it was, neighbors in and out of each other's houses, and hoped that he could provide the best of that for his child in this very different world.

He had lots of ideas on how to be a good parent, and so did Helen. Like every couple before them, they talked about what their own parents had done right, what they had learned from the experience of being a child and from living in the world as adults, what they hoped for.

Mostly, they agreed.

He fully participated in the pregnancy and attended all of the Lamaze parenting classes. When the day came, he was present during the long hours before Helen gave birth. She suffered through back labor, but finally their baby was born. Jonathan Salvatore, named after Sal's father and Jack Murphy, was 8 pounds six ounces. They were both ecstatic, and after holding the baby in his arms, Sal rushed to the hall phone and announced his joy to their families.

The month after the birth of your first child is anything but easy, but thanks to the guidance of Mary Contini, they weathered all the new experiences. Helen breastfed Jonathan, but Sal took the midnight feedings and often drove the car around the block so the baby would stop crying and fall asleep. Sal loved being a father and loved this particular baby, who was an exceptionally adorable, intelligent and all-around remarkable boy, as both parents affirmed to each other.

Eighteen months later, they were blessed with a second child, Marisa. She was nine pounds and had a full head of dark hair. Helen had been a little too casual with her timing and almost gave birth in the hospital parking lot. "Did you want to have to tell your daughter she was born in a car?" he teased her.

"Better than being conceived in the backseat of one," she retorted.

"It wasn't!" he said, and she dissolved in giggles.

Toddler Jonathan was fascinated with his sister and only a little jealous. Sal once caught him explaining to the infant that Sal and Helen were really HIS parents; she was just visiting.

Sal loved watching all the experiences of childhood through his children's eyes. There was an enormous sense of awe and magic as they saw the world through the prism of their innocence. It was more than refreshing for him to come home at night and have them regale him and Helen with their views and questions. They were fully at home in nature and found charm and beauty in the simplest experiences.

Jonathan was the more physically active of Sal's children. Sal's brother once referred to him as Felix Unger, a character from the play *The Odd Couple.* He was in constant motion and thoroughly enjoyed being a partner with his father in the attempts to plant and maintain their large garden. It was a long way from the cobblestone streets of Jersey City to the suburban setting of Cupertino, and Sal enjoyed the work. One day it was time to fertilize the plants, and Jonathan, ever Sal's shadow in the garden, had a quizzical look on his face while his father was doling out the fertilizer. Sal knelt and asked, "Jonathan, is there something you want to ask me?"

He furrowed his eyebrows and said, "What are you putting on the plants?" He was not old enough to understand the word fertilizer, so Sal chose to explain it in terms he was sure he would understand.

Sal said, "Jonathan, I am putting poo-poo on the plants so that they will grow."

He smiled, and his response made such sense and warmed Sal's heart. "If I take a lot of poo-poos, I will grow!" So wonderful and literal. Sal let his understanding stay where it was.

Marisa was equally wonderful but more pensive and reflective than Jon. She had inherited her mother's hatred of the cold. At the outdoor sessions at daycare during the winter, she displayed total disdain for this part of her day. At this early age, she asked great questions, and usually had a marvelous follow-up to Sal's first attempts to respond. A peek into her personality happened very early on when she took something that rightfully belonged to her brother. Sal asked her to give it back. This was met with no response as she tenaciously held onto the forbidden object. Sal then moved to the wondrous concept of sharing, which once again fell on deaf ears. Finally, in a strong tone, he said: "Marisa, you have two choices; give that back to Jonathan, or I will take it from you and give it to Jonathan." She looked at Sal almost with pity and said: "I have three choices. I can give it to Mommy, and she can give it to Jonathan." Sal knew then that this would not be the last battle with this exquisite child.

Helen and Sal loved living in California but wished their children could know their families on the East Coast. Helen's parents lived in Troy, New York, and it would only be a two-hour drive to their home from Boston. Helen was one of four daughters, and after the youngest was born, her father bought an Irish setter and named him Edward Martin Murray Junior. He loved his daughters but laughingly admitted that Junior gave him some aid against the female entourage in his home. He was an adoring father but knew little of the daily expenses of four daughters. His wife purchased all of the children's clothing at an upscale store in Albany, The Geranium Tree. One evening when her father was writing checks he came to a rather large bill and inquired, "Heavens, Dorothy, how many geraniums do we need?"

Elaine's mother was charming and had an elegant but inviting presence. Dorothy was the local unofficial marriage and guidance counselor for all of the young women at the Troy Country Club. Helen had received the best of both worlds from her parents. She was academically brilliant but had the grace and communication skills of her mother.

Sal decided to seek opportunities to return, but it was difficult to secure a position of vice president in the Boston area. One evening, while they were visiting, his sister-in-law invited Sal to a party at the University of Massachusetts. Sal became engaged in an animated conversation with Doctor Greg Arnold, the Massachusetts Commissioner of Education. Sal passionately conveyed the opinion that educators were woefully neglecting the needs of children with handicapping conditions. The commissioner listened intently, then asked Sal for his phone number. The next morning Commissioner Arnold called Sal and offered him a position heading up a new program at the University of Massachusetts in Amherst. The commissioner informed him that he would have a partner, and the focus would be on changing the culture of secondary schools regarding handicapped adolescents. Sal was dumbfounded. He told the commissioner that he was seeking a senior position in a corporation and could not consider his offer. The commissioner, with a certain degree of sarcasm, responded by saying, "I gather your passion last evening was more based on rhetoric than a desire to change the system."

Sal was greatly disturbed by the conversation and shared the incident with Helen. One of his biggest concerns was that they had agreed that Helen would not practice medicine full time until both children were in grade school. The salary at the University was paltry, and they would be living on a constrained budget. She told him that if he wanted to do this, she would be supportive. Sal called the commissioner and said that he would take the job for a definite period with specific caveats. The staff had to be diverse, and Sal needed the guarantee that he would have the absolute right to hire and fire. He also requested a certain budget and control over the candidates who would be selected for the program. The last point that needed to be discussed was Sal would only be available for a three or four-year period. The commissioner agreed to all of the requests.

It was the sort of opportunity that rarely comes along. His partner, Maddie Bragar, a Ph.D. in special education from the Syracuse University, and Sal had the challenging task of assembling a team to approach the issues concerning those with handicapping conditions in secondary schools. The program was to be centered on a one-year master's program for high school principals and superintendents. The primary goal was to help them understand what the issues were regarding students who had previously been labeled as slow, retarded, emotionally disturbed and physically handicapped.

. At graduation, the best tribute came from one of the principals in the program. He said, "I came into this program primarily because I wanted to get a master's degree. However, I have been changed for the better. I have always cared about every kid in my school, but this program has changed me. I now understand more fully the challenges that kids with special needs and their families face every day."

34

MAY 1984

Another Adventure

ONE OF SAL'S FORMER PARISHIONERS HAD become the CEO of a Johnson and Johnson company. He called Sal and requested his assistance in pulling together his management team. Sal was thrilled at this opportunity yet rather apprehensive. He had been a consultant and executive in a major corporation but was concerned after his years at the University that working in a corporate environment might create a conflict of values. There was a strong bias in the academic world that people in corporations were not as ethical as those who labored in universities. Sal knew this was false in his prior employment but was concerned that his experience might not be typical across the corporate world. This concern quickly vanished. Little did he know that this would be the beginning of how he would spend the next twenty-five years of his life. Dave Collins, the CEO, was an incredibly talented leader, and the entire senior management team developed under his deft guidance.

Sal was responsible for the development of the company's strategic plan with the senior executive team. He had learned this process from his time at Dymo. Collins and he had planned to move executives out of their departmental sandboxes by cultivating opportunities for them to work on cross-disciplinary challenges. The positive results of this approach were that eleven of his team became company presidents and the twelfth became in charge of all research and development. The values that had been at the forefront in the parish were still operational, and Sal found that perhaps because of his background, many people appeared to immediately trust him. Sal learned a great deal from David and employed much of what had worked in the settings of other Fortune 500 companies. He loved developing organizational structures that could meet the needs of the companies and provide leadership opportunities at every level. With each of his international clients, he was able to employ the theory and benefits of Roving Leadership. On one occasion, a pharmaceutical company was having serious problems with the manufacturing of their lead compound. The pills were disintegrating before their ordinary expiration expectancy. The management team decided to award a major contract to a mechanical engineering firm to solve the problem. Sal agreed but offered the opinion that the operators on the machines that manufactured the pills should also be on the team. Some members of the management team scoffed at this, but Sal convinced them that no harm would be done by this addition. The first day they were trying to address the source of the problem, one of the engineers was in conversation with an operator and was told that in the final process of heat and reduction of air, one of the valves was sweating. The engineer was amazed because this seemingly trivial information was vital to the solution. The engineer offered that it would have taken them significant tests and probably two weeks before they discovered what the operator had observed.

35

1994

A Bridge to Nowhere

R OBERT MCNALLY HAD ENDURED YEARS OF surgery and physical rehab since the fateful accident in New York City. Initially,
there appeared to be brain damage as well as the physical disabilities, but speech therapy had altered this concern and Robert had
an unusually high IQ. His parents recognized early on that his
artistic ability was exceptional and would provide many opportunities to use his mind and spirit, especially during the periods of
prolonged surgery. He had lost his spleen in the accident, but the
real hardships were the surgeries rebuilding his legs and hips. At
one point, it was thought that he would require the amputation
of his right leg, but that concern had been alleviated by a combination of physiotherapy and antibiotics. His education at the
Pennsylvania Academy of Art under the tutelage of great teachers

like Seymour Remenick helped him develop a painting style that was impressionistic. His expertise was in plein air towns and landscapes of marsh settings. He had won several prestigious awards in the past seven years.

Arlene had spent much of her summer at their home in Long Beach Island. Robert also was staying at the beach house and had three galleries in the neighboring communities featuring his art. It was thrilling for both she and Michael to see the professional growth of their youngest child despite the years of surgeries and ongoing physical therapy.

However, the joy of their one son did not mitigate the ongoing separation that existed between Michael and Michael Jr. Arlene McNally found herself in the middle of a feud between her husband and son. Since Michael Junior announced to the family that he was gay, there had been almost no contact between father and son. They were both locked into intransigent positions, and it broke Arlene's heart to know that there appeared to be no bridge for them to cross to each other. Her husband was a wonderful father who loved his son, but because of deeply held religious convictions could not condone his son's homosexuality.

Arlene had kept in frequent contact with her son who lived with his partner Ted near San Francisco. In the spring of 1994, she decided that she would spend a week visiting them. She had made frequent trips to San Francisco through the years but had not met Michael's partner. She informed her husband of her intention but in no way sought his permission.

Michael Jr. and Ted lived in Sausalito on the other side of the Golden Gate Bridge. They owned a duplex that had fantastic views of the bay as well as San Francisco. Michael was the principal of a startup technology company, and Ted was a professor of Italian Art at Berkeley. Arlene was most impressed by Ted. He was clearly brilliant with an engaging personality. More importantly, it was obvious how much he cared for her son. They had been living together for a year and a half.

In the middle of the visit, Ted had a full day workshop in the city and suggested that mother and son should have some quality time alone. Michael Jr. played the role of tour guide perfectly in the city and made a late luncheon reservation at the wondrous Alta Mira Hotel and restaurant in Sausalito. Seated at one of the premier window tables, Arlene marveled at the wondrous views of Tony Bennett's city.

She quipped, "I may also leave my heart here." Michael Jr. laughed and said, "The city is often referred to as Bagdad by the Bay."

The brunch was exquisite, and the accompanying white wine perfectly complemented the food. Michael Jr. asked dozens of questions about his siblings, but there was no mention of his father. Arlene filled him in on the family. Michael Jr. had frequent conversations with his siblings, and all had visited him while in San Francisco on business or pleasure. His being gay was not a problem for any of them.

"Aren't you going to ask about your father?"

Michael grudgingly said, "How is he?"

"He is well."

"What did he say about visiting the prodigal son?"

"His literal words were goodbye and hope you have a wonderful visit." In fact, he had only said goodbye and had offered no hope for a wonderful visit. Arlene sipped her wine before speaking again. "You may not feel it, but he is your father and deeply loves you."

"Mom, at some level I believe that, but I cannot stand to be around him. He makes me feel like I am evil incarnate. Two years ago at Long Beach Island, he seemed consistently to avoid me."

Arlene understood this, but it wounded her heart, and she wished to create some hope. "I can only imagine how hard that is for you, but he also suffers. He is between the love for you and his faith."

"Mom, I get that. If it's okay, I would like us to end this topic." Arlene understood that any further words would spoil the wonderful time they were sharing.

When Arlene arrived at the airport at the end of the visit, Ted hugged her and said, "I am thrilled to have had time with you. I clearly understand why Michael is so terrific. He had wonderful roots."

Arlene kissed Ted on the cheek. "Take care of him, Ted. It has been a blessing meeting someone he loves so dearly."

Ted picked up Arlene's suitcase while Michael said goodbye. "Mom, it was wonderful having you here. I was so happy that you could meet Ted and spend quality time with us." As they hugged, it was apparent that they might not see each other again for months.

Arlene kissed him and made one last attempt. "Is there any possibility that you will come to Long Beach Island this summer?"

Michael frowned. "Can I bring Ted? You don't have to respond, Mom, I know the answer. I will never come unless I can bring Ted." They hugged again, and Arlene slowly walked to the door of the airport.

Arlene decided instead of heading directly to the beach from the airport she would spend the night in New York. She set her alarm and drove from the city at 3 a.m. to avoid the rush hour traffic. Once on the island, she stopped for gas, coffee, and a bagel. She arrived at the beach house, gently opened the door and walked to one of the bedrooms on the first floor. She was certain that Michael was still asleep in the master bedroom on the second floor. The sunlight was peeking through the blinds, and she loved the sound of the waves as they caressed the beach.

She put on sandals and made her way to the deck and then onto the sand. The beach was almost empty except for a solitary figure walking a golden retriever. The only sounds were the sea gulls and the waves. She walked to the water in bare feet and stuck one foot in the water. She giggled because the temperature was far below her standard for swimming. She realized that the ocean had not had the essential two months of pulverizing sunshine. She bent down to pick up an interesting piece of driftwood and began to reflect on her time in San Francisco. Suddenly she heard someone calling her name.

She turned and saw Michael on their deck frantically waving his arms. He hurriedly came down the steps and hustled to meet her. When he was close, he opened his arms and kissed her. "I heard you come in, but by the time I put on shorts and a tee shirt you were already gone. How was your flight?"

This question did not sit well with Arlene, and she sharply responded, "Is that the most important question you can ask me?"

Michael was surprised at her reaction. "What is that supposed to mean?"

"It means you are ignoring where I have been and who I went to visit."

Michael became very defensive. "We haven't seen each other in a week, and this is the response I get? Instead of being present in this glorious place, you start out with the past."

"It is not the past, Michael, it is the present."

"Okay, calm down. What do you want me to do?"

Arlene began to cry. "I want you to love and accept your son."

"That is unfair. I love him as much as you do, but I cannot accept the way he leads his life. Arlene, it is an issue of right and wrong, and I cannot be a hypocrite."

"You talk about what he has chosen as if he woke one day and decided to shatter your heart. He is who he is, and he suffers from your rejection."

"Am I expected to join the crowd and throw the teaching of my Church overboard?"

That statement sparked anger and Arlene forcefully stated, "Michael, I am no less a Catholic than you, but I will not believe that Jesus wants me to shun my son. I just spent a wonderful week with him and Ted. It breaks my heart to know I may not see him for years. He will not come here alone because he cannot."

"Arlene, I never want him to be unhappy. I have every day searched my soul and prayed for guidance. If I accept this person Ted as a member of our family, I would be a hypocrite."

Arlene felt drained and decided any further discussion would be in vain. Neither one knew what to say, so they walked back to the beach house in silence.

36

JUNE 2000

A New Adventure in New Brunswick, New Jersey

WHEN SAL LEFT NORTHAMPTON, IT WAS important to him that Helen also have equal career opportunities. Within three weeks she had a bevy of job offers; Helen transferred from Cooley Dickinson Hospital in Northampton and took a position in the ER at the Robert Wood Johnson Hospital in New Brunswick.

Helen had always put her needs on the back burner due to her generosity of soul. She was a marvelous parent and had supported every adventure that Sal had cultivated over the years. She was an outstanding professional but always maintained the ability to share any professional successes with others. Physicians and nurses gravitated toward her, and she often became their mentor, sometimes in nontraditional ways. It was truly amazing that she could juggle personal and career responsibilities and meet every deadline.

Even when she experienced breast cancer, she went for her radiation treatments and then immediately went to work. Her schedule, despite the drain, anxiety and loss of energy, literally changed nothing in her dedication to her work and family. Helen was a remarkably independent woman; whose strength was in her loving devotion to others.

They purchased a foreclosure in Yardley, Pennsylvania, that had, in the words of enthusiastic naïve amateurs, "potential." The large English Brick Tudor was one of seven large homes on Greenway Avenue. The houses were situated two blocks above the Delaware River and had once been an exclusive neighborhood of wealthy factory owners. The home had beautiful hardwood floors, chestnut bookcases and a chestnut staircase that had layers of oil-based paint. They worked tirelessly trying to improve the house, but Helen was more committed to extended work schedules than Sal. One night, after working on the bookcases and staircase removing layers of lead paint, Sal said he had enough and went to bed at midnight. Helen, covered with paint, continued to work on the staircase, removing the paint by using a heavy solvent.

Two hours later she hurried up the staircase to the bedroom woke up Sal from a sound sleep. "The staircase is on fire!"

The solvents had created a chemical reaction. Sal raced to stifle the smoke by activating the fire extinguisher. This temporary setback did nothing to prevent Helen from continuing the next day to clean the staircase, but this time she was armed with a fire extinguisher.

Despite extensive national and European travel on Sal's part, the relationship between him, Helen and the children deepened.

Sal attempted to arrange his travel schedule around the children's school and athletic events. Helen, in her usual fashion, had cultivated a group of dear friends and she even found time to start a book club. Sal marveled at the schedule she kept but at times was worried because she got by so little sleep. Somehow, she was unwilling to let anything go to the back burner. One of their friends said, "Jesus takes care of seventy percent and Helen has the rest."

Adolescence was a whole new adventure for the La Greca's. Sal had a wonderful loving relationship with his youngest, Marisa, but was warned by his brother, who had four daughters, that soon the aliens would visit. He contended that at age fourteen they kept the physical image of the child but left an entirely different person. Sal laughed at this and did not realize that his relationship with his daughter was about to change.

Marisa was enrolled at Stuart Country Day School of the Sacred Heart in Princeton and thrived academically. She was president of her class and an accomplished actress and singer. At her first performance, Sal and Helen were shocked at her beautiful singing voice. Other parents asked who her vocal teachers were and Sal humorously quipped, "The shower." The raves by her teachers were wonderful to hear, but their experiences were different from the ones Sal had with Marisa at home. She was never disrespectful but aloof in their interactions, and Sal recalled his brother's counsel. Fortunately, Helen and Marisa had an outstanding relationship, which made for numerous chats in her room at all times of the day and night.

Jonathan was enrolled at Holy Ghost Prep and was caught up in sports and the debating team. This was a pleasant surprise for Sal because Jonathan had been rather shy. The debate team eventually led him to his choice to pursue a career in TV sports.

Freshman year in college was a difficult time for Jonathan and the family. When he returned from Ithaca at the Christmas break, Helen was shocked at his appearance. She confided to Sal that she feared Jonathan had leukemia or diabetes. Sal pooh-poohed her impression and suggested it was too much coffee and late-night paper writing that caused his drawn demeanor. Unfortunately, Helen was right, and it was determined that Jonathan had type 1 diabetes. Sal was devastated, and the following year was a nightmare. Jonathan continued to lose weight. Fortunately, the Joslyn Institute placed him on an insulin pump, which dramatically improved his health. He graduated in four years and started his TV career at a small station in upstate New York.

Marisa was accepted as a finance major at Georgetown and continued the family's female tradition. Her mother and aunt had also attended Georgetown. She thrived in the academic environment and went on to be the CEO of the student-run bank at Georgetown. She had eight job offers when she graduated and became a financial advisor for Legg Mason in Baltimore. After three years, she took a job in business development and eventually settled on studying law in Boston. The early loving relationship between Sal and Marisa was fully restored when the aliens returned her at age nineteen.

The family stayed in the area for thirteen years before Helen was appointed Director of Emergency Medicine at Beth Israel in New York City.

There is an old joke that certainly was true for Helen and Sal in the New York opportunity. "Life begins when the children leave home, and the dog dies." New York was the culmination of Helen's medical career. Beth Israel was an outstanding medical complex that was a forerunner in many health areas. Helen, as the head of emergency care, had an excellent staff and generous resources in developing the premier area of emergency health care in Manhattan. Helen's philosophy permeated every aspect of emergency care. She completely understood the complexities of emergency room medicine, but she was committed to having kindness be the mantle that covered all interactions with patients. She believed that kindness not only benefits the patient but the healthcare provider as well. Current techniques, tests and pharmaceuticals help heal, but the intangible of kindness plays a vital role in healing the whole person.

Helen's position at Beth Israel offered them an opportunity to live in a city they both loved. They thoroughly enjoyed spending so much time together, and besides being husband and wife, they were each other's best friend. Sal had largely curtailed his international travel, and this offered the perfect opportunity to fulfill a promise that he had made to his mentor Viktor Frankl. Having met so many of the Holocaust survivors through Frankl, he had been encouraged to one day become a public witness. He took this seriously but had been so busy with career and family responsibilities that he had not yet fulfilled this commitment. He decided that he would write a novel in remembrance of Frankl and those who had suffered and perished.

For months, he wrote and rewrote and finally believed that the story was ready to be published. In his naiveté, he expected an immediate acceptance from a publisher, but in fact, he was disappointed at the avalanche of rejection letters. He even received a three-page letter from an agent telling him that he loved the book. However, he stated, "I can't represent you because you are a nobody."

Finally, it happened; he received an inquiry from a small publisher who was enthusiastic about the work and wished to publish it. Six months later, which was record time in the industry, he and Helen were standing in front of a fiction section in Barnes and Noble. They were there taking pictures of the novel with a host of their friends. The book was exceptionally well received, especially by the Jewish community, and afforded Sal many opportunities to speak about the Holocaust in the States as well as Europe.

37

50th High School Reunion

MICHAEL AND ARLENE LEFT NEW YORK at 3 o'clock on their way to Jersey City to attend their fiftieth high school reunion. As they drove through the Lincoln Tunnel, they were trying to recall the first names of their classmates. Arlene was holding the yearbook and would provide Michael with a classmate's last name. He was expected to recall and give the person's first name. Michael failed miserably on the first few attempts, and Arlene began to tease him. "You are much more talented as a surgeon than a name re-caller."

Michael scoffed at this evaluation and said, "When we get through the tunnel, you can drive. Then with the yearbook in my hand, we will see whether your memory is better than mine."

"Just keep driving, Doctor, and stop trying to protect that male ego."

Michael smiled and said, "I am sure that some of the class has already passed away."

Arlene concurred. "I am aware of a few deaths, but I'm sure there are more. When we get close to the school, let's stop for coffee. I don't want to be the first ones at the party."

The neighborhood had changed dramatically through the years and many of the traditional businesses had closed, but they were able to find a Dunkin Donuts. West Side Avenue, which had been a thriving business community, was now a series of low-end businesses, and many storefronts had boarded windows and were empty. They had heard that the neighborhood was somewhat economically depressed and one of their classmates had recently visited the area and told them, "If you leave a B29 on West Side Avenue it will be gone in an hour." Seated in the rear of the shop they focused on their expectations for the event. Arlene said, "I hope Elizabeth is there. Did you know that she married Frank Felice?"

Michael said, "No. Didn't his father own a bar on West Side Avenue?"

"Yes, and Frank was the class ahead of us. They began dating after Sal went into the seminary."

The sound of Sal's name was difficult for Michael. He had written a letter to Michael when he left the priesthood, which he had never shared with Arlene. Michael had trouble accepting Sal's decision and never answered the letter. He now realized that this had been a mistake. He sorely missed Sal.

"I am sure you hope that Sal will be at the reunion. I only hope the two of you clowns behave yourselves." Arlene opened the yearbook to Sal's page. "He was such a comedian, and I was truly shocked when he went into the seminary. I know he left the priesthood, but I wonder where he is now."

Michael was uncomfortable with the conversation. Taking the yearbook into his hands, he began to turn the pages.

As they drove up to the school, there were balloons and signs telling them where to park. The main building had seen better days. The exterior had some missing bricks and was in dire need of a sandblasting. The windows were coated with dirt, and the sidewalks were all cracked, which made walking quite perilous. The gym was decorated with a large fiftieth- anniversary banner and there were photos of each member of the class on the walls. They were warmly greeted by Janet Kelly. She was two years ahead of them and was the most loyal student of the alumni. She worked tirelessly to promote the alumni group and had raised substantial funds, which allowed the high school to remain open. After placing their nametags on, they began to mingle with the crowd. Almost immediately Michael spotted Mike Henry at the other end and went to greet him. Arlene found her friends and said, "I will see you in a bit."

Mike had been a fireman in Jersey City and was now living down the shore. "How the hell are you, Michael?" his buddy bellowed.

"Great. How about you?"

For the next twenty minutes, they traded high school stories and memories. At one point they shared the fact that golf was the most difficult game they had ever played. Mike still played regularly, but Michael had not played in years.

"Do you ever see any of the old crowd?" Michael asked.

"Yes, some of them are actually neighbors. I see Maddy and Ropey regularly. Maddy will be here, but I doubt that Ropey will make it. He has had some physical problems."

"When you see him, give him my regards." Michael scanned the room, but the one person he really wanted to see was nowhere in sight. "Have you seen Sal?"

"No, and unfortunately Janet said he will not be coming. Apparently, he is speaking at some conference in Germany. I know

he is married and for a while was living in California." Michael
dropped the subject and began to talk to more of his classmates.
He never mentioned it to Arlene but was feeling guilty and sad
that he hadn't responded to Sal's letter.

38

The City that Never Sleeps

S AL HAD CURTAILED MOST OF HIS international consulting
work and was focusing on the Holocaust presentations that
he seemed to be giving monthly. He had written a series of novels
and articles about the Holocaust and was making presentations
largely to Jewish communities. They had moved to New York in
January of 2011. Both children had left the nest, and the cultural
life in New York afforded he and Helen endless opportunities.
Manhattan was open twenty-four hours a day, and they could
step out of their building for any given need day or night. It was
a city filled with the promise that anything is possible.

Sal grew up across the river in New Jersey and knew the belief
that the residents are cold and aloof anything but the truth. The
area around 96th and Third had been a welcoming neighborhood, and in many respects, they felt like they were living in a

small village. The sheer energy of the city propelled Helen and Sal into endless moments of joy. They had season tickets to the opera and frequently attended cultural and sporting events. The only negative was that Sal was a Red Sox fan and feared for his life at Yankee games. Sal mentioned to Helen that living in New York had felt like an ongoing vacation. But now, they were discussing the next phase of their lives. They agreed that soon they would spend a year or two living in Italy. They had often vacationed in various parts of Italy, and Helen was enamored with Rome and many of the villages in Tuscany.

That future came to an end one day in September.

It was their custom on Wednesday afternoons, after Helen had finished her shift at the hospital, to meet for an early dinner and either a movie or a play. One Wednesday morning, before Helen was leaving for work, she said, "I would like to take in that new Tom Hanks movie." Sal agreed and kissed her as she prepared to leave. He finished his coffee and went upstairs and began to do research for his new novel. In the middle of the afternoon, the phone rang. It was Doctor Harriet Shackles from Beth Israel. After he answered, there was a long pause. Finally, Doctor Shackles said, "Sal, I am sorry to tell you that Helen collapsed in the ER and is in Intensive Care."

The rest of the conversation was a complete blur. Sal raced downstairs, grabbed his coat and hailed a cab. Arriving at the hospital, he was met by Doctor Shackles, who took him to the ICU. He was overwhelmed to see Helen on a respirator, with a host of tubes penetrating her body. After sitting by her bedside for twenty minutes, he was invited to a small conference room where three physicians explained in detail that Helen had experienced a brain aneurysm. Her prognosis for survival was dismal. The amount of brain damage was massive, and if she survived, which they doubted, there was little hope for any progress.

After two days, the situation had deteriorated further, and Sal knew that removing her form the respirator was the only decision that he could make. He sat by her bed joined by Jonathan and Marisa and decided that it was he who should pull the plug. He was assured that she would feel no pain, and after a short period of time, she passed peacefully. His children wanted him to stay with them, but he wanted to be home. He would contact them and requested their aid in arranging the funeral.

Her death cast Sal into a spiral of sadness and ultimately depression. The nights without her were awful, and he dreaded the endless hours as he often drank too much wine and stumbled his way to bed. He had always imagined that he would go first because of the twelve-year difference in their ages. Despite the support of his children, he felt more and more alone. He often sat in his office reading cards and notes that Helen had sent through the years. He also had saved all of the personal memorial cards that were received when Helen died. He took momentary solace in the wonderful ways she had touched so many lives, but it was not enough. Writing offered temporary hours of flight, and a few too many glasses of red wine dulled the pain but could not replace what he had lost. There were moments when he felt as though the grief had plunged him into quicksand, and nothing could rescue him from being submerged.

Being no stranger to death, he was still stunned by the intensity of the toll grief takes on the body. His gait was slowed, and at times he was so wrapped up in thoughts of Helen that he would lose his balance. Accepting her death was like falling down a mountain, hitting layers of rock on the way. It was an endless array of psychic bruises that appeared to have no end. There was no taming the grief. What appeared as anger really was a mask for the depth of loneliness of life without her.

39

The Golden Years

MICHAEL'S WORLD HAD CHANGED FOR THE better over the last few years. He had become emeritus at the University of Cornell surgical department and had greatly reduced his teaching schedule. Still on the board of directors at two nonprofit organizations, he felt that the next phase of his life was unfolding smoothly. He was unable to perform major surgery due to failing eyesight but often gave lectures on the concepts of superb surgical care to the new residents. Long-term residents of New York, he and Arlene had no intention of leaving their home, but they began to make significant plans for travel and longed for the opportunity to get away from the Northeast in the winter.

Wednesday, which was almost a religious date for many of his surgeon friends regarding golf, was the opposite for Michael.

For years this was a day that he spent away from the stresses of medicine and was devoted solely to his family. Ever since their nest emptied, it was a weekly ritual that he and Arlene left the city during the fall months and traveled to Spring Lake for lunch and a walk on the beach.

In the past few weeks, Arlene had been feeling quite tired. She believed the fatigue had started the weekend that she and Michael babysat Mary's four boys. Yesterday while having her roots done at the local salon on East 53rd Street, she had a bit of a fainting spell, but realized she was dehydrated. It was very arid in the shop due to the hair dryers. A small bottle of water quenched her thirst, and she revived quickly.

The Jersey Shore was part and parcel of their youth, and for many summers the family had spent weeks at a clip on Long Beach Island. Michael loved the company of the children and especially loved the hours of fishing with the grandchildren and the nightly visits to the boardwalk for ice cream and kiddie rides. Until recently, Michael could not afford extended times away from his surgical practice but arranged his schedule so that he had more than an occasional three-day weekend during the summer months. The last few years had been especially fulfilling as he had the opportunity to spend more time with his children and grandchildren at the beach.

The only member of the clan who never showed up was Michael Jr., who lived in San Francisco and had never had a close relationship with his father. It bothered Michael, but over the years he had accepted the distance and understood that despite the lack of closeness, his son was firmly loved and accepted by his wife and other siblings. He was aware that his son Gene, a Southwest pilot, had arranged flights for his sisters and brothers to spend time with Michael Jr. on his most recent birthday. Mary frequently called her brother and had him visit without mentioning it to her father.

Driving over the George Washington Bridge, he and Arlene were struck by the physical beauty of the city on this majestic fall day. The sun was glistening off the construction site of the new World Trade Center, and the sky was without a cloud. Traffic was unusually light, and they chatted about a host of hopes and dreams on their way to Spring Lake. Arriving at their destination, they were greeted by Antoine, who graciously ushered them to their favorite table overlooking the ocean. The Golden Lantern restaurant was close to the beach, and their custom was to have lunch and then kick off their shoes and walk for miles along the coast.

Scanning the menu, Arlene jokingly noted, "The last thing that I need is another wonderful meal. It took me longer than usual today to find an outfit that actually fits. I have lost the same twenty pounds for the last thirty years, but they always make their way back. Oh, the hell with it. I don't even know why I look I always get the crab sandwich and the clam chowder." As they ordered, Arlene appeared to have a hacking cough attack but waved it off as something going down the wrong pipe. The rest of the meal was uneventful, and they chided each other as they scanned the dessert menu. Arlene, ever the chocolate maven, decided on the seven-layer cake, and though he teased her, Michael was thrilled because he would have the opportunity to share the dessert.

As the cake appeared with two cups of decaf, Michael held Arlene's hand and said: "Hope you have the generosity of spirit to leave me a few bites." Arlene laughed and passed a fork to Michael. She had begun to eat the delicacy when suddenly she turned ashen. She gripped her side and felt excruciating pain. She attempted to stand but almost fell as she pushed her chair away from the table. Michael was stunned by this turn of events. "Arlene, what is happening?" he asked. The pain had somewhat lessened, and she sat back down.

"I don't know, Michael, but I had a severe pain in my side."

"Are you okay now?" he inquired.

"Yes, I am fine," she said, and trying to make light of the situation continued, "I was more frightened that you would eat the entire cake while I was distracted."

Ever the physician, Michael pressed for information about the pain and surmised that Arlene was experiencing a kidney stone attack. The rest of the meal was without incident, and yet Arlene suggested that they pass on their traditional post-lunch walk on the beach. Michael agreed but strongly suggested that she make an appointment to see their internist and his close friend Doctor Vic De Fino. "It is probably nothing," he said, "but you haven't had a physical in a while, and I would feel better if Vic examined you."

The mood on the ride home was quite different than on the way to the shore. Michael had an uneasy feeling about what had occurred. When they reached Manhattan, he excused himself with the pretense that he was going downstairs to see if any packages had arrived. In fact, he called Vic De Fino.

"Michael, what a pleasant surprise. Are you in Spring Lake?"

"No, I am back in Manhattan. I know that you have a tough teaching schedule on Friday, but could you find some time to see Arlene?"

There was a pause on the line, and Vic asked: "Is she alright?"

"It is probably nothing, but something happened at lunch that alarmed me. I just want to check it out."

Vic scanned his cell phone for Friday's schedule and said, "I could see her at my office around four-thirty."

Michael paused. "I will be teaching. Is there any other time?"

Vic teased Michael and said, "It would be best if I saw her alone the first time. I will call you after."

"Okay. This may be much ado about nothing, but I want to stay on top of this."

Vic said, "You are probably right, but I don't think I have seen her for over nine months. It is reasonable to do a complete physical. I will call you after I see her."

"Thanks, Vic, talk to you on Friday."

Arlene's blood tests were confusing, and it was difficult to make a definitive diagnosis. However, the ultrasound indicated there were small masses in the pelvic and lung areas. It was imperative to perform a series of procedures and a biopsy to define whether this indicated cancer, which stage, if any, and whether it had metastasized. When Michael and Arlene showed up at Vic De Fino's office, he was in the waiting area and ushered them into a room away from other patients. Michael realized that this attempt at privacy did not augur well. Vic sat close to both of them and presented the results.

As he finished, Arlene said, "Vic, do I have cancer?"

Vic sighed and answered, "We don't know that yet. I need you to spend an overnight in the hospital. I have contacted Doctor Clive, who is the finest gastroenterologist in the area, to perform the procedure, and we will biopsy the small masses. All of this will be performed under anesthesia." Michael had a thousand questions but deferred them so as to not share his panic with Arlene. He trusted Vic and knew of Doctor Clive's outstanding reputation.

The next day Michael escorted Arlene to the hospital. Immediately upon entry, they were treated as dignitaries. Michael was so loved and respected that everyone in the surgical area pledged to do everything in their power to make the day a seamless success. Arlene was given a private room on the eighth floor with a view of the East River. After she was prepared for the procedures, Michael hugged and kissed her, and then found his way to Vic De Fino's office. The next day and a half was longer than he could imagine; Arlene handled the waiting period better than him.

The day after the tests came back, Vic De Fino opened the folder with the results and almost wept. It was never easy for him to view such dooming indicators, but it was beyond painful to discover that someone he loved had stage 4 cancer. The results from Arlene's tests, as well as the procedure performed by Doctor Clive, left little doubt that Arlene had adenocarcinoma, and apparently, the primary tumor in her esophagus had metastasized and spread to other organs.

Vic could find little hope in the results. In an hour Arlene and Michael were to be in his office, and though he often had the painful task of giving bad news to patients, this was emotionally excruciating. Not only was Michael one of his closest friends and colleagues, but Arlene was one of the most special persons he had been privileged to know.

Exactly at ten minutes before nine, Arlene and Michael arrived and were escorted into Vic's office. It was apparent from Vic's demeanor that the news was not positive. Michael immediately launched to a series of specific questions, but before Vic could answer, Arlene spoke. "Vic, I have been around medicine for a good part of my life, and I need to have you answer one question. Do I have cancer?"

Vic looked down at his hands but knew he could not avoid answering. "I'm afraid you do, Arlene." Michael began to ask for the specific results of the tests, and what the experts had recommended as a treatment protocol.

Although stunned, Arlene placed her hand on Michael's and said, "I know I will be in good hands, so let's begin to explore where we go from here." Both Michael and Vic, who were distraught, could not get over the grace and courage with which Arlene handled the news. For the next hour, they discussed treatments. Doctor Clive had recommended immediate surgery in order to contain the spread and hopefully enhance her quality of life.

40

OCTOBER 2014

No Magic Bullet

ICHAEL HAD SPENT ENDLESS HOURS GOING over every alternative therapy for Arlene's cancer. There was no getting around that, statistically, she had less than a ten percent chance to survive a year. The cancer had progressed to many vital organs, and the chemotherapy, which had almost killed her, had produced no significant change. Obsessed would have been too weak a word to describe Michael's state of mind as he explored, for endless hours and days, every novel and innovative treatment he could find. The irony was, as a physician, he would have dismissed out of hand some of these holistic remedies, but this was the most special person in his life, and he would leave no stone unturned. His consult with oncologist Jim Kuhn one afternoon left him depressed, and without warning, after Jim left, he began to sob. Quickly trying to gain control, he decided to go home early, and spend the rest of the day with Arlene.

Arlene entered the bathroom and began to run the hot water for her bath. As she undressed, she glanced at the mirror and barely recognized herself. She had radiation marks on her body and had lost considerable weight. Much of her beautiful hair had vanished. She poured her favorite bubble bath into the tub and slowly entered the warm water. As she slowly glided into the foam, she was caressed by the warm water and for a fleeting second had no concerns or pain. The heroic attempts to at least slow down the cancer had all failed. She had pondered her choices for weeks and concluded that she no longer would participate in any new therapy. No more endless hours of nausea and bowel discomfort.

Having made this decision, Arlene spent almost all of her day reading and corresponding with her many friends across the country. She and Michael had been guarded about her prognosis with the children and close friends, but now she decided it was time to make the children aware of the seriousness of her condition. Michael entered the bedroom and found her nodding off on the chaise lounge. He gently kissed her forehead, and she responded by placing her arms around his neck.

"You are home early."

"I wanted to have an early intimate dinner with my best gal."

"Oh really, what time will she be here?" she teased.

"She arrived over forty years ago, and I had the good sense to keep her."

"Wow, you are the romantic today."

"Do you feel up to eating?"

"I think I could handle one of your omelets."

"Omelets? How can you call my wonderful frittatas omelets? I will forgive you this one time."

Arlene laughed as Michael made his way to the kitchen. He donned an apron that the grandchildren had given him for Father's Day. Opening the refrigerator, he asked Arlene whether she wanted two or three eggs.

"I think you had better go with two. I fill up rather quickly."

As Michael whisked the eggs and poured a slight bit of milk into the batter, Arlene moved to the dining room table, grabbed a pillow and adjusted it behind her back. Michael lit the candles and poured a glass of red wine for Arlene.

"I have been saving this wine for a special occasion. I would like to toast the love of my life."

They clinked glasses, and slowly Arlene began to eat her dinner. Michael cleared the table and Arlene went to the library and sat on the chaise lounge.

"Do the dishes later," she said, beckoning Michael to come and share her seat. "Michael, I have given things a lot of thought, and I want to discuss some issues with you." Michael dreaded what was to follow.

"I no longer have any illusions about the fact that I am going to die. I don't want any more chemotherapy or other radical treatments. I understand the reality, and I want what little time I have to be quality time." Michael, though silent, completely understood her decision. However, the finality of it tore his heart to shreds. "The second issue is I want everyone here for Thanksgiving, and that includes Michael Jr. It is time to tell all of the children what we both know. I think Mary is aware, but they all need to hear it from us. I would appreciate it if you personally invited everyone. Some of the children can stay here, and we can rent some rooms for the overflow." Michael gently caressed her hair and fought back tears. The love of his life was going to die shortly, and there wasn't a damn thing he could do to stop it. Arlene took a sip of water and continued, "I need you to repair your relationship with Michael Jr."

Michael paused, "I would love to, but I don't think he wants any part of me."

Momentarily irritated, Arlene said, "That's nonsense; he needs you. Let's talk about the elephant in the room. Our son is gay. That is no reason not to love him."

"I do love him but cannot accept his lifestyle."

"The hell with his lifestyle; love him for who he is."

Michael could see that Arlene was irritated but chose to be frank, "If I accept his being gay, I would feel like a hypocrite."

"Michael, there is no hypocrisy in loving him. He is our cherished son, and he needs to be loved totally by you. Promise me that you will try and reconcile."

Michael nodded to show that he would try.

Arlene smiled and said, "We are coming to the final two requests from my bucket list. I have always wanted to see the Cliffs of Moher, so right after Thanksgiving, I want to go to Ireland."

Michael knew that Vic De Fino and Arlene's oncologist would think that was madness, but he agreed. He would do whatever it took to make her last days happy.

"The last item may be the most difficult for you, but it is vital for me. After my death, I know you will be sad, but please go on with your life. It would be easier for me to die if I knew that the road ahead would still have meaning for you."

This request was one he could not guarantee, but, beginning to weep, he embraced her and in a barely audible voice said, "I will try."

41

NOVEMBER 2014

Thanksgiving

THANKSGIVING WAS ALL THAT ARLENE HOPED that it would be. There was a period of overt sadness and tears when Arlene confided to the family that her illness was terminal. However, the family rose to the occasion, and the next four days were days filled with laughter and love. Michael Junior and his father behaved admirably around Arlene, and she held the false impression that many issues had been resolved. In fact, nothing had changed, and after the holiday, they went back to their prior relationship.

As wonderful as the family gathering had been, it taxed Arlene both mentally and physically. She had become incredibly frail but was determined to make the trip to Ireland. Despite the protests of her oncologist as well as Vic De Fino, Arlene and Michael decided that this was so important to her that nothing should stop them from seeing the Cliffs of Moher. As Michael prepared for the trip, there was a twinge of regret. He thought they should have made this trip years ago when things would have been much easier for her. They had traveled to many national conferences and had visited Rome once but never found the right time to visit Ireland. Well, now was the time. Michael spent hours preparing for the trip. With his usual bent towards research, he gathered every conceivable piece of information about Irish pubs, restaurants, and lodging. This had to be, within the confines of her physical ability, a fabulous trip.

Arlene refused to be escorted to Kennedy Airport in an ambulance, so a stretch limo was hired. Upon arrival, after going through security, they were welcomed by Air Lingus personnel and escorted to the VIP lounge. Arlene quipped, "I am being treated as if I am the Queen of England."

Michael smiled and said, "Be careful with those British references, my dear, they may not go over well with the Irish." Once on board in the first-class cabin, Michael contacted the flight attendants and told them, "I am a physician, and my wife has been recently ill. She will be taking sleeping pills and will not require any food or drink during the flight. We are on our way to see the Cliffs of Moher, and complete rest is essential before we arrive."

Fortunately, the flight was without turbulence, and Arlene slept until the cabin lights went on for breakfast. She could have some tea, biscuits and fruit. Her level of excitement was boundless. Wearing a heavy Irish knit sweater and a beautiful green scarf, she could have been the poster woman for the Irish tourist board. There was a wheelchair waiting for them at Shannon Airport, and after going through customs, they saw a giant of a man holding a sign reading: "Welcome Dr. and Mrs. McNally." Daniel Finnerty came to them and said in a glorious brogue, "Welcome to the land of your heritage. I will be your driver and guide for the next four days."

42

Damn Hard-Boiled Eggs

F IT WEREN'T FOR THOSE DAMNED hard-boiled eggs, I wouldn't be in this predicament." Sal was packing two suitcases as he prepared to leave for Fox Run, the assisted living place that had been selected by his children. In the last two months, on three occasions he had completely forgotten that he had put hard-boiled eggs on the stove. The first two incidents were minor, but the last one did him in. Having placed the eggs on the stove, he went out to get a newspaper. Sitting blissfully in Starbucks, he heard the sirens but thought little about them. By the time he returned home, the pot had exploded, and much of his condo was engulfed in flames. This was the last straw for the condo board. Though they loved Sal, they could no longer tolerate the danger that his behavior presented to the rest of the residents. The president of the condo board had notified Sal's son Jonathan that it was time for an intervention.

Momentarily placing the suitcases near the door, he opened the desk in the hallway and started to remove the contents. In the top drawer was a box containing many cards that had been sent by him and the children through the years to his wife. He had been spared going through Helen's clothing because his daughter had volunteered to take on the task, but touching mementos that she treasured caused a pain that seemed to elevate his grief. One graying item in the box caught his eye, and he took it out and momentarily smiled. It was a menu from The Greek Taverna, the restaurant where they had gone out on their first date. On the back, in her inimitable handwriting, were the words, "The night I fell in love."

He could still see her that night at the Greek Taverna and despite his pain smiled at how ridiculous his attempts at Greek dancing were. He could recall her marvelous laugh. She was one of those rare persons that cared about you and what you had to say. She was in the last year of her residency at USF. Little did he know that night that they would spend the next forty years together.

At first glance, it appeared they had nothing in common. She was from some Podunk town in upstate New York, and he had lived his life mostly in the New York City vicinity. She was attired beautifully, design and fashion at the forefront. He smiled at the thought of how he was dressed at their first meeting. He had bell-bottomed purple pants that, if caught by a stiff wind, would have carried him out to sea. His leather belt was so wide it could have held up the Brooklyn Bridge. His psychedelic shirt was only outdone by his platform shoes. She was coiffed perfectly, with not a hair out of place, while he had a red beard and hair to the middle of his back. There was no way that these two would wind up together, but they did.

She was the love of his life, and he could not fathom going on without her. They had been more than husband and wife and had shared so many happy and silly moments together. He was no stranger to death, but he had lived with the illusion that he would go first and be spared this most intense grief. Not in his wildest fears did he imagine that overnight she would be gone. She was physically absent and yet ever present, and the wound opened each day with a fleeting memory, a place, song, or the sight of someone they both knew. He kept her voice on his cellphone and frequently called her number.

Jonathan, an NBC sports broadcaster, had just returned from doing interviews before the All-Star basketball game, which was to be held in New York. Living in New Jersey now, he was regularly able to stop in New York to see his father. He had noticed at Thanksgiving that there were some physical changes occurring in his dad, and he worried that since his mother's death the changes were becoming more significant. It was difficult for Jonathan, as with all children, to watch his father age because Sal had always been such a vibrant, dynamic force in his life. As recently as two weeks ago, he had discussed the situation with his sister but had no immediate thoughts that the hard-boiled egg incident was not an isolated event. After significant conversations, the siblings decided to spend some time with their father and try to convince him to move toward a more appropriate setting.

Sal was aware that the hard-boiled egg incident was merely the tip of the iceberg. Everyone elderly experiences some 'senior moments,' but lately they were more frequent and at times confusing. Life had not been the same since Helen died, and he blamed a lot of his difficulties on the grief process. There was no way, under any circumstances, that his life would not been dramatically changed by her loss. It was not only the fact that she died, but that it happened so abruptly.

Now, since her death, the words kept going over and over in his mind as if there were a hydraulic drill piercing his brain. "Helen is dead. Helen is dead."

He kept imagining that the whole situation was a dream and that Helen would be coming for dinner soon. The reality was he was alone, and there was no substitute that could replace the wondrous experiences and love that he had shared for over forty years.

There was a knock at the door. Slowly Sal closed the suitcase, walked down the corridor and turned the doorknob. His son Jonathan was standing there sheepishly. "Hi, Dad," Jonathan said as he embraced him in their usual fashion. Salvatore squeezed him harder than usual and felt the glimmer of a tear in his eye.

"I guess it's time to say goodbye to this place where I have lived with your mother for over twenty years."

Jonathan shrugged and said, "I know it must be tough, Dad, but I think that the place you're going is quite terrific. I remember Mom at one point saying that in the future she thought Fox Run might be an appropriate place for both of you to spend your golden years."

"Golden years?" Sal snorted. "Jonathan, you can do better than that. What the hell is so golden about the fact that I'm leaving a place I love, where I spent years with your mother, to go to some old-age farm where my primary responsibility will be to wait for the Grim Reaper?"

Those words struck Jonathan, and he was somewhat at a loss for a reply. What could he say? What would make a difference at this moment? He thought perhaps he just should keep silent. He picked up two of the suitcases and said, "The moving van will be here tomorrow to take the rest of the furniture and art work that will go to Fox Run. The remainder will be kept at my home, and you can decide later what pieces should be brought to Fox Run. Marisa will be here to make sure it all goes well."

Closing the door, Sal turned the key and started toward the elevator, but wistfully turned once more to gaze at the home he was leaving forever. He momentarily thought he should change his mind and stay in his condo. Certainly, there had been senior moments, but he was not senile. Why should he go to a place that was not of his choosing? These thoughts were not powerful enough to change the plans, so he reluctantly agreed to go to assisted living.

The ride to Fox Run was only about twenty minutes, but the traffic was extremely heavy. The conversation between Jonathan and Sal seemed stifled and almost unnatural. They had always had a very warm, loving and open relationship, and Jonathan sensed his father's pain and anxiety. With his mother dead, his father was being stripped of all that was known and natural. The twisted look on his father's face mirrored the anguish of his soul.

The trees were starting to change on both sides of the Parkway and the colors of green, orange and red were beautiful, but they paid scant attention to the vista. The constant bumper-to-bumper traffic finally opened, and Jonathan exited the Parkway. The tension grew as they neared Fox Run. Salvatore remained silent. Looking at his grieving father, Jonathan remembered that he was always the life of the party.

A friend of his once commented: "Your mother is the heart of the party while your father is the one that makes the house filled with laughter." Jonathan always remembered his home as filled with chatter and laughter. A specific incident stood out in his mind. One fourth of July, when he and Marisa were probably about ten and eleven, Sal led a parade from their house on Greenway Avenue around the block. He kept playing on his clarinet "When the Saints Go Marching In" over and over. When he started, there were only the children and Helen, but when he looped around, thirty neighborhood children and had joined the joyous festivities. Growing up, he believed that no matter what challenges he might face in life, there would be a way to handle it. All that seemed so distant and remote, and he wished he could turn back the clock. He felt chagrined that he was consigning his father to a place where the older man did not want to go. Both he and Marisa had offered to have him move in with them, but Sal dismissed the offers out of hand. He appreciated their generosity but said that there would be no way that he would inflict that kind of responsibility on them.

They made a left turn off the main road, passing the large sculpted gate at the entrance of Fox Run, and cruised down the road to the main entrance. Jonathan heard Sal's sigh as his father closed his eyes. Parking in front of the entrance, Jonathan went to the trunk to remove the two suitcases and gently placed them on the curb.

"Dad, wait here," he said, "I'm going to park the car and then we can walk in together."

Sal opened the car door, gingerly stepped outside, and glanced at the lovely manicured grounds. *Well, I guess this is better than prison. Somehow, I thought I would escape this. But here I am: from happiness with a loving wife to a sanctuary, merely marking time.*

Jonathan quickly picked up to suitcases, and they entered the front door of Fox Run. In the vestibule, Sal barely noticed the sculpted plaster ceilings and the large crown moldings that held beautiful Hudson River paintings. The antique Chinese vases with flowing plants near the center of the office would have caught Sal's eye in the past, but now all of it seemed sterile and unappealing.

Almost instantly, Sal and Jonathan were met by the directress, Mrs. Blanche Boyer. "Well, good morning," she said. "I gather this is Doctor. Salvatore La Greca. Welcome, Doctor. I presume that you are his son Jonathan. Again, welcome. Please follow me to my office and we can chat about some of the benefits of living at Fox Run."

Sal turned to Jonathan, saying: "You don't have to stay, Jonathan. I know you have things to do. Say hello to Amy and Erica."

"Okay, Dad," Jonathan replied. "If you need anything at all, just let me know. We are not that far away, and I know this weekend both Amy and Erica would love to come down. Maybe we could go out to lunch."

With that, the two men embraced. Jonathan turned and walked to the door, and again Salvatore felt that he was all alone.

As she escorted him through the place, Mrs. Boyer made rapid conversation, "Well, let's start with the preliminary. What would you like me to call you? Doctor, Salvatore, Sal, what is your preference?"

In his grieving state, Sal was frustrated with this woman who was trying to get him to speak. "It would be fine if you called me Sal," he replied.

"Okay, then, Sal it is!" she said, handing him an envelope. "This is a packet of information regarding most of the things that you will need to know about living in Fox Run. We hope this place offers ample opportunity for you to maintain the lifestyle to which you have become accustomed in your home. We request that some of your furniture and artwork or whatever is most appropriate be placed in your condo so that you will feel more comfortable."

Sal, only half paying attention, muttered, "Fine. I will read this later, whenever I get to my room."

The directress continued with her machine-gun speech, "Alright. In the meantime, it might be beneficial for me just to give you a quick tour of the facility and show you some of the amenities that we hope that you will be able to utilize during your stay here."

That last part hit Sal like a ton of bricks. "Your stay here" sounded like a euphemism for some sort of confinement. Sal knew he was being petty, but somehow this whole thing was rubbing him the wrong way.

After handing him his packet of information, Mrs. Boyer stood and said, "Let's start with the music room." Opening the door, she said: "Here you will find all sorts of CDs. We have a piano, and fortunately, three residents are accomplished pianists, and often we have sing-alongs!" Salvatore rolled his eyes at the thought of singing show tunes with a group of tone-deaf old people.

"Next is our arts and crafts room. Here we have all sorts of opportunities for people to use their skills and talents." Sal glanced at the five souls busy making Christmas ornaments or stringing beads. *The day I wind up in this damn room will be the day the world ends.*

The tour continued for the next twenty minutes, but Sal heard barely any of it. It was a rare opportunity to be grateful for his poor hearing. Finally, the tour ended, and he was shown to his room. Closing the door, he lay on the bed. *I haven't been this anxious since that first day at Darlington seminary.*

43

2014

The Old Sod

THE LIMESTONE LODGE WAS A LOVELY inn near the town of Doolin, eight kilometers from the Cliffs of Moher. The driver, Mr. Finnerty—or Big Fin, as he preferred to be called—suggested that they rest for a wee bit, and then he would pick them up and drive them to a pub for lunch in the quaint town of Doolin. He proudly boasted that Doolin was the center of Irish music, and they were fortunate because Sean Doyle, the famous singer and tin whistle player, was in town for a three-day stint at Gus O'Connor's pub. He also suggested that they go to the Cliffs in the morning because the forecast was more favorable.

The accommodations were excellent at the Limestone Lodge, and Arlene was thrilled that despite the overcast day with drizzling rain, she could see the Cliffs of Moher from their room.

After a shower and a short nap, she informed Michael that she was "raring" to go to Doolin. Fortunately, Ireland had a non-smoking rule, so there would be no difficulty with her breathing at the pub. She had a portable oxygen canister but preferred not to use it unless it was necessary. The driver, who had been waiting for hours in the lobby, immediately responded to their phone call and, holding an umbrella over Arlene's head, gently assisted her into the back seat. The ride to Doolin was rather harrowing due to the narrow lanes, but nothing could upset Arlene because she was in the land of her family, and this was a dream come true. Michael, on the other hand, grimaced every time another car coming the other way at great speed barely squeezed by them.

Gus O'Conner's pub was a throwback to the eighteenth century. The interior of the pub was unique and very traditional. Pitch pine walls taken from St. Aidan's monastery had been recrafted and used throughout the bar. In the middle of the pub, there was a little snug which provided separate seating for women in the old days.

Arlene smiled, inhaled the smells, and embraced the character and visuals of a place frozen in time. She loved the walls graced with some of Ireland's historical characters and heroes. If God were to create a pub, Gus O'Connor's would be the model. The menu was filled with all sorts of fish and bangers. Unlike in the States, the beer was at best lukewarm, but even that did not take way the joy of the McNally's lunch. Arlene passed on the beer, instead choosing a cup of Irish coffee. The bonus of the lunch was that Sean Doyle and his three friends were practicing for opening night, and the sounds of the tin whistle and song filled the pub. When Doyle played "Whiskey in the Jar," the place erupted in spontaneous applause. He followed by singing "Galway Gal," and the silence in the pub during the song made it truly an emotional experience. It was a magical afternoon for the McNally's.

Arlene had loved her first day in Ireland, and fortunately, she was relatively pain-free and slept soundly. The next day had been as forecast, windy but clear, and the vistas from the breakfast room were breathtaking. Michael was more apprehensive about today than yesterday. His research beforehand alerted him to the reality that the Cliff excursion would present challenges for Arlene. Finishing his breakfast, he urged Arlene to stay and soak up the views for the next fifteen minutes. He went to the lobby and was preparing to contact Fin by phone when he spotted him having coffee and reading a newspaper.

"Good morning, Doctor. I believe we have the perfect day to see the cliffs. I would advise you and Mrs. McNally to put on every piece of warm clothing because it can be quite chilly at this time of the year." Michael thanked him for the advice and said: "Fin, my wife is seriously ill. It has been her dream to see the Cliffs, but I am worried that it may not be possible because she is limited as far as walking."

Fin listened intently and responded, "Doctor, my mother died last year from cancer, and she loved this area. A week before she died, I took her to her favorite spot and carried her up the steps so that she could see the full view. That memory fills my heart on the days I most miss her. It will be my honor to make sure it works perfectly for your wife." Michael was so touched by this response that he could not speak and warmly shook Fin's hand.

Bundled up with blankets, Arlene and Michael were captivated by Fin's running commentary on the history of the area. The road to the Cliffs of Moher was narrow and very scary with sharp switchbacks. It was known as the wild Atlantic Way. The ride, though somewhat hazardous, was breathtakingly beautiful. Michael spent more time looking at Arlene's beaming face than the phenomenal views. Patches of treeless rock mountains and herds of cows and sheep appeared around each bend in the road. Arlene said to Michael, "It is too bad there is not a place to park because these scenes would make wonderful photos."

Fin turned and offered, "Mrs. McNally, there will be great places for photos once we reach the Cliffs."

"Thanks, Fin, but please call us Michael and Arlene."

Once they arrived at the parking lot, Fin assembled the wheelchair and handled Arlene a thermos. Wrapping the blanket around her, he winked and said, "The thermos is filled with holy water which turns into Bailey's whiskey once you say a silent prayer. You can use a sip or two to warm you."

Walking from the parking lot to the cliffs, they saw a beautiful green field with paths in several directions, and cows grazing in the fields right up to the paths along the edge of the cliffs. There were steps that went to the left or right, and Fin chose to take the stairs to the right that climbed up to the O'Brien Castle. Fin locked the wheelchair, lifted Arlene into his arms and said, "This is going to be a long climb, but you and I are going to the top." Michael was exceptionally nervous about the hike and very focused on climbing the steps. When he turned around, his mouth dropped. He had never, ever, seen such an incredible sight.

The beauty was beyond imagination, but he was also frightened when he realized that the ocean lay seven hundred feet below. There was very little space between them and the edge, just a low stonewall. On the opposite side, which was even higher, there was nothing along the path, just the edge. Once they reached the top, Arlene spent a very long time taking photos. Below there was a smaller rock formation covered in grass. This was Goat Island, home of hundreds of puffins. The ocean was quiet, despite the winds, and they were able to see hundreds of beautiful white birds perched on the edges of the rocks. They looked like little white specks from so far above.

Along the paths there were many people playing instruments: flutes, accordions, and harmonicas. Within a few minutes, they heard two different renditions of "Danny Boy" and "When Irish Eyes Are Smiling," adding to their total experience.

When they returned to the parking lot, Arlene kissed Fin on the cheek and said, "You will never understand what this day means to me." Fin smiled and eased her into the wheelchair. Arlene had no way of knowing that for Fin it was like a beautiful day with his mother.

The time in Ireland had been exhilarating for Arlene but had considerably drained her energy. Over the last few months, she had been having difficulty walking and often experienced a lot of pain. Michael had insisted that the day after the venture to the Cliffs of Moher, she sleep in and have a late breakfast. Arlene followed Michael's advice but in the afternoon pleaded with him to call Fin and arrange for lunch and a brief shopping excursion in Doolin. On the way to town, she asked Fin if there was a shop in town that specialized in Irish wristwatches. Fin immediately responded that McCrory's, a jewelry shop near Gus O'Connor's Pub, had an exquisite assortment of watches, but the prices were quite high. "While you are at lunch," he said, "I will walk to the shop, and make certain that they will be open after you finish your lunch."

Gus O'Connor's Pub was crowded, but apparently, Fin had some pull with the owner because, on arrival, Arlene and Michael were seated at a table with a reserved sign on it. Arlene's appetite had almost completely vanished, but she managed to eat some Irish soda bread and half a bowl of soup. As before, she nursed a glass of Bailey's whiskey and ate a bit of Michael's chocolate cake.

After lunch, Fin met them at the front door and drove the two blocks to McCrory's Jewelry Store. As Arlene exited the car, Fin asked if she wanted to ride in the wheelchair, but she said, "I would prefer to walk because the handsome man next to me has been flirting and wishes to walk arm and arm with me."

Michael said, "You have inherited the Irish Blarney, and by the way, Fin, it is she who is flirting with me."

Fin loved the playful banter and could only imagine how painful her death would be for Michael.

Donald McCrory, the proprietor, was pleased to show Arlene a bevy of top-of-the-line Irish watches. He insisted that they were finer than any timepiece that could be found in Switzerland. "They have better marketing, but our watches overall are finer and less expensive."

Michael looked over her shoulder and whispered in her ear, "I hope, my dear, that you are not going to buy me another watch. I already have four that you have bought me through the years."

Arlene asked for a chair to be brought to the viewing area and said to Michael as she sat, "You are such a vain creature. What makes you think that this watch is for you? Perhaps it is for my secret admirer. Now be on your way and go to the front of the shop." Michael laughed and made his way to the large black leather chair in the side room and dutifully waited for her to finish.

Arlene chose a beautiful watch that had dials for the time, date and weather. She asked Mr. McCrory if it was possible to have the watch engraved that day because she was leaving for America the next day. Mr. McCrory was thrilled to make such an expensive sale and informed Arlene that an engraver was on the premises. She would have the watch by eight o'clock that evening. "It will be delivered at your hotel. Is it a gift?"

Arlene nodded and filled out the form for the inscription. After the purchase of the watch, they returned to the Lodge, and Michael insisted that Arlene take a nap before dinner. She agreed and after a light supper spent an hour writing postcards to the children and grandchildren.

When Michael came to bed, she was reading an Irish novel. Placing the book on the nightstand, she reached for a pouch that contained her rosary beads. As Michel sat next to her on the bed, she took his face in her hands and gently kissed both his eyes and cheek. "Michael, I am so glad you resisted all the advice from our doctors and allowed us to share this wonderful vacation. My life with you has been blessed beyond measure."

Michael returned her kiss and said, "Medical advice is valuable, my dear, but at times advice from the heart is more important."

"I agree, and I would like to end this splendid day by our saying the rosary in gratitude for all we have."

The last morning at the Limestone Lodge found Arlene and Michael having a leisurely breakfast. A messenger from McCrory's had brought the watch the prior evening, and instead of packing it, Arlene had placed it in her handbag. Michael, witnessing her putting the gift box away, requested that she give him the name of her secret admirer so he could challenge him to a duel. "We Irish do not take lightly to someone trying to carry our woman away." Arlene refused to bow to the pressure and steadfastly kept the suitor's name a secret.

At approximately 10:30, Fin knocked on their door and asked if he could place their luggage in the car. He started to carry the suitcases out when Arlene requested that he return after loading the car. Michael made a sweep of both rooms to ensure that nothing would be left behind. He helped Arlene into a lounge chair to "rest for a few minutes while I go pay the bill."

As he left, Fin re-entered the room, and Arlene asked him to pull up a chair and sit next to her. Fin had many tourists in his ten-year stint as a driver and tour guide, but none had touched his heart like the McNally's.

Arlene had a small gift box in her hand and said, "Fin, this has been one of the most special experiences of my life, and you are largely responsible for the joy we have experienced."

Fin blushed at this statement and said, "It has been my pleasure."

Arlene took the gift box and placed it in Fin's hand. "Please open the box because it is a small token of our appreciation."

Fin was overwhelmed when he opened the box. "Arlene, I don't know what to say," he murmured.

"Look on the back, Fin."

The carved inscription read: "To Fin, who fulfilled a dream for me at the Cliffs. Love, Arlene."

Fin was speechless as Arlene reached out to hug him. He was not a man who easily cried, but as he helped her into the wheelchair, a tear dropped down his cheek.

It is not uncommon for someone who is dying to muster the energy to attend some special event. In Arlene's case, it was the trip to Ireland. Almost miraculously, the trip went off without a hitch, but at the end of the trip, she was barely able to function. She slept most of the flight back to the States and had to be carried to the limo at Kennedy Airport. For eight days after, she was either in bed or on the chaise lounge. Her breathing became labored, and she required oxygen both day and night.

One McNally family custom was the trimming of the tree at the beginning of December with the grandchildren. The date was set back due to their vacation, but Arlene wished to carry on one of her favorite traditions. The children arrived on Saturday, the fifteenth of December, and the most enthusiastic of the grandchildren was five-year-old Timmy. Racing into the bedroom, he gazed at the tree, turned, and ran to his grandmother who was sitting on her chaise lounge. After hugging her, Timothy looked perplexed. "Why do you have on pajamas, Nana?"

Arlene smiled and said, "I have been sick, Timmy, so I keep them on all day."

This information seemed to agree with Timmy's experience. "When I am sick, I stay in my pajamas, and Mommy lets me stay on the sofa and watch TV. Sometimes I throw up." Arlene loved how literal children are at this age and smiled at Timmy. He continued to engage her in conversation. "What's that up your nose?" referring to her source of oxygen.

"This helps Nana breathe."

That input did not register with Timmy. He could not fathom why something up your nose helps. "Sometimes I stick my finger up my nose to get a booger, but it doesn't help me breathe." Arlene had to cover her mouth in order to repress the urge to laugh. After kissing Arlene, the rest of the children had begun to trim the tree, but Timmy was more interested in continuing his chat. Sitting beside her, he asked: "When will you get better, Nana?"

These were the difficult questions to answer for a five-year-old, and Arlene struggled with her response. "I am not sure, Timmy." With that, Timmy joined his siblings and on more than one occasion almost knocked the tree over in his attempts to place ornaments on the high branches.

After an hour, Michael came into the bedroom bearing brownies, cookies, and hot chocolate. Most of the children sat during their snack break near the tree, but Timmy apparently had some unfinished business with Nana. Chewing on a brownie, he asked: "When I get sick, I always get better. Can we give you soup to make you better?" Arlene patted his head. She did not wish to lie to him because soon she would be gone.

"Timmy, Nana may have to go away to get better."

Timmy had never gone away when he was sick, so he needed more details. "Where will you go?"

She slowly began, "I may have to go to a place like Disney World."

Timmy's face beamed. "Can I come with you?"

"No, it is only for grown-ups."

"Will Mickey Mouse be there?"

"No, but there will be angels."

Timmy thought that was cool. He turned and pointed to the top of the Christmas tree. "Like the one on top?"

"Yes, Timmy, like that one."

"Can I come and see you there?"

"No, but I will ask Grandpa to give you a big picture of me. You can put it in your room and talk to me whenever you want."

That offer seemed to satisfy Timmy. Knowing that Nana was in good hands with the angels, he was sure that she would get better.

As Timmy put on his coat, he remembered what he had in his pocket. "Nana I forgot to show you this. He held a brand-new dollar in his hand.

"Where did you get that, Timmy?"

"I got it from the tooth fairy."

"Wonderful."

"I saw the tooth fairy, Nana."

"You did? What did she look like?"

"She looked like Mommy, but she was naked." Arlene turned away and did all she could to stifle the laugh at this wonderful innocent moment.

After the children left, Arléne recounted the morning inter-action with Michael. Her appetite had vanished, but she was constantly thirsty. She thought it was time to discuss getting Michael some help with her care. Vic De Fino had suggested that they employ hospice care, but Michael had, up to now, resisted that idea. Arlene believed that his refusal hinged on the finality of her situation. Having a hospice nurse in the home would signal that the end was near. She was gentle but firm in her decision, and Michael realized that it would be beneficial for both of them.

With Christmas rapidly approaching, Arlene wished to have daily visits from family and friends. Michael felt at times that he was arranging the schedule for a dignitary because there were dozens of requests. Arlene was dying the way she had lived her life. Attentive to each visitor, she continued to have that rare gift that made everyone believe that he or she was her best friend. She was by nature and temperament a giver, and even cancer could not rob her of who she was. In the summer, realizing that her time was limited, she had earmarked all of her most prized possessions for those who held the most important portions of her heart. Each of the children and grandchildren, as well as Michael, had been given a gift and an accompanying note.

Three days before Christmas, the physical changes became more noticeable. Unlike her normal outgoing personality, she would at times withdraw from conversation and have periodic bouts of staring into space. She often would have no recollection of these times. On December twenty-second, she called out to Michael who was in the kitchen making himself a cup of coffee. She screamed, "Michael, Michael, where are you?"

He rushed to the bedroom, and when he entered, she said, "Donny and Danny were just here. I saw them, and they talked to me." Michael knew that visions and hallucinations were not unusual at this stage. He did not deny their presence. His acceptance seemed to comfort Arlene. He gently stroked her arm and listened as she repeated the story over and over again. She was having difficulty swallowing, so he pressed the control of the hospital bed and raised her head. He coated her lips, which had become rather dry, and placed a few tiny ice chips in her mouth. The pain had become constant, and she required increasing amounts of morphine.

Between long bouts of sleep, she would awake and inquire about the date. Michael had requested his friend Father Ray Aumack to visit the morning of December twenty-third to perform the anointing of the sick. Arlene was conscious and immediately recognized Father Ray. She was able to have a short conversation with him, and as he anointed her, she seemed peaceful. Outside the room, Father Ray put his hand on Michael's shoulder and asked, "How are you holding up?"

"As usual, I naively thought that knowing she was going to die would help, but it really doesn't. I don't want her to suffer, but the thought of going on without her is impossible."

"I am always available to you, Michael, and when she dies, I would be honored to be one of the concelebrants at the funeral Mass."

Michael embraced his dear friend and said: "Thanks, Father, I certainly would love to have you on the altar." Saying those words was another step in the realization that his emotional anchor was slipping away. She had been his rock through the tremendous pain and confusion of losing his mother and brothers. She had been there to comfort him years ago, when his father died, and it was hard to imagine life without her. Arlene had been his haven for love and understanding, and probably in a few days she would be gone. He walked Father Ray out and went back to the bedroom. Arlene had slipped into a deep sleep. He sat on the bed holding her hand for the next few hours.

Christmas Eve Mass had always been one of the highlights of the season for the McNally's, and even though Arlene was in and out of a coma, Michael decided to have the Pope's Christmas Eve Mass on the widescreen TV. The hospice nurse, Mary Anne Ryan, had coffee with Michael that morning, and he asked her, "How long do you think she has?" He was aware of all of the indicators of immediate death but respected the opinion of someone who dealt with this daily.

"Michael, you know it is always difficult to be precise, but seeing her this morning, I believe it may be sometime today."

They chatted for a bit, and Michael excused himself. He went to the bedroom and found the channel that was presenting the Pope's Mass. He responded to every part of the liturgy as if he were present at St. Peter's. Knowing that hearing was the last faculty to go, he spoke to Arlene during the liturgy. They were both great fans of the current Pope, and he hoped that she could hear the loving words of the Holy Father during his sermon. As the liturgy progressed, her breathing became more and more shallow. Mary Anne, also an Irish Catholic, had entered the room and crossed herself as she sat in the chair nearest to the bed.

Just before the kiss of peace, Michael heard a few sounds that he knew were indicative of the final moments. At the kiss of peace, he touched her face and placed a kiss on both cheeks. Arlene appeared to exhale, and there was a long breath and then silence. Mary Anne rose from the chair and listened for a pulse and a heartbeat. She turned to Michael and said, "She's gone." Michael collapsed in uncontrollable sobs, and Mary Anne cradled him, beginning to cry as well.

44

The Pain of Loss

Michael spent Christmas day with Mary. The delight of the children opening presents took a slight edge off the reality that Arlene had died. Michael stayed through lunch but returned to his townhouse late in the afternoon. The day was bitterly cold, and Michael was overwhelmed by the sadness that gripped him as he entered the foyer. Every item in this beautiful residence reflected the loving touch of Arlene. There was no scent of illness in the library, and Michael detected the faint smell of Arlene's perfume. The townhouse was the home that Arlene had created through the years. The paintings, furniture, drapes and even the Venetian chandelier had been selected by her.

He had been involved in some aspects of restoring the historic house, but Arlene had been in charge of planning the renovations with the architect and selecting the decor. He sat for a while in the library, which had become Arlene's bedroom, and stared at the slight indentation in the leather chaise lounge where Arlene had spent much of the last few months. The overcast sky and encroaching darkness seemed to reflect the state of his emotions. He finally hung up his overcoat and made his way to the kitchen. The phone rang. It was Mary making sure that he had arrived safely at home. She told him that she would come by early in the morning to pick up Arlene's dress, even though there would be a closed coffin. He was so grateful to Mary, who had stepped immediately into the breach and taken care of all the funeral details. Before ending the conversation, she informed him that Michael Junior would be arriving that night from San Francisco, and Tom would pick him up. He was glad that his son was staying with his sister because he did not have the energy to engage him that evening.

Michael rose early the day after Christmas and began to organize himself for the first day of viewing at the funeral parlor. He turned on his cell phone and saw that his messages were full to overflowing. It did not seem imperative that he answer any of them, so he decided to shower, dress and attempt to prepare himself mentally for the afternoon. Mary, Tom, Michael Junior and Robert arrived a little after noon. Reminded of Arlene's last request, Michael warmly greeted and hugged each of them. There was small chatter about Junior's flight and his adjustment to the time zone, but little else. Mary had brought sandwiches and suggested that it would be worthwhile to eat before leaving for the funeral home.

As Michael and the family entered the funeral parlor, conversation completely ceased. They had arrived one hour before the visitations began and took turns kneeling before Arlene's coffin. Arlene had requested a closed casket, so Mary had selected photos of her life and a video that had been shot at their home on Arlene's seventieth birthday. Michael immediately went to the kneeler in front of the casket and silently asked his Lord to give him strength to get through the next few days. He rose, gently touched the casket, and made his way to one of the front chairs. The children followed suit, and before long the endless line of visitors began to enter the funeral parlor. The noise level at one point was so loud that Mary was annoyed and considered saying something, but Michael reached out and touched her hand. He cautioned her, saying, "It is not a sign of disrespect to your mother, Mary. All these people loved her, but they have not seen each other for months, and this is just the way of their reconnecting."

The visiting line went on for over three hours. There were colleagues, friends and people whose lives had been changed by Arlene's many volunteer activities. Each of them had a story that reminded Michael what a tremendous gift Arlene had been in his life. Mary had arranged for the family to have dinner near the funeral parlor. The evening was a repetition of the afternoon, and Michael was finally home by 10:00. He listened to the messages that had been left on the phone. With each one, it was driven home that Arlene was truly dead. The mind in the grief process is overwhelmed with memories, and each call conjured up moments of their life together. The last few months had taken a heavy toll on Michael, and it was imperative that he get to bed. He knew that the next few days would be emotionally and physically draining.

The most difficult moment came on the morning the second day of Arlene's viewing when all the visitors were asked to leave. The family spent a few minutes alone in the room, saying their goodbyes. As they were escorted to the limousines, they waited for the flower car to be filled. Michael glanced out the window as Arlene's casket was placed in the hearse. Mary leaned her head on his shoulder, and suddenly there was complete silence in the limousine.

Arlene had requested that she be buried from the Jesuit church on 86th Street, Ignatius Loyola. They had visited Rome in 1977 when Michael had attended an International surgical council and it reminded her of Il Gesu, the mother church of the Jesuits in Rome. As the family entered the church, they were struck by the beautiful combination of American, European and African marbles employed throughout the entrance and sanctuary. One of the most striking parts of the church was the three- dimensional replica from the Roman Church ceiling of a fresco painted by Baciccia. As they walked up the aisle to the front pews, the organ filled the church with the beautiful notes of the Prayer of St. Francis.

Michael was holding Mary's hand as the procession from the back of the church began. They all stood as Arlene's casket was followed by the priests and altar boys. There were five priests on the altar, and all had a personal connection to the family. Father McNulty, a lifelong friend, though ill, was to be the main celebrant of the Mass. He began the liturgy by facing the congregation and saying, "We are here today to celebrate the life of our beloved Arlene. It is a day filled with tears but also joy because there has never been anyone worthier to enter the kingdom of heaven."

The readings were delivered by Mary and Tommy. After the gospel reading, Father McNulty ascended the pulpit to deliver the eulogy. Father McNulty's words were touching because he truly knew and loved Arlene. One of the heart-wrenching moments of the liturgy was the presentation of the gifts by Robert and the grandchildren. Michael was touched by the beauty of every aspect of the liturgy. The only moment of fleeting anger for Michael came at Communion time when his son Michael Junior remained in the pew and made no attempt to receive Communion. Michael couldn't believe that, even now, he would not give an inch.

Michael had asked to speak at the end of the Mass. He had written the eulogy because he was fearful that he would break down and not be able to keep his focus. He ascended the pulpit, took a deep breath, and began to read "Funeral Blues" by W. H. Auden, only changing the pronoun.

Stop all the clocks, cut off the telephone,
Prevent the dog from barking with a juicy bone,
Silence the pianos and with muffled drum
Bring out the coffin, let the mourners come.

Let airplanes circle moaning overhead
Scribbling on the sky the message 'she is Dead'.
Put crepe bows round the white necks of the public
     doves,
Let the traffic policemen wear black cotton gloves.

She was my North, my South, my East and West,
My working week and my Sunday rest,
My noon, my midnight, my talk, my song;
I thought that love would last forever: I was wrong.

The stars are not wanted now; put out every one,
Pack up the moon and dismantle the sun,
Pour away the ocean and sweep up the wood;
For nothing now can ever come to any good.

"If I were to end the eulogy with the words of that meaningful poem, it would only be half of the story, because in this shattered heart there is the strongest conviction that all who were privileged to know her have been blessed beyond measure. In the last year, despite her weakened condition, she continued to put everyone else first. Even the nurses at the hospital were part of her ongoing group to be loved and cherished. Arlene had a heart that continuously expanded and included everyone she met. Of all who knew her, I have been the most blessed because I met her in the fifth grade. She was first my friend, then my love, a marvelous wife, mother, and grandmother. The one thing that she brought to every role was her love. She had that rare gift of making everyone feel special. What consoles me at this moment is the reality that one day we will be reunited with her in heaven. For now, I pray that the memories will sustain us as the reality of her loss settles in. She was and is one of a kind, and I would like to close with a line from her favorite play, *Les Miserables*: 'To love another person is to see the face of God.' Everyone in this church has seen the face of God because of her love."

45

MAY 2015

The Deer

MICHAEL WOKE TO THE SOUND OF the wind brushing the tree branches against his bedroom window. He instinctively reached for Arlene in the bed but realized he was alone. Slowly, with great effort, he pushed himself into a sitting position and placed his tearful face into his hands. After a few stationary moments, he reached for his glasses on the bed stand and tried to focus his thoughts. Taking a deep breath, he composed himself and swung his legs out of the bed. He longed for life to be normal again.

The townhouse, which had been his haven away from the rigors and responsibilities of his surgical world, now became a place of haunting memories. Arlene's presence was everywhere, in a vase that she loved, in the color of the walls and the selection of her favorite paintings. He often sat in the library and cherished all the wonderful moments they had shared in the townhouse.

The early evening with increasing shadows of darkness engulfed him into a loneliness that often led to his leaving the building and wandering around the neighborhood for hours. He never wished to frequent the little restaurants and bistros that had been their regular stops and found that Café Nero was a preferable choice. He often would sit there until closing and then take the longest route possible home.

The following months after Arlene's death were not anything new as far as the intensity of loss, but this time it was different. One of the keys to working your way through the grieving process is to have an ally. When his mother had died, Arlene had been there. She was not only his rock but became a second mother to his young, vulnerable brothers. When Donald was killed in that horrible accident at the beach, she was the glue that held them together. When tragedy struck again, and Danny died in his arms on the basketball court, she was the one who absorbed his tears and allowed his pain and confusion to surface. She had been the safe harbor, and now when he needed her the most, she was gone. Her death stole his biggest ally to combat pain, and he was stripped naked before the endless torture of her absence.

One bright Tuesday morning, Michael decided that moping around the house feeling sorry for himself was a strategic mistake. He had given up his consulting and charitable work once Arlene was diagnosed with terminal cancer. Their last months together had been so intense, with so much love, old jokes and new conversations. Arlene had found beauty in almost every moment—a song on the radio that they had listened to in their teens, the afternoon light falling in gold rectangles on the floor, the smell of a Christmas fruitcake baked by a dear friend—and would draw his attention to each one.

Michael had found himself wondering why he had never noticed these things before, or never so profoundly. Most of all, he had the great opportunity to care for his beloved, to fulfill her wishes, big and small. It had been an exhausting period, full of dread of what was coming, but now he missed it terribly. Now there was nothing.

He had no illusions that he could dismiss his grief and instantaneously get on with his life, but he needed more social contact. Mary and the rest of his children were consistently a presence, but he needed to allow them to get back to their own lives. Scanning his cell phone list, he stopped at the number of Jim Tracy, his accountant, who lived in Nanuet. Jim had called almost weekly, inviting him out to lunch. Today he decided to join Jim in Nanuet.

The traffic was light as he crossed the George Washington Bridge and entered the Palisades Parkway. His eyesight had been failing over time, and he was having difficulty with the glaring sunshine. For the past two miles, he had frequently drifted into the speed lane. On each occasion, a blaring horn had startled him, and he made a sharp turn back to the inside lane. The next time he drifted, the move back was too radical; he hit the curb on the shoulder and lost control. He was wearing a seat belt, but the car crashed into a tree, and the impact launched him toward the door. The front windshield was shattered, and shards grazed his face and forehead. Witnesses to the accident stopped, and someone called 911. Before long he was placed in an ambulance and whisked off to Good Samaritan Hospital.

"That deer jumped right in front of me, and that is when I lost control of the car."

Michael McNally told the same story repeatedly to explain his accident. In fact, there was no deer; this fabrication was his way of saving face and avoiding the reality that his sight was severely impaired. He had hidden the recent diagnosis of macular degeneration from his family, but they were aware that his eyesight was failing. His daughter Mary had been worried about him, especially since the death of her mother. The last two years had been a drain on his vitality as he cared for Arlene through the final stages of her illness. The foundations of his world had vanished.

The injuries from the accident were not life-threatening, but because of the concussion, the attending physician decided to keep him overnight for observation. Mary arrived at the hospital. "Dad," she began, "I know that this was not your fault, but I would feel more at ease if I knew that you were safe and secure."

Michael winced because he knew where this conversation would lead. "Mary, this was pure and simply a case of a deer jumping in front of my car."

Mary knew that a frontal assault on this story would be in vain, so she attempted a roundabout incursion. "I know that, Dad, but I have had concerns about your staying at home, and though you know Tom and I would love to have you live with us, the boys would drive you crazy." Mary was referring to the four hellions, aged five to eleven, who made living in the house an adventure.

Michael smiled. "I love them, Mary, but there is no way that I will live with you. I would like to remain where I am."

Mary, tenacious as a barnacle, tried again. "Dad, you know that there are places where you could keep your independence but would have fewer responsibilities. I know that Mom had a friend who lived at Fox Run and loved it. When you are released, I would like us to explore the options." Michael knew that Mary, like his wife, was like a dog with a bone, and there was no way she was going to abandon this issue. Reluctantly, he agreed, but there was not a twinge of enthusiasm for leaving his home.

Doctor Vic De Fino had been a cherished friend and colleague of Michael's for over thirty years and was privy to the medical changes that had occurred the last year. Entering the hospital room, he greeted Mary with a kiss and hug. Turning to Michael, he said: "Well, is it true that you are going to apply for the NASCAR tour?"

Michael smiled and quipped: "You and the white horse you rode in on."

"Well, I can see that despite the poor quality of medical care here, you have survived your encounter with Bambi."

"I am sure you think that's funny, but it is a simple fact. No one could have avoided losing control of the car."

Doctor De Fino smiled, turned to Mary and said: "Mary, could you please step outside for a few minutes while I examine this curmudgeon?"

Mary picked up her sweater and said, "I will go to the cafeteria and be back in a while, Dad."

Once Mary left the room, the gloves came off. "Michael, I don't know whether there was a deer or not, but you can no longer hide the fact that you have lost significant vision. Driving a car is no longer an option. I have been silent up to now but can no longer allow it."

Michael knew this was true but felt a wave of anger toward his colleague and friend. "Are you a member of the vision police?"

"Cut the bullshit, Michael. If the roles were reversed, you would take the same stance. It is time for you to face the reality of your situation."

"Alright, but don't say anything to Mary. You and I can discuss it next week."

"Alright, good buddy. I know you are pissed at me for bringing it up, but together we will find ways to handle all of your needs."

46

OCTOBER 2105

Fox Run

THE SMELL OF BURNING LEAVES DRIFTED through Sal's window as the evergreen trees danced in the breeze. Fall was so beautiful in the luscious grounds of Fox Run—the magnificent array of colors of oak, maple and beech against blue sky created wondrous vistas. It had always been one of Sal's favorite seasons, but the few times he ventured outside to walk the grounds, he barely noticed the glorious pageant of nature.

It had been anything but a smooth transition for Sal. Unlike his entire life before, he fell into a pattern of solitude. The first four months at Fox Run, Sal had gone from a deep depression to a reluctant acceptance that this was his only choice. There was no sense fighting it; this was the end of the road. His life was over, and so he bowed to the reality that this high-priced warehouse was the last stop. He envisioned that his knees would go, followed by hip and shoulder problems and the inevitable loss of memory. Eventually, they would carry him out feet first. Initially, he ignored the available activities.

He hid out in his room and, despite the pleas of staff, took all his meals by himself. Feeling isolated by this strategy, he reluctantly started to appear at meals and joined one of the bridge clubs. Purpose and meaning had infused every decade of his life, but now he felt adrift in a current where he had no real value. The computer became an extension of his personality, and he spent endless hours on games and searches. It filled the time but was another reminder of the life that he had lost. In the past, being social came relatively easy to him, but the ever-looming grief of missing Helen wove through his daily routines. This place would be idyllic if she were here with him because she had such social grace and kindness that by now he would be immersed in a plethora of social activities. Despite her hectic schedule, Helen could juggle twenty balls in the air without one falling to the floor. Her giant heart could always make room for a new person or cause. Among the many things he missed about her was her ability to almost go into a trance watching people.

From the moment he awoke, he grappled with her absence, but today was one of those days when grief was especially strong, and he dismissed the myth that he could integrate her death into his life. Friends had ceased mentioning her, fearing that the sound of her name caused him pain. Others urged a stiff upper lip; it was time to give up the grief and move on. All of this was well-intentioned, and he realized it was more about their discomfort, so he usually graciously accepted their attempts to ease his pain.

Today was just like any other day and, had it not been for the calendar on his watch, he would have no sense that it was

Wednesday. The office had left a note under his door informing him that there would be two new residents arriving today and if he could, he was to join the committee in the late afternoon to welcome them. He mused, "The word 'residents' should be changed to 'inmates.'" This made him chuckle as he made his way to breakfast. The room was filled with canes and walkers and was an instant reminder that one by one the normal functions of life were being stripped from the residents. The smell of Lysol was overpowering in the dining area. First, it was the inability to drive, then painful joints and an array of illnesses. The only thing left was the ability to eat endless amounts of sugar in cookies and ice cream. It was in those brief moments alone that the pleasures of life were savored.

Sal tried never to sit at the same table, but this morning he committed a serious infraction of the unspoken rules. Sipping his coffee, he became aware of someone standing over his shoulder. "I believe you are sitting in my seat." Somewhat stunned, he looked up at a well-attired gentleman with a scowl on his face and a large wooden cane in his hand. The man continued grumpily, "Everyone knows that five of us sit at this table at every meal."

Sal's initial Jersey City reaction was to tell him to shove that cane up his ass and find another seat, but he realized that all activity in the dining room had come to a screeching halt. All the residents appeared to be gleefully hoping for a major verbal confrontation. Sal resisted the rude response, put his hands on his creaky knees, apologized, rose and moved to an empty table.

After breakfast, Sal picked up his mail and daily newspaper and headed for the library. Reading his *New York Times*, he heard a voice at the doorway that had the distinct accent of his birthplace. He put his paper down, turned to the sound of the voice, and with usual Jersey City sarcasm, uttered, "Oh, Jesus, look what the cat dragged in. Michael McNally!"

Standing in the doorway was someone he had not seen for over forty years: A tall, elegantly dressed man in a blue blazer with a striking Notre Dame tie. He had streaks of white in his black hair and deeply set warm, dark brown eyes. The humor masked the immediate thrill of having a buddy at Fox Run. "I hope you are only visiting," he continued. Warmly shaking the hand of his long-lost friend, he asked, "How the hell are you?"

Michael replied, "Oh, don't tell me that they let guineas live here. I thought this was a high-class place. I may have to request my deposit back. Obviously, if they checked references, you would never be allowed in."

Sal laughed, thrilled that someone from his past, someone he could relate to, would be a neighbor. "Michael," he said, "I am surprised you passed the vetting process. Do they know that you were once part of a group of degenerates who spent most of their lives hanging around on a corner? That shirt and tie may fool these hicks, but I know that deep down you were part of the infamous 'St. Al's seven.'" Sal was referring to seven attendees of St. Aloysius High School who were inseparable, and to hear it told, about twenty-five minutes from being residents in the local reform school.

Motioning for Michael to have a seat, Sal began the process of indoctrination for the new resident. Placing an imaginary list in front of him, he began to read in a very solemn tone, "If you really are one of the inmates, as a member of the friendship committee, I must welcome you to prune juice heaven. The staff will be devoted to keeping you dry and moving your bowels on a regular schedule. The focus around here is urine and excrement control. You are to suppress all sensual thoughts, and farting on the elevator is strictly forbidden. These rules are unchangeable, and violations are subject to a public stoning." Putting down the imaginary list, he asked, "When did you arrive?"

Mike took out a cigarette and realized by the apoplectic look on Sal's face that smoking was not allowed in the library. He dutifully returned the cigarette and confessed that he had never been a smoker but had lately decided that the Grim Reaper was going to get him one way or another.

"I visited last Thursday, and with a lot of arm-twisting from my children, I decided that this probably was better than most places that warehouse old farts like us. I loved where I lived in Manhattan but was highly pressured to leave."

Sal was thrilled that part of his vibrant past would be living at Fox Run. There was nothing more comforting than knowing that the culture you grew up in is known and loved by a buddy. "The way I remember you best is you and Gerry Pier pitching pennies on the corner."

Michael shook his head in disbelief. "There's a name I have not heard in a century. Do you recall your comment about him in Sister Angela's class?"

Sal laughed, and though he could vividly picture Gerry Pier in his mind, that was all. "Hell," he said, "I can't remember what I had for breakfast."

Michael chuckled and began to set the scene. "It was one of the hot Indian summer days, and, even with those God-awful Catholic uniforms the girls wore, it was obvious that Mary Ann Gallo was hugely endowed. Gerry was staring at her breasts when he was called upon to read by Sister Angela. He had an erection, so he kept his hand on it trying to hide it. Sister Angela demanded that he take his hand out of his pocket. When he did, you said, 'Hey, Gerry, you forgot a finger.' The good sister raced down the aisle and whacked you five or six times and demanded that you go to confession."

Sal was doubled up with laughter but would give no credence to the event. "I'm a good Catholic boy, and I am sure you are

342 | S.J. TAGLIARENI

making that up. Speaking of getting whipped by the good sister, has the warden shown you all of the facilities yet?"

Michael scowled at that question. "Do you mean the Directress, Mrs. Boyer? She has the personality of a shut door. Her face looks like she has a migraine and bleeding hemorrhoids. Is she always so formal and aloof?"

"Wait until you're here a while; she will really tick you off. The woman has more rules than the government. Sometimes I feel like I am in the third grade being scolded by one of the nuns. Speaking of nuns, I will never forget your Mother's Day caper. You asked Sister Michaela for permission to take a collection for the unknown soldier's mother on Mother's Day."

Incredulous that Sal remembered that, Michael smiled and replied, "Yes, I actually made one hundred and six dollars until Father Kelly found out about it. Not only did I have to give the money back, I had to make a public apology to all those I had fleeced. After I apologized, he read the riot act to me and said he would be watching me. He scared the hell out of me. I always thought that the discipline was only because it was expected, but now I think he got a kick out of it. Sal, your remembering that indicates that at least you still have all your marbles. Walking around this morning, I had the distinct impression that a lot of people are just sitting on their asses waiting for the Grim Reaper. Though I prefer those who are out of it to the breakfast crowd discussing every freaking part of their body and what ails them. The news that I was a surgeon must have been leaked out."

Sal nodded in agreement. "Yeah, I know that feeling. I never thought the main topics of conversation would center on the ills of the aging process. They should change the name of this place from Fox Run to God's Waiting Room. Some people in life check the baseball scores; we check the number of those that have made it through the night."

Mike tapped his fingers on the table, a nervous habit he didn't even notice. "How long have you been here?" he asked.

Giving a gesture as though he was a prisoner in chains, Sal responded, "Almost seven months. My kids thought I needed a safe environment. The precipitating event was one day I forgot that I had started something on the stove. I went out shopping, stopped at Starbucks and while reading the *New York Times* heard one fire engine after another whiz by on Eighth Avenue. When I returned, my condo was on fire, and there were fire trucks around the entire building. The pot exploded and did significant damage to the kitchen. The curtains caught fire, but fortunately, most of the damage was in the kitchen and foyer. Despite this, the condo board thought I was an arsonist and notified my children and me that it would be best for all if I found a new living environment. Well, that is my saga. What misdeed brought you to our hallowed haven?"

"I had an accident on the Palisades Parkway. That was the tipping point for my kids, especially my daughter Mary. While driving in broad daylight, I went off the road and hit a tree. The damn tree had the whole world to grow in, but it had to grow right in front of my grill. Pretty much totaled the car. I made up a bullshit story about a deer running in front of me, but neither the cops nor my kids bought it. The kids had been after me for a while to give up the car and find a place that I would like and be safe. I guess the old reflexes aren't what they used to be. I can't see worth a shit distance-wise."

"Were you living alone?"

There was a pause. Taking off his glasses, Mike appeared to wipe a tear from his eye. "Yeah, Arlene died last year after a long bout with cancer."

Sal recollected that Irish beauty who was also a person of exceptional kindness and warmth. "Sorry to hear that. She was the most beautiful girl in our graduating class."

"She wasn't only beautiful, Sal, she was a terrific person. How about you? I heard somewhere along the way that you were married . . ."

Sal reached into his back pocket and took a creased, slightly torn picture of Helen out of his wallet. "Helen and I were married for forty years. She was an emergency room physician. One day she was treating a patient and just keeled over. She had a brain aneurysm and died soon after." He still had difficulty talking about her death. No matter how many times he made that simple statement, it still jarred him emotionally.

Mike could feel that, like himself, Sal had not been able to move past his wife's death. "You sound as lost as me. I still find it hard to believe that she's gone. Occasionally, I find myself dialing my home number to talk to her, and then I realize again that she's dead."

"Boy, I get that. I always thought that it would be me that would die first. I was twelve years older than Helen. I guess I lived with the myth that the age difference would allow me to skip the pain of her dying first."

Starting to feel tears in his eyes, Mike tried humor to soften their grief, "My God, you don't look a day over ninety. Do you sleep in formaldehyde?"

"You always were a smart ass. If I remember correctly, you are six months older than me."

The banter about age allowed Michael an opportunity to voice one of his pet political peeves, "Don't say that out loud, Sal, or the Obama death panels will come after me. The best way to cut the cost of health care is to start eliminating the elderly. When you sign up for Medicare, they put you on the list."

Sal raised his hands toward the ceiling in a gesture of total confusion. "Oh God, I've been cursed to spend my waning days with a right-wing nut."

Michael immediately responded, "Don't tell me that you are one of those bleeding-heart liberals. It's people like you that elected this disaster. The only good thing about being a senior citizen is that I won't be around to see the damage Obama will wreak on our future. This deal with Iran is probably the biggest foreign policy giveaway ever. You had better get a prayer rug because he is so damn weak that the terrorists are taking over the entire Middle East and eventually America."

Sal was now fully engaged and immediately shot back, "Well, I have to tell you that after eight years of dipshit Bush, it's refreshing to listen to a president who can speak in complete sentences. If brains were dynamite, Bush couldn't blow the ass off a flea."

Leaning closer toward Sal, Michael came back with, "At least Bush was a citizen. Obama should be recalled because he has not proven that he is a bona fide American."

"I see that you have the full-blown insanity. Do you really believe that bullshit?"

"If it's bullshit, why can't we see the documentation that proves he is a citizen? The guy is suspect at every level, and I'm not even sure that he isn't a Muslim. Hell, check out his middle name: Hussein."

"Yeah, my middle name is Joseph, do you think that I'm the Virgin Mary's husband? Mike, these charges are the result of a fringe group that finds fault with everything he does."

Mike started to barrage Sal with data, "Yeah, just like your so-called fringe group did with Bush. Their behavior was unpatriotic and did nothing to support our troops. Obama is dismantling everything that we knew and loved as kids."

Sal had heard this over and over from members of his family so it was not a great shock, but he inquired, "Like what?"

As if a file had been opened, Mike responded, "The government is going to control everything in our lives. Christ, he owns the banks, the car companies, and he hasn't done shit about the illegal immigrants. I'll bet that he grants them all immunity. Fortunately, Donald Trump has the balls to build a wall and deport them. There is a great deal of righteous anger, and Trump has the guts to voice what a lot of us are feeling. Not only that, Obama hasn't done one thing to defeat Isis. Trump won't be a weakling like Obama."

Sal raised his eyebrows, incredulous. "Trump? Are you kidding me? The guy is a loose cannon who has alienated every group except the angry white people in our age group. The latest insanity is that he has resurrected that train wreck, Rudy Giuliani. The way to stop Trump is to give him an enema and then bury him in a shoe-box. This may come as a shock to you, Mike, but your grandparents didn't come here from Iowa; they came from Ireland."

Seeing a real opening to control the debate, Mike raised his voice, "They came as legal immigrants who followed all the rules. They did not sneak in and soak up all the benefits. My family worked their asses off and devoted themselves to making a better life for their children. In just two generations, they changed the course of history in this country. I, as a physician, am a living example of what love and devotion to country can achieve. The liberal bullshit is giveaway city. Carter, Clinton, Gore, and now Obama are willing to give away the store if they can steal some votes. I will cut Clinton some slack; he was only interested in getting laid. The new nut Bernie Sanders is an avowed Communist and looks like the character from the Muppets. Everything will be free soon, and poor bastards like you and I will have to give till it hurts. When the hell did you think that an avowed Communist would run for the presidency? And then there is the Dragon Lady herself. I would sooner trust the words of a serial killer."

Sal waved off the barrage, responding, "Yeah, the hypocrites that espouse a morality that is purist in theory but garbage in practice. The crowd that was so outraged by Clinton were balling everything that moved. Your current presidential line-up, hangers-on and moral majority supporters are stacked with candidates who have been married a bunch of times and had more affairs than Clinton. They don't believe in science and think every woman should be pregnant and silent. What about Cruz? Talk about a scary guy. A couple of weeks ago, he said there is no place in America for atheists and gays. Some of the things that come out of those presidential debates sound as though they come from people who have no understanding of our heritage. Trump is my favorite, though; he just makes so-called facts up. Is this what I have to look forward to every day: the parrot version of Beck, Limbaugh and Hannity?'"

"Not as badly as those jerks on MSNBC. The so-called Reverend Al Sharpton and Rachel Maddow defend the indefensible like the riots in Ferguson and Baltimore. They act like every cop has a hunting license to shoot innocent civilians."

The confrontation had now become very heated. Sal sought to defuse the situation. "I think that if we continue this partisan stuff, we are both going to have elevated blood pressure. I seriously doubt that either one of us is going to have an aha moment and move to the other side. Obviously, we both feel passionately about these political issues; maybe we need to discuss other things. Hell, I haven't seen you in years, and I don't want this to be a contentious relationship. We were great friends in school, when we hung around on the corner. I would rather spend time on what we have in common, not what separates us."

Sitting down and wiping the perspiration from his brow, Michael agreed. "I think you're right; I am getting a little hot under the collar. If you agree to put your *New York Times* under the table, I will agree to be civil."

"I'll make you a deal; I'll never read the *New York Times* in your presence if you agree never to turn on Fox News in the game room."

"Can I read Sean Hannity's book out loud?"

"You do, and I'll have Hillary Clinton come to our speaker's program."

Somewhat shocked, Michael asked, "We have a speaker's program here?"

"Yeah. Last year we had Barbara Streisand, Michael Moore, and Barney Frank."

Michael made the sign of the cross. "Christ, shoot me now."

"Just toying with you, Doc. Let's go to lunch."

47

On the Corner

EVER SINCE MICHAEL HAD ARRIVED, SAL felt more connected to Fox Run and life in general. He had stopped eating alone; he and Michael spent a large part of each day together. This morning they had breakfast in the main dining room, being extremely careful not to occupy any of the seats assigned by God to certain territorial residents. After breakfast, they moseyed down to the mail center and then took up residence in the poolroom. Sal shuffled through the usual countless requests for funds, and the holiday greetings from everyone who had ever had his name in a file for a purchase. Michael, on the other hand, seemed absorbed in a letter, and his smile turned into a belly laugh.

Pushing aside his boring correspondence, Sal asked, "What the hell is so funny?"

"A letter from Jimmy Manning."

"Maniac? Is he in prison or has he been granted asylum by Putin?"

"He's as nutty as ever. Listen to this. Only Maniac would write in this vein:

Dear Mike,

You are the forerunner of legions of old people that eventually will be prisoners like you in Fox Run. You must lead a good example by living the tenets of behavior that you learned in Jersey City. Because of your advanced age and limited mental capability, you may have forgotten the tenets, so I have enclosed them.

Never trust anyone under seventy-five.

If you have hair growing out of every orifice, shave your ass and walk backwards.

Never pass a bathroom.

Never waste an erection.

Never presume it is just a fart.

If you live by these tenets, your waning days will be golden instead of yellow or brown.

I will visit you as soon as I remember who the hell you are.

Love and kisses,

Jimmy "Maniac."

Sal took the letter from Michael and laughed out loud. "Boy, does that bring back memories of the gang on the corner. He was the craziest bastard in the whole neighborhood."

Both men were laughing, and Michael had trouble speaking. Finally, he gained control. "You don't know the half of it. He was a genius at walking backwards and sneaking into Madison Square

Garden. Also, he often brought strangers to my house and left them there when he knew I was out. My mother would feed these total strangers, thinking they were friends of mine." Slapping his knee, he wiped the tears from his eyes.

Sal was equally giddy at the thought of that local lunatic. "Just hearing about him gets my juices going."

Pensive for a moment, Michael placed the letter on the table. "Like you, I miss those days. There was such togetherness with all the guys on the corner. I would not have known enough to call it community then, but that's what it was. I always felt like I belonged to something special. It was like that sitcom *Cheers*, a place where everybody knew your name."

Sal was touched by Mike's words. "Yeah, every guy was a part of my family. I don't think I ever had it to that degree except for my personal family. My suburban life consisted of being nice to a group of strangers. Hell, I spent more time talking about my lawn than anything else."

"That's true, Sal. I was blessed with countless friends along the way, but except for Vietnam, I never felt as rooted as I did on the corner."

"It's amazing. Your coming here has unleashed a ton of memories and stories about those days. I've had names pop into my head that I haven't seen in over fifty years. Turtle, Chinkie, Beaky, Octopus, Dinty and Lodi. Of all of them, I most remember Lodi. He constantly walked as if he had a load in his pants."

"Yeah, a lot of our characters had politically incorrect names, but they fit like a glove, especially Dinty. We thought of him as one of us even though he was mentally challenged. He was a living example of how the neighborhood took care of its own."

The memories were exploding; it was as though Maniac's letter had triggered an immediate connection to their past. Sal offered, "My favorite Dinty story took place one year at Midnight Mass.

In the middle of the service, which of course was in Latin, Dinty stood up and shouted, 'Speak English, you sneaky bastard. Why are you wearing nice clothes and I have these rags on?' Everyone laughed, even Father Reynolds, and those around Dinty politely asked him not to do it again."

"We all watched out for him, and when his father died, Bert Burke and I offered to be pallbearers. After his father was buried, he lived in the same house. He never actually worked, but people brought him food every day. He died ten years ago, having never spent a day in an institution."

Looking at his wrinkled hands, Sal shook his head. "God, so much time has passed since the Dinty days."

Michael agreed. The banter became slower and more thoughtful as each man reflected on the value of those days and perhaps for the first time felt a yearning to be rooted again. "We were together every day, and then suddenly we were all scattered."

Wistfully, with a touch of guilt, Sal said: "I kind of lost track of you after that lunch in New York."

"As I did you after I went to Vietnam."

Trying to probe his memory, Sal thought of what information he had received along the way. "Years ago, I heard from Johnny Wochna that you had completed your surgical residency and were practicing in New York. I thought: 'Oh Christ, I hope he doesn't kill someone.'"

Smiling, Michael decided to break the rules, reaching for a cigarette. He took a long drag, saying. "You don't know the half of it. By the time I was a resident in surgery, I was quite competent. However, the last two years of med school were somewhat of a disaster. My internship began with a stint at Lankenau emergency room. A cab driver brought a woman in, and she was about six seconds from delivering. I positioned myself, and the baby comes out, and I missed it. It went right into the pail. The woman is asking is it a boy or girl as I'm trying to retrieve the baby from the pail."

Sal covered his ears. "Christ, you were a disaster!"

"After my initial successes in cardiology and child delivery, I moved to attending broken bones. I put a cast on this guy's leg and forgot to put the gauze on before the plaster. When the poor bastard came back to get the cast off, I took tons of skin with the plaster removal. The guy says, 'Does it always hurt this much?' I lied and said it's usually worse. I topped this orthopedic feat by building a walking cast for a middle-aged woman. I couldn't get both sides even so I kept adding plaster. The damn thing was so heavy that when I finished, she couldn't lift her leg. I gave her crutches until she got used to the cast. Though it did get better, and at one point I was no longer a public health menace."

"When you finished, where did you go?"

" You knew that I did a residency in surgery at Bellevue. Are you going senile?"

Sal laughed and said, "Sorry, I forgot. It was a senior moment.

Mike put out his cigarette and although it was quite cold out opened the window and attempted to wave the smoke out of the room. "How about you. Was your beginning in the parish as much of a disaster as my initial ventures in the emergency room?"

"I think nervousness occurs in every occupation. In my case, it was fueled by my enthusiasm. I was so rattled my first time at the cemetery that as I was reading the prayers, I stumbled into an open grave. Fortunately, the family was still in the limo. I climbed out and dusted myself off without anyone knowing what happened."

"God, even then you were out to lunch. Sal, can I ask you a tough question?"

"Sure, why not?"

Hesitating, Mike asked, "Did you leave the priesthood because you lost your faith?"

Not the least bit surprised or annoyed by the question, Sal responded with a question of his own. "What do you mean by faith?"

"Come on; you know what I'm talking about. The Catholic faith that we both grew up with. Did you just lose that along the way?"

"It depends on how you define faith, Mike. I never bought into a lot of the rigid hocus-pocus stuff. For me, it was all about the Beatitudes, the words of Christ in the Sermon on the Mount and the sacraments. It was the joy of truly being involved in every aspect of the parishioners' lives that I found so fulfilling. The rest of the trappings were part of the official institution that I never believed in, especially some of the Church's policies. As the years went by, I could not live within those parameters. It wasn't out of anger, but I felt that for me to continue would have been hypocritical. I don't believe that I ever lost my faith."

Somewhat skeptical of Sal's response, Mike continued, "That seems like you became a cafeteria Christian, picking out only the things you liked, and you gave up the baby with the bathwater. I don't understand how you could walk away from such a gift; we all revered the priests when we were kids."

"Should I have stayed because of the expectations of others? Don't conscience and personal responsibility have a part to play?"

Mike frowned, obviously annoyed by Sal's response. "There is too much of that personal responsibility bullshit in the world today. I think that whenever we are faced with tough moral choices, it's fashionable to fall back on the conscience bit. Do you still believe in God?"

Sal paused. "It depends on which day you ask that question. There are days when, down to my socks, I am convinced that there is a God, and other days when it all seems like a fairy tale. It's not that I don't want to believe; I do, but it comes and goes. When I was in the sixth grade, I was to serve the early bird Mass. It was winter and the night was still and beautiful. Walking from my home, I gazed at the stars and was mesmerized by their beauty. There were millions of them. When I reached the church, all the candles were lit, and it was almost a mystical moment. When I went out on the altar, I had a feeling that God was on my shoulder. I would love to have that feeling every day."

"But maybe you can have it. Pride and intellect may be in the way. I can't prove the existence of God in some scientific way, but I believe, and that belief is a leap. That's what faith is. Maybe it's time for you to come back, Sal. You're not getting any younger, and this may be the perfect time to reconnect."

"In a way, I envy you, Michael, because your belief allows you to have a place to put everything in your life. If there is pain, you can offer up the suffering. If there is joy, you can thank God for your blessings. The absence of that is not something I relish, but I can't buy in because it takes away all the questions."

"I just don't get why you would discard this wondrous gift that has been given to you. Hell, you're obviously a guy who gives a shit about everyone, so I am not making any judgment about your character. If you said that you gave up the priesthood because of celibacy, I could understand that, but doubt is part of being a believer. It would be too easy if there were some magic trick that God could perform to convince us."

"Celibacy did not play a major role in my decision. I had already left the ministry in my heart and head before I met Helen. Saying I left the ministry is not entirely true. I left the formal ministry, but feel as deeply obligated to live the spirit of the gospels as when I was an active priest."

"The Church is my rock, Sal. It got me through major personal losses as well as Vietnam. I experienced things there that still cause night sweats. Prayer and faith allowed me to work daily on the mangled bodies of young men. And one of the joys is that I believe that I will see Arlene again when I die. It is such a comfort for me to know that."

"Your answer for what happens after death is one of the great bonuses of being a believer. There are days when I feel that I will see all of my loved ones again and days when I think it's all a fantasy."

"But, Sal, that's what faith is, a leap into the unknown. What harm is there in letting yourself go? You once believed this with all of your heart, and if you are willing, He will touch your heart again. You may think it's corny, but I pray that you will find the gift again."

"I don't think it's corny, and I appreciate it."

"Christ, maybe I should have been the priest."

"With your religious convictions, there would be more children in the world. You would have all of the Catholics in your parish playing Catholic roulette. Do you know what they call the "Rhythm method? Pregnancy."

Michael laughed sarcastically, saying, "Let's go have lunch before I wring your liberal neck."

"Before we do, it is my turn to ask a question."

Michael sat down and said, "Shoot."

"When I left, I wrote you a letter because as my best friend I did not want you to hear the news from anyone else. I never received a response and candidly was quite hurt."

Michael grimaced and did not immediately reply. "Your letter came at a time when there were personal family issues that were deeply troubling. I don't want to go into it now, but I guess I felt betrayed by your decision. I have regretted not answering your letter and never told Arlene that you had reached out. All I can say now is that I am sorry."

Sal felt the sincerity of Michael's words. "Water under the bridge, Michael, but thanks for telling me you are sorry."

48

MARCH 2016

Unfinished Business

E VEN AFTER MONTHS AT FOX RUN, Michael did not fully adjust to assisted living. Sal was worried about him and, without being too bold, frequently encouraged Michael to talk about his new life. He made it a point to engage Michael every morning and help him organize the day. Sal believed that if he could participate in some of the Fox Run activities, he would adjust more easily. Knocking on Michael's door on his way to breakfast, he entered Michael's room and shouted: "Come on, sunshine, let's see who bought the farm during the night." Michael laughed, went to his closet and put on his blazer. He straightened his tie and brushed a piece of lint from his shoulder.

Sal said, "They are not giving out best-dressed awards, dummy."

Not to be outdone, Michael responded, "I gathered that from the outfit you are wearing. You could easily be taken for a homeless person."

Arriving at the dining room, they quietly went through the food line and, after pouring themselves coffee, found two seats at an empty table in the rear of the room.

Michael stirred his oatmeal and said, "Christ, it's so boring here. Every day seems like a month. The food is so damn ordinary, and outside of my room the air is filled with pungent chemicals to neutralize the smells of the aged."

"How are you really doing?"

The smile faded, and Michael admitted, "I am bored to tears. It seems like I've been here for years."

"That's because you haven't completed your project in arts and crafts."

Looking at his hands, Mike shook his head. "These hands have performed lifesaving surgery, and now they are only good for stringing beads. Do you believe that crap? Making useless junk just to keep us busy. I was a professional with a huge practice, making life and death decisions, and now I'm gluing popsicles sticks together."

"What else could you do?" Sal asked.

"That's just it; you can only read so much or watch so much television. Conversation in the great room is like my first days as an intern. Everyone is sharing their medical history in the middle of burps and farting sounds. I'm beginning to think that going home is less dangerous than the daily gas attacks in that room. Talk about carbon limits. Cows don't give off as much gas as the residents. One of the worse parts is the realization that each day we are losing more and more of our mental and physical capabilities. I am still fairly fit, but when I see how age erodes the bodies and spirits of so many here, it worries me. What the hell do you do all day?"

"I mostly spend time on my computer. It's an endless source of information, plus I keep up with friends and colleagues on email."

Michael shook his head. "Baloney. You probably watch porn all day."

"You don't have to watch porn on the computer, just look at the ads on T.V."

"Yeah like the boner ads—the real reason the guy can't get it up is that he's sitting in a tub of cold water. His pecker has shrunk from the cold."

"And how about the part that talks about the problem with a four-hour woody? Call a doctor? Shit, call an ambulance for his partner. She's probably dead."

"Four hours? Hell, you could do the whole neighborhood."

"The pharmaceutical business has more syndromes than one could imagine, shaky leg syndrome, limp dick, bleeding hemorrhoids, constant belching and farting, frequent or infrequent peeing. The side effects are death, diarrhea, or you can't poop for a year. Then they tell you this rarely happens. Hell, the cure is worse than the syndrome. So much of it is marketing hype."

"You think that's new information for me? I consulted for major pharmaceutical companies. Some of the drugs are lifesavers, but there's a lot of me-too compounds that aren't any better than the competition."

"We are digressing, Michael. What could make it better for you here?"

"If I knew that, Doctor Phil, I would not be climbing the walls."

Attempting to connect Michael to his incredible life history, Sal pursued options. "Have you thought about writing your memoirs? You have had a very interesting life: med school, being a surgeon, Vietnam, father, husband, die-hard conservative."

"Funny, when you are going through your life, you don't think that there is anything unique about it, and then you get to our age, and you think, 'What the hell happened? Where did it all go?' I think there is also the conviction that it's all been said. What the hell do I have to offer?"

"I don't believe that it's all been said because your experience is singular. No one has ever lived and perceived life exactly as you have."

Michael raised his eyebrows at the astute approach of his buddy. "Christ, Doctor Phil, you are really good. How much do I owe you for this counseling session?"

Sal immediately responded, "Just leave a sheaf of unmarked bills in an envelope on my bed."

"You can take the man out of Jersey City, but you can't take the Jersey City out of the man. Did you know that my whole family at one point had no-show jobs working for the city? My cousin Tommy was appointed the commissioner of weights and measures. At his first news conference, a reporter asked him jokingly: 'Tommy, how many ounces in a pound?' My dumbo cousin thinks it's a real question and answers, 'Hey, first day on the job, give me a break.' If you put him and his three brothers together, you would have one brain."

"That's what I'm talking about. Tell us the stories of Jersey City."

"A lot of the stories center on our parish and the corner."

"I have a few of my own. Do you remember Father Reynolds?"

"Yeah, he was a great guy and a magnet for people who were a little off center. His confession line was always long because he was kind to everyone. Almost like our crowd going to the Polish parish to confess to the Polish priest. Do you still go to confession?"

"It's been quite a while."

As the weeks went by, Sal was gratified that Michael seemed to be adjusting more and more to Fox Run. He became involved in a few of the clubs, and both men took advantage of some of the activities that the residence provided offsite. They attended two plays and, though embarrassed to admit it, took the bus on one occasion to Atlantic City.

Fox Run had excellent facilities, a large swimming pool with an adjacent hot tub, a beautiful library with literally thousands of books, a game and hobby room as well as a music room with a genuine antique Steinway piano. It was an elegant environment, but one that was without a meaningful schedule. Those present had been separated from the vitality and challenges of occupations, raising families and having an impact on their world. Now they were reduced to coping and waiting for the inevitable. Each day chipped away at their physical and cognitive abilities, and the loneliness of loss was ever present.

Sal was playing a solitary game of pool when Michael entered the game room.

"What's the reason for the grumpy face?" Sal asked.

"I was bawled out this morning for smoking in my room. I was told that if the smoking continues, I'll be in violation of the bullshit paper I signed when I came here."

Sal imitated being handcuffed. "The smoking police will find you no matter where you go."

"It reminds of when we were kids in the drugstore. You could out loud order cigarettes, but you had to ask for condoms in a whisper. Now you can loudly order condoms, but you have to whisper to buy smokes."

Sal shared some spicy gossip. "One of the nurses told me that the directress caught two of the residents making love in a bedroom yesterday. She informed their families that they were engaging in inappropriate behavior."

"When you first come here, Mrs. Boyer is so friendly and charming, but that fades fast. After a while, I got the impression she thinks her job is to treat us like children. I would like to find a way to torment her."

"I may become your accomplice because she pisses me off also. As a way for you to chill out now, I think you should take this quiz with me."

"What quiz?"

Sal picked up a copy of *Family Circle* and opened to the main feature. "This one in the magazine; it is based on Dickens's *A Christmas Carol*."

"And I thought Boyer was a pain in the ass."

"Come on; it will take your mind off all this trivial crap."

Michael reluctantly sat down and covered his face as though he was in extreme pain. "Maybe they should have three classes of people in this zoo. Those who are out to lunch, normal people like me, and touchy-feely nerds like you."

"Come on, Scrooge, participate. First question, looking back on your past, when were you the happiest?"

"When I wasn't forced to participate in bullshit quizzes."

"Come on, be serious."

Mike paused, thinking. "I guess there were a couple of times. When we were hanging out as kids on the corner, and when I was first married."

"Second part of the question is, what made those times happy?"

"I guess it was like being part of a place where people really knew and cared about you. There was a commonality. Everyone was kind of equal and cut from the same cloth. Our lives were simple, but we always had each other. Do you remember when we had six guys in a car all smoking at the same time? We would cruise the streets looking to pick up girls. If anyone had been crazy enough to get in the car where the hell would we have fit her?

"The other time was the days and months right after Arlene and I were married. We didn't have a pot to piss in, but every purchase or event seemed special. I remember one time we went to the Philadelphia airport to watch the planes land and take off. We sat there mesmerized for hours and didn't spend a penny."

Sal listened intently to Michael's choices, and they triggered his own memories. "I can relate to those experiences, but for diversity's sake, I will choose when my kids were small. In the beginning, I was terrified, but once Jonathan survived and was thriving, my confidence as a father grew. Both kids were such joys, and I loved watching each day be a new adventure for them. I think part of that wonder rubbed off on me."

"The other time was when I taught high school juniors."

"What's so great about teaching kids? Isn't it just hormone control at that age?'

"For one thing, when you teach kids, you see things that you thought you understood in a deeper way. Also, the kids I taught were bright and challenging."

Sal picked up the magazine and continued, "What are some of your regrets?"

"That's easy. I regret meeting Sal La Greca because if I didn't know him, I would not be subjected to this stupid quiz."

Sal shook his head and responded, "I will ignore that remark and continue with the questions. I am sure if you pondered the question for a while, many would jump out. There are two that are immediate for me. The first is when I was eleven years old. One night about nine-thirty, my friend Bobby Smith came to my house. When I opened the door, he said, "My father dropped dead, and my mother sent me to the store to get a quart of milk."

I said that I was sorry but did not know what to do. He stayed for a couple of minutes and then left. I have regretted to this day that I did not go to the store with him."

"But you were just a kid."

"I know that, but the memory sticks in my gut to this day."

"What was your other regret?"

"I adored my grandmother, but she could not speak any English. One day she was taking me to the Italian section of the city for food shopping. She loved to make me homemade pizza. While we were waiting for the bus, two teenage boys started making fun of the old guinea lady. She smiled and thought they were being friendly, but they were taunting her. I was embarrassed and afraid, so I acted as if I didn't know her. This loving person had never done anything but care for me, and I denied knowing her. I felt so guilty and mad at myself for not sticking up for her."

"Again, you were a child, and it was an unrealistic expectation for you to be a hero at that time. You always tease me about Irish guilt, and I have my share. One of my biggest regrets is not taking Arlene to Ireland until she was dying. In the beginning, I didn't have the money, and later, I didn't have the time. We made the trip just before she died and despite her deteriorating health, it is a wonderful memory for me."

"Any other regrets from the past?"

Michael paused and appeared uncomfortable. "There is a major family issue that I'm not ready to discuss."

"Go ahead; it will do you good."

It was obvious that Mike was annoyed at Sal's persistence. "I don't want to discuss it, and that's that."

"Okay, Mike, I understand."

"I think I've had enough of this quiz," Michael said and walked away.

49

Lingering Grief and Guilt

THE WEATHER CHANGED FOR THE BETTER, and the winter was slowly giving way to the promise of spring. Mike and Sal were having coffee in the late afternoon on a patio outside the dining room. Michael said, "I saw a woman in the lobby this morning that looked just like Arlene when she was fifty. I was stunned by her appearance. It set off all kind of memories."

Michael stopped talking, and there was a long pause. Sal waited. "It's the little things that I miss. Like her touching my hair as she passed when I was reading in a chair or meeting her for a movie and sandwich after work. It's the nights that are the most difficult. It's amazing how lonely you can be in your own home. Everything in that place was a constant reminder that she was no longer there. Sal, when does it stop hurting? There isn't a day that goes by that I don't miss Arlene. There is always something that reminds me of her."

Sal shrugged his shoulders to indicate that he had no answer. "I still have Helen's number on my cell phone. There are times when I forget that she is dead and go to call her."

Michael nodded in agreement. "The good part for me is that I always knew that I was the luckiest man alive. The bad part is that I still feel guilty about my inability to save her. Christ, I probably know more about her type of cancer than anyone alive. I spent endless hours trying to find a glimmer of hope, and every time I thought I was on the right track, I would run into a blind alley. I took her to the best oncologists in the country, but it made no difference. I even looked at every homeopathic treatment as well as nutritional and herb medicine, but none of it mattered."

"I'm sure that you did more than anyone could do."

"I even resorted to bargaining."

"Bargaining?"

"Yes, bargaining with God. If he spared her, I would commit myself to being a better person. In the end, all I wound up with was a sense of failure and guilt."

Sal was briefly silent but then added, "At a serious moment like this I hesitate to tell you that Italians do not suffer from the disease of guilt. We have willed it to the Irish and the Jews."

Brushing aside the humorous comment, Michael sought common ground. "Did you feel anything like that when Helen died?"

"I experienced an anger that was totally foreign to me. I was angry at everything and everybody. Hell, I was even angry at her for dying. How stupid is that?"

"Gee, I thought I was the only one that felt that way. What did you do with that anger?"

"Initially, I buried myself in writing. I would drink a little too much wine. The wine consumption didn't last long because I recognized that was a road that led nowhere. Spending time with my kids helped a lot because I could see the wonderful job that Helen had done with them. They both reflect all of the great qualities that she possessed."

"Do they have any of your qualities?"

"I'm sure they do, but they are more like their mother."

"You would think that with our backgrounds, death would be something we would understand and deal with better than most."

"I think it's a false idea that being a priest or doctor insulates us from pain. We are just like anyone else; when death comes, it sears our souls. I first learned that when Jack died at age twenty-nine in an auto accident."

"Who was Jack?"

"He was a priest that I was stationed with in the parish. Murph, as I affectionately called him, had this angelic Irish face but in many ways, he was like our friend Maniac. I had left the parish for graduate work in Rome when I received the news about his death. It hit me like a brick. I went home for the funeral, but it was months later that the grief overwhelmed me."

"Were you in Rome on vacation?"

"No, I was in Rome at the University but soon went to Vienna to study with Doctor Viktor Frankl."

Michael was surprised to hear Sal's response. "The guy who wrote *Man's Search for Meaning*?" Michael could not believe Sal's connection to Viktor Frankl. "You sent me his book after Danny died and along with a priest, Father Hudson, it helped me through the losses of my mother and brothers. I read *Man's Search for Meaning* repeatedly."

"That book also got me through Jack's death! I was his teaching assistant in Vienna. One night I went to his office and for two hours just dumped my heartache and confusion in his lap. Now, you must realize that not only was he in four German concentration camps, but he also lost most of his family. He listened and never said a word until I was done, and then he said two things that changed my life. He said: "You feel such pain because you loved Jack. There will come a moment in time when you will have to choose between getting in the grave with Jack or choosing to live again. From what you have said, if you choose to bury yourself with him, I don't think you understood what a life force he was."

"God, that's profound."

"That night was the beginning of my living again. His words also helped me with Helen's death.

"I'm intrigued with your affection for Jack. What was he like?"

"I could regale you for hours with Jack stories."

"Regale me; all I have is time."

"A perfect example of his zany quality occurred while we were on vacation in Greece. We arrived at the dock to catch the boat to Hydra a few minutes late. Jack bribed a local fisherman to catch the large ship. When we got to the ship, he told me to put on sunglasses and wait until he returned. After about ten minutes, three sailors came down the ladder and escorted me to a private deck. Jack had told the captain that he was forbidden to tell them who I was because of national security. The entire trip people were leaning over the deck to take my picture."

"I think that Jack would have fit into the old neighborhood."

"In some ways, he was like Father Reynolds. Jack was a magnet for anyone who was a little off center.

"When someone like that dies, a piece of you goes with them. Death was a frequent part of our lives, but it's different when it's someone you love.

"Helen's death was so much like Jack's in that it was a total shock. I could not bear the early evening without her. The loss was enormous, but the months after the funeral were worse. I realize now that I did everything possible to avoid going home at night."

Michael was gripped by the similarity of experience. "It's so hard to visit places that were special for us. Her favorite restaurant at the shore was the Golden Lantern. We used to eat there at least twice a month, but I haven't been near the place since she died. I feel incomplete without her. I don't brood about it, but the ache is always there."

"So true. The pain comes and goes, with no expiration date. It's not just the holidays; it could be a song, a place or seeing someone that we both knew."

"In our culture, you are allowed a brief mourning period, and then everyone goes back to their routines, leaving you to grieve by yourself. I have been through so many personal tragedies, and Arlene was my anchor going through the grief. Now my anchor is gone, and it is so foreign not to have her with me. My kids help, but there is no replacing her."

"My daughter Mary looks so much like Arlene, and has so many of her qualities."

"That's true of my kids also. They are the image of their mother. Those Irish genes overshadow the Italian names I gave my kids."

Michael saluted Sal and said, "That's because we are a superior people."

Sal did not respond with a snide remark, caught up in the seriousness of what they were sharing. "There are not a lot of opportunities to talk about my wife anymore. The kids talk about her, but no one else mentions her."

"I think people believe that it will cause us pain to talk about them, so they avoid it."

"Yeah, when I mention her, there is usually silence or a quick change to another topic."

"Part of the problem is that Arlene was involved in almost every part of my life. I knew her since the fifth grade. She was connected to every stage except this one."

"You know what I miss the most? Helen's laugh. She thought I was the funniest man alive and would howl at my stories even after she had heard them many times before."

"I used to marvel at how many people were in Arlene's network. She was constantly on the phone counseling or listening to the joys and woes of her friends and family. At her funeral, it seemed that everyone said that she was their best friend. The outpouring really helped, especially for the kids."

"It is amazing how many lives they touched. Helen's colleagues at the hospital regaled us at the funeral home with stories about how she was always calm even during the emergency room crises. For weeks after the funeral, we received notes from grateful patients she had treated."

Michael appeared to be very serious and paused before he spoke, "You know, Sal, there are not many opportunities to talk about these things. I feel like I am talking to myself with you because you have so many similar thoughts."

"I think it's a guy thing, Mike. We were not raised in a world where men talked about loss and feelings."

"I think the kids today are different and talk about things openly that we would have never considered raising. Even with Arlene, my kids would discuss topics that my parents would have been shocked to hear."

"It's all about comfort, Michael. Helen had great antennae for what was going on with our kids. She had a real skill to get them to open up and confide in her."

"I have great antennae also, but I never knew how to approach the kids."

"That's where I believe our wives were different. They plowed through the discomfort, and we retreated from it."

Michael was hesitant but finally asked, "Do you think our kids knew how much we loved them?"

"Depends on whether we told them and showed them that it was true."

"I think that I was an excellent father, but I wish that I had been more open with my kids. It seemed that there was never enough time. When I think of the hectic schedule that I kept for years, it's hard to believe that I have so much free time now."

"Tell me about it. As a business consultant, I averaged one hundred and sixty thousand air miles a year. In those days, I longed for more time to engage in hobbies and other pursuits. Be careful what you wish for, Michael."

"What hobbies and pursuits?"

Trying to move away from the serious, Sal quipped, "I longed to spend the rest of my days writing the definitive tome on Irish cooking delights. I was going to explore the seven hundred ways one could prepare corned beef and cabbage."

Not to be one-upped, Michael responded, "Funny, I was thinking of devoting my golden years to writing, *How Liberal Views Kill Brain Cells.* Come on, smart ass, be serious."

"My first hobby was golf, but it didn't take me long to realize that it was too late. My aging body could not make a proper turn for a beautiful swing. I hacked around for a few years but finally accepted the inevitable."

"And what other pursuits?"

"Mostly languages. I speak Italian and some German and French but wanted to upgrade my skills. What about you?"

It was Michael's turn to add a caustic comment. "I wanted to discover a vaccine that would prevent adults from being infected by the liberal virus. Once onset occurs, rational thought ceases, and senility directs all behavior."

Sal made a guttural sound. "Sometimes I wonder why I even grace you with my presence. How the hell did you get through med school?"

"I picked out an upperclassman with an Italian name, and thought if he can make it there's no problem for me."

"Do you have any cyanide capsules on you? I need immediate relief from your delusions."

"In fact, I feared the so-called 'golden years.' My work meant everything to me, and it gave me such purpose. The day I stopped practicing medicine was the beginning of a minor depression."

"Why did you leave the practice?"

Michael appeared to be cataloging the reasons in his mind. "Because I couldn't physically keep up with the schedule and because my eyesight began to fail me. I realize now that other opportunities were available, I could have become a full-time mentor to the younger surgeons, but I didn't take the time to explore it. Also, I wanted to spend every waking moment with Arlene."

"Is it too late now to find alternatives?"

"What would I do, old buddy? Like you, I am a prisoner of limited eyesight and creaky knees. The days of opportunity are gone. The train has left the station."

"Maybe you could assist the nurse practitioner here."

Michael shook his head: "Besides giving the directress heart failure, I don't think the board of directors would be crazy about that possibility. Besides, I am a surgeon, not a gerontologist." Michael appreciated Sal's constant attempts to have him be more adjusted at this stage of his life. "I know that you are trying to help me find some purpose."

Sal said: "Remember, I am also a doctor.'

"A Ph.D. does not count. You are not a real doctor."

"But I am a hell of an imitation. Would you like to explore your possibilities?"

"I would love to have something meaningful to do, but there is nothing available."

"Alright, Doctor, it's time for role reversal. What would you tell me if I were in your shoes?"

"With your fat feet, I would advise you to go barefoot, or buy new shoes."

"Why do I bother?"

"Because I am so cute and charming."

"In reality, you are fat, have a bald spot and smell like Bengay."

"If you think you look better than me, can I borrow your magic mirror?"

"God, do I look as bad as you?'

"You were unanimously voted ugliest resident on your wing."

"With your endearing personality, I am going to recommend that you become a member of the welcoming committee. You will certainly keep the place from overcrowding."

"You are already on the committee, and the limit is one pathetic member."

"Back to reality, Doctor. Let's find something meaningful for you."

"Who died and put you in charge of my future?"

"The Wizard of Oz gave me this task before he passed on. I must find where you fit into the universe's eternal plan."

"Your eternal purpose is to annoy me. I pray every night that we don't die on the same day. I would go nuts spending eternity next to you."

"Wouldn't you feel better if you had a schedule with some meaning?"

"There is no one in the world that doesn't want a purpose, but my life is over."

That phrase made Sal shudder, and he responded with a vigorous denial. "It's only over if you will it to be over. With your skills and experience, there is at least one more challenge."

"Yeah, like avoiding Depends."

"Maybe what you need is a companion."

"Is that code for 'Maybe you need a woman?'"

"Now that you've mentioned it, yes."

"Did you have anyone in mind?'

"Not really, but there are some lovely women here."

"It has been a dog's age since I did any of those dating rituals. The 1950s, to be precise. I must have gone out with all of three girls before Arlene. Wondering if I'd ever get to second base. Jesus. I wouldn't know where to begin. Why are you laying this trip on me? What about you? You're also single."

"It has crossed my mind, and like you, I am also somewhat shy. I am going to dinner in five minutes with the number one goal of finding you a love interest."

Michael sighed and said, "If you embarrass me tonight I will muster what energy I have left and kick your ass.

50

MAY 2016

Memories of Fathers

IT BECAME PART OF SAL'S MORNING schedule to knock on Michael's door and accompany him to breakfast. One morning he knocked and knocked and suddenly had a panicked feeling that something had happened to his friend. He hurried to the front desk and asked if anyone had seen Doctor McNally. The person at the desk informed him that Doctor McNally took a cab about fifteen minutes ago. Sal surmised that he probably went to morning Mass. Later that day, Michael called Sal and asked if he would like to join him for lunch. "Where were you this morning?" Sal asked. "I missed you at breakfast."

"I took a cab and went to the local Catholic Church for Mass. Today is the anniversary of my father's death."

"Were you close to your dad?"

"I hardly knew him growing up. He was rarely around, always working. He seemed like such a dour guy. He suffered losing my mother and my brothers almost back to back. My grandfather was the most negative person in the world. My father told me that his father said, 'Life is a shit sandwich, and every day we take a bite.'"

"Boy, I can't even imagine that; my father was just the opposite."

"I remember your dad; he was always smiling every time I went to your house."

"He had a lot of little boy in him. When he was seventy-seven, he had a hernia operation at Bayonne hospital. When the surgeon visited him after the operation, he asked the doctor: 'Doctor, when I get home will I be able to play the piano?'

"The doctor replied: 'Certainly.'

"'That's funny,'" my dad said. 'I couldn't play it before the operation.'"

"So that's where you learned to be a clown."

"You don't know the half of it. Another time he was in the hospital having a pilonidal cyst removed, and the day after the operation he was roaming the halls as a goodwill ambassador. He spots a guy with a worried look on his face and decides he will find out what the guy is worrying about. He asks the nursing attendant what operation the person in 514 is having. He finds out that the woman in 514 is having a pilonidal cyst removed. With this information, Dad moves in and tells the guy in great detail that he had the operation, and it was a breeze; he's fine. The guy is looking at him like he's nuts. The nursing attendant had the wrong room. The guy's wife was in 516 and was having a hysterectomy."

"It's true that you guineas can't tell your ass from your elbow."

Sal changed the topic to Michael's father. "Did your dad act like life was a shit sandwich?"

"No, I wouldn't say that. He loved my mother, was grateful to her. But I can't remember that he ever hugged me growing up. He wasn't mean or anything, just not very demonstrative, except that one time when Danny died. He shared some of his feelings, and we began to relate at a different level. Another time I was in the Marines and on my way to Vietnam. When I was leaving, my aunt was crying, and I put my hand out to shake my dad's hand. He grabbed me and hugged me for what seemed an eternity. When he finally let go, I could see the tears in his eyes. I realized how much he loved me. He just couldn't show it in the way I expected him to show it. After I came back from Vietnam, the two of us spent more time together than we had before. When he retired, I got him to play golf. He was a terrific grandfather, and my kids loved him."

"Tell me about your kids."

"I have five kids. Michael Jr. is the oldest. He is single and runs a technology company, whatever the hell that is. He lives in the San Francisco area. Mary Rose is next and is married to Tom, a physician. They have four kids. I see her more frequently than any of the other kids. Evelyn, like Michael Jr., is also single. She teaches music at Seton Hall University. Gene is a pilot for Southwest airlines. He's married and has a four-year-old son. He visits me every time he flies into La Guardia. The youngest is Robert, whom we adopted when he was five. He has some physical difficulties but owns an art gallery in Summit and is an outstanding artist."

"Do you see your kids regularly?"

"They all have busy lives, but I do see them fairly regularly." Michael paused. "All of them, that is, but Michael. We butted heads for years, and now he lives in California. The rest of the kids keep in contact. Outside of Arlene's funeral, I haven't seen him in years."

"Do you know what caused the breach between you?"

"One of the problems was that anything that I valued seemed to mean nothing to him. I tried to interest him in sports and frequently took him to sporting events. He would act as if he couldn't wait for the games to be over. He was a terrific swimmer but wouldn't even try out for the swimming team. I even got him golfing lessons, but that didn't work either. I could never penetrate the shell with him. Another problem was that he was so damned liberal and thought that everything I believed in was horseshit. We argued about everything. You would probably love him. He's more liberal than you."

Sal sensed that Michael was skirting the real issue. "Mike, is there something more to it than the whole political difference?"

"It's not just political. He has completely abandoned the Church. Even as a kid, he resisted everything Catholic. He was always bright, and yet he flunked out of Regis prep. I always believed that he did that deliberately. He never even considered a Catholic college and does not buy into any of the Church's beliefs. The rest of my kids are practicing Catholics, and I take great heart in that fact."

"I get the feeling that there is something more to your split than you're telling me."

Michael glanced away from Sal, becoming increasingly annoyed with where the conversation was going. "I'm not sure I want to talk about it because I just don't get it." Michael played with his coffee cup, turning it around in a circle several times. He wished that he could end the conversation, but also longed to talk about it.

"Mike, don't make me be Sherlock Holmes. What don't you get?"

"It's not easy. . . . I don't know whether I should tell you."

"Come on, spit it out: "

After a long pause, Michael groaned and softly said, "My son is . . . gay. God, I hate that word. I just can't accept it."

"When did you find out?"

"I think I always knew but didn't want to believe it."

"Why not?"

"Hell, you wouldn't understand. I've been through so many difficult things in my life, but I can't get a handle on this. This blows me away, and the thought that he is so different kills me."

"Did Arlene know that Michael was gay?"

"She knew and had no problem with it. That's where we were so different. She could accept anything."

"What is the most difficult part for you?"

"I just don't get how the hell it happened. We raised him the same as the other kids."

"Did you ever discuss how you feel with him?"

"Discuss is the wrong word. Every attempt leads to the same result. I lose my cool, and he clams up. The kid does not believe in rules. You would love him because he's so goddamn liberal."

"No rules?"

"He thinks the Church is bullshit, and rejects the Church's position on homosexuality. I tried to get him to talk to a priest friend of mine, and he comes back with, 'Dad, do you know how many Catholic priests are gay?' "

"Where was Arlene when all of this was going on?"

"She tried many times to bring us together, especially when she was dying. I think that both of us loved her so much that we put our best foot forward in front of her, but it didn't last. Even at the funeral we somewhat avoided each other. It has completely gone downhill since then."

"What do you think you can do about the situation now?"

"I don't know how to fix it."

"Fix it?"

"Yeah, fix it. I want the magic wand that will make him straight. I'm sure you think that's awful."

Realizing how electric this discussion could become, Sal gingerly continued, "Mike, I have no right to think that your feelings are awful, but I come at it differently than you. I don't want to get into a whole religious/ political argument with you."

"Tell me what you think. I won't lose my cool."

"I don't think being gay is wrong."

"But it's unnatural."

"Who decides that?"

"The Church for one and every civilization in history."

"Mike, it has been a reality for thousands of years."

"So, has murder, but that does not make it right."

"What's so wrong about two people loving each other?"

"It's against nature and is morally wrong."

"I don't buy the unnatural argument. People don't love each other based solely on gender."

"What the hell does that mean?"

"It means that gay people don't have any more choice than straight people. I'm not straight because I'm better; it's just the way I'm wired."

"Maybe you believe that because you can accept anything."

"The fundamental difference between us, Mike, is that I don't believe that being gay is immoral."

"Sal, gays are so promiscuous."

Sal shook his head in disagreement: "Michael, I know straight guys that would screw a snake if you held it still."

Michael was silent for a moment. "Sal, the Church has been and is my anchor; how do I throw the teaching overboard?"

"I don't think you throw it overboard, but I know that you love your son, and that has to be the most important ingredient in all of this."

"It's not a question of love. It's a question of right and wrong."

"I don't buy that, Michael—it's deeper than that. It's a question of love overcoming difference."

"I love him but can't accept his lifestyle."

"Is that going to change him?"

"No, but why should I be the one to change?"

"Is being away from him working for you?"

"No."

"Then what are your choices?"

"I don't have any."

"Really?

"I'm not sure."

"Mike, we are not getting any younger, and this is a time when we need to look at what is really important to us before we go."

"This is so damn hard:"

"I can only imagine."

51

MAY 2016

Medical Diagnosis

S AL MET MICHAEL IN THE HALL as he was headed for the mailroom. "Missed you at breakfast this morning," he said. "Where are you going with the suit and tie?"

"I have a doctor's appointment this morning and then probably off to the hospital for some tests in the afternoon, but I will be back in plenty of time for the karaoke program tonight."

"Do you believe that we have been reduced to the ancient order of Hibernians karaoke night?"

Michael gave a shrug and said, "If that one jerk who sings in the great room all day gets up to sing, I may have one of your people take him out."

"Enough with the mafia references. What kind of tests are you having?"

"Just the usual G.I. tests and a few others that your feeble mind cannot comprehend."

"Oh, I forgot, you as a physician are all-knowing and a high priest in our culture."

"Jealousy is a terrible disease and will consume you unless you accept that there are people who are superior to you."

"Kiss my ass."

"Where would I begin? You're all ass."

"On a more serious note, why are you having all these tests?"

"I have had some G.I. discomfort, but I don't think it's anything major. There is the slim possibility that there is a small obstruction and these tests will determine whether it is the cause of my symptoms."

"If my Uncle Joe were alive, you wouldn't need all the tests."

"What the hell does your Uncle Joe have to do with my medical condition?"

"When my father was diagnosed with a terminal illness, Uncle Joe showed up and requested that we give him my father's car. My brother, sister and I agreed that would be a nice gesture. When my sister was diagnosed with terminal leukemia, Uncle Joe showed up again and requested that we give him Tina's car. My brother and I once again decided to give Uncle Joe the car. After my sister's burial, I said to my brother if you ever have a serious illness and they tell you that you're are going to be fine, and you see Uncle Joe in the hallway, forget it, you're toast and will die. Give him the car keys, make an act of contrition and close your eyes."

"Christ, your uncle is the Italian equivalent of my great Aunt Mary. She was ninety years old, and whenever anyone went to visit her, she would start sobbing and say, 'I will never see you again.' Everyone thought that was her way of telling you that she was going to die. In fact, it meant that the visitor was going to die. My father never let her run that routine on him."

"We're the progeny of witch doctors and witches. What time do you expect to be back?"

"If it's before the karaoke hour, I will tell them that I feel weak and they should keep me overnight."

"You mean you would rob all of the residents of your heart-breaking rendition of 'Danny Boy?'"

"You and the white horse you rode in on. Are you interested in going out for dinner tonight?" Michael asked. "I would like a break from this place."

"Sounds like a good idea. What did you have in mind?"

"Nothing formal. I thought perhaps a pizza and a couple of glasses of wine at the new pizzeria in town."

"How about at 6:30? I will call an Uber."

Michael scoffed at Sal's ability to adjust to the modern world. "You are a social media nut," he said.

"Hell," Sal responded, "if it weren't for me, you'd be with the crowd gluing popsicles together in the arts and craft room. Get out of here before I wring your neck. See you later."

Michael was a little early for his appointment, but when Vic De Fino entered the office, he motioned for Michael to join him. Taking off his coat, he hung it up and asked, "How about a cup of coffee? I invested in this contraption, and after years of drinking sludge, I can make real espresso." Michael appeared impressed with the machine and, like Vic, drained a cup of espresso.

Vic began the conversation by inquiring as to how Michael had adjusted to Fox Run.

Michael answered, "It has been vastly better than I expected. One of the bonuses is that an old buddy of mine from Jersey City is there and it helps to have someone who has a connection to my past. Also, Mary and the rest of the family regularly check in, and I have been fortunate in getting out more than occasionally."

Vic went back for seconds on the espresso, but Michael refused a refill. "Don't think it would be wise to have another."

With that remark, the conversation moved from banter to inquiry. "Why it that, Michael?"

"I have had some stomach issues lately."

Vic began to gently probe: "How have you been feeling in general?"

"Pretty well, actually, except for the occasional stomach discomfort.

Over the next thirty minutes, Vic examined Michael and, at the conclusion, said: "I find nothing that indicates that your over-all stomach issue is anything but perhaps a hiatal hernia, but it is time for you to have a full workup. Let's schedule blood work for you this week, and then we can chat on the phone. Also, I ran into Bob Gussin last week. He was asking for you. He is the new medical director at Beth Israel. Maybe I can set up a lunch for the three of us."

Michael agreed.

The afternoon after Michael had tests and blood work, Vic was reviewing the results. "Jesus, when is this guy going to get a break." He took off his glasses, greatly disturbed at the lab results of his friend. After thinking about his next steps with Michael, he decided to call and set up an immediate appointment.

Michael answered his cell phone. "Good morning, Vic."

"Hi, Michael, would it be possible for you to come and see me this afternoon?"

Michael knew that this type of inquiry indicated that something was drastically wrong. "Vic," he said, "we have known each other too long to pussyfoot around your request. Is this about my blood work?"

Vic hesitated to take a deep breath and then responded, "Yes, it is, Michael." Vic began to explain the results. "I want to have you in the hospital overnight to take the entire battery of tests to find out exactly what is the primary issue."

Michael asked directly, "Do you think I have pancreatic cancer?"

"I am not sure. Until we have all the data, I will not speculate."

Michael appreciated Vic's professional way of handling the diagnosis, but in his heart, he was sure that the worst-case scenario was what he was facing.

That evening over a few glasses of wine and a wood-burning stove pizza, Michael told Sal that he would be hospitalized in the morning.

52

MAY 2016

Terminal Disease

MICHAEL WAS SEATED IN THE BREAKFAST nook, staring out the window. Sal entered, poured himself a cup of coffee and sat down next to Michael. "God, what the hell's the matter with you?"

Michael started to answer and paused: "I . . . got my test results yesterday afternoon."

"And?"

"It's pancreatic cancer."

Sal slumped down in his chair, stunned at the terrible news. "Oh, damn it, is there anything they can do?"

"Radical surgery, but even with that, it's still hopeless. I am not going to go through all that Arlene experienced."

"What exactly did they tell you?"

"They did the usual mumbo-jumbo dance when I asked how long do I have. Somewhere between five minutes and two hundred years. Being a doctor, I've heard that so many times, it's not funny."

"Seriously, Michael, how long do you think?"

"The longest would be two years, and the shortest would be six months. It's funny; when they told me the prognosis, all I could think about was Vietnam."

"Vietnam?"

"Yeah, in Vietnam, you lived with death every second, even in the medical units. One day I was coming out of the latrine, and two seconds later it was hit, and two friends of mine were killed. I hadn't thought about that for years, but last night I dreamed about that day. It's not death that scares me; it's the process of dying. I saw Arlene go inch by inch."

"Will you be able to stay here?"

"Yeah, they have hospice here, so I won't have to be moved, even at the end."

"Can I do anything?"

"Let me win at gin rummy."

"Come on, be serious."

"I don't know. But having you here kind of connects the dots for me."

"How?"

"The rest of the people here are nice, but they are still strangers. You go all the way back to the corner. You are a connection, and there are so many things that we have in common. You instinctively know where I come from and how I see the world."

"Mike, in the immortal words of Yogi, 'It isn't over till it's over.'"

"Things must be pretty desperate if you're quoting Yogi."

"Who else would you quote to a Yankee fan?"

"Don't go sad face on me. I don't want to be reminded daily of my impending doom."

"O.K., but what can I do?"

"Just be there. I can't tell you specifics now but . . . knowing that you care helps."

"Don't make me constantly ask what you need—you have to tell me."

"It hasn't fully set in yet, but I will be straight with you about my needs."

Sal hesitated because he feared Michael's reaction to a burning question he needed to ask. "Are you going to tell your kids?"

"I guess I have to."

"Does that include Michael?"

"I probably will let Tommy tell him. They are very close."

"If I am over the line, tell me, but I think it would be better coming from you."

"Why?"

"Because maybe it will be a chance for the two of you to fix things before the end."

"I wouldn't know how to begin."

"Mike, tell me what you want to happen between you and Mike Jr."

"I at least don't want him to hate me."

"I'll bet he doesn't hate you—he loves you. Give him a chance to express the love he feels for you."

"I wish that I could believe that he still loves me."

"He needs this more than you do. Remember how you felt when your father hugged you before you went to Vietnam? No man can be whole without the love of his father."

"I don't think that I can approve of his lifestyle."

"Mike, give him all the love you've been saving for him. You don't have to approve; it's bigger than that. Ask yourself what Arlene would want you to do."

"I think that I am more afraid of this than the cancer."

"What's the worst thing that can happen?"

Michael took a deep breath and sighed. "That he doesn't care because it's too late."

"You will free all of your kids if you try, especially Michael."

"What if he won't come here?"

"At least you will have tried, and he will know that you still cared."

"I'm not even sure how to reach him."

"Tommy will know."

"You're like a goddamn dog with a bone on this."

"That's because you need to do this."

"If he comes, will you hang around while I see him?"

"Absolutely. Where the hell would I go?"

"Thanks, you're not as big a jerk as people say."

Sal shook his hand and said, "Wait until you get my bill."

53

JUNE 1916

Last Attempt at Reconciliation

MICHAEL JR. ADJUSTED HIS TIE AND gathered his belongings and prepared to leave his Manhattan hotel. His brother Tommy had called and informed him that their father wished him to visit Fox Run. Michael Jr., who was in New York on a business trip, had no intention of visiting his father, but Tommy insisted. There had been almost no communication between the two men since Arlene's funeral. Junior loved his father, but he was fearful that another heated session between them would change nothing.

Seated in the media room, Michael found it ironic that on this day that his son was to visit, the airways were filled with a story about a clerk who refused to issue marriage licenses to gay couples. He mused that this was the last thing he wanted to see on the news today. The basic position that he held about homosexuality had not changed, but he was profoundly sorry that his relationship with his son had caused so much family pain.

One of the staff tapped gently on the door and said: "Doctor, your son is here to see you."

Michael rose and extended his hand. Mike Jr. responded, but they both appeared to be physically uncomfortable.

"Tommy called me and said you wanted to see me," Mike Jr. began. "I had to be in New York for a conference, so I extended my visit."

"I'm glad you came. . . . How have you been?"

"Fine."

"It's been a long time."

Michael Jr. appeared nervous and resorted to small talk. "How is it living here?"

"It's okay. At least I won't kill any deer."

Smiling, Junior added, "I heard about that."

"It is great to see you." Michael decided it was time to address the elephant in the room: "Your mother could always find the words even in difficult situations. I . . ."

"Dad, I'm not sure why you asked to see me. Tommy was secretive about it."

"It's very complicated, and I don't exactly know where to begin."

"Just say it."

"I wasn't feeling well for the last few months and I . . ."

Junior became apprehensive. "Are you sick?"

"Yes, I just found out that I have pancreatic cancer."

Junior was momentarily speechless. "How bad is it?" he asked.

"Really bad. It has already spread."

"Isn't there anything that they can do?"

Michael said sadly, "I know what the reality is. I've been this route with your mother; the only hope is that they can slow it down."

Looking for a ray of hope, Junior asked, "Have you gone elsewhere to get a second opinion?"

Michael understood that the news was shocking, and this was his son's initial attempt at denial. "Mike, I'm well versed in this. Second opinions are not going to change the prognosis. I've accepted it, but . . . I did not want your brother to tell you. I wanted to tell you myself."

"Thanks . . . I don't know what to say."

"I know that there has been a lot of distance between us, and I needed to talk with you."

"About what?"

"About the past and what happened between us."

Junior didn't want to repeat the shouting matches of the past. "Dad, I don't want to go over that again."

"But I need to. Honestly, I can't let this opportunity pass."

"What's the use? We'll start out calmly, and then you will lose your cool and start yelling at me."

"I can promise you that will not happen this time."

"Why not?"

"Because this may be my last chance."

"I don't know what to say, Dad . . . I am who I am, and that's the way it is."

"I could say the same thing about me, but that is not good enough now."

"What do you want to talk about?"

"Let's talk about what we have avoided for years."

"What . . . the fact that I am gay?"

"Exactly. I want to understand it."

"Understand it? It is what it is. There's no explanation. You obviously think it is a disease that can be cured."

"Give me more credit than that. I'm . . . boxed in by my life. Everything I was taught . . ."

"The bottom line remains the same. You can't accept me as I am."

"That's not true. It's not who you are, but what you have chosen."

"Who I am and what I have chosen are the same. Being gay is not something I put on and then take off. It's the same as you being straight."

"Can you understand why that is difficult for me?"

"Why the hell do you think I never told you?"

"Maybe if we had talked more, it would have been different for us."

"I doubt it . . . there was too much pain in your rejection."

"Do you think it was a picnic for me? There is no preparation for something like this."

"There's no short course on my side of the fence either."

"Mike, I want to move forward. It's really important to me now."

"How do we move forward?"

"You need to know how much I worried that you would be hurt because of your lifestyle."

"Lifestyle?" Junior said angrily. "What the hell does that mean?"

"Maybe that's the wrong word. Ah, hell. Let's be honest. AIDS."

"Straight people get AIDS."

"Yes, I know."

"A lot of my friends died, Dad. It was rough. I used to talk to Mom."

"But not to me. I'm sorry. I know . . . I know grief is the pits. I wish—. Shit, I don't know the right words. I grew up with things being so clear, and now nothing seems clear."

"What do you mean?"

"I was taught that homosexuality was wrong."

"Do you believe that now?"

"I don't know. Something like that gets in your head. Even the Pope seems to be nonjudgmental, but I do know that if I had a choice, you would not be gay."

"So, you would like to fix me?"

"I love you, Mike. Is it wrong to want good things for you?"

"What good things?"

"Being the same as your sisters and brother. Hoping you would have a family."

"I do have a family and someone who loves me."

"It's not the same."

"It's not the same in your book, but love and family are bigger than sexual preference."

"I wish that I could agree, but it would make me a hypocrite."

"I don't want you to agree, but I still feel that you are rejecting me."

"That's not true . . . I . . . I've always loved you, and it breaks my heart to have you distant from me."

"Then love me for who I am."

"I do. Why do you think I wanted you to have a family? There's nothing fiercer—more joyful, more painful—than the love of a parent for a child. I haven't done everything right, and I'm still struggling with this, but my love for you is greater than what has gone wrong between us. I know that one conversation can't make everything perfect, but I need to find again what we used to have . . . however that would be expressed now that you are a man . . . that relationship we had before we drifted apart."

Michael paused, then looked up, his eyes meeting his son's. "I will do whatever it takes to have you back in my life."

Those words touched Junior, and he sensed the sincerity in his father reaching out. He put his hand briefly on his father's arm. That arm, once so strong—lifting him up to his shoulders as a little boy, supporting him against the waves at the shore. He used to feel so safe in his father's arms. Now the muscles were wasted, the skin loose. "Dad, I have to catch a flight back tonight, but I'll be back here in a month. I know that this hasn't been easy on either of us, but thanks for taking the first step."

Junior stood up, embraced his father, and left. Shortly after he left, Sal entered the room. "How did it go?" he asked.

"I think for the first time we both got past the hurdles to become father and son again. I realized how much I missed him. It was almost like before all of the issues that divided us. He seemed relaxed at the end, and I'm convinced that we will stay in touch. The only good thing that has come from my illness is that I have been given my son back."

"I'm thrilled for you."

Exhausted but at the same time exhilarated, he said, "Sal, it seems strange because I haven't changed my convictions, but Mike seems happy and knowing he has someone who cares for him doesn't seem wrong. I am grateful to you because, without your consistently prodding me to reach out to my son, today would never have happened."

54

The Fox Run Gang
Strikes Again

THE MEETING WITH HIS SON HELPED Michael deal with his impending death. After he broke the ice, they began conversing frequently, and Junior came twice to visit him. Despite his terminal illness, Michael's mood remained upbeat. One morning at breakfast, as Michael smiled and hummed, Sal asked what was making him so cheerful.

"After talking with my son yesterday, I feel like I'm getting all of my ducks in a row. I have made a list of things that need my attention before I reach the pearly gates. There is one that requires your assistance."

"Shoot, master, your request is my command."

"The Red Sox are in town next week, and I would love to go and see the new Yankee Stadium."

"That's doable; I have a friend who is an executive with the Sox. I'm sure he can come up with a couple of tickets. How will we get there?"

"We can drive."

"Are you nuts? How the hell can we drive? You see poorly, and I am too damn weak to drive. Remember, Mr. Rocket Scientist, you are here because you hit a tree."

"First, I did my research; there are no trees on any roads between here and Yankee Stadium. And if there were trees, what the hell is the worst thing that could happen? We hit the tree, and we die. Big deal, I'm already going, and you're probably not too far behind."

"Okay, Einstein, where will we get a car? No one in their right mind would rent us a car. I can just see the Hertz guy saying 'Sir, you two turkeys will need a Seeing Eye dog and a nurse before we rent you a car.'"

"Who said anything about renting a car?"

Slightly fearful about Michael's plans, he asked, "What did you have in mind?"

"We borrow a car."

"Borrow as in steal?"

"No, a short-term loan."

"And where is this insane person that is willing to loan us a car?"

"In the directress' office."

"Mrs. Boyer? Are you crazy? She would cut our nuts off if we asked for her car."

"Big loss—they're useless anyway at our age. We aren't going to ask her. We are going to presume she would lend us her wheels."

"We are going to steal her car, and she will be thrilled and not cut our nuts off? Do you realize that this constitutes grand theft? We could go to jail."

"Nah, she will avoid the bad publicity. We would just have to put up with that sour puss and the lecture."

"My ass, we'll wind up in prison.'"

"I'm sure they have hospice in prison. What the hell can they do to us? We'd become legends, the male versions of Thelma and Louise. Hell, they'll probably make a movie about us. Every old fart in this place will revolt against the dictator."

"I don't know, Michael; this could have serious consequences."

"Look, if you're squeamish about this, I will tell them that I kidnapped you at gun point."

"This sounds like something that Maniac would do."

"Or your friend Jack."

"How will we get her car keys, and won't she know immediately that the car is gone?"

"I've already figured this out. She parks her car in the back lot, so she won't know for hours that it's gone. She never leaves work before 7. The game is at 1:00 so we'll be back before she knows what happened."

"How do we get her keys?"

"She keeps them in her purse, so early on game day, we walk past her office. I fake a temporary weak spell. I ask her to get me some water, and when she goes for the water, you take the keys from the purse."

"But what if the keys are attached to her office keys?"

"As a super sleuth, I have already checked. They are separate."

"I think I'm as crazy as you."

"This will become a legend at Fox Run. The boys from the corner strike again. I can see the headline: 'Given up as past their prime, the two criminals pull off the impossible.'"

"On my last day of freedom can I at least root for the Red Sox?"

"You do, and I'll have some tough Yankee fans kick your ass."

"What kind of a car does she have?"

"A BMW sedan. Why?"

"I'll go online and get the story on all the operating procedures."

"Great, I can see that you're already getting into the plan."

"The only consolation is that Maniac and Jack would think this is a great idea."

After a sleepless night, Sal hoped that Michael had changed his mind. He heard a knock on his door. Michael's decision obviously had not been altered.

"Are you ready?"

"What time is it?"

"10:00 a.m."

"Is there any chance that we can change our minds and watch the game on cable?"

"This is the moment to be bold and strike a blow for all the downtrodden souls in the world."

"What the hell do you think this is, the French Revolution? You crazy bastard, we will either be dead or in prison by nightfall."

"Have no fear, my man. We are about to pull off a caper that will be recounted here every day for years to come. We will give hope to all those seated in the great room who long for one more shining moment."

"Boy, those pain pills you're taking create wonderful delusions. I may need those in prison when one of the inmates decides he wants to play house with me."

"It's time to go get the keys, Sal. Get your jacket, put on your driving goggles."

The ploy worked, and once the keys had been borrowed, they started towards the back-parking area.

"It's cloudy out. Maybe we should check the weather forecast. The game may be rained out."

Michael began to sing as they left the room, "Take me out to the ballgame. Take me out with the crowd."

The two aging car thieves approached the caper with very different demeanors. One, fully dressed in Yankee paraphernalia, was almost giddy. The other appeared frightened and less than excited about their forthcoming career in crime. Michael flipped Sal the car keys, which Sal dropped. The keys bounced under the vehicle. Michael sighed with disdain and said, "Hard to believe that you once were an accomplished athlete." Sal now went down on all fours to retrieve the keys. Finally, he fished them out and opened the car doors.

Michael rolled down the window, eager for a quick getaway. "Come on, let's get going. What the hell are you waiting for?"

Sal hardly heard his accomplice's plea because he was trying to get the GPS on his phone to work.

"Who the hell are you calling?" Michael asked.

Sal turned toward him and said: "No one. I am trying to get the GPS to work."

"What the hell is a GPS?"

"It is the app that will give us directions."

Finally, Sal punched in the pertinent information and put the car in gear. The voice on the GPS told them to make a right turn. Michael quipped, "At the pace you are driving, we should have left yesterday." Sal made the right turn, gripping the wheel in fear. Now that they had left, there was no pretending that the theft had not happened.

The GPS told them to take a right on Route 9 and in six miles stay in the left lane and get on the Palisades Parkway. Mike let out a war whoop. Sal was keeping up with the traffic. The Parkway was relatively empty, and with the aid of the GPS, there was growing confidence that they would reach the stadium in one piece. They begin to chatter as Sal became more comfortable with the drive. As they approached the George Washington Bridge, Sal removed the E-Z Pass from the sun visor. "Why the hell are you removing that?" Michael inquired.

"Because it will indicate that the car has been used on this date. We have to pay the toll in cash."

Michael smiled, "You are not as dumb as you look, Sherlock."

Suddenly on the horizon, the House that Ruth built appeared, and they dutifully followed the signs to the VIP parking. As they handed the attendant the car keys, Sal slipped him a twenty-dollar bill and said, "We will leave early, and there is another twenty if we are immediately ready to go."

The attendant pocketed the twenty and happily said: "You will be right in the front, Chief."

As they entered the stadium, they were directed to an area right behind the visitors' dugout. Sal's friend had given them seats two rows behind third base. Michael turned and said: "I knew that someday I would be happy that you are my friend."

As they were seated, Michael turned to their neighbors and stated, "This poor thing that I am with is a Red Sox fan, so please feel free to verbally abuse him." Sal got into the act, stood for a bow and was barraged with humorous abuse. It was almost game time, and as they stood for the national anthem, both men were no longer worried about the car incident. They had made it this far; there was no reason to believe that they would not return undetected.

The first three innings indicated that this would be a close game because both pitchers set down the first nine batters in order. In the Red Sox fourth, the game began to change, Pedroia led off the inning with a single to right field. Mookie Betts followed with a line single to center, and Sal elbowed Michael in the ribs, saying, "Your beloved Yankees are going down."

Not daunted by the current situation, Michael shouted out, "Let's get two." Sabathia pranced around the mound and picked up the rosin bag. Ready to pitch, he went into his stretch, checked the runners, and proceeded to walk the next batter on four pitches. The Yankee pitching coach came out and attempted to settle Sabathia down. Up next was Yankee nemesis 'Big Papi' David Ortiz. Waving his bat in a menacing way toward the pitcher, Ortiz took the first pitch for a ball high and outside. Sabathia crowded Ortiz with a slider inside, and the count was now two and zero. Sabathia threw the next pitch, a fastball on the inside corner, and Ortiz crushed it. As the ball soared into the second deck in right field, Sabathia picked up the rosin sack and slammed it to the ground. The Sox led four to zero.

The Red Sox dugout was ecstatic, and Sal smirked while Michael appeared sullen and forlorn. As the next batter stepped into the box, Sabathia let loose with a fastball that hit him in the rib cage. He went down writhing in pain, and the Red Sox bench began to hurl insults at Sabathia. Defiant Sabathia came off the mound and returned obscenities in kind to the Red Sox. Both benches cleared, and there was a full-fledged brawl. Once order was restored, Sabathia and two Red Sox players were ejected. The Red Sox scored four more runs. At the end of the fourth inning, the score was Red Sox eight, Yankees zero.

After a beer and a couple of hot dogs, Sal decided that they should leave after the sixth inning so that there would be no traffic as they exited the Stadium parking lot. Michael concurred, and as they were leaving, Michael stopped and said, "I have another idea."

"What the hell are you going to do now?"

"Why don't we get a beer and some nachos? We can spill a little in the trunk and place some nachos between the seats in the back. The smell will drive her nuts."

Sal laughed. "Boy, I hope I never piss you off, because you are the devil incarnate."

Arriving at the car, they poured a little beer in the trunk and spread the nachos way under the seat. Discarding the rest of the beer in a trashcan, Sal set the GPS, and the car thieves set out for Fox Hill. The ride back was uneventful, and, while Michael asked the directress to join him in the library because he had a suggestion that he would like to explore, Sal placed the keys back in her purse. The Fox Run Two had pulled off the perfect crime.

55

OCTOBER 2016

Saying Goodbye

T HE WEEKS AFTER THE YANKEE STADIUM caper saw a downhill spiral in Michael's health. He had tremendous difficulty
standing, and required the aid of a walker to navigate his room.
For all practical purposes, he was unable to leave his room, and
Sal was his constant companion. They had requested that Sal and
he share all of their meals in Michael's room. It was becoming
more apparent each day that the end was near, and Michael consented to move to the infirmary wing and have hospice care. In
the following week, his condition worsened, and Michael was
now confined exclusively to bed.

There had been a constant flow of family and friends visiting
the past few days. The high point was when Michael Jr. and his
husband spent time with Michael. It was such a relief to Michael

knowing that he had restored his relationship with his son and that all the hurdles had disappeared. He imagined Arlene smiling down at him in approval. He took pleasure in knowing that he had completed her bucket list.

One morning after breakfast, Michael was informed that a former Marine was here to see him. Michael asked to raise the head of the bed so he would be able to converse with his visitor. A middle-aged man with two prosthetic legs entered the room and said, "Hi, Doc, remember me? I was Corporal Jon Gibbons in Vietnam." Immediately, as if it was yesterday, he recalled the young Marine who had begged him to die. "The last time I saw you, I was so pissed, and I guess you bore the brunt of that anger. I thought my life was over. I laid a ton of guilt on you."

Michael shook his hand and said, "I felt terrible that morning and have never forgotten you."

"I was so goddamn bitter, but despite all I lost, life has been good to me. I have a wonderful wife and three great kids. They are adopted, but I could not love them more if I were their biological father. I tried to track you down and finally found out from your old hospital that you were here. I just want to thank you, Doc. I know you have others that want time with you, so I will leave." Michael reached out his arms. The former Marine hugged him and left the room.

Michael was energized by the visit of the Marine and later in the day shared the experience with Sal. "Nice to know that you made a difference, Michael," Sal said as he sat on the edge of the bed. He reached for Michael's hand. "There are so many people whose lives you touched, and you should be comforted by that reality." Sal could see that Michael was on the verge of tears and, trying to inject some humor into the moment, asked: "Did you see the video where your candidate talked about grabbing women by the pussy?"

Michael shuddered and said, "That is the last straw. Arlene would be horrified if I voted for him. Still can't vote for the Dragon Lady, so I guess that I will have to do a write-in. One of the bonuses of death is that I will not live to see either in the White House."

Michael's dying was particularly difficult for Sal because their time together had been so special. Their political differences meant nothing because the friendship was a monumental gift for both. The partisan exchanges were amicable and tinged with humorous banter. Their time together had given them a plethora of moments where they shared themselves at an emotional level that was rare for men. Sal had found some of what he had lost—a connection to the world—and had begun to live more fully.

Michael asked Sal to refresh his pillow. Once this was done, Michael said, "Thanks to you, my son and I are together again. I am most pleased that I have fully restored my relationship with him. I will not die and leave him with a lifetime of guilt."

Michael rearranged his position in the bed and seemed momentarily pensive. "Sal," he asked, "there are a couple of requests that I have for you."

Sal immediately responded, "Anything you ask, I will do."

Michael motioned for Sal to give him the glass of water on the bedside table. Sipping the water through a straw, he continued, "My first request may seem odd, but I can assure you that I have completely thought this through before asking. I would like you to give me the last rites."

Sal was stunned by the request. "I am not sure I can do that because I am no longer an active priest."

Michael waved his hand to dismiss the objection. "You forget that I have a superior knowledge of theology. 'Tu es sacerdos in aeternum.' You are a priest forever."

Sal asked, "Why not have Father Riordan, the local chaplain, perform the rite?"

"Because he is a stranger, and you are my best friend. It would have great meaning for me if you would do this."

Sal could not deny his friend. He told him that he believed that somewhere in his room there was a priestly stole and he would improvise with the blessed oils. "What is the second request?"

"I have discussed this with my kids, and they agree. I want you to give the primary eulogy at my funeral Mass."

On the brink of tears, Sal nodded in agreement. In a choked voice, he said, "It would be my honor."

Michael patted Sal's hand. "I am not afraid and so ready to see Arlene and my family. I know there is another life waiting for me, and I will even get to meet your Helen. I am sure she has a mansion in heaven, having put up with you for many years."

Sal went back to his room. High up in his walk-in closet was a box that contained a priestly stole and a small gold vessel filled with holy oils. Sal placed the stole in his pocket and reached for his cell phone. Over the next two days, he called Michael's children and requested that they come as soon as possible. When the entire family had arrived, but before they entered the hospice area, Sal tried to prepare them for the reality that Michael might not be able to recognize them. As they walked across the main living area to the infirmary, all were touched, realizing that this truly was the end. Sal was deeply emotional but also felt eternally grateful that he could perform this ritual for his dear friend.

As they entered the room, the only sound was the oxygen machine that was providing breathing assistance to Michael.

Slowly they approached the bed. Michael was not moving, but he seemed comfortable and peaceful. Sal counseled the group that there was a strong possibility that Michael could still hear, so he encouraged each family member to kiss him and whisper in his ear. Sal was touched by the love of each child for their father and began to cry himself when Michael Jr. spoke to his father. When Junior left his father, he aided his brother Robert in leaning over the bed and hugging his father. Robert's physical impairments made it difficult for him to bend without assistance.

When they had all finished, Sal in a loud voice said, "Michael, we are here to give you the last blessings of the Church that you loved and served so well." He then dabbed the holy oils on Michael's eyes, ears, forehead and lips. A deep and profound spiritual feeling grasped him as he led the family through the prayers. After ten minutes, he came to the end and said, "Michael, may the angels come to greet you and may Arlene embrace you with her arms wide open as you enter the gates of paradise."

Again, each child took a turn at kissing their father and whispering in his ear. Michael Jr. came to Sal, hugged him and said, "I am eternally grateful to you for giving me back my father." Sal was the last, and he could not contain his tears as he cradled Michael in his arms. The nurse practitioner had been in the back of the room for most of the ritual and now came to Michael's bed and checked his vital signs. She blessed herself before removing the oxygen from his face. She then walked over to Sal and whispered in his ear, "He is gone."

THREE DAYS LATER

Sal ascended the pulpit at St. Ignatius Church. Gazing out at the filled pews, he began his eulogy, "Good morning and my condolences to all who loved Michael, especially his wonderful family. Everyone here this morning has known and loved Michael as a father, grandfather, physician, and friend, and I am sure that each of you has a bevy of warm and loving memories. He touched so many lives, and, despite the tragedies that he experienced in his life, he was a magnet of caring and compassion. He cared for his brothers after his mother's sudden death and weathered the sudden, tragic deaths of those wonderful children. He was a man of deep faith, and he took the pain of his losses and wove it into his ability to care for everyone that he met. He was a living legend at the hospital. Patients and staff held him up as the model for outstanding health care. He had the ability and desire to see beyond physical organs to the person who was undergoing surgery. His golden hands were outmatched only by his caring heart. A nurse once told him that he should leave surgery. Michael was stunned by this remark, believing that he was more than competent as a surgeon. The nurse added, 'You have exceptional surgical skills, but you also have an outstanding, loving personality and surgeons don't ordinarily have personalities.'

"To talk about Michael without mentioning his soul mate, Arlene, would be an unforgivable oversight. Over and over in our time together at Fox Hill, he would regale me about their life together. She and those here present in the first two rows were the greatest gifts of his life. There are so many dimensions to this giant of a man that I can't capture, in this brief time, who he was. However, there was a side of Michael that his saintly Irish face hid from the public." With that statement, Sal reached down to the bottom of the pulpit and placed a Yankee hat on his head. He then, in detail, to the amusement of the congregation, revealed the Great Yankee caper.

412 | S.J. T<small>AGLIARENI</small>

"In the twilight of my life, Michael was a gift that rescued me. I had reluctantly entered assisted living with the belief that my life was over. He brought the spice of political difference, and initially, we argued about a host of current societal issues. I teased him about being to the right of Genghis Khan, and he gleefully referred to me as his wayward Communist buddy. But his passion for social justice and magnetic ability to care for those who have been marginalized every decade of his life ignited the embers in my soul. He connected the dots of our youth with the memories of all the magnificent career and personal journeys we had shared. His faith in God uncovered the dormant spiritual needs that became alive and once again vital in my soul. This was a giant of a man with a humility and kindness that allowed me to share all of my concerns and fears. As my friend, he encouraged us to leap over the forbidden barriers that men are not supposed to cross. We shared our pain and confusion at the losses of our wives, and I found the will to live more fully again. He was my teacher at the end with the way he handled his illness and death with grace and courage. I am a better person today because of Michael, and I realize now through his eyes the immortal words of Yogi Berra, 'It isn't over until it's over.' In conclusion, I would like to add that I will miss Michael for all the days I have left, but I will be fulfilled and sustained by knowing that he is ever on my shoulder and in my heart."

Weeks after Michael's funeral, the sounds of the wind and whirling snow hitting the bedroom window slowly awakened Sal from a deep sleep. He lay in bed for twenty minutes, going through the thoughts that had dominated his mind since Michael's death. Certainly, there was sadness at losing his best friend, but it was much more than that. As he rose, he smiled, remembering the Yankee game escapade. It had been a long time since the little mischievous boy in Sal had found a partner in crime. The absolute joy of recounting that tale at Michael's funeral warmed his heart, and he gratefully chuckled that the news had not made it back to Fox Run.

Shaving and showering, he spent more than a few minutes selecting his breakfast attire. For the past weeks, he had worn a blue blazer and slacks to breakfast instead of a sweatshirt and jogging pants. Despite the loss, something was happening within his heart and mind that brought forth new energy. Residents and staff were overly solicitous, and that was part of it, but there was more: he was truly alive again. When he came to Fox Run, he had in many ways resigned himself to merely marking the days until his passing. There were no more goals, no aspirations, no challenges. The man who had almost from birth been an adventurer had become a settler. No more days of big dreams and mountains to climb. He was loved by many, but in reality, he was a shell of himself. The risk-taker who was always willing to take the path less traveled was now merely one of the herd.

Somehow, his relationship with Michael had peeled back the layers of acceptance. The friendship, despite their many differences, was such a gift. He once again bore the mantle of helper in working tirelessly to mend the relationship between Michael and his son. There was also the burst of spirituality that had raced through his veins as he anointed Michael and prepared him to enter the gates of heaven. Michael taught him that even though he was no longer on the active clergy list, in the eyes of God, he was a priest forever. These realities were leading him out of a tunnel into the light, and he could hear the voice of his mentor Viktor Frankl, "Salvatore, there are always choices."

Sal took pen in hand and began a process that he had employed with literally thousands of others in the past. He started to develop his goals and bucket list. The energy of the adventurer had come back, and he dismissed his age as a barrier to the selection of the goals. He worked for hours, and when the entire process was finished, he went into his closet and took out his vintage bottle of Brunello wine. He had saved this bottle for a special occasion. This was that moment. He poured himself a glass and toasted Helen, Michael and Arlene. "My dear loved ones, thank you for all the love and life you have given me." He then read the following goals out loud.

1. I will put my unit at Fox Run up for sale.
2. I will spend the spring and summer in Sicily.
3. I will discover the life and culture of my father's village.
4. I will write a novel about my Sicilian father and his life in two worlds.

The new adventure had begun, and even though many would think he had gone senile, he knew that the best days were yet to come.

The End

ABOUT THE AUTHOR

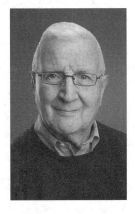

SALVATORE J. TAGLIARENI is an expert in Leadership and has developed the dynamic practice of Roving Leadership, a system based on the principle that every person at some point can lead in the search for outstanding organizational results.

He is a story teller, writer, business consultant, art dealer, and former Catholic priest. For over 25 years he has successfully engaged private and public companies in their search for outstanding strategic performance, and has the ability to create processes for the positive transformation of organizational cultures.

A gifted speaker, he is blessed with a great sense of humor and can invigorate an audience with insights on life and leadership. Salvatore was profoundly influenced by his relationship with Dr. Viktor Frankl, the celebrated psychiatrist and author of Man's Search for Meaning. He is the author of *Roving Leadership, Breaking through the Boundaries* and the novels *Hitler's Priest* and *The Cross or The Swastika*.

Salvatore is the former president of Next Step Associates a Strategic organizational consulting firm. For 25 years he has performed strategic planning and organizational design and implementation for many large International companies such as Johnson and Johnson, IBM, Hoffman La-Roche and Boston Financial, as well as nonprofits such as The National League for Nursing and The Independence Foundation.

As a young Catholic priest studying theology in Rome, his life was forever changed when the tragic and unexpected death of his best friend led him to seek and gain mentorship from Dr. Frankl. Dr. Frankl and other Holocaust survivors changed the course of Salvatore's life as they shared their personal horrors under the Nazi regime.

After leaving active ministry as an ordained Catholic priest in 1970, Salvatore went on to earn a PhD in Leadership and Human Behavior. He is a sought after keynote and motivational speaker.